No Place Like Alone

Travels in the Covid Wagon

ISBN: 979-8-9916354-0-0 (Paperback)
ISBN: 979-8-9916354-1-7 (E-book)
ISBN: 979-8-9916354-2-4 (Hardcover)

Any references to historical events, real people, or real places are used fictitiously. This story is based on real-life events, but names, characters, places have been changed for a better reading experience.

Read more of Oscar's work at dogblog.wf.

For Willy
who was with us every step of the way.

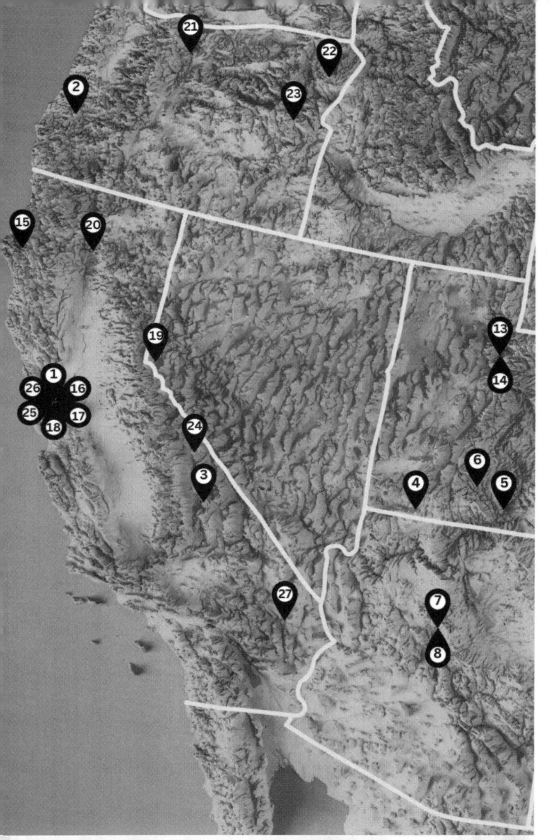

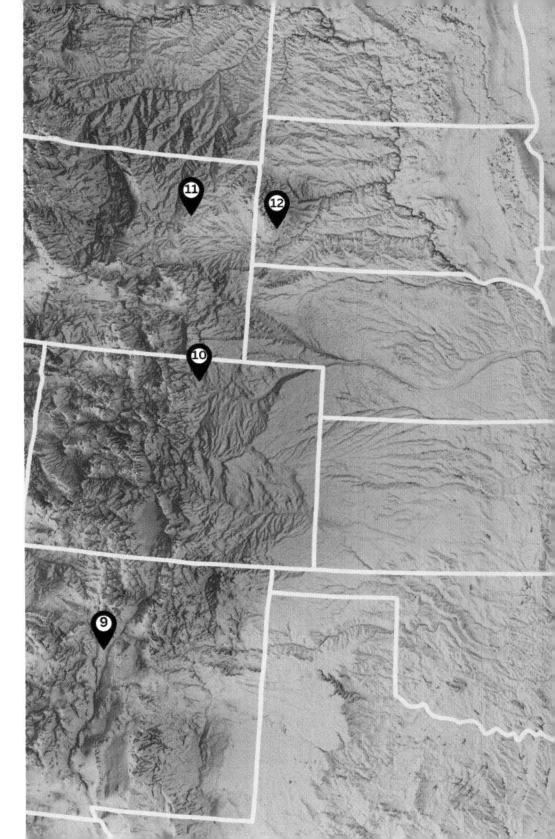

Part 1
Doomed

see more photos

Chapter 1

Impending Doom

People talk about "the dog who caught the car," as if nabbing cars were the point. A dog knows that the thrill is in the chase, so who cares if you actually catch anything? But our companions at the other end of the leash aren't so wise.

Humans, or *people* as they call themselves (as if dogs couldn't be people, too), get so distracted trying to solve the mystery of what happens next that they don't notice all the fun they're missing along the way. It's not the *wondering* so much as the *wandering* in search of answers that gets them into trouble. My life partner, who I call Mom, wandered onto the road once and actually caught the car. Some dreams are more fun when they don't come true.

It all began right after she started molting. Every few years, Mom goes through a phase where she puts our life inside a box, shakes it up, and puts everything away in a different house than where it belonged before. Humans molt other things, too, but a house is easier to see than what's inside their heads.

As a dog who spends more time with humans than I spend by myself, I'm an expert in human behavior. I can read what's in their thought bubbles by watching the way they move, where their eyes are pointing, and listening to the sounds they make. Mom and I go almost everywhere together, including the places where dogs don't usually go. We even work together. Or, at least we did back when there were still jobs for office dogs, before the City emptied out so they could tear it all down. But no one knew yet that the whole world was about to start molting, too. Mom and I just thought that we were going on a quest to get Mom out of her rut and would come home to a different job, in a different office, with a different pack of collies for me to manage.

On my last day as a business dog, I ran across the slick office floor like a cannonball to greet one of my best collies at the door. I slid the last few steps and stopped against her shins, doing a hello jig to keep her from walking away without petting me. The clicking of my toenails bounced off the brick walls, filling the office to the rafters with the sound of joy.

"Hi, Oscar!" Jackie squealed, crouching to scratch my muscular booty with both hands. "Are you excited for your trip?"

"I'm excited if you're excited." I wiggled my stubby tail in rhythm with her scratching.

As if I hadn't heard her the first time, Jackie asked again, "Who's excited? Are you excited?"

I didn't mind that she couldn't understand my accent. Any attention is good attention. "It's me! I'm excited!" I aimed a grin toward Mom to invite her into the conversation. She lurked in the corner, trying to shrink herself down even smaller than she actually was, but her face reflected my smile.

With all that baby talk and repeating everything over and over, it's no wonder that humans have a reputation for being dimwits. Some people think that dogs are dumb, too—as if anyone who can't count past ten doesn't count at all—but they usually think that about anyone they don't take the time to understand. Humans only talk like tea kettles to us dogs because they want so badly to be understood. If you pay attention, you'll find that they have a much bigger vocabulary than sit, stay, and do you wanna. After spending so much time studying them, I've learned to understand the more subtle vocalizations that they use with each other. There are still some words that don't fit easily in a dog's head, but you get the hang of them with practice.

Take the word collie, for example. When I first became a business dog, I was confused about why all my new Friends kept talking about their collies. Since Mom and I worked together, I naturally assumed that everyone's canine life partners must come to the office with them. I expected Lassie to burst out of one of the glass doors at any minute to herd her team into a meeting. Maybe I just started on a slow day.

The next day I was still the only dog under the lunch table, and the next, and the day after that. So I listened more closely and noticed a pattern. Every time someone used the word, their eyes shifted to someone else and softened with something like friendship. Over time I worked out that, just like a friendly person becomes a Friend as you learn more about them and collect memories together, a *collie* is a Friend you make at work.

Mom was too clumsy around people to make Friends without supervision. That's why I was hired. I was what they called a *reasonable amomodation*, which means a dog who trains a reactive human to behave around other people. It's not like Mom was aggressive or anything. She liked other people—or at least the idea of company—but she wasn't very well socialized and other people made her nervous. Without me to show her how friendly the world could be, Mom would be chewing on the furniture in no time.

Jackie looked up at Mom and her voice stiffened to a human register. "You sure are lucky you're leaving the City when you are. It's coming…" She paused for a meaningful look and her eyes added, *You know what I'm talking about and how monstrous it is.*

"What's coming?" I asked. "The boat?"

For weeks, everyone had been talking about a boat full of people possessed by some unspeakable evil. The sailors wanted to go home, but no port would let them in, even in the places where they belonged. So they'd been floating on the high seas like pirates until someone figured out what to do with the wickedness inside of them.

"You can't leave people to drift around the ocean just because you don't have a perfect solution to their problems," Mom said with a wag of her head. "Did you hear that they're thinking about actually closing schools because of this nonsense? Since when do we call a state of emergency over germs? Kids get sick. That's what they do. I'm glad we'll be out of the City till this whole thing blows over."

Mom never met a problem she couldn't solve by running away. Being trapped with her problems was the worst torment that she could imagine, even worse than being trapped with other people. Her mind had been chasing the same stale thoughts for so long that she didn't even need to think them to be exhausted. When a dog or a mind won't come when it's called, the only way to get their attention is to run away. A mind, like a dog, loves to chase and no adventure ever got to *happily ever after* without a quest. We were leaving on a quest that very afternoon to give Mom and her mind space to find each other again.

"Well, I'm glad that you'll be working right down the street so I can keep seeing this guy when you get back!" Jackie turned up the vigorousness on her butt scratching to show she was talking about me.

"You should come with us!" I channeled my excitement into the corner where Mom was hiding. "Wouldn't that be fun, Mom?"

Mom's face clenched. After a too-long pause, she said, "Maybe we can come over for lunch every other week."

"You promise?" I wagged. If Mom had her way, she would work inside a computer so she never had to see people at all. Luckily, jobs like that were as rare as unicorns, and harder to catch than a car.

The buzzer announced that someone else was about to open the door. I turned to see who it was. "Denise!" I squealed, launching toward her as fast as I could on the slick floor. I was just about to hit cruising speed when there was a thump behind me. The leash snapped taut, holding me fast to the spot. When I looked back, Mom was standing on the other end, trying to look busy.

"Good morning, Jackie," Denise said as she walked into the kitchen. "Good morning, Oscar." She leaned over to give me a stiff pat.

"Good morning, Denise! How was your—"

"Come on, Oscar," Mom interrupted. "We've got some things to wrap up before lunchtime."

Denise may have been my Friend, but she was Mom's nemesis. No matter what Mom did, Denise came along afterward to tell her all the ways it was wrong. Except when Denise liked what Mom did and took credit for it herself, like the dog at the park that pees on everything right after someone else does.

I wouldn't have needed to choose between Mom and my career if Denise hadn't come between us, but there wasn't room enough in this office for the two of them. After Mom left her last job—the lonely one that thought dogs belonged at home—she made a solemn vow to never let work come between us again. She found our job with Jackie and the others so I could work with her. We worked hard to keep each other on our best behavior at the office, but Mom wore out her welcome before I did.

"Bye, Denise!" I wagged as Mom dragged me out of the kitchen. "I'll see you at lunch after our quest."

Dogs don't like to travel the same way as our human companions. We prefer to bark in hotels rather than sleep in them, and if you think airplanes are cruel for humans, try flying like a dog. So instead of traveling the usual way, Mom and I toured the world in an ancient minivan with just enough room for a dog and his Mom to live in the back. Because it was white, round, ancient, and held our whole lives inside as we traveled the west in search of a better life, I named our car-house the Covered Wagon.

The Wagon wasn't always a car-house. Before it met us, it was a mailman van that used to carry its villain from house to house as he hunted for families without brave dogs to protect them. Now the Wagon was reformed. It kicked the mailman out of its cockpit, ripped off its tattoos, and filled its heart with warm blankets and nourishment. Like Mom, the Wagon still showed signs of a rougher past. Its postal tattoos hadn't come off without a fight, and there were long scars on its flank where the tattoos ripped the skin away to show the raw metal underneath. The sicko who used to drive it would watch the Wagon's butt as he drove, and now Mom didn't know how to remove the camera or the satellite-dish-sized mirror sticking suspiciously off of its back. Mom kept the bars in the windows that defended the Wagon from vulnerability but used them to hang lights and other useful things where she could find them. To protect the Wagon's privacy, Mom had the windows tinted as black as sunglasses. With time, the scars, bars, and extra doodads became endearing quirks that made the Wagon easier to find in a crowded car kennel.

With the Wagon as our car-house, we could travel just about anywhere and be ready for whatever we found when we got there. I was the captain, responsible for making sure that each day had a happy ending. Mom was my skipper, driving the Wagon, making food, and talking us out of any trouble we met along the way.

Unlike Mom, I never dreamed of running away from work or the fiddy collies I managed there. Meetings were the best part of my job because people weren't supposed to touch their keyboards in a meeting. I wandered the room in search of restless hands, offering my head for a pat any time I found one. Lunch, when everyone came together to drop food on the floor, was the best meeting of all.

I was enjoying a last lunch with my collies when Mom called for me to *c'mere*. I pulled my face out of the lap it was resting on and followed Mom toward a room where nobody was eating.

"This had better be important," I said, looking back at my collies, still pushing food meant for me around their almost-empty plates.

"It is. We've got to do my exit interview so we can hit the road." Mom closed the door. "We've got a long drive tonight and an early start tomorrow."

I was about to ask why we had to be up so early if we didn't have to go to work when Boss Charming came in. My questions would have to wait.

Boss Charming was a great leader. He knew how to motivate each member of his pack to bring out their best. Mom gets job satisfaction from fancy words, so he sat at one end of the long table politely listening to her stack one big word on top of another while at the same time praising me with pats on the back.

At the far end of the table, Mom's speech went something like, "Blah, blah, blah, synergy…" I recognized the words *cattiness* and *territorial*, but I wasn't really paying attention. If only Mom hadn't had neglectful bosses in the past, she might not want to run away from Boss Charming's pack. But like a kicked puppy can grow up to be a dog that runs away from even a good home, Mom's need for escape was stronger than her need for a pack.

"… agile methodologies to deploy new features without running it by the QA team…" Mom droned, while under the table I worked hard to earn Boss Charming's respect in a different way. "… devaluing the impact on cross-functional— Is my dog licking your leg?" she interrupted herself.

"Yes, he is," Boss Charming said with the confidence and grace of a natural leader.

I listened to them look at each other for a few licks, but stayed on task.

"Would you like me to make him stop?" Mom asked.

I moved on to a fresh spot as Boss Charming shifted in his seat and tilted his head to give Mom's question the consideration it deserved. "No," he said after careful thought. "I'm wearing jeans."

The wet smacking of my hard work filled the room as they looked at each other for another beat. Mom resumed, "… dynamically integrate client-centered methodologies…"

After a while Mom's fancy words wound down and everyone relaxed a little.

"How long are you taking off before you start the next job?" Boss Charming asked, leaning back in his chair to show he was asking as a Friend.

"About a month. I start on April 6," Mom counted.

I knew that *six* meant *some, but not too many*, but when she strung six together with a whole lot of other numbers, I got confused. Numbers were Mom's way of organizing her life and testing the trustworthiness of others. If she said, "I'll meet you at *six*," and the other person solved the riddle and showed up where she expected, then she knew that they were safe. *April* was a number used to count time, but only a human could understand its true meaning. When Mom said *April*, her thought bubble might show anything from daffodils to taxes.

"What are your plans for your time off?" Boss Charming asked.

"We're headed up to Oregon tonight, then going on a road trip through the southwest." Her finger danced through the air like an orchestra conductor to show what a long way we planned to go. "I've always wanted to see Devil's Tower in Wyoming, but I keep getting distracted in the Four Corners area and wind up spending more time in Canyon Country than expected."

"I've been to all the far corners of the earth," I bragged, "the corner of Utah, the corner of Arizona, the corner of New Mexico, and... that's four, right?"

"Isn't Oregon a little out of the way?" Boss Charming asked.

"I've been there too," I bragged.

"A little," Mom admitted, as if she couldn't hear me. She did that a lot when other people were around. "But I committed to run this race a few months ago so we could meet one of Oscar's social media followers." I had to make all of Mom's Friends for her, even on the internet. I think she preferred making Friends on the internet because unlike in real life, the internet let her share only the parts of herself that she wanted people to see. "We'll run the race and book it down to Death Valley the next day so the detour won't put us behind schedule," she explained.

"Isn't it shorter if you come through Salt Lake?" Boss Charming said. "Idaho and Montana are beautiful."

Mom bristled at being told something that she already knew, so I jumped in to save her. "Who ever heard of changing your plans just because something is convenient? You can't let the world push you around like that. Isn't that right, Mom?"

"March is too early in the season for the mountains," Mom agreed. "The Sierras, Cascades, and Rockies are still going to be covered in snow and the back roads will be closed." She waved her hand through the air like someone unbothered by inconvenience. "What's an extra 1,000 miles anyway? It only takes about 15 hours to drive from Florence to Badwater."

"It can get pretty cold in the desert this time of year, too," Boss Charming warned, as if we didn't already know that, too.

"That's what blankies are for," I told him.

"It's not so bad." Mom shrugged. "I've got a couple of 0° sleeping bags. It's pretty cozy with enough extra layers, a hat, and the dog. We've slept through plenty of single-digit temperatures that way. At least I don't have to worry about finding ice for the cooler in wintertime. Summer's much worse. Especially before I got the air conditioner fixed."

Boss Charming looked at Mom with something like concern to show how impressed he was. "Don't you ever worry about traveling alone in all those remote places?"

"Nah." She flapped a limp hand to show how silly it would be to worry about a little thing like that. "I like being alone."

"She's not alone," I promised. "I'll be with her the whole time."

"Good thing you've got Oscar with you," Boss Charming agreed. "People will hesitate before messing with a big, black, barking pitbull."

"Don't worry. I'll have Mom to protect me," I told him. "I run faster than her, so they'll eat her first."

"What do you do for food?" he asked.

"I have a cooler and a little camp stove that I set up on a TV dinner tray," Mom said modestly. "I keep about a week's worth of soup and trail mix in the van and usually pass through a town big enough for a supermarket every few days. If not, there are always truck stops."

Boss Charming looked even more impressed than before. "Be careful in those places."

Mom's shoulders stiffened. She shifted into her expert voice to show that she didn't need anyone's advice on how dangerous other people could be. "Truck stops get a bad rap. They have pretty much anything you need: cheap gas, sparkling water, bathrooms, showers, laundry, and hot dogs for this one." She tilted her head toward me.

"Truck stops are the best," I wagged. "They're like people; always surprising you with delicious treats, as long as you don't expect them to be something that they're not. Searching for the best in exotic and unfamiliar places is what makes traveling fun."

"I guess you won't find anything more dangerous at a truck stop than you would in the street outside this office," Boss Charming said with a shrug. "You'll probably be safer out there than around here for the next month. That cruise ship is supposed to be docking in Oakland today."

I wanted to find out what Boss Charming knew about the ghost ship, but he opened the door and the smell of sammiches rushed in. A new group of collies sat unsupervised at the lunch table, probably dropping chicken and hamburger on the floor.

"You'll fill me in later, right Mom?" I called over my shoulder before resuming my post under the lunch table.

Mom's voice came from outside the wall of legs. "C'mon, Oscar, it's time to go."

"I'm busy," I said, using the same excuse she uses to overrule me when I want to go for a walk. I backed deeper under the table and checked the floor for crumbs, cleverly moving my collar out of her accomplices' grabbing range. I didn't see the problem with my plan until it was too late.

The leash!

Mom's shoe reached under the table and hooked the loop. I clamped my butt to the floor and braced all four legs. The leash pulled taut and my collar dug into my neck.

"Come on, adventure calls," Mom grunted.

The smooth floor betrayed me as the leash pulled me toward the wall of legs against my will. "But people are still eating," I begged. Two unmatched legs pulled aside and the leash dragged me into the light.

Mom kept pulling me toward the door. Without turning around, she raised her free arm and shouted, "Bye everybody!"

"Bye Oscar!" my collies called after me. The last thing I saw before the door closed were my collies' hands petting the air above their heads.

Mom stalked purposefully toward the car kennel, careful to keep her eyes on the sidewalk in front of her. I could never get used to how everyone in the City put on an invisibility cloak as soon as they stepped into the street. Mom's invisibility cloak covered me, too. No matter how hard I tried to catch someone's eye, no hands ever reached down to pat me and no strangers' voices told me how cute I was.

"Boo!" A stray human popped out of a doorway, waving his arms and howling.

I jumped behind Mom so he would eat her first, but Mom walked past him as if he were a ghost. She simply stepped aside as casually as if she were avoiding broken glass on the sidewalk. The stray drifted on to start an argument with a parking meter instead.

Now that we were alone, I finally had time to ask the question that had been bugging me all day. "Why's everyone so scared of that boat?" I asked. "What's on it? Pirates? Ghosts?"

"Its passengers have a virus that no one's ever seen before. It's killing people and they don't know how to contain it."

TV and movies are a great way to learn about things no one's ever seen before. I'd seen this movie and knew just how to fix it. "All they have to do is get on the lifeboats and make sure the virus doesn't come with them," I said. "It's like in *Titanic* when Billy Zane heroically uses his gun to keep the lifeboat safe from that little girl with the sniffles. When all the good guys are on lifeboats, you just have to sink the ship with the bad guys on it. Easy peasy."

"A virus isn't something you can drown or wave a gun at, Spud." Mom calls me *Spud* because my body is the same shape and hardness as an uncooked potato. My official breed is *potato beast*, but Spud is easier to say. "Viruses live inside people and ride from person to person in invisible droplets. Sometimes you don't even know that someone's got it until it's already spread. Then it's too late."

"Ah. It's invisible you say?" I asked knowingly. I'm an expert at sniffing out invisible villains and barking at them any time I detect one, especially in the middle of the night. "You're talking about a boogeyman. Or… not a man. A boogey*virus*."

Mom didn't even slow down to appreciate my wisdom. "They want everyone to stay on the boat so they won't bring the virus ashore and spread it to the rest of the country. Luckily, we'll be long gone by the time the boat germs spread to the rest of the population. Since it needs people to spread, the safest place we can be is where there are no people."

I didn't like the sound of that. "What do you mean by the *staying away from people* part?"

Mom wiped her wallet against the box next to the car kennel door until it clicked. When she opened door, the familiar smell of human pee filled my nose.

"It won't last long, sadly," she said.

Sadly-sadly-sadly, the stairwell echoed.

"This is just one of those things that they make up on TV so life seems more exciting," Mom went on. "A handful of people will get sick and the news will make a big deal about it for a couple of weeks until the next scandal comes along. Don't worry."

Worry-worry-worry, reassured the echo.

"What if the evil has already gotten off the boat while no one was looking?" I asked.

"You remember that emergency meeting last week? Apparently all you have to do is wash your hands." Mom pulled out the keys and the Wagon's lights waved hello.

"Aren't you supposed to do that anyway?" I asked.

"Exactly," Mom said, like I'd agreed with her rather than asking a question. "It's just to fill airtime. Since we're gonna be out of town, we'll miss the whole thing."

Chapter 2

Doomed

Despite what she told Boss Charming, Mom didn't like going out of her way for anything, so it was strange that she decided to start our desert adventure in the rainforest of Oregon. There was nothing desert-like about the atmosphere the next morning when Mom burst into the Wagon as soggy as if she'd showered in her clothes. She plugged the key into its slot behind the driving wheel and set the blowers to *dryer* mode. I had an urge to shake out my fur just looking at her.

"You don't actually plan to go out in this, do you?"

Mom glowered at the waterfall pouring down the front window. "It's important to keep your commitments."

"Yeah, but you hate Oregon."

"I don't *hate* Oregon. I just don't like that they don't let me pump my own gas. What kind of place makes it illegal to do something for yourself just so some poor soul can make 11 dollars an hour sitting in the rain waiting for me?"

"The rain is another excellent reason not to come to Oregon," I reminded her.

"I know, I know. I fell for it. But there aren't that many races that allow dogs. Once I saw the pictures, I couldn't resist." She woke up the Witch that Lives in her Phone and held up the screen to show me an endless dry sea covered in waves of sand.

The Witch was always scheming to steal Mom's attention and telling lies to lure us into disaster. The old *cool picture* prank was one of the Witch's favorites. Mom fell for it every time. She's a sucker for dramatic landscapes, so the temptation of a sandscape where she wouldn't have to follow anyone else's path was an irresistible Mom trap. This time the Witch's dastardly plan would backfire for sure, though, because like all wicked witches, the one in Mom's phone was allergic to water.

"See?" Mom held up the Witch to show me a droopy runner and a whole lot of sand. "The website said we would run through sand dunes. Doesn't that sound like fun?"

"You think doom sounds like fun?"

Mom petted the Witch's screen fondly as her thought bubble inflated with possibilities. "I bet they're not that big, though, and we'll mostly see them from a distance while we run on a paved beach path or something."

She tapped the screen and a squiggly line filled the Witch's face. Mom squinted at it like she was peering into a crystal ball. "Look, the course is almost completely flat."

"It looks like a porcupine with its hackles up," I said.

"That's just because of how flat it is." Mom always believed what the Witch said rather than what she could see with her own eyes. "When there are no major hills, it makes little inconsequential stuff look like a big deal."

"How long is this race?" I asked suspiciously. If the Witch could lie about hills, maybe the length of the line was a lie, too.

"It's a 25K," Mom said, without explaining how long that was.

I've been a runner since I was practically a puppy, so I knew that the *kay* meant kill-mom-meters. *Killmometers* are like miles, except they're imaginary. While a mile always beeps in the same place no matter how many times you run there, killmometers are for special occasions, and grow or shrink depending on how hard the race is.

16

"How long will it take us to run twenny-five kay?" I asked.

"Less than 3 hours on a course this flat," she calculated, "even if we stop to take a lot of pictures."

"Oh goody! A three hour tour! Nothing ever goes wrong on a three hour tour," I wagged.

Mom reached into the sack she'd brought back from the rain. She pulled out a bunch of pins hooked together like a tiny keychain and a piece of paper. She peeled through layers of shirts and jackets before finally pinning the paper to her shorts, where it would be visible no matter how hot or cold it was. Finally, she pulled a plastic bag from the secret compartment under the front window and zipped the Witch inside where she would stay dry even if Mom and I didn't.

Mom unscrewed the key from its slot and sat for a moment listening to the rain on the roof. "3, 2, 1…" She paused as if she'd forgotten her line. "3, 2, 1, GO!" She reached for the door and dove into the rain before she lost her nerve, pulling me along on the leash behind her.

Mom and I stood apart from the people-pack gathered near the starting line. They huddled together like the penguin pod in that nature documentary, taking turns in the warm spot in the middle. "No, you're faster. You go in front of me," one would say, pushing a fellow racer toward the edge to take their spot in the middle. "I'm only using it as a training run. You go ahead, I insist," said the next runner, pushing the first out of the way and cozying into the center of the huddle.

"Why don't we smoosh in with the other people where it's warm?" I shivered.

"Because you think they're all here to see you," Mom said, like she thought they weren't. "And I don't think it's a good idea to pack in so close with that many people right now."

Mom always preferred to freeze alone than stay warm together, but lately everybody was saying that sort of thing. I shook off the rain and looked longingly at all the runners making friends without me. Together they made an umbrella for each other, but a dog and his Mom aren't enough to make an umbrella all on their own.

"Don't worry, Mom. It's safe," I told her. "It's called *herd immunity*."

She gave me a funny look. "What the heck is *herd immunity*?"

I'd learned about herd immunity late one night from one of those documentaries that plays after Mom's show ends and she's too asleep to turn it off. Anything that I couldn't learn by watching Mom I learned from TV.

"You know how wildebeests run in groups so that it's harder for the lion to pick just one of them? *Herd immunity* is science's word for safety in groups. " Smarts are how Mom shows dominance, so it was fun to be the one who knew about science for a change. I tried not to let my tail wag as I 'splained, "It works on raindrops, too. See? The rain can't find the people who are bunched together, so it's all falling on me instead."

Just then, a man walked to the far side of the starting line and shouted something at the crowd. They all turned away from the warm spot to look at him as he howled a word… then another… then another… When he barked the loudest word of all, the pack spilled over the starting line where they turned back into individual runners. I shook the wet out of my fur one last time and waited for the last person to cross the line so Mom would tell me to *on-your-mark, get-set, go.*

Tripping someone with your leash is a foul, so Mom made me give everyone a head start. Mom's loser attitude isn't such a handicap in a road race, where there's space for many people to run side-by-side. But on a trail that only fit one runner at a time, getting stuck behind the wrong runner could turn the best part of a race into a walk. Good thing I knew how to use the course to my advantage. I leaned hard into my collar, zigzagging around the competition.

"Make way!" I wheezed. "Comin' through!"

Instead of tripping my rivals, I used the leash on the curves to edge them into bushes. On a normal run I would have stopped to let them pet me, but dogs know the difference between a run and a race by instinct. I stuck my nose into the cracks between runners and wedged them apart like a cannonball, dragging Mom apologizing through the hole behind me. When the trail was an Oscar-wide line of mud and puddles, I sped up to claim the solid mud so my competition would get puddle in their socks. Anyone who stepped back onto the trail too soon was fair game for my leash, which I stretched high and long back to Mom like a clothesline.

Right when I'd cleared the perfect spot in the pack with no one too slow ahead and no one too fast behind, the trail-choking trees parted and the runners ahead slammed to a stop. Ahead, the sand was piled so high that it filled the whole world. Runners plodded single-file up its face in a curling line toward the clouds. This must be the doom the Witch used to lure Mom here.

I charged up the hill, trying to make up for Mom's plodding pace, but the sand spread and smeared under my paws, making her too heavy to move. No matter how hard I pulled, the sand just sagged underneath me like a dreadmill so that each leaping bound just brought me back to Mom's side. I pulled mightily until the trees were below us, and then I pulled some more. I hauled Mom up the doom until there was nothing in the world but sand and sky.

As suddenly as it started, there was a crease in the sand and the doom ended. On the far side, the first rays of sun fell from the clouds onto a dry, sandy sea so vast that it filled the world in every direction. Runners fanned out of each other's way and bounded down the steep slope in whooping leaps. Mom swung her free knee like a jet booster as she leapt into empty space. She hung in midair for a long moment before her foot fell from the knee like landing gear and she touched down, letting the sand cushion her fall before launching the other leg into another falling leap. I followed, whole legs disappearing as the dooms caught my tremendous speed.

At the foot of the doom, my body settled to a stop but my insides were still weightless. Being surrounded by so many Friends, the thrill of the race, learning to fly... I couldn't contain the excitement any longer. I stopped mid-stride and squatted.

Mom stopped behind me, scanning for looky-loos. "Good thing I brought a bag," she said out loud, which was strange. Mom and I didn't need words to communicate, so the only times she ever aimed her voice at me were when she was giving orders. But it's rude to boss someone around when they're going potty. Most of the time, Mom only talked out loud when she wanted other people to hear her. "Ah! Here it is." She shook out the bag like a magician pulling a handkerchief out of his sleeve.

"That's just for sidewalks," I whispered. "You don't have to pick up poo when we're on a trail, remember?"

"You just took a dump in the middle of the race course with a dozen witnesses." Mom looked around trying to catch a witness's eyes as she fitted the bag over her hand like a puppet.

"Running away is what you're *supposed* to do in a race." I blasted off in a post-poo sprint, but the leash held me fast. "Come on! Let's flee the scene. It'll be fun."

"Oh great. I can't wait to carry this poop *all the way to the next aid station.*" Mom paused to give someone time to laugh. When no one did, she moved the conversation back inside her head where only I could hear.

The pack broke up like the clouds and spread out across the sand until we were practically alone under the strengthening sun. With the sand swallowing Mom's footsteps, only the rustling of the poop bag told me that she was still behind me. Instead of a trail, we followed a never-ending series of posts sticking like buoys out of the sand. They were spread out so that each buoy seemed like the last until you were close enough to sniff it. Only then would another appear in the distance, the ribbon on its tip fluttering against the sky.

On every climb, Mom shook the fist holding the poop bag and whispered threats about the nasty things she would do if the dooms didn't cut it out. Mom often confuses planning with predicting and thinks that she can shame the world into amomodating her plans if she can just prove it wrong. When growling didn't work, she bargained like the earth had made a promise with its fingers crossed behind its back and she could still change its mind. At long last, the dooms gave in to Mom's dragon voice and retreated into the trees.

"Finally!" Mom gasped. "It feels like we've been wandering through the desert for 40 years."

"Trees don't grow in sand," I agreed. I thought I heard a snicker, but maybe it was just the wind rustling through the leaves.

The sand lay in ambush among the roots, less steep than before, but just as deep. Everywhere we ran it was sand, sand, sand. No trash cans, no water bowls. Nothing but sand. Now that the sun was out, there was no time to dawdle. Even in the trees its gooey, sluggish heat stuck to my back and made it feel like I was

21

running through syrup. I peeled my tongue from the roof of my mouth and let it flap as I jogged.

Eventually, we reached the only road of the day. A glorious, swimming-pool-sized puddle glistened in the middle of the block-long strip of asphalt. Puddle water doesn't bother me, but Mom is more squeamish.

"Eew, don't drink that," Mom said. "You shouldn't drink water with rainbows in it."

I'm colorblind and don't believe in grey-nbows. "This is no time for your superstitions," I slurped. "There's plenty here for the both of us." I waited a moment for her to join me, but Mom is stubborn. "Suit yourself," I shrugged, and drank my fill.

The road led into a car kennel. Mom took the lead, pulling me on the leash for the first time all morning. "Hallelujah! A trash bin," she said, holding out the sad, mashed bag.

The trash can closed its mouth with the same sound that jail cells make. When Mom turned to face what was beyond the car kennel, her face made the expression of someone on the wrong side of the bars. A trail-marking ribbon flapped from a stick stuck in a beach covered in—what else?—deep sand. Mom made a whimpering sound and staggered onto the beach.

Mom almost never runs with a water bottle, especially in a race, when people volunteer to serve her. But we'd been wandering through dry sand all morning without aid. Perhaps I should have insisted that she drink out of the puddle.

I was starting to wonder whether a tongue could get sunburned when I spotted a shelter in the distance and caught the faint smell of fresh water. I gave Mom a *catch me if you can* look and led the way. Mom's ragged breath behind me proved that she was lying about feeling too tired to run anymore.

Under a canopy, a picnic table overflowed with treats like pretzels, peanut butter sammiches, M&M's, and chopped-up granola bars. Like a gentleman, I let Mom do the begging while I sat in the shade waiting for her to bring me a snack. But even with everything her heart desired spread out in front of her, Mom hesitated to touch any of it.

Her pincher fingers pulled a single chip out of its bowl like a Jenga piece. She held it up to her face, but her mouth wouldn't open. She offered it to me instead. "Do you want a potato chip? I probably shouldn't eat anything someone else might have touched." She pointed a longing look at the trail mix before reaching past it to pick up a banana instead.

Mom scraped her tongue across her lips as she watched a creature wandering among the picnic tables. The creature looked just like a man, except that he had pitchers at the end of his arms instead of paws. Inside Mom's thought bubble, I watched her tackle him, rip his pitchers from his arms, and pour both of them greedily down her throat. Mom tore her shark eyes off the creature, pointed them at the lady behind the table, and hid her bloodthirstiness behind a smile. "Do you have any cups?" she asked politely.

"I've got just the thing," the lady said, picking up peanut butter jars and jelly knives until she found a rubbery bag about the shape of a tube sock. It dangled like a dead fish as she held it out.

Mom held up the sack by the stiff ring at the top and inspected the sad, floppy pouch dangling from it. "So I'm supposed to drink out of this?"

"It's reusable," the lady said, like it was a priceless treasure and Mom wasn't worthy. "It's made to fold up easily into a pocket while you run."

Mom relaxed. "So I get to keep it? Thank you."

The woman stiffened in the way people do when they find out that Mom is a selfish person who is only acting polite to deceive them. "Ed can fill it for you, but you've got to give it back when you're done."

This wasn't the first time that Mom had made the mistake of believing that helpers would help her, too. Today, the help was meant for people who brought their own bottles. It's awkward for everyone when you accidentally try to take help meant for someone else, which is why Mom tries to never rely on anyone. Just in case.

"Is it, like... um... has someone else... erm..." Words spun through Mom's thought bubble as she tried to find the combination that didn't sound ungrateful.

"She's asking if it has cooties," I translated.

"You'd be surprised how many people don't bring their own bottle and expect us to provide one along the course." The woman shook her head to show what she thought of litter bugs like Mom.

"*I'm* not surprised. The question is, why are you?" Mom said in her head, where only I could hear her.

"Is there any water for me?" I panted.

When the lady looked from Mom's sour puss to my grin, her smile got as big as her face. "Hi there, big guy! There's a dog bowl right over there."

Eddie Pitcher Hands slopped water from his paws into the sack. Mom dragged her goopy tongue over her lips again and lifted it toward her mouth.

"No, Mom! The boogeyvirus!" I reminded her. "Don't do it. You'll die!"

"Ssssh!" Mom thought at me. "That was down in San Francisco. I'm sure it's not in Oregon yet..."

She closed her eyes and drank the water down. She looked at the last jellybean of water at the bottom of the sock and only hesitated for a moment before asking Eddie Pitcher Hands for a refill. She didn't even hesitate before asking him to fill it the third time.

When she was finished, Mom gave the pouch back for the next thirsty runner and turned her attention to the unprotected snacks. All the runners ahead of us had already used their paws to wipe slime off of their faces before sticking those same paws into these bowls and stirred them around. Mom looked at the pretzels and M&Ms as if one of them might bite her. She carefully picked up a peanut butter and jelly sandwich by the crust and took a delicate bite.

We left the boogeysnacks and ran through miles, and miles, and miles, and miles, and miles, and miles (six more of them) of sand. We ran on beach sand, grass sand, and woods sand. By the time we got back to Eddie Pitcher Hands, Mom looked like a cartoon crawling tongue-out through the desert. This time she didn't even ask before reaching across the table for the drinking sock and slurping down water as fast as Eddie Pitcher Hands could pour.

By the time we emerged from the sandy forest back into the sea of dooms, the excitement was gone for me, too. Dogs can't smell the future like people can, so all I had to do was worry about putting one paw in front of the other until someone told me I was done. Since Mom could count the gap between her and the future, each of her steps was burdened with the distance still to go. We trudged on without a thought of running as the weight of all of Mom's steps not yet taken added to the sorrows of all the steps behind. The sun had long ago erased all signs of the morning's rain from the sky, and I missed Eddie Pitcher Hands.

"How far have we gone?" I asked when even Mom's thought bubble was silent.

"We just hit 13.1 miles," she sighed. "If this were a half marathon we'd be done by now."

When Mom seemed ready to crawl on all fours like a sensible runner I asked, "It's not much longer, right?"

"We've gone 15.5 miles!" she moaned in despair. "It should be over now."

"But look, it's not over yet." I looked at the next far-off sand buoy to show her what I meant.

"This isn't right!" Mom snarled like she wanted to teach someone a lesson. Since I was the only one around, she taught me a math lesson. "25K is only supposed to be 15.5 miles. No more, no less. We should be done by now! But there was almost a mile of trail through the trees before the dunes and I can't even see the damned trees, which means we've still got a mile to go. At least!"

"But Mom, nature doesn't come in units that are the same every time. You can't make the finish come closer just by counting."

"Okay, fine. It's not the course that's too long, it's the measurement that's wrong. If your race isn't 25K, then call it a 27K, or whatever distance it actually is. That's the agreement!"

Sometimes Mom's rules make my head spin. "What do you do when someone breaks an agreement?"

"The agreement ends and you don't have to do your part anymore."

"So if you agreed to run twenny-five killmometers, and we've run twenny-five killmometers, then I guess we're *all done*. Shall we have some drinks and snacks?"

"The drinks and snacks are at the finish!" Mom howled. "They tricked us and now we have to keep running against our will. There's no justice in this world!"

"I know how to fix it," I said. "How about we decide to keep running because we want to?"

"But I don't want to. I just want it to be over."

"Well that's your problem."

"It *is* a problem! The laws of math and science are what hold the world together. You can't just decide that your kilometers are 15% longer today. It's... it's..."

"Lawless?" I suggested.

"Exactly!" She scowled, retreating back inside her head.

If you're not a runner, you may not know that *almost there* is a lot closer to the finish line than most people expect. *Almost there* doesn't come when you've got more distance behind you than what remains, and it's not the last mile. Every step in a race adds to the tiredness of the last, so the struggle grows as the distance left to run shrinks. You are always in the hardest moment of the race as long as there are more moments ahead.

Almost there is the place where you finally see the finish line and all the soreness goes on mute. Your suffering bursts like a blister. Relief drowns out the tired as you outrun your misery and the whole world cheers for you. Then you cross the finish line and the tired catches you and turns you into roadkill.

We weren't *almost there* yet when trees appeared at the foot of the final doom. The course continued to put killmometers between us and the finish, and Mom filled them each with curses. I *almost* thought we were *there* when I spotted the first car through the trees, but the trail curled up on itself to squeeze even more killmometers in the space it still had.

Mom tallied up the race's broken promises as we ran the long way round the car kennel. "We've run more than 17 miles through deep sand and now they're making us run around in circles?"

"And look! After a three hour tour, we're right back where we started," I marveled.

"More like 6 hours. It's like they're tacking on distance just to mess with us."

Finally, we rounded the last bend to *almost there* and I crossed the finish line to the thundering applause of the two people who noticed.

On the far side, someone finally handed Mom a cup-shaped glass of her very own. She staggered toward the tanks, filled the cup and emptied it down her throat, refilled it, and held it down for me. When my tongue could no longer reach the water at the bottom, she refilled it and took another turn herself. When we'd both drunk enough to leave water in the cup at the end of our turn, Mom led me back to the Covered Wagon.

I wanted to *lay down* and take a nap, but no one can sleep through the tussle of Mom changing clothes in the Wagon. She dug through the suitcase like a dog on a beach, throwing t-shirts, sweatshirts, dry socks, and clean underwear over her shoulder. Once she'd found all the ingredients for a new outfit, she peeled off her soggy shirt, squirmed out of her wet sports bra, and wrestled a clean one over her sticky skin. She leaned back to lift her hips enough to pull off her shorts, kicked her legs, and wriggled the sweatpants back over her hips. When she was finally dressed again, she leaned away one final time to put her soggy clothes in the laundry bag. I stretched out in bed and closed my eyes.

The door rumbled open and I waited for the driving hum of the Wagon to lull me into a long nap. But the door didn't slam shut again.

I opened one eye to see Mom waiting expectantly at the door. "Are you coming?"

"I'm sleeping."

"I've got a surprise for you. A real treasure."

Mom had been talking so much about the race's broken promises that I'd almost forgotten she'd promised me a surprise after the race, too. I sat up. "Does it have to do with that cookout I smelled at the finish line?"

"No, but it involves dinner later." Mom pulled something sparkly from behind her back. It was my mermaid costume from last Halloween. She strapped the seashells across my chest and fastened the fin around my waist.

When I was a puppy, the feeling of having something on my head used to turn me to stone. All I could do was plead helplessly with my eyes until Mom removed the hat and lifted the spell. The trouble was that turning me into a statue made it much easier for the Witch to take pictures, so Mom started bringing hats and other costumes with us on all of our hikes. She actually liked how the different costumes helped tell our adventures apart when she and the Witch looked back on them.

Even after the curse was lifted and I learned how to move under hats, Mom kept bringing costumes on our hikes. I didn't mind so much because if anyone caught me wearing a stetson at the edge of a cliff or a beret on a mountaintop, they were more likely to notice what a *good boy* I was and reward me with extra pats. Now my "hats for pats" schtick was famous and people came from all over the internet to tell me how handsome I was.

"What do mermaids have to do with treasures?" I asked as Mom clicked the walking leash onto my collar. "All they do is flirt with princes."

"It'll be extra sparkly now that the sun's out, so that's a bit like treasure. We want you to stand out, don't we?"

"It's the treasure that sparkles, not the treasure hunter," I reminded her. "Why don't *you* wear the sparkly clothes for a change?"

"Don't be silly," Mom said. "You're the star of the show."

I couldn't argue with that.

Mom led me back to *almost there* and stiffly lowered herself onto a log. "This way people will see you at the best moment of the whole race," she explained.

We clapped for all the twenny-five killmometer and fiddy killmometer winners as they burst limply into the finish area. We'd already cheered for many winners by the time a tall lady I'd never seen before came around the corner.

She perked up like her finish line came sooner than everyone else's. "Oscar!" she said, with the energy of someone who hadn't been running through deep sand all day.

All it takes for me to fall in love at first sight is someone noticing that I'm a *good boy*. Mom dropped the leash and I sprinted into my true love's arms, plowing like a cannonball into her heart.

"Who the heck are you?" I squealed, wagging my fin and jumping around so she could pat both my head and my butt with the same hand.

"Oscar! Oscar! Oscar!" my Surprise said.

"My name's Oscar too!" I told her. "It's a very good name."

"No, she's saying *your* name," Mom 'splained. "This is your friend Lily from the internet. She's the one that got us into this mess."

"Hi, Lily!" I screeched. "Come on, I'll show you the way to the finish line. I thought there was treasure there, but now I know that the treasure won't arrive until you do."

I set Lily free to discover the finish on her own. Mom found a table close to the water jugs and I sat beside her, sparkling to make it easier for Lily to find us again. She appeared with one plate and two sammiches and sat down, forgetting to put the second sammich—my sammich—where I could reach it.

"Hey, aren't you forgetting something?" I screeched as Lily took another bite without offering me one.

"Oscar, quiet!" Mom scolded.

Lily handed me a piece of turkey anyway and took another selfish bite. "Sharing is caring," I reminded her in an even louder voice. Mom shushed me a second time.

I'd seen this movie before. Mom had put me under a silence spell so Lily would pay attention to her instead. If I wanted my voice back, Lily would need to give me the kiss of true love.

I gently kissed Lily's sweaty knee through her tights. "You're very beautiful," I thought at her. When she put a bite of sammich in her mouth without giving me any, I used body language to get her attention instead. I rested my head in her lap and shimmied my hips suggestively.

"Oscar! Be polite!" Mom squawked. She yanked the leash, pulling me away from my new-true love's leg.

But Lily thought my twerking was quite fetching. She leaned over to let me lick the salt from her face. With the kiss of true love, the spell was broken. My soulmate peeled back the bread on the second sammich, letting the turkey drop onto the ground as if by accident. I cleaned it up before Mom could scold her for making a mess.

"Let's go find some real food," Lily announced.

"I thought you'd never ask," I wagged, leading the way back to the car kennel.

I escorted Mom and Lily to a restaurant to complain over chicken fingers. The complaining was Mom's reward for all that running, the chicken fingers were my reward for listening to her all over again, and Lily ordered chili.

"I thought that the dunes would only be a small part of the race," Mom whined. "I didn't know that 80% of the course would be through deep sand!"

Numbers are the only way Mom knows to tell other people how she feels. She never says, "It's raining," she says, "There's a 90% chance of rain" to remind herself that there's always a chance that the world will go back to how she thinks it should be. She says "Quiet! It's 2 o'clock in the morning," as if the number should make me extra sorry for saving her life when she'd rather sleep than hunt ghosts.

"… And the course was long!" Mom went on. "Like *really* long! 25 kilometers is like…" her face squished as she tried to convert mental suffering into miles. "… like 15-something miles, and my watch said more than 17 and a half. That's like… um… like 10% longer than it should have been." Numbers are also how Mom tells right from wrong. The first person to make a number that everyone agrees with is supposed to be crowned *Right*. If Lily agreed with Mom's numbers, perhaps it would erase the extra miles altogether. But all the day's suffering would be for nothing if Mom's numbers didn't convince Lily.

"And I only ran half as far as you did… less!" Mom looked at Lily's face and nervously awaited her verdict.

"It was pretty long, wasn't it?" Lily said to show that the numbers were right, but not necessarily Mom's feelings.

To my surprise, Mom nodded. "You're much more polite about correcting Mom than the Witch is," I told Lily, marveling at how Mom seemed to find letting go of her outrage soothing. "Do it again."

"And what's with only having 2 aid stations?" Mom blustered with slightly less force. "I can go 6 miles without water, but not when it takes 2 hours to cover the distance."

"The 50K came through the aid station four times, but I visited five because I thought I lost my phone," Lily recounted.

The horror of losing the Witch lured Mom's attention away from the numbers into real concern for Lily's safety. "Oh no! What did you do?"

"I noticed it was missing more than a mile from the aid station, so I ran all the way back, looking for it on the ground the whole way. When I got there, someone pointed out that it was in my pocket the whole time."

"Your witch is a trickster, too?" I asked. "I bet you were real disappointed when you found out you hadn't lost her after all. Aren't witches awful?"

"So wait, you ran an extra 2 or 3 miles, on top of the 31 miles it was meant to be, and on top of the 2 miles that weren't supposed to be there?" Mom sputtered, trying to count Lily's attitude in a way that made sense.

"Yes, it was a long day," Lily said in a voice like it hadn't really been such a long day after all.

"Are you sure you don't want a pitchfork and maybe to light someone on fire?" I asked supportively. "Don't you think someone should pay for this?"

"I would have given up right then and there," Mom said. "I was having a real pity party for those last few miles."

"You weren't partying," I reminded her. "You were grumbling and bellyaching like every doom had been put there to make   your   life   harder."

Mom ignored me so as not to lose track of her rage. "And I didn't have to start in the pouring rain like you."

"It was a beautiful course. I came for the scenery and the challenge, and I got both," Lily said. "Sometimes things don't work out perfectly. That's life."

"Ah! That's where you're wrong," I said, glad that I could share my life coaching skills. Lily seemed to think she was a dog. It was time somedog loved her enough to remind her how to behave like a human. "In our house, we get frustrated when life doesn't go our way because we know that things could always be better. That's called *standards*. Whenever you start to feel too good, remind yourself that you have standards and you'll be back to normal in no time."

"I would've lost my ever-loving dog doo and thrown a temper tantrum," Mom said. "You can't give people wrong information and send them off into the wilderness. What if they act on that bad information? Someone should pay for putting us in that situation."

"You *did* throw a temper tantrum," I reminded her. "But you held onto your ever-loving dog doo for several miles, remember?"

"Well," Mom said, warming up for a goodbye. "We should probably…"

"You've had a long day. Why don't you at least stay the night?" Lily said. "There's an extra bed in my hotel room."

Nothing makes Mom more anxious than a kind invitation. She ground her teeth, searching for an excuse.

"It's not just you," I reassured Lily. "Changing plans makes her nervous, in case she has fun and it proves her plan wrong."

"It's a 15-hour drive to Death Valley," Mom said eventually. "I'd like to knock out a few hours before bed tonight. It was nice to meet you."

Chapter 3

Outlaws

In a world crowded with so many interesting people, Mom must go to lengths to avoid the choking grip of friendship. Part of the reason she decided to drive such a long way from rainforest to desert was that a big drive makes for a good excuse to escape.

It's easy to count the hours between Oregon and Las Vegas to impress someone, but it's more difficult to sit through them. I fell asleep as Oregon disappeared from the tail window. The trees had disappeared by the time I woke up again. Then the grass went away. The mountains came, turned white, and then bald until the only thing left outside the Wagon windows was dirt and bare rock. I was starting to think we were going to stay in the Wagon until the whole world disappeared when Mom suddenly perked up.

"I've always wanted to visit that place with the walking rocks," she said.

"The walking what?" I asked. "It sounded like you said *rocks*."

"There's this dry lakebed where rocks move on their own. No one has ever seen it happen, but they leave grooves in the ground to show where they've been."

I imagined a scientist studying the lake floor with boulders charging toward him like a game of redlight greenlight. "That sounds dangerous. What if we get run over?"

"In pictures, none of them look any bigger than a basketball." She cupped her paws awkwardly around the driving wheel to show how big a basketball was. "I think they did eventually figure out how they move; something about wind and rain. The only reason they didn't figure it out sooner is probably because it's so hard to get there."

"Where is it?" I asked, expecting somewhere imaginary like Narnia, Middle Earth, or Milwaukee.

Mom flapped her hand toward the naked mountains outside her window. "They're right over there in Death Valley."

I imagined a rock rolling out of those mountains and myself down below, escaping with the aplomb of Indiana Bones. "That sounds like just the kind of adventure we've been looking for. Let's go!"

"I looked it up before we left. Death Valley is a National Park. No dogs." She looked around mischievously. "But this place doesn't look too closely monitored, does it?" She held the Witch to her mouth and commanded, "Give me directions to Racetrack Playa."

My tail twitched rebelliously. "But I thought Parks were forbidden."

"The rule is that dogs aren't allowed on trails, but they *can* go on roads! That means that we can visit so long as there's a road that goes there. If we happen to take a few steps off the road for a good picture, well… Everyone gets a little lost sometimes."

"Won't we get vaporized or something if we step off the safety of the road?"

"Listen, National Park rules are for 2 things: to protect the wildlife and to protect the Park Service from liability. The wildlife in Death Valley are things like lizards and beetles, not fuzzy, chasable, edible, or infectible critters. We won't be outside the van for very long and I'll keep you on leash. So that takes care of the wildlife."

"What about the lie-ability? Isn't it sort of like a lie if we go somewhere we know we shouldn't?"

"Liability means they don't want anyone to get hurt, but it's not like there will be crowds of tourists all the way out there. You and I are experienced hikers and we'd be taking the same risks outside the Park as in it. Where's the harm?"

"In two miles, turn left," the Witch butted in.

"Really?" Mom held the Witch on the driving wheel so she could read and drive at the same time. "Well I'll be darned. It looks like we don't even have to go through the main park entrance to get there."

"Turn left," the Witch commanded.

Beside the road, a teepee-shaped sign guarded a dusty car-trail into the desert. The Wagon didn't click, or even slow down. The car-trail zipped through the windows front to back.

"In one thousand feet, make a U-turn," the Witch scolded. Mom hit the *shut up* button.

I watched the teepee-sign shrink in the back window. "You were supposed to turn. Didn't you hear her tell you to turn?"

"Do you know what that sign said?" Mom tested.

Dogs can't read, so she was asking me to tell her something she wanted to hear. "Does it say, *Dogs allowed this week only*?"

"It said the road was blocked 22 miles ahead."

I wasn't about to give up on my excuse to get out of the Wagon that easily. "That means we'd have twenny-two miles to figure out what to do next."

"It also said NO ACCESS TO DEATH VALLEY."

"Excellent! That plays right into our plan. If anyone gets mad at us for sneaking in, we can blame the sign that told us we *weren't* going to Death Valley!"

"You can't close nature." Mom wagged her head like it was silly to even try. "It just means that the road is so poorly maintained that it's easier to put up a sign than raise the money to fix it, which could take years."

"It could be a decoy. Maybe they knew there was a brave dog coming who wouldn't take *no* for an answer."

"It's a public road, so it's not like they're going to lock you up just for being there," Mom said, like the solution to one problem was just a warmup to an even bigger problem. "But you can't count on anyone to come out there and rescue you if you get in trouble."

The Wagon pulled to a stop across the beginnings of a dirt road beside the highway. It wasn't really a road, since a gate blocked its path a few steps from the copilot's window.

"Are we there?" I smooshed my nose against the window and searched for clues about the adventure to come.

"No, I just need to think." Mom never thinks for herself, so she called on the Witch for help.

"Mom! Mom! Lookit the size of the chain on that gate! Do you think it's locked so the rocks don't get out? Hey, are you sure this is a good place to stop?"

"I just want to check something before cell service drops out again."

"Won't someone wonder what we're doing, and be mad when they find out that we're here for no reason?"

"I haven't seen any *NO STOPPING* signs," Mom said without taking her eyes off the Witch's screen to check. "I'm out of the road and it doesn't seem like anyone's using that gate, so I don't think we're breaking any rules. I doubt anyone will even notice."

"Phew. I thought so. So how long is the hike to the walking rocks?"

"The drive takes 4 hours from here, and it's… 60 miles long!" the Witch said through Mom's mouth. Mom translated, "The road must be really gnarly. That's an average of 15 miles per hour! The van would never make it."

"High clearance and four-wheel drive are a *must*," the Witch added smugly.

"We don't have either of those." Mom sagged so hopelessly in the driving chair that she looked like she never planned to get up again.

"We have four wheels," I reminded her. "What if we just walked in? I'm a very strong dog, remember? I ran the world's longest twenny-five kay yesterday."

"It's much too long to run. What if we got stuck 50 miles from the nearest road? It says here there's no cell service along the way."

You don't usually see whales in the desert, but just then a killer whale breached the hill behind us. It stopped across the driveway with two wheels still perched rakishly on the road, flashing the lights on its back to call even more attention to itself. I watched Mom's eyes in the mirror as the whale flapped a fin and a Law climbed out of its finpit. Mom rolled her eyes and rolled down the window.

The Law paused to check out the Wagon's butt. He clutched at a big button on his breast, tucked his chin, and whispered into it. It let out a squawk.

"Don't worry, Mom. I've got this one," I whispered.

When the Law was finished preening, he strutted toward the cockpit, checking himself out in all the windows along the way. His shirt filled Mom's window and my hackles prickled.

"Is everything okay?" the Law asked.

"I WAS *ON THE LEASH!*" I barked at the top of my lungs.

Mom covered the ear closest to me and flinched. "Oh yeah, just fine. I'm trying to decide whether to stop in Death Valley to camp or carry on all the way to Las Vegas. I stopped here because there's cell service."

Dog doo! That sounded like something a guilty person might say.

Mom tested his bluff. "Have I done something wrong?"

"Oh, no. Nothing wrong." He leaned back on his heels to check himself out in the back window. "I just wanted to make sure you're okay."

"Yup. Just fine," Mom reassured him. Then, remembering that an excuse is never finished until you say when you plan to move along, she added, "I was just looking at the different routes into Death Valley."

"The turn-off is about twenty miles up the road that way," the Law waved in the direction we were all facing.

A man-dog must never accept directions, especially if he didn't ask for them. "We know where it is," I barked. "We already know about the secret passageway and everything, so buzz off."

"Ow!" Mom held her my-side ear again and scowled. "Get in the back, Spud. You're not helping."

Once he saw that Mom was listening again, the Law continued, "… and then you're going to make a left."

"Great. Thank you. But I'm okay parked here, right?" Mom made her face do a smile. "Just until I have my route programmed into the GPS?"

"There's almost no cell service in the Valley," he said, leaving the *little lady* part silent.

"Yes, I know. And is it okay if I sit here, just while I wait for my offline maps to load?"

"Yup. I'm just making sure you're okay."

I poked my head over Mom's shoulder. "You already said that!"

Mom grabbed my face and shoved it behind the driving chair again.

The Law looked the Wagon up and down nosily while Mom and I argued. He inspected the camera periscope and the dish-sized mirror on the Wagon's backside. "So what's up with the car? Are you filming something?"

"It came that way," Mom explained. "It's just an old Postal Service van I got on Craigslist so I could camp in the back." She remembered that it's illegal to be poor in some places, so she added, "… when I'm on vacation. Like today."

"Oh, cool," he said, still not going away.

"So… if I stay here, is that cool?" Mom asked again. "I'll be gone in like 15 minutes. As soon as the maps, y'know, finish downloading."

"Oh yeah. I was just checking to make sure you were okay." The Law waited for Mom to ask him to rescue her. When she didn't, he said, "I'll let dispatch know you're okay."

"Thanks." Mom eyed the Witch on the copilot's chair but remembered her manners. She kept her hands on the driving wheel until the Law crawled back into the whale's finpit and they swam away.

The Witch went back to singing and Mom went back to poking. The Witch hadn't even finished a whole song when another killer whale prowled past. It made a tight turn and beached itself in the same place as the last Law-mobile. Mom rolled her eyes again, rolled down her window again, and waved again.

This time, two Laws got out and stood one on each side of the Wagon.

"I was *WEARING* a *LEASH!*" I bellowed even louder to be sure they could hear me.

"Hi." Mom spoke first to establish dominance. "I just spoke to your colleague a few minutes ago. Am I in anybody's way?"

"Nope, we just wanted to make sure you weren't in trouble," the New Law said.

The Other Law checked his hair in the copilot's window.

"I don't want to be any bother," Mom promised. "*Am* I in trouble?"

As Mom explained all over again about Death Valley, and Witch service, and where we were going, and why the Covered Wagon looked that way, I barked all the important parts with her for emphasis.

"Working PERSON!" I screeched.

"A WOMAN who doesn't need directions!" I bellowed.

"MailMAN's CAMERA!" I screamed.

"It's not hooked up to a TV!" I shouted.

"Thank you for the directions," Mom said when the interrogation was over. "I think I can find it without the GPS now. I guess I'll just be moving along, then."

The Other Law bragged into his shirt about bravely rescuing a lost tourist as they walked back to the whale. Mom waited until the fins thumped before waking the Wagon.

"What was all that barking about?" she asked as the Wagon led the whale back onto the highway.

"*Person, woman, man, camera, TV,*" I said. "Remember that magic password any time someone thinks you're a dummy. It instantly shows people you know what you're talking about."

"What, like *supercalifragilisticexpialidocious*? You do know that song is about how people who use big words are full of crap, don't you?"

"You'll see."

But Mom wasn't about to accept that the walking rocks were out of reach just because it was dangerous, a really bad idea, and the Law had already investigated us twice for even thinking about it. Her eyes kept slipping off the road toward the miles of desert between us and the walking rocks. "The part that gets me is that more people are hurt every year in Parks where Rangers are nearby than in all the other public wilderness lands combined."

"Defund the Rangers!" I agreed. To hear most humans talk about it, the wilder-ness is a dark and frightening place, but really it's just what's left over outside civilization where no one gets to make rules and anything can happen.

"What a strange thing to say. We can't get rid of law enforcement or we'd descend into chaos. Rules are the only way to keep everyone safe when you can't trust their judgment. You've got to protect nature from people, and people from themselves."

I tried to picture the Law's pestering as affection. "Nah, some people just think the world is their own territory and make it their mission in life to keep everyone else off the furniture. What kind of freak uses rules as their love language?"

"The Park Service, the EPA, people with clipboards outside the supermarket…" Mom sighed. "They're just trying to preserve nature. Sometimes the best way to protect something is to keep your distance."

"I see." I paused thoughtfully and waited for the ideas to come together. The Law couldn't get enough of us, and yet we weren't in trouble. No matter how many times Mom told them we were okay, they only became more interested. "So that's why the Law looks for people who *aren't* in trouble," I solved. "Because they're staying away from anyone who's really in danger. To protect them."

Mom looked longingly at the desert slipping past the windows faster than she could store it in memory. "Life is so much simpler in the wilderness where there's no responsibility and you only have to look out for yourself." She sighed. "The problem is that Park rules give people the illusion of security. If there's someone to enforce the rules, that must also mean there'll be someone to help when they take dumb risks. It ain't Disneyland out there, folks. You can't count on anyone to come and rescue you."

Humans live under a magical spell that makes them the most powerful of all beasts, strong enough to defeat any danger. They can conjure enchanted screens that become any toy they want to play with and magical travel machines to take them anywhere they want to go. They call the spell *civilization* and use its magical powers to fill their food fortresses with treats and build great buildings to keep them warm, protect them from the rain, and give them light at night.

To keep the spell alive, everyone must say or do the same thing at the same time, like a worldwide game of Simon says. They create rules to keep it going, but it takes a lot of work to keep everyone playing by the rules. So Simons print their rules on signs to recruit people to play with them. They put their rules on the internet so witches will tell far-away Simons all about their accomplishments. They write them on papers and make you paw-tograph them to remember forever the time you played by the rules together. Professional rulers even hire the Law to act as their Simon in case anyone misses the signs, and papers, and witch warnings.

Most people spend so much time in civilization that they forget it's all in their imaginations and they can step out of it at any time. If there were no civilization at all, wildness would just be a fact of life, but the wild feels wilder right after you've broken the spell. That's why they call it the *wilder-ness*; because it's both a place and a way of being.

I nudged Mom's elbow. "Let's make a break for it."

"I'm stubborn, but I'm not stupid," Mom said, proving that she couldn't see the future as well as she thought. "It's not worth the risk of needing to call for help. Let's push on toward Vegas so we'll have time to do something fun tomorrow."

Chapter 4
Weather Jinx

It was dark outside when the Wagon pulled over.

"Are we here?" I searched the window for signs of adventure, but only the ghost of a handsome dog stared through me from inside the glass.

"No, this is just the Park boundary." Mom stepped into the night, leaving the door open for me to follow.

"Hooray! I knew you could find it. Are we going to sneak to the walking rocks by the cover of night?"

"No. I was trying to avoid it, but the most direct route to Utah from here is through Park land. I was hoping to get to the far side tonight, but the damned Park is bigger than Rhode Island and I'm too tired to drive that far." She walked toward a screen glowing in the darkness. Even here in the middle of the wilder-ness Mom could find a screen. "We probably need a permit to stay overnight."

Like in the City, people and wagons need permits and passes to excuse them for taking up Park space. Parks can sneak up on you like this one did, so part of Mom's wilder-ness preparedness plan was always to keep her National Parks pass up-to-date, even though we weren't allowed out of the Wagon in most of them.

The screen sat majestically within a post the size of a totem pole, as if a parking meter could rule the entire world if it were big enough. Mom poked at it, whining half in her thought bubble and half out loud about, ". . . have one already… where do I… oh come on… that's not fair… *how* much?"

The machine chirped, its belly whirred, and it laid a top-secret message. Mom pulled it out of the secret compartment below the screen and waved it defiantly. "Stupid thing didn't even ask for my annual pass. Cost me 30 bucks for a mucking slip of paper."

"Don't they know who you are?" I said in the offended voice that Mom expected.

She placed the paper ceremonially on the front windowsill and tapped it a couple of times to prove it was there on purpose. "Think of it as double-paying in protest."

"That'll show 'em."

"At least a parking pass is cheaper than a campground." Campgrounds came with all kinds of nastiness, like noises, long walks to the potty, and rules about leashes. We came to the wilderness to get away from all that. "If anyone asks why we're not in a campground, we can just tell them that we weren't planning to spend the night. Which I suppose is true, when you think about it."

"Who's asking?" I squinted nervously into the darkness.

"The rangers. Or just busybodies."

"Say no more," I said sagely.

Dogs know all about silly rules for where you can and can't exist. Some people just can't enjoy a place unless someone else isn't welcome there, so they pen in nature with gates, railings, and fences and think it means they've tamed nature. They mark their territory with signs that dogs can't read that shout orders without saying *please*:

"KEEP OUT: SENSITIVE WILDLIFE AREA"

"USE BEAR BOXES TO KEEP BEARS OUT OF CAMPGROUNDS"

"LOWER LID TO KEEP OUT FLIES"

"STAY AWAY FROM CLIFF"

"STAY ON TRAIL"

"TRAIL CLOSED"

"DON'T TOUCH"

"CAMP ONLY IN DESIGNATED AREAS"

"CAMPGROUND FULL"

"NO CAMPING"

"NO PARKING"

"NO VEHICLES"

"NO DOGS"

Whether you're standing, sitting, walking, snacking, going potty, finding a place to hitch your Wagon, or sleeping quietly inside of it, they'll find a way to tell you you're doing it wrong.

With our *Get Out of Jail Free* Card on the front windowsill, the Wagon plunged into the deathly blackness of the valley in search of a place to hide for the night. The wilder-ness summoned every car in the valley into a train behind the Wagon. They shone their extra-bright eyebeams into the mirror, making the darkness even darker. If that weren't enough to keep me up all night, the curses Mom growled into the mirror while missed sleeping spots flashed in the darkness were enough to give me nightmares.

It's harder than you think to find a place to sleep in the wilder-ness. Car-trails make excellent sleeping spots, but the same darkness that makes them so good for sleeping also makes them very hard to see from the road. The moment you start looking for one, the zillions of cozy spots that were there during the day disappear.

"Well at least the *NO CAMPING* signs make it easy to spot the pull-offs," Mom muttered as the Wagon swooped into a roadside cubby to let an extra-bright pair of lights pass.

The moment the Wagon pulled back onto the road, another pair of dots appeared in the blackness behind us. The mirror caught their light, spotlighting Mom's squint as she searched the front window for escape. The Wagon slowed its roll and began to click. Harsh light filled the cockpit as the beams bore down on us. We made a hard turn into the safety of a car kennel and darkness washed over me.

"Phew! That was a close one," I said. "Nice find, Mom. Look, there's a people-potty and everything."

But Mom didn't look because her eyes were stuck on a sign in the Wagon's eyebeams. "Phooey! *NO CAMPING.* I think we're going to have to sleep in a campground tonight."

"Don't give up so easily," I encouraged. "The ground beside the road looks like the same stuff they make car-trails from. I bet it's great for sleeping."

"There was another sign that said *OFF-ROAD DRIVING PROHIBITED.* National Parks are the worst!" She pulled out the Witch and demanded, "Take me to the nearest campground."

"There's a campground twenty minutes away," the Witch taunted.

"We came from that way! Driving 20 minutes in the wrong direction adds 40 minutes to our trip," Mom whined. "We've been in the car all day. What else you got?"

"This place is forty minutes away and also in the wrong direction," the Witch said.

"Fine. We'll go back," Mom humphed.

We drove half a Rhode Island back to the campground and found the biggest sign yet waiting for us when we got there. "Thank goodness!" I wagged. "What does it say? Does it say *WELCOME OSCAR?* Or *CONGRATULATIONS FOR SURVIVING A WHOLE DAY IN THE WAGON?*"

"It says *CAMPGROUND FULL*," Mom read. "It's a Sunday night, for heaven's sake. If they want you to follow the rules, they've at least got to give you a chance to do the right thing."

"What do we do now?"

"If you can't make good, you've gotta break bad." Mom checked over both shoulders to make sure there were no witnesses. "I saw an unpaved service road back there. Let's just drive far enough that we won't be visible from the road and spend the night there."

The Wagon returned to the darkness beyond the reach of the campground's lights and crept off the pavement. The road ended under one of those man-made pole-trees and we finally stepped into the fresh air. The night crackled with an eerie feeling that made my fur stand on end.

I sniffed one of the tower's metal paws. "I don't think this thing is going to give us much cover," I whispered. "You can see right through it. Look, I can see the road from here."

"Why did it have to be a full moon? This white van sticks out like a beacon for miles around," Mom groaned. "No matter how hard I try to stay out of people's way, there's always something to draw someone's attention. I can't wait till we're out of California where the rules don't follow you off the road."

Mom stayed on guard all night, waiting for the Law to knock on the window to ask if we were okay. For me, the race ended in Oregon, but Mom lived every day like a race, rushing from one thing to the next and planning what she would do if something tried to slow her down. A full night's sleep is no way to get ahead. Instead, Mom used the nighttime to think about everything that could possibly go wrong so she could have a plan and a backup plan for each expected disaster. Of course, when one thing goes wrong, other wrong-things soon follow, so each plan and backup plan had to fit with the others. Sometimes it took the whole night to put it all together.

Mom passed the time strategizing with the Witch, *rolling over* every time she needed to rearrange the thoughts in her head. It was hard to sleep through her restlessness. Mom and I had to sleep like puzzle pieces to fit in the snug space inside the Wagon. Any time either of us moved, the other had to adjust to find that perfect fit again before we could rest.

It was still nighttime when she patted me awake. "Rise and shine, Spud. We've gotta get an early start if we want to get to the Valley of Fire before it gets too hot."

"But it's still dark." I burrowed deeper into the blankies.

Mom took her post behind the driving wheel. "Fine, you get your beauty sleep. You're gonna need it with all the pictures I'm going to take. This time, it's gonna be epic."

Everyone has at least one superpower. For example, I'm supernaturally handsome with bottomless puppy eyes that a girl can lose herself in. Once the ladies have fallen under my spell, they're helpless to resist my charm. They beg for kisses as they drop bits of their lunch under the table until I oblige. Not every superpower is as useful as being Dog Juan, but even people who are nothing special like Mom have a superpower if you look for it.

Mom's superpower is that she brings unseasonably severe weather wherever she goes. Mom's vacations bring the first rainy day in a ten-year drought. The race she trained for all year brings headwinds that blow your hat off and rain that soaks through your pelt. Mom can turn an Arizona summer day to Oregon in February, and bring a blizzard to Albuquerque in June. That's why Mom's superhero name is the Weather Jinx.

I'd been to Las Vegas many times before, but I'd never visited Las Vegas when it was dry because I always travel with the

Weather Jinx. The last time we visited the Valley of Fire, Mom brought so much rain that it put the fire out. The rain stopped by the time we got there, but the valley was still so filled with steam that there was nothing for me to pose in front of but fog.

The Wagon pointed its nose toward the part of the sky where the stars were disappearing. As the sun climbed out from inside the earth, so did we. It lit the heavy clouds with the neon greys of the Las Vegas strip, and gathered them around like a cozy blanket as it climbed higher in the sky. Soon enough, the only thing left of it was a pale, groggy light.

"Welcome to Nevada!" the Witch announced. Maybe Las Vegas wouldn't have noticed that the Weather Jinx was in town if the Witch hadn't opened her big, fat mouth.

As soon as our cover was blown, the clouds over Nevada went from cozy to nasty. It only took a few more minutes for them to gather a storm. Paw-sized raindrops rushed to turn the road into a river.

"Dog doo! This storm wasn't supposed to come through until this afternoon," Mom accused the sky, like the storm was the liar and not the Witch.

"Oregon, Las Vegas, you keep taking us to places where it rains all the time," I said "Maybe we should aim for somewhere that isn't as wet rather than wishing a place were different."

"You think Las Vegas is a rainy city?" Mom asked, like I was the crazy one.

"It's been rainy every time I've been here."

"That's not true. There was the time..." Mom tilted her head and thought for a moment. "Hunh. You're right."

I let her think for a few thumps of the wipers before asking, "Where to now?"

"I guess Las Vegas isn't going anywhere." Mom sighed and set her eyes back to the line in the middle of the road. "We'll be back again someday. Let's just push on to Utah. At least this will give us more time in Canyon Country."

Beyond Las Vegas, most of the West is wild and untamed, even in modern times. It's a land so fierce that even the plants have claws. The sky is full of sun and stars, and isn't concerned with serving witches. Wild one-eyed dogs with peg-legged limps roam the roads like pirates searching for buried treasure in the food wrappers and bottled messages thrown from wagon windows. Car-trails run naked without pavement to hide their bumps and potholes. Even the road signs have bite marks like bullet holes.

Mom is at her stillest when traveling. Her thought bubble shows nothing but static and a minute grows to fill a lifetime while a whole lifetime can fit into a minute. Now that we were beyond the land of traffic and rules, Mom settled into a road trance. Sometimes I thought she could drive round and round the world like that for the rest of her life, only stopping at a gas station a few times a day.

We all get treats at the gas station: Mom gets bubbly water and bubblegum, I get cheese sticks or hot dogs, and the Wagon gets to fill up. The Wagon lived on an all-juice diet, feeding through a straw while Mom was inside the potty-and-cheese-stick shop. In northern Arizona, I sat in the driving chair supervising the Wagon's snack time and spying on the people at the other juice boxes while Mom was inside. The shelter over the juice boxes muted the banging of rain on the roof, so I could hear their conversations through the closed windows.

"We're just picking up some essentials before we go into quarantine for a few days," the one from the car full of people puppies said.

"They're already out of canned soup and toilet paper in there," the one with the pickup truck said. If Mom were one of those hikers who mark her territory with a tacky white flag, we'd really be in trouble. Mom hates to run out of things, so it was a good thing I'd taught her how to find toilet paper in nature.

"… We were only supposed to come for the weekend, but my sister's refusing to come back to Boulder with me until Colorado is as safe as Utah," a woman with a bike rack on the back of her car told a woman whose car was covered in bumper stickers.

As my ears roamed juice boxes, my eyes stayed stuck to the door where Mom had disappeared. Every time the door opened, instead of Mom, a bandit or a veterinarian came out carrying big bags of loot. I'd learned from movies how masked bandits roam the desert with bandanas over their faces, but I'd never heard of bands of veterinarians sticking up a train. Veterinarians give me the willies. You can't trust anyone who covers their smile before patting you. Sure, they *seem* nice… until they take you into the back room where Mom can't protect you. Whose temperature did all these veterinarians come to this gas station to measure? And was Mom okay in there without me?

Mom finally appeared in the door with a spooked look on her naked face.

"Oh, thank dogness you're safe!" I wagged. "I thought the place was being held up by a band of swashbuckling veterinarians with a bad case of diarrhea. I was afraid they were holding you hostage for a toilet paper ransom. By the way, what does *quar-unseen* mean?"

"Where did you hear that?"

"The people in the next car were talking about it while you were inside. They said they needed lots of toilet paper because they were going into *quar-unseen*. Is that when you're alone in the bathroom and no one can hear you call that the roll is empty?"

"*Quarantine* is when you have to stay away from people because your presence could kill someone," Mom explained like there was no need to be so dramatic. "These people are talking about locking themselves inside their houses starting tomorrow. They don't even know when they'll come out again."

"And they'll be spending all that time in the bathroom? Is that why toilet paper will save their lives?"

"Nah, people just don't know how to deal with scarcity. When they think about what they can't live without, their first thought is the experience that makes them feel deprived most often. And do you know what the most lonely, isolated feeling in the world is for an American?"

I imagined my own worst feeling. "Getting snacky when the treats are on a high shelf and you can't reach?" Too late, I remembered that unlike dogs, humans can climb on counters to reach the highest shelves. "No, wait. Just kidding. That's not my guess." I thought through my years of Mom observations trying to figure out the one thing she couldn't live without. It wasn't thirst, because humans can conjure water inside their stuck houses. "Their witches!" I guessed. "Final answer."

"Good guess, but the only situation where you feel more desperate and alone than when there's no cell service is when you're in a public bathroom and you realize too late that your stall is out of toilet paper. Nothing makes you feel more unclean and alone."

"Did you notice the disguises?" I asked. "They must be doing it so no one can identify them when they kill someone with their very presence. Don't they realize that a veterinarian running loose through the desert is bound to raise suspicion. If you need to disguise your face, you should do it with a bandana."

"Yeah. That was weird, wasn't it? People wear masks in the City all the time, but I've never seen it out here in Navajo country." Mom thought for a second. Outside the windows, the town petered out into clusters of small houses. "Do you know why there aren't more Native Americans around?"

I knew the answer to this one. "Because they were eaten by dinosaurs and went exstinked!"

"What a horrible thing to say! Of course not. The Europeans brought deadly germs on their boats when they came to America. Their diseases spread over the continent faster than the Europeans did. By the time the colonists caught up, 90% of the native population was already gone. Can you imagine what that must have been like?"

"Yeah, but what are the chances that a deadly disease—the likes of which no one has ever seen before—will come across the ocean to kill Jillians of Americans again?"

"If people are starting to quarantine, we probably shouldn't draw attention to the fact that we're traveling. It couldn't hurt to keep a low profile and be a little more sensitive to the communities that we visit."

"Turn here," the Witch interrupted. The Wagon did as it was told. "In three miles you will arrive at your destination," the Witch added without noticing that the Wagon was already stopped.

In front of the Wagon's nose, a cattle catcher was halfway through its transformation into a swimming pool. Water more than a cow's-ankle deep filled hole underneath, and it wouldn't be long before the bars would be underwater, too.

"Well this changes things," Mom said.

"Do cows know how to swim?" I asked hopefully. A bovine lifeguard-dog who spent his days barking at cows would be an excellent second career with my cattle dog heritage.

"The rain is turning these dirt roads into mud. This is a van, not a submarine," Mom said. "If the mud doesn't get us, the temperatures will drop overnight and turn the rain into snow and ice. I don't want to get stuck out there."

"Where will we go if we can't leave the road?" I asked.

"I guess we'll have to go to a campground. A shower would be nice…"

"Going to a campground will blow our cover!" I yipped. "Everyone will know we're travelers. What if they think you're possessed with boogeyvirus?"

"Oh dog doo. I hadn't thought of that. I don't know."

"Whaddaya mean you don't know?" I asked, even more nervously than before. Knowing things is what Mom does. She knows how to drive the Wagon and how to convince the Witch to take us places none of us have ever been before. She knows how to tell if a store is open or closed before we get there. She knows how to talk to the Law so they don't send us to the pound. She knows how to open the Food Fortress, and how to use money to fill it with delicious snacks.

"I've seen and heard so many impossible things over the last few days that I don't know what to expect anymore. It's like everyone started playing by a different set of rules overnight, and no 2 people are playing the same game anymore."

The Wagon tiptoed into a campground across the street from a supermarket and the type of restaurant that serves bacon all day. Usually, we would need a reservation at a fancy downtown campground with a shower that didn't run on coins, but today the only car-houses in the campground were the kind that dream of being stuck houses someday.

Mom dismounted the Wagon and hunched to hide from the rain. A chihuahua and two ladies sat on a porch. The ladies sucked on their smoke sticks and watched Mom skulk toward them. Only the chihuahua gave any hint of what he thought of her.

"Are you open?" Mom shouted over the rain.

"WHO GOES THERE?" overreacted the chihuahua.

"Sure we're open," the bigger lady said, like it was a silly question. "We just haven't had many people passing through because of this storm."

"I thought it was because of the coronavirus," Mom said. "I came from San Francisco through Nevada and Arizona, and it seems like everybody's closing down over this thing."

"You're in *You*-tah!" the smaller one declared. I wasn't sure what she meant, but by the way she stomped her foot, punched the air next to her hip, and straightened her spine, I guessed it had something to do with being tough and darned proud of it.

"Are there any tent spots available?" Mom asked.

The ladies waved their arms at the rain to show which puddle was our camping spot while the chihuahua warned us not to try any funnybusiness.

After exchanging cards and clipboards for a few minutes, Mom came back to the Wagon and guided it into our puddle. When she returned from the shower a year or two later, her hair was as wet as Utah and smelled of anti-frizz and coconuts. We spent the rest of the evening quarunseeing in the Wagon and waiting for Utah and Mom's hair to dry. By the morning, both Mom's hair and the ground were still wet and stiff with cold.

"Luckily we're only doing a small hike today," Mom said. "There's supposed to be a break in the weather later this morning. Wanna risk it?" It may have sounded like a question, but suggestions are just decisions in disguise when you know how to drive.

The rain beat on the roof as the wind rocked the Wagon like Noah's Ark.

"How about we take a nap day?" I suggested back, letting the racket on the roof back me up.

"The trail is at higher elevation. There'll be snow…" Mom tempted.

"Yippee skippee! You promise?!" I wagged, throwing off the blanket and jumping into the copilot's chair.

Snow is the word for the sparkly bits that flake off of clouds and turn everything underneath fluffy with white dirt. White dirt has magical properties that regular dirt doesn't have. It smells like freezer burn and zambonis. It preserves a perfect buttprint when you roll in it. It cools you down on hot mountain hikes. It's a great kisser. You'd have to be a real fuddyduddy to dislike white dirt. Mom can't stand the stuff.

The village looked like a ghost town as the Wagon rolled through empty streets. The buildings disappeared at the edge of town as suddenly as if Mom had changed the channel on the front window. I watched the rain trying to turn to snow as the slush under our wheels got chunkier and grew a white crust. Usually, Mom's eyeballs stay stuck to the road when the weather threatens to yank it out from under her, but this time her eyeballs slipped around the desert.

"I think we've been here before," she said. "Remember that time we wound up on the wrong side of the Grand Canyon?"

That was during our first expedition in a borrowed carhouse, before we met the Wagon. We were so new to traveling that we didn't know about AllTrails or saving mapps for when the Witch wasn't talking to us. Back then, Mom didn't want planning to ruin the surprise of what the trail had in store, so we drifted through the desert, hoping adventure would find us. With so much emptiness and no plan, most of what we'd seen of the West in those early days were its roads. We hadn't yet learned that the best place to hunt the wilder-ness is away from pavement, signs, and other things to mark the way.

"You thought the Wagon would die if its paws touched anything but pavement, remember?" I said.

"Back then my biggest fear was not having cell service," Mom said like she was remembering a cute puppy. "Everything I knew about the wilderness came from Hollywood. I thought if I left civilization I would immediately have four flat tires, get mauled by a bear, have to crawl through frozen rivers, and sleep in rotten logs like in *The Revenant*. It took a lot of experience to figure out what was fiction and what was reality."

It was too hot to hike the last time we were here, so I'd lain in the shade under a tree and waited for Mom to come to her senses. I tried to find the pygmy tree whose shade I'd panted under that day, but today the trees were disguised under heavy cloaks of white dirt and there was no shade anywhere in the gloomy morning. Now that we weren't searching for significance by the side of the road, the place looked like any other spot between here and there. It's funny how a place changes every time you see it, as if the place isn't as important as the self you bring to it. I still wanted to flop down under the trees, but this time to wallow in the white dirt and make a snow angel.

"Just think; we were surrounded by trails that day and had no idea," Mom said.

"Travel takes practice, doesn't it? Remember how you thought that a trail too technical for running was a waste?" I remembered something even funnier. "Remember how you thought you needed to take a shower every day?"

"Cleanliness is a lot more important when you've lived your whole life with pavement between you and the earth," Mom said. "With no real danger indoors, you need to find something to fill the time, and some people find meaning by cleaning. Showers every day, washing the dishes after dinner, changing the sheets every week, folding your laundry… that's the sort of nonsense that gives life meaning in civilization."

"There are people who change their sheets every week? Do they throw up in them that often?" I asked. Maybe Mom was testing if I knew fiction from reality. She looked like she meant it, but it was just too incredible. "Nah, that's fake news," I decided. "Whoever told you that must have been in the pocket of Big Soap."

The Witch commanded the Wagon to turn into a car kennel. It obeyed, aiming its nose between where the parking lines might be. The ground was hidden under white dirt, and the rest of the world was swallowed by a smudge like an overexposed photo. Moving through it, I began to make out the difference between the grey sky, the grey snow falling from it, and the white ground it was falling on.

"It's mountains of white dirt!" I squealed, executing an expert somersault-hole-digging combination. Then I discovered something even more exciting. "And there's sand under here!"

"They're coral-pink sand dunes," Mom corrected me.

Being colorblind means you never know if your grey is the same as someone else's gray, or if your white is someone else's coral pink. "Whatever you say, Mom," I rolled my eyes and then I rolled my body in the white—I mean "pink"—dirt again.

I sprinted in loops, leaving pawprints, buttprints, and backprints all over the dooms. The whiteness blended ground into sky and gradually filled in my pawprints as if it meant to offer a fresh page for each dog to make his own mark on the world. I smelled no sign of anyone else, but it was hard to know that somedog wasn't doing his own gymnastics routine just out of sight over the next doom. Behind me, even Mom was doing her best to disappear.

"This sucks," she sniveled. "I was really looking forward to the contrast of the sand against the sky in photos. There's no contrast here, just grey."

"No, Mom! This is awesome!" I corrected her. "It's better than awesome. It's… There's no word for how awesome it is in your language." So I barked the word in my language and did a cartwheel followed by a sprint to show her what it meant.

When I was done, I slowed down to walk with her. "Weather is part of Nature, you know."

"I know, but rain and snow aren't supposed to happen in the desert," the Weather Jinx accused. "That's what makes it a desert."

"You're not exactly a ray of sunshine either," I told her. "Just like how a trail reflects your mood depending on the eyes you brought that day, Nature brings her own moods. You wouldn't trust weather that's always pleasant and mild because you'd be a little suspicious of what it's hiding."

"Of course I appreciate weather that's constantly pleasant and mild," Mom said. "That's why we live in San Francisco."

"But if you only go out on nice days, you'll miss the exciting episodes that make Nature a kickass show season after season." Just like how the best jokes are the ones with unexpected punchlines, our most fun adventures were the unpredictable ones when Nature was feeling punchy. But Mom has no sense of humor when it comes to planning. If she could, Mom would put Nature on *do not disturb* mode so the weather would never interrupt. "Isn't it just a *little* fun when the wind is so strong that it sends you chasing your hat down the trail?" I coached. "If all our stories were predictable, no one would want to hear them, not even us."

"I suppose. Our best memories *have* come from the days that didn't go to plan." Mom looked around the dooms to make sure that no one had heard her admit she was wrong.

"Nature doesn't show this side of herself to fair-weather friends, you know," I reminded her. "You've got to accept the gloomy days and a few rainstorms to show you love her just the way she is. If you don't judge her temperature swings or try to change her thunderstorms, she'll open up and let you see things that she doesn't show to just anyone."

"I'm here, aren't I?" With her paws in her pockets, her shoulders in her ears, and her eyes on the ground, Mom looked very much like someone trying not to be there.

"Wishing you lived in a world without weather is a waste of a wish," I said. "Making Friends with Nature means accepting her wicked sense of humor and laughing at yourself when she shows that she doesn't give a cat's sass about your plans. That's how you make Friends. If you try to learn how to enjoy every day as it is, maybe Nature will stop messing with you."

Ahead, the Wagon's white flanks emerged against the white background. "I think we've proven ourselves for today," Mom said. "The sun had better come out tomorrow."

Chapter 5

Out of Harm's Spray

Now that we'd earned Nature's trust, she cleared the skies over Utah to let us in. The sun may have been shining and the white dirt gone from the mashed-potato-shaped rocks, yet Mom was still waiting for the other poo to drop. Some families sing or play license plate bingo on long drives, but my family plays a different game. Mom thinks of something that could go wrong, and I have to think of a reason why it's going to be okay. Mom's a really tough competitor because she practices her worrying constantly. If she doesn't have anything obvious to worry about, she invents an imaginary worry to practice on.

She'd been honing her worries about our next trail since before our trip began. Every time she convinced herself to stop worrying and go for it, she thought of something new to worry about and the disaster movie in her thought bubble would start again from the beginning.

As we got closer to a little town called Escalante, Mom invited me to play the worry game with her. She made the first move. "Now that I think about it, 60 miles is a really long way on a dirt road. What if we get stuck?"

"If the Wagon is injured and no nice whales come along to help, we can always walk out. It would be a fun adventure."

"You can't walk that far," Mom doubted.

"We'll take our time. I bet that with enough naps and snacks we could walk around the whole world."

"I can't carry enough water to get you that far."

"In one thousand feet, turn onto that sketchy dirt road over there and drive on it for sixty miles," the Witch said.

The Wagon swerved the wrong way and pulled into a gas station instead.

In the voice she uses when she's definitely not making an excuse, Mom said, "We should stock up, just in case."

"If they have hot dogs, you should buy them all. Just in case," I called after her.

She came out a century or two later, grinning and holding a heavy-looking box like a prize. She hoisted her trophy into the bed, where it crashed heavily into my sunspot.

"Whatcha got there?" I sniffed.

Mom puffed out her chest like she'd outrun a jackalope for the last box. "It's a 24-pack of fancy juice-water." She ripped open the side of the box and pulled out a can. "They'll make a nice treat after a hot, thirsty hike."

"But what about regular water?" I asked. Usually the packet of bottles took up most of my sleeping space, but I'd had plenty of room to stretch out the night before.

Mom fanned my worry out of her ear. "I'm sure we can make it 1 more day on what we have in the van." She opened the juice-water and took a self-satisfied swig.

I looked at the squashed plastic skin that the bottles came from. I would have guessed that there definitely wasn't enough left, so I was glad that Mom knew what she was talking about.

Mom started the Wagon and picked up the worry game where we'd left off. "But what if we hit a sharp rock and get a flat tire or something?"

"Turn right," the Witch commanded. This time, the Wagon did as it was told.

"Can't the Witch call for help or something?" I asked.

"You think there's going to be cell service all the way out there?" Mom challenged. "We just left the only town big enough for a stop sign for 100 miles in any direction."

Despite Mom's worrying, the road was tame at first and the wheels on the Wagon went round and round without any of Mom's worries coming true. It wasn't until the second hour that we crossed the wrong cow catcher and a herd of highway bandits ambushed us. Without saying a word, they blocked the road with their beefy bulk, threatening us with stares as sharp as knives.

The Wagon halted and I ran to every window, trying to bark at all the cows at once. They had us surrounded. The Wagon honked its horn and the chief bull lifted his head to show that he had horns too.

"Quiet, Oscar! Don't upset them," Mom hissed.

I ignored her. "What's the matter with you?" I barked. "Shoo! Shoo! Get outta here! Coming through!"

The cows stood their ground, as if they couldn't hear me at all.

After a long standoff, the Wagon took a tiny, submissive step forward. The bully chewed his cud menacingly and gave the Wagon a hard look to show who was in control. After several chews, he took an unhurried step to the side. As the Wagon crept past, Mom tried not to make eye contact with the bull as his breath puffed a small cloud onto the window beside her.

"What if one of us gets hurt and we can't get back to the road?" she asked with eyes stuck straight ahead.

"We could get hurt on any of our adventures. That's why we're careful," I told her before going back to cow-barking.

"What if we get lost and can't find the road?"

"We get lost on every adventure. You and the Witch always find a way out."

When even Mom was running out of new things to worry about, the road under the Wagon turned into machine guns and the rocks into landmines. *Ratta-tatta-tat, boom!* the floor thundered. Each time the road kicked the Wagon's belly, Mom groaned like she was the one kicked.

"The road sure is getting rocky," she said. "I hope we don't have car trouble all the way out here."

"You already used that one." I played along anyway. "Someone will help us. There are lots of people out here. Why, I think I've seen three other cars today!"

"Yeah, but they were going in the other direction."

"They were coming from somewhere," I said. "Probably the same place where we're going. Maybe we'll even make a Friend."

Much later, the road became so steep and rocky that the Wagon whined its suspension and stomped its tires against the potholes, begging to turn around.

"Maybe this isn't such a good idea," Mom said, hanging onto the driving wheel like it was her life preserver in a rough sea.

"Don't be such a Chicken Little. I'm sure it'll get better up ahead. Things are always at their worst before they get better."

"I'm quite sure it won't get any better from here," Mom said, like everything getting worse was already part of the plan. "But there are only 5 miles ahead and 55 miles behind us. My nerves are too fried to drive back over all that after what we've been through. We might as well keep pushing."

"See?" I said. "You're almost there. *Almost there* is when everything gets better."

A rock kicked us hard and the Wagon let out a metallic groan.

"What if we have car trouble, *and* we get lost, *and* hurt, *and* we run out of food and water, *and* my phone dies?" Mom asked.

"That's cheating."

"No it's not. Haven't you ever noticed that bad things pile up? Once one thing goes wrong, everything goes to hell."

"Nothing in real life is ever as scary as the things you make up to worry about," I reminded her. "Most of your worries don't even happen."

"It's not nice to belittle someone's worries just because they're not real." Mom lifted her chin and half-closed her eyes snobbily. "Maybe it's my worrying that *prevents* bad things from happening. Did you ever think of that?"

"My turn! I have a bad thing," I said. "You could stop worrying, and then we'd *really* be in trouble!" Mom had no comeback for that one.

My bones had shaken loose and shuffled into the wrong body parts by the time the Witch started counting down our last mile. My tail perked up between where my ears used to be and I wagged my knees when the Wagon stopped. Mom's nose reached for the front window as she X-rayed a puddle blocking the Wagon's path.

"Nah, I'm not risking it," she decided, settling back in the driving chair.

"Oh fun! Driving back over all of that in the dark is gonna give you all kinds of new things to worry about."

"Nah, we're less than ½ a mile from the trailhead. We can walk from here. I guess this is home sweet home."

The Wagon pulled off the road and Mom pulled the *that'll do* lever behind the driving wheel to hobble it. The Wagon sighed and settled with an exhausted *tick-plunk* as we each searched our new home for a potty that suited each of our styles.

By the time darkness fell, Mom's jitters had settled and there was room in her thought bubble for boredom. As we ate our dinners, she searched the Witch for something that she could doom scroll without the internet.

"How about we look at the reviews on AllTrails for inspiration?" the Witch suggested.

"No fair!" I said. "You can't copy other people's problems. That's against the rules."

Mom caught the Witch's pass and ran with it anyway. "The trail *is* the river. I repeat, you will be hiking *IN THE RIVER*," she read. "What do you suppose that means?"

"Don't let her get to you, Mom. She's probably up to her old tricks. Maybe it was flooded that day. What time of year are rivers the biggest?"

"Maybe in winter, because of the rainy season? Or it could be spring, when the snow melts."

I could never figure out how seasons work in places that have four of them. At the Stuck House we only have three seasons that we call by different names: *morning, afternoon*, and *night*. "What season is it now?" I asked.

Mom did some quick calculations. "It's mid-March so that's… winter. Or spring? Right between winter and spring."

"Oh good! You're right either way!"

"Yeah, but what do you think they meant by hiking *in* the river?" Mom pressed.

"That's called swimming," I yawned. "You can't trust a review from someone who doesn't know the difference between hiking and swimming."

"But what if the water is high and we aren't prepared. We could drown."

"I know how to swim," I said. "I just don't *like* to. Do *you* know how to swim?"

"Of course I know how to swim."

"And who's gonna push us into the water if we don't feel like swimming?"

"No one's going to push us," Mom said. "But water can be unpredictable in the desert."

"You think the river is gonna jump offsides and tackle us?"

"Well, no. Not like a flash flood. But what if there's water blocking the trail? That could happen."

"So?"

"So… we'd have to cross." She turned her nose up a few degrees. "You wouldn't know this because you never played *Oregon Trail*, but bad things always happen at river crossings."

"Like wet socks?"

"Among other things…" she said mominously. "You know that feeling when you're swimming in heavy clothes?"

"I'm a runner not a swimmer, Mom. And I don't wear clothes."

"Oh, right. Well, getting into trouble isn't the scary part. At first, the extra resistance doesn't seem like a big deal. You get so wrapped up in a fight that you forget to check if something is worth fighting for, so you keep swimming until you're in too deep. By the time you realize that you're bogged down, it may be too late."

"Ah yes," I yawned again, in case she hadn't noticed the first time. "It's important to stay out of bogs."

"The terrifying part is the moment when you realize you've gone too far and might not have the energy to swim all the way back to shore. I worry about what *might* happen so I can recognize it early. That way, I use up all my fear when I'm safe so I can think clearly in the face of danger. That's how my anxiety keeps bad things from happening, you know."

"Okay, so what if the trail disappears behind a puddle and there's no way to cross it without your socks getting wet? What then?"

"We'd have to turn back, I suppose."

"Is that better or worse than dying?"

She gave it some serious thought. "That's a tough one."

"I'm tired," I said. "Can we finish worrying in the morning?"

"By morning it'll be too late," she said urgently.

"Why's that?"

"We need to get an early start, and you can't worry properly once you've taken action."

Mom asked the Witch to wake us up before sunrise so we'd have a full day to get hurt, lost, suffer a Wagon injury, and die before sunset. She was still playing worry solitaire as I drifted off.

I woke up to Mom packing the bigger, tougher packpack she'd bought especially for today by lantern light and wondered if she'd slept at all. She checked and double checked that we had plenty of fruit and nuts for her, brunch kibble for me, and an extra juice box for the Witch. Once she was satisfied that she hadn't forgotten any emergency supplies, she reached for the water bottles to fill the remaining space in the packpack.

"Oh dog doo!" she said when she pulled back the blankets and saw the water bottle husk looking like a toy with all the stuffing pulled out. "We only have like 8 bottles left."

"Yay! We're saved!" I yawned, glad Mom had planned ahead and conserved water.

"I don't know if that's enough for you, me, and second-coffee," Mom counted.

"What about your fancy canned water?" I reminded her. "How about I drink the bottles, and you drink the cans."

"Eew, warm raspberry water? Gross."

"That's what I thought, but you were excited about it yesterday. Isn't this just like the survivalist challenges you've always dreamed about? You've got to go to extremes to find out what you're really made of. Like drinking warm fuzzy water."

"Worrying about scarcity is only a waste of time if you survive. Do you know what happens when you lose a survivalist challenge?" Mom asked, like I'd never watched an episode of reality TV.

"Of course I do! They turn off your torch and send you home. But first they stick cameras in your face so the world can watch you cry. The episode ends with a scene of you eating hot dogs with your Friends so your fans can see how different you look after a shower. How about I take the hot dogs and you do the crying and shower bit."

"There are no TV producers in the desert, Spud. I'm afraid it's a little more depressing than that."

"Silly Mom. Nothing is more depressing than a failed reality star."

There was no canyon at the trailhead, only a flat and wide frappuccino-colored river under an enormous sky.

"See, Mom? There's nothing to worry about," I said, claiming big points in the worry tournament. "The river will never get us with all of this flat land next to it for us to escape."

"Do you know where canyons come from?" Mom asked, cheating as usual. Whenever she gets stuck, she uses science to invent some improbable story because she knows a dog can't argue with science. This time, she didn't even wait for me to guess. "Rivers dig canyons over millions of years."

"You're pulling my tail," I said. "How can water do a thing like that?"

"Erosion. It's very scientific. You wouldn't understand," Mom boasted, claiming a bonus point for being so smart.

"Nuh-uh! I may not speak science, but I know a thing or two. The desert is full of canyons, but you said yourself, there isn't supposed to be water in the desert. Rivers are made of water, so you could never get enough of it in the desert to dig a canyon, even if that *were* how they were made. So there." I hoped she would award my points before she remembered about the river right next to us.

"You wanna bet? If there's no canyon, I'll buy you a hot dog."

"You're gonna be jealous of my delicious hot dog when all you have to eat is your words."

The river sank as we walked, but not nearly deep enough to call it a canyon. It was more like a furrow. The bank we were walking on stayed flat, but farther from the river, the ground began to slant. The slant became a slope and started to close in, squeezing us closer to the river with every step.

When the slope was twice as tall as Mom and far too steep to climb, the river made a sudden move. It veered off the lazy line it had been following all morning and made a sharp bend, cutting us off. It rushed head-long into the slope, carving away the sand to show the smooth wall of rock underneath. Only half a mile into our hike and both Mom's socks and my hot dog were in danger.

Mom's eyes bounced around the cramped furrow, searching for a way to keep her socks dry. The river closed in from two sides while the wall-like slope blocked our escape on the other side. To turn back after driving all this way was a fate worse than death. The panic on Mom's face reminded me of the feeling I get when she calls me to the people bathroom, closes the door, takes off my collar, and turns on the shower.

Mom's eyes caught on something and her frown turned upside-down. "Look over here, there's a side trail!" she said, eyes pointing at a patted-down line in the dirt. It was just wide enough for a fluffle of rabbits, as long as they hopped single file.

"That's definitely not where you're supposed to go," the Witch corrected. "You're supposed to hike in the river. Weren't you listening last night?"

Mom took one last look at the mapp, put the Witch in her pocket, and followed the rabbit trail topside. I watched her go as the river's gurgling swallowed the sound of her footsteps. All the scent tracks told me that the trail was underwater, but there was no other choice for a couple of landlubbers who hate dampness. Mom would never go anywhere without a plan, so I followed her to higher ground.

"How do you know we won't get lost?" I asked when I caught up.

"I have a theory." Mom looked into the deepening rut beside us. "This trail follows the river's path almost exactly, except that it's a few feet to the left. Canyons can mess with GPS signals."

"I wouldn't call it a *canyon*. It's more like a…" I searched the scene ahead for a different word to save my hot dog. *Gully?*

Gorge? Gulch? "… a *ravine*," I decided. "A ravine is smaller than a canyon, you know."

"Okay, well maybe the *ravine* caused a GPS error that mapped the path just to the right of where whoever recorded it actually was."

Left and *right* were numbers that confused me. I knew that Mom always wanted to be *right*, but it seemed like *right* went in a different direction every time. Maybe Mom's riddle was a clue. I studied the squiggles that the rim and river made. They were the same shape, but the rim was high and the river was low. With every paw we put in front of the other, the river went farther down and the path went farther up. If the river was *right*, then why were we up here on top of a cliff when Mom hated heights even more than wet socks? I needed a hint.

"You said that *right* was the one that goes *down*?" I asked, like I was just testing her.

"Get back from there!" Mom squawked.

I forgot. Mom would never, ever look down. She was even more afraid of heights than she was of wet socks. Whether it was because she couldn't face the river or all that terrifying height in between, it amounted to the same thing. One look down through all that empty air to the sock-soaking river and there would be no turning back. The height would hang onto her curiosity, turning her body to stone as her imagination was sucked over the edge. I'd had to coach Mom back from the brink many times when her legs became too weak to pull her mind out of the abyss.

The river became smaller and less scary as the height grew in between. Although it was still right next to us, it was impossibly far away. All it had taken to save us from soggy socks was a slight turn and a few steps up the slope. If a single step had made the difference between danger and safety, how many other invisible disasters had Mom's worrying sidestepped?

That must've been what Mom meant when she said she could stop something bad from happening just by worrying about it. If you don't sharpen your eyes with worry, you might miss the rabbit tracks and walk blindly into misfortune.

We walked until the path only existed in Mom's imagination and the soft dirt smeared our paws closer to the cliff with every step. Seeing no trail that didn't lead over the edge, I walked behind Mom as she fought the sucking danger. The height got into her legs and each step became smaller and stiffer than the last, as if she could hold back all that ghastly empty space if she resisted hard enough. She shuffled forward in teency steps, keeping both paws locked to the ground.

When she's like that, she screams at me if I pick up too many paws, or so much as look at a cliff. It's stressful because which spots are "safe" are always changing, and it's hard to move in slow motion when you keep getting startled by screams. When Mom was too much of a lunatic for either of us to take another step, we turned and lurched back toward ground she could trust.

It's funny how things stretch out the first time you see them, but seem a lot smaller on second view. Once the earth was solid enough that Mom didn't have to project manage every step, it took us no time to return to the spot where rim and river parted.

Mom let her eyes float upriver for a long moment before yanking her gaze away like the leash behind a squirrel. She dropped the packpack to the ground and pulled out all of the empty bottles, lining them up in the sand. She dunked one in the river until it was full of cloudy frappuccino-grey water.

"What are you doing with that?" I asked.

"I saw a sign on the way in for a trail that I've always wanted to visit. This way, we'll have enough water to stay out here for another day before we go back to town." She unscrewed the cap of the next bottle and dunked it. "You drink this, I'll drink the raspberry water, and that way there'll still be enough fresh water for me to make my coffee." She proudly polished the sand from the frappuccino-filled bottles before packing them back into the packpack. "It's called being resourceful."

A question was still bothering me. "Was today a good adventure or a bad adventure?"

"What do you think?" Mom asked, as if I could decide something that important all by myself.

"You were afraid that eighty miles would be too long for me, and we didn't have to go eighty miles after all. So that was... um... good, right?"

"It was only 18 miles, but yeah. It was disappointing, but probably for the best."

"And you were afraid that no one would be around to help if we got in trouble, but we didn't see a soul. So that was... bad? Right?"

"But we didn't get in trouble, so not seeing people was nice."

"You were afraid of running out of water, and then there was more of it than we knew what to do with. So that means it was good, right?"

"That was a relief," Mom agreed. "But it did cut our hike short."

"You were afraid of getting your socks wet and your socks stayed dry. So that's good, right?"

"I suppose. There was no way to keep my socks dry *and* see what we came here for, so I made a choice."

"And you worked so hard to get all your worrying out of the way ahead of time, but you got scared anyway. So that's bad, right?"

"I'm afraid of heights, but I love the views. You can't have a thrill without fear."

"But we didn't get to see the part of the trail that we came to see. So that was bad, right?"

"That was disappointing, but there's no sense in worrying about things you can't change," she said like she'd known it all along. "Maybe we'll find another way on another day."

"But you said it yourself, this river's been here for millions of years. It'll probably still be here if we ever come back."

"Maybe I'll figure out how to make the river less wet, or part its waters like Moses. If that doesn't work, maybe I'll choose to toughen up and carry on with wet socks. Perhaps the barrier isn't the river itself, but what I think the river means."

"Is falling in a river better or worse than falling off a cliff?" I asked.

"Tough choice, but falling off a cliff is a lot more final."

"How do you know? Maybe you'd discover that you can fly the second you let the fear go."

"Best not to find out. Sometimes things are *worse* than your fears, you know."

"Sometimes things don't work out the way you want and still aren't as bad as you expect," I said. "If you're always avoiding things that worry you, how do you know whether you're on the right path or just the one that scares you the least?"

Mom held up a finger as if she'd already won the point. "If I hadn't worried so much about water, I wouldn't have thought to drink warm raspberry seltzer all day or refill bottles from the river." She shook froth back into a frappuccino bottle to make her point. "Because of my heroic worrying, we have enough water for one more hike before we go back to town. In your face, Mr. Know-It-All."

Chapter 6

Sand Trap

The next morning, Mom and I slept in until sunrise. Although it was bumpy, now that we knew there wasn't anything along the way that we hadn't overcome already, the ride back hadn't been nearly as scary. Now, we were in a luxurious car kennel halfway back to town where the people-potty still had toilet paper and the Witch had a clear view of the internet. There had even been another car when we got there, although it was gone now. We sat in bed while Mom savored a cup of poop juice made from the last bottle of fresh water.

"Get a load of these rock formations!" Mom held out the Witch so I could admire the stripes on her screen. "And slot canyons!" She flicked a finger, and I saw what looked like rocky curtains. Mom can't simply enjoy an adventure as it rolls out around her without stressing about the meaning of it all. These days she decides the meaning ahead of time so it won't be distracting when our paws hit the dirt. That way, she doesn't get overwhelmed trying to notice all the cool things she didn't plan for. It's not till afterward, when the Witch beams Mom's memories back at her that she's able to take it all in, stop grieving that it didn't go as planned, and enjoy the experience as we lived it.

"You're not gonna fall for that one again, are you?" I yawned. So soon after the dooms of Oregon Mom had already forgiven the Witch's dirty tricks and forgotten the heartbreak of broken promises yet again. "What do the reviews say?"

"Who cares?" She turned the Witch protectively toward herself, like I was too dense to understand her genius. "It says that they're filled with water for most of the year, but after yesterday I'm not about to let a little water get in the way of something I've always wanted to see. The photos look pretty tame and most people are babies. I'm sure it's not that bad."

She stuffed the packpack with as many bottles of river water and cans of raspberry water as it would hold. Finally, she laced up her running shoes and we jogged eagerly into the morning.

I trotted with my nose high and ears flopping as the dirt turned to sand. Rocks the shape of gumdrops, decorated with the wispy stripes of candycanes poked out of the sand. They were the size of cars at first, but grew to the size of trucks, then buildings as we ran.

Mom dashed from one interesting rock to the next like a game of tag, asking me to *up-up* on each one so she could take Jillians of pictures to capture the memory for later. Every time Mom started running, another rock caught her eye and we had to stop again.

"I don't get why you take so many pictures," I told her as I posed dauntlessly on top of yet another ice-cream-shaped rock. "Are you going to forget what I look like?"

"If I take more pictures, there's a better chance that one will turn out the way I want."

Dogs don't take pictures, but Mom had tried to explain it before. "Doesn't a photo capture exactly what the world looks like?" I asked, showing her my bored look in profile. "Instead of taking a hunerd pictures, you could just take one and look at it for longer."

"Most of the time your subject is in shadow or blinking, and it ruins the whole thing." She looked away from my face in the Witch's screen only long enough to take a knee. "*Lookit me.* If I take dozens of versions of the same picture... *Lookit me*, Oscar, over here… and then edit and crop them, I can usually make one look the way I want. Then I can relive the experience with all the parts I didn't like cropped out."

Mom stood up, so I released my pose and followed her to a different rock whose colors swirled differently. "That's silly. Why work so hard to gather zillions of memories if you're gonna ignore the versions you don't like? What's wrong with the world as it is?"

"A photo doesn't just show the trail as it is, it shows my impression when I saw that spot. *C'mere, up-up.*" She waved her fingers higher on the rock to show where she wanted me to sit. "Things look different depending on where you stand."

"But your version is so small that it goes into your pocket and you never look at it again. That's like having a perfect bone and then forgetting where you buried it." I half-jumped half-fell off the rock and followed Mom through the sand. The candy-cane walls were beginning to close in, giving her fewer places to stop. "Maybe if you didn't spend so much time trying to freeze the perfect moment, you could live *all* the moments in your life at full speed."

"That's ridiculous. We don't run so fast that we can't see stuff," she said. "If I look faster, I don't have to move so slow."

"But the beak on that silly hat blocks your view. When you're looking for where to put your paws, all you see is the trail right in front of you."

"If you go through life treating every moment exactly the same, life would be as meaningless as this sand we're running on. The moments you choose to remember determine the path you follow and the person you become."

"It's hard to know what you want when you're living in the past and the future all the time."

Mom turned a ferocious look on me and snarled, "Don't you start that mindfulness crap with me."

I decided that Mom had had enough life coaching for the day and ran ahead, eager to turn the future into the present. The rocks on either side gradually pinched closer together, covering the sand in shadow and bathing them in a damp coolness. Mom stopped looking so hard for memories and faded into the world inside her hat.

Without warning, my leg disappeared up to the knee into the sand. I pulled it free and ran back to the safety of Mom's side.

"What the goose?" I checked that I still had all four of my legs before looking back to where it happened. Everything seemed normal other than a fading paw-shaped puddle marking the spot where my leg had vanished.

"What happened?" Mom asked the moment before she lost a foot into the earth.

"What is it?" I cringed heroically, knowing that looking irresistibly pathetic was the only way to lure Mom to safety.

"I think it's… quicksand."

"I thought quicksand was make-believe," I said.

"What else could it be? At least now we know to be careful."

I got better at spotting the quicksand with each leg it stole. The trick was to look near puddles for wet sand and steer well clear. But as we walked deeper into the canyon, the walls closed in and there was less dry sand to escape to. When the passageway narrowed to a few Oscars wide, the quicksand slurped all six of our paws at once. I escaped back to the solid sand while Mom continued forward, fighting through the sucking ground toward its puddle, which filled the whole floor of the slot.

"Come back!" I barked. "There's nothing but wet socks that way."

"My socks are already wet," Mom called in a voice that bounced back hollow from the canyon walls. She leaned over to roll up her pants above shoes that were already half-swallowed by the sand. "Maybe it's not that deep."

Mom waded in. On the first step, the water swallowed her socks completely. With the second, it licked at her cuffs and slurped toward her knee.

"If you don't come back soon, I'm gonna have to come in and get you!" I shouted.

Gonna get you - gonna get you - get you, the canyon mocked.

She swung her leg around looking for the third step. After a time, her paw came back to its twin. "Damn. Too deep."

"Ohhhhhhhh, darn." I tried to make my tail wag in a disappointed way as I ran back up the canyon.

When we stepped out from between the tight walls of the canyon, Mom pulled out the Witch for advice. That traitor had promised two slot canyons, so who knew what kind of prank she had planned for the second.

"It says here that we have to walk halfway back to the Wagon before the turn, and then we'll walk that same distance again in a different direction." She looked back down at the Witch, swiveled a few ticks, and looked up to see what the Witch was pointing at. "But it looks like there's a trail that cuts the tangent and comes at it from the other direction."

"What's a *tam gent*?" I asked, sounding out the unfamiliar word.

"It's a loop, see? The shortcut will take us over those cool rocks. We'll get to see more than if we came in and out on the same trail. It's perfect."

"Why do you suppose they built that fence across the perfect trail?" I asked.

"That fence isn't meant for us. It's only there to keep the cows from wandering off. Come on, let's check it out."

Mom slithered through the narrow space between the last fence post and the rock wall and I ducked underneath. We climbed the steep sides of a candy cane rock and came out onto its flat roof. From the sandy canyon bottom, the rocks had seemed like buildings in the City—close together, but each one standing on its own. Now I stood on top of a smooth tabletop that stretched for many blocks in each direction. The canyon we'd just climbed out of hardly seemed like a scratch in the middle of all that flatness.

There was no sign of a trail, only the rock's wavy pattern, whose stripes made no more sense than the whirls on a piece of wood. The only things on the ground were bonsai cacti growing in tiny dimples in the rock and a bajillion meatball-shaped stones scattered everywhere. Some of the meatballs were cracked open and hollow as a spent tennis ball inside.

"I wonder what these are." Mom poked one with her toe to see how it rolled. "They look like they're from the center of the Earth or something."

"Don't be silly," I scoffed. "They're dinosaur eggs. From the chicken-sized dinosaurs that no one talks about."

"Dinosaur bones aren't the only interesting thing inside the Earth, you know," Mom said, obviously annoyed that I was trying to take her job as the smart one. "Mysterious things happen down there at a scale you can't even imagine. If you know how to read their language, rocks can tell epic stories." She looked at the rocks sinking into quicksand in the middle distance and added, "The kind of legends only a planet can tell."

"Dinosaur stories are more exciting," I said, "on account of all the bone crunching and blood."

"There's plenty of crunching in geology and the earth bleeds lava. Isn't that interesting?" It did sound pretty cool, until I remembered that Mom's lava doesn't even glow. Every time she promised a visit to a volcanic eruption, we were millions of years late to the action and all that was left was a black mess like a crushed freeway. Mom had a very active imagination when it came to rocks.

I followed her as she hiked across the flat roof, holding the Witch in front of her like a compass. The Witch directed us to a scar in the rock that deepened to a crack, then spread to the width of an alley before disappearing around a corner.

"This is it," Mom said, putting the Witch back in her pocket and stepping into the crack. The stripes made a kind of staircase to the bottom. I followed her into a canyon as cluttered as nature's basement. Rocks and branches lay in unsorted piles against the walls and scattered among the puddles on the ground. Obviously, no one expected visitors on this side of the canyon.

Another challenge was waiting for us when we came around the bend. A pool of water the creamy grey of poop juice filled the canyon floor from one wall to the other.

"Oh well," I said, "I suppose we'll have to— Hey! Where are you going?"

Mom already had her pants rolled up and was wading away from me through knee-deep water.

"If you don't come back soon, you're gonna be sorry!" I shouted.

She kept wading. The puddle caught her pants and started climbing up her legs. With each step, the wet line on Mom's jeans climbed a little closer to her butt pocket, where the Witch lived. Rather than dissolving in worry when the line got to the Witch's doorstep, Mom just pulled her out of that pocket and held her high in the air for safety.

"Come and get me, unless you're too chicken," she said without turning around.

You're too chicken-chicken-chicken, taunted the canyon.

I waded in socks-deep just to prove it wasn't funny anymore. "Don't make me come over there and get you!"

Mom sloshed onto the bank. "Fine. Stay there. See if I care."

I had to think quick or else she might wander away without me. I took another cautious step. When she didn't turn around, I took another. On the next step, the bottom disappeared. I splashed in up to the collar and swam the rest of the way.

"Thank dogness that's over!" I said, shaking the puddle out of my fur like a shampoo model. But when I looked around for adoring fans, Mom was already gone.

I found her around the next bend studying a wall of boulders clogging the canyon as if she were contemplating a painting in a museum. The bottommost boulder was taller than Mom with a face as steep as the canyon walls it was wedged between. There wasn't even enough room for an ant to walk around. Smaller boulders were piled on top of it nearly to the top of the canyon, which was deep enough to swallow a house by now.

"Oh no," I said, perfecting my most disappointed wag. "I guess we'll have to go back now." I turned and led by example.

"I'm just planning my route." Mom was silent for another thoughtful moment. She patted a divot in the stone. "*Up-up.*"

I took a running start and followed her instructions. Once I'd caught my balance, I asked, "Now what?" but she was already tap-tapping another flatter spot higher on the rock. This time I was too high for Mom to reach the next step, so she told me to stay and climbed ahead to the top of the base, using all four of her paws like a lizard. From there, she reached down and tapped a spot that was too small to balance on, but would give me a jumping-off point to scramble up next to her.

Mom continued pat-patting the jumble of rocks where it was flat enough to fit at least three paws. I took flying leaps between them until we were nearly level with the top of the canyon and there was only one rock on the pile above us.

I looked at the gap between my toes and the topmost boulder and thought for sure it was the end of our adventure. The rock I was standing on slipped steeply into a gaping hole as wide and black as a Tyranasaur's gullet. The overbiting rock on the far jaw leaned highly and steeply over the hole like a roof. The rock under my paws was too steep for a jump not to become a fall, and the gap was too big to step across. I was sure Mom would notice the trap and turn back, but to my horror, she picked me up and carried me into the hole.

"For the love of Dog, let me go!" I squirmed.

"Hold still." She squeezed me tighter. "I might drop you if I lose my balance."

There must have been a tongue in all that blackness, because Mom was standing on something. Her whole body was swallowed in darkness, but her head still stuck out of the hole. One bite, though, and she'd be a goner. I craned my neck to make sure my own head stayed out of the hole and flailed my paws toward the far rock, trying not to look down. Mom lifted me with a grunt until my front paws could reach the top of the overhanging rock. With my front paws in place, she grabbed my butt and pushed until all four paws were underneath me.

I watched her climb out, not to help, but so I'd be ready to shout *told you so!* into the abyss if she slipped. Hanging from her front paws and using her back paws as wedges, she smeared and flapped, pushed and flopped onto the rock beside me.

We both looked down the far side of the barricade. The rock dropped cliff-like into a moat as wide and depthless as the last. Mom patted little ledges just wide enough to catch my paws on the way down until there was nothing left to do but dive into the puddle. I belly-flopped the last step and swam to solid sand.

Mom splashed out of the moat behind me and gave me more kisses and snuggles than she usually does when we're in *badass* mode. "It's a good thing that this is a loop," she said, "because I don't know how we'd get back over that in the other direction."

Before long, we arrived at the main feature: a place called Tunnel Slot, which turned out to be a butt-hole-shaped crack between cheeks of solid rock. A dingy puddle that started two Wagon-lengths in front of the entrance filled the tunnel clear through to the other side.

"Maybe it's not as bad as it looks," Mom said hopefully.

"*Not as bad* is still bad," I reminded her.

Mom waded in with her shoes on, still fearless after our death-defying escape. She lifted her arms for balance as the puddle sucked up her ankles and shins. She used her free leg like a blind person's stick to see the puddle bottom as she tapped her way deeper. The next step would have wet the Witch's pocket if it weren't soaked already. Mom didn't take the next step. She stood knee-deep in the puddle and squinted through the butthole to the tiny star of light on the other side. "We could maybe swim…"

"No!" the Witch and I screamed together.

"… but I don't know how we'd get our stuff across," Mom finished. Her body sagged.

"No way, uh-uh. I'm not going in there!" I repeated, backing out of the shadows into sunny safety.

Mom reached her neck toward the darkness to make the distance a little shorter. "It's only the length of a swimming pool, I bet." The Witch and I waited in suspense.

Mom reached down toward her pants cuffs. Was she rolling them up higher to go deeper? Her hand kept going. She reached past her socks toward her shoelaces. Was she taking off her shoes, the better to swim with? She missed her shoes and grabbed the packpack strap instead. She swung it onto her back and turned away from the tunnel with a sigh. "Fine," she said. "Let's go."

Overflowing with relief, I turned my tail toward the creepy hole and pranced manfully back up the canyon. Then I remembered. The moat. The boulder pile. The Jaws of Death!

I ran ahead to get it over with. My coat couldn't get any wetter than it already was, so I splashed into the moat and swam around looking for a place to *up-up*, but the big rock made a wall even taller than the other side. When I clawed at the rock trying to lizard-climb like Mom, I only sank deeper.

I was still paddling around when Mom caught up. I swam back to shore and whimpered for her to fix it and the canyon mocked my cries.

She held out her shovel-arms and squatted. "Don't worry, Spud. I got you."

"That's not what I had in— Let me go!" I struggled mightily, but the more I wriggled the tighter Mom held me.

Puddle water squeezed from my fur into the few pieces of Mom's clothes that were still dry as she staggered into the water. A roly-poly rock rolled under her foot and she lurched, dunking my nose before she caught her balance again.

"You're doing it wrong!" I whined, struggling even more mightily to free myself. Water squelched from my fur and dribbled down my belly into her hoodie as she hugged me tighter.

When we were below the lowest part of the wall, she hefted me up until my front paws landed where the wall wasn't as steep. But it was still too steep to hold me.

"I can't do a pull-up," I wheezed assertively. "Try something else."

"I got you," Mom grunted reassuringly as she shoved my butt like a bulldozer.

I looked back to make sure she was serious. The quicksand under the puddle swallowed everything below her knee. The more she pushed, the more the quicksand squished, and I was no closer to the top.

The pushing turned into pinning as Mom used one paw to keep me from falling while the rest of her took another baby step closer to the wall. When her nose was touching the rock, she started to climb. She smooshed her toes into knicks and used her free paw to hang on for balance, all the while balancing my butt on one shoulder like a waiter holds a tray.

With every step, I rose a mini-meter higher. I scrambled and scratched, trying to stick long enough for Mom to climb another step and bring me closer to flat ground. Finally, one of my paws stuck to the rock. Then another. Mom spotted me until all four of my paws were underneath me, but it only lasted a moment.

I felt one, then the other back leg slip out as I began to slide back toward the puddle. For a moment, I thought all was lost. Time slowed down, and I had a chance to wonder if Mom would catch me or if I would knock her down so we both fell in together.

I felt two paws on my butt, but not in the usual way. Instead of lifting me like an elevator, Mom crammed me hard into the rock.

With Mom's pushing, my paws stuck just enough to scramble like a lizard onto a precarious balancing spot, where I faced the Jaws of Death. Without even checking to make sure Mom was behind me, I took a leap of faith.

I thought I had it for a second. One and then the other front paw landed on the steep slope, but my back leg landed in a wobbly place. The last one didn't land at all, but hung over the void. The hole grabbed my loose leg and started sucking me in. My life passed before my nose as another leg lost contact and slipped down the monster's gullet.

Just when I thought that all was lost, firm claws clenched me under the legpits and pinned me back onto the rock. Mom must have jumped in to choke the hole and caught me just in the nick of time! Of course she did. Because true love means not letting your life partner fall into a bottomless pit.

Mom boosted me out one scooch at a time until I could stand on my chest and use my front paws to pull my back legs under me. I needed all four of my legs to run up the steep slide before it sucked me back toward H-E-double-hockey-sticks. I aimed for the place where the rock met the wall, where there was a notch just wide enough for an Oscar. It was low enough to save me a step or two, which could make all the difference.

I ran, but just as I reached the notch, I slipped again. I landed hard on my belly. I was beached, with back legs still hanging over the hole, front legs hanging on the other side of the notch, legpits wedged between rock and canyon wall, and my belly doing the standing.

I hung there for a second, watching more water from my belly fur dribble down the rock as I tried to figure out what to do next. Mom grunted behind me. Before she could make the situation worse, I slithered my chest to freedom and let falling do the rest of the work of getting my legs back under me.

"I aced it, didn't I?" I wagged as Mom plopped down the last rock behind me.

Once Mom had cleared up any confusion about who was a *good boy*, we climbed back out of the crack in the same place we'd come in. This good boy had had enough of Mom's leadership. When we were safely back on clear ground, I kept running straight past the chickensaurus nest back the way we'd come.

"Where are you going?" Mom called after me.

"Back to the Wagon," I said over my shoulder. "I've had enough."

"You're running the wrong way," Mom corrected. "That way goes deeper into the canyon, remember? The van is this way."

I stopped running. "How do you know?" When I looked back, her arm was pointing away from me toward more unknown rocks.

"It's simple. The trail is shaped like a Y."

"What does a *why* look like?"

"Like this," She held her arms above her head like she'd just won. "The Zebra Slots were over here." She waggled one of her paws above her head. "And the Tunnel Slots were over here." She waggled her other paw above her head. "We walked this way to get here." She took the Tunnel paw and moved it back and forth above her head from the Zebra paw back to where it belonged. "The van is over here." She shook a soggy foot. "So if you run that way, you'll be running into the desert until you fall into the Grand Canyon." She pointed her chin toward the unknown rocks again. "That way is a shortcut."

"I don't like your shortcuts." But there was no one else to jump into a monster's mouth to save me, so I followed her anyway.

Mom took a bearing from the Witch and walked across the naked rock as if it were a trail. This time, when a cow fence blocked our way, there was no way around. We were probably the first not-cows to try to cross here since chickensauruses ruled the earth.

"What do we do now?" I asked.

"This is nothing. We've solved problems way worse than this before," Mom said, forgetting that way worse problems meant way worse solutions.

She walked along the fence, checking its feet for signs of weakness. The fence was made from three wires: the top one too high to step over, the bottom one too low for Mom to climb under, and the one in between was there so you wouldn't get any ideas. Finally, Mom found a place where the ground dipped to make a gap under the bottom wire. Here, there was enough space to lose not just a tennis ball, but a basketball under the fence. Mom took off the packpack, threw it to the other side, and lay face-down like a chalk outline. She slithered underneath with much grunting and cursing. When she stood up on the other side, I looked both ways for tattletales and ducked under the fence to join her.

We finally walked back into Quicksand Wash wet, dusty, and with specks of cow dung and blood on our coats. My chest filled with relief knowing that the only traps between me and the Wagon were a few puny patches of quicksand. Suddenly, a little quicksand didn't sound so dramatic.

"Where does quicksand come from?" I asked as we trudged through the miles of sand between us and the Wagon.

Mom tilted her head to think. "It's been a long time since my 8th grade geology class…"

"Cheesology? That sounds like the hobby for me. I have a talent for anything cheese-related."

"Geology is rock science," Mom said, shoving her science between me and cheese. "The quicksand was like an upside-down puddle with the water pooling under the surface instead of on top. All the rain from the storms last week must have raised the water table until it's level with the surface."

I knew that the Weather Jinx could pull water from the sky, but I had no idea she was powerful enough to pull water up through solid earth. "Did it come for you out of revenge because you escaped the river yesterday?" I asked. "No wonder you were so scared on top of that cliff. The river could have reached up through the rock and grabbed us at any second."

Mom modestly shrugged off her bravery. "We probably won't have to worry about quicksand much anymore, though. The rainy season is almost over and the drought is so severe that most of the underground lakes are starving."

"Is that why it's eating legs instead?" I asked.

"It didn't *eat* our legs," Mom lied.

"How can you say that? It's eaten like nine of them today."

"We got them back. The worst thing that happened was that my socks got wet."

"I thought wet socks *were* the worst that could happen."

"It seemed like that yesterday, but once the worst had already happened, there was nothing I could do about it. It was like a burden had been lifted." A peaceful half-smile snuck onto Mom's face. "After that, wet socks were the least of my problems."

"If you can pick your problems," I coached, "maybe you shouldn't see wet socks as a problem at all. You would have less to worry about if dry socks weren't something that you expected from life."

"What? And worry about things I can't control instead? Are you crazy? If wet socks feel like the end of the world and I'm the only one who can control whether my socks stay dry, then only I can save the world from disaster."

"That's a big responsibility," I agreed.

"It sure is, especially since quicksand, puddles, and rivers are never going to listen to me. Maybe that's why it felt so good to let the responsibility go."

"Oh good! So if all the quicksand is going away and wet socks aren't a big deal anyway, then the world is safe. What will you do with all your free time now that you don't have to play the worry game anymore?"

"There are always things to worry about. It's even worse when the groundwater dries up, you know. Do you know what a sinkhole is?"

"The hole in the sink is called a *drain*, Mom."

"Not a sink hole, a sinkhole…"

"What did I say?"

"When the water table dries out, it leaves empty cavities underground. Without water holding up the ceiling, the ground above it collapses. Anything that happens to be there is swallowed by the earth, never to be seen again. Southwestern cities like Tucson, Houston, and San Bernardino are already sinking."

I had no idea that the Weather Jinx's superpower was so important. "Not Saint Bernardino, the gateway to the Inland Empire, home to the world's first McDonald's, the only city whose airport is named after a fart!" I gasped. "The West is going ex-sinked and people are worried about a little virus?"

I was so absorbed in the story of Middle Earth, that I hardly noticed that we were almost back to the road. As soon as we stepped into the car kennel, the Witch came back to life and began buzzing red alert. Mom's face did perplexed as she read what the Witch had to say.

I flopped down in the shade of the Wagon and waited for Mom to unlock the door, but she was still standing halfway across the car kennel staring at the Witch.

"What does she want now?" I asked, not because I cared but because I wanted Mom's attention back.

"What the heck does *shelter in place* mean?"

Part 2
Referees

see more photos

Chapter 7

Referees

"Is *shelter in place* the one where you're supposed to climb under your desk and hold your head?" I asked.

"I think you're thinking of *duck and cover*," Mom said. "I've never heard of *shelter in place* before, but Lily said that they've closed down Portland and she thinks San Francisco is shut down too. Imagine that! A whole city shut down. The world has gone absolutely crazy!"

When I tried to picture it, my imagination turned black. "What does that mean?"

"Like people are grounded and can't leave their houses."

"Oh, I get it." I half closed my eyes the way smart people do to show they understand. "So they can think about what they've done."

When I was a puppy, Mom used to put me on *time out* in the people bathroom to think about what I'd done. The trouble was, no matter how hard I thought, I never could figure out what made Mom turn into a dragon. Many times she would come in the door smiling and *poof!* she transformed into a fire-breathing monster, fuming about slippers, or trash on the floor, or whatever. When a Bad Dog comes to the Stuck House these days, Mom just makes me *sit-stay* to watch her be a dragon while she incinerates everything on the floor. Sometimes it feels like the fire breathing will never end, but if I sit with my ears back and let my eyes get big like a Japanese cartoon, the fire eventually burns out and Mom kisses it all better. Then it's peaceful and I have time to think about the things that Bad Dogs do.

How bad would a dog need to behave to send the whole City on time out? How many I-turned-my-back-for-one-second sammiches would he need to swipe to cancel walks for every dog in the City, and their people too?

"But what did they do wrong?" I asked.

It was Mom's turn to think. "Be disease vectors, I guess? Breathing, touching, snot, and face-scratching are a fact of life. It's like they're saying we're unclean in some fundamental way."

"How many minutes are people grounded for?"

"I have no idea! Not minutes, that's for sure." She said it as if my wrong guess was someone else's mistake. "Days? Weeks even? They've even closed down schools and businesses. Can they do that? I don't think they can do that."

"No, they can't do that," I said, proud to share my people-behavior expertise. "If people don't go to work, they can't buy dog food or anything. Then they die."

"Exactly!" Mom said, like she'd known it all along. "Speaking of which, we should probably find a town to pick up supplies."

She finally opened the Wagon door and we sat inside while she had an emergency conference with the Witch. "There wasn't much besides that gas station in Escalante. They probably have big supermarkets in Page or Kanab…" She sliced her finger around the Witch's face. "If we're going into town, I could really use a hot meal that didn't come from a can."

"Dream on. That didn't even exist *before* the boogeyvirus."

"I know." Mom slumped miserably. Mom was an herbivore, and everybody knows that there are no plants in the desert. She had to graze far and wide to find a restaurant that serves vegetarians.

"Have you ever tried a hot dog? They're not really made from dogs, you know."

Mom brightened. "I have an idea!" She pulled the Witch to her mouth like a police walkie talkie. "How far is it to Sedona, Arizona?"

"Traffic to Sedona is light, so I'm estimating six hours and thirty-seven minutes," the Witch taunted.

"Do you know what's just 350 miles away in Sedona?" Mom said in the same tone I use when I know she's hiding a toy behind her back.

I tried to remember what I knew about Sedona.

". . . where can we find wifi, somewhere to sit, and all the hot food required for happiness?" Mom hinted.

In Sedona we'd found the Law, white dirt, brick-grey dirt, and the most delicious warm meal that a rambling dog could possibly hope for.

"In Sedona there's a…" Mom drew out the *aaaaaaaaa* for suspense, which meant I was supposed to guess, but I already knew the right answer.

"McDonald's!" I cheered at the same moment Mom exclaimed, "Whole Foods!"

The excitement dropped out of Mom's face when she heard my guess. "McDonald's? You can get that anywhere. This is the only Whole Foods between Las Vegas and Albuquerque."

"If McDonald's is so common, why don't we go more often?"

"I'm sure there's a McDonald's in Sedona, too." Mom said dismissively. To the Witch, she ordered, "Take me to the Whole Foods in Sedona, Arizona."

"Continue east for two hundred and seventy-four miles," the Witch commanded.

Mom spurred the Wagon with the key and it giddyupped back onto the car-trail. "I knew something terrible would happen if I went out of cell range for too long," she said. "I leave civilization for 2 days, and look what happened."

"Why is it your job to fix… whatever it is?" I asked.

"It's not my job. There's nothing I can do. Absolutely nothing. But if they're shutting down entire cities, who knows what they'll try next. I don't even know if we'll get in trouble for not being home."

"But you *are* home. Home is wherever the Wagon is. You can do nothing from here, can't you?"

"I don't know *what* they can do. They're already saying that people can't earn a living, go where they want to go, and see who they want to see. It's like they're trying to outlaw our very existence. I've never seen anything like this in real life."

"They're outlawing friendship?" I whimpered. I would never be able to hide my friendliness for long enough to stay out of trouble. "They can't really send you to the pound for charisma, can they?"

"It's more like house arrest," Mom said dismissively, as if *I* was the one missing the point. "It'll never work. They can't send you to prison just for having a body like you can take a dog to the shelter if you don't like how much he sheds. That's some toxic shame, original sin nonsense." Except she didn't say *nonsense*.

"Neener, neener, neener! You can't house-arrest someone who doesn't have a house. Suckers!" I agreed.

"Who knows what rules they'll come out with next. The next piece of news could be something that lands us in jail for being so far from home."

"You can't change the rules in the middle of a game," I reassured her. "The rules *are* the game. There's no winning without rules to play by."

"Right! See? Even a dog gets it. What ever happened to life, liberty, and the pursuit of happiness? It's a virus, not a... not a..." Mom stuttered while her imagination sputtered to come up with something powerful enough to stop the whole world. Her imagination pooped out. "This isn't Hollywood," she finished un-grandly. "But if they can prevent people from working, buying useless junk, or coming and going as they please, maybe they *can* force us into house arrest."

Mom took a deep breath to turn down the movie in her head: "Let's think about this: If the reason they want everyone to stay home is to avoid contact with the virus,

"and the virus is in California...

"and the virus needs people to spread...

"and there are more people in the cities...

"... then we're safer in the wilderness out here than a city in California, don't you think?"

"Good idea! We can live in stone houses in the cliffs like the Anaschnozzy people used to. It'll be fun. Haven't you always been curious about what you'd do in a survival situation?"

"This isn't a run-for-your-life kind of survival situation. It's more of a stockpiling thing. Plus, it gets cold out here at night."

"You're supposed to build a fire, duh. You know how to make fire, Mom. You just pull the trigger on the flamethrower and *woosh*, the stove is hot."

"Ah yes, the traditional Bic long-neck lighter of the ancient Anasazi civilization." Something about the way Mom said it made me think she didn't mean it. "The people who knew how to survive out here lived a very different life from how we live today."

"Don't be breedist. Humans aren't all that different from each other. Even the ones that are ghosts."

"No, I mean they were mostly hunter-gatherers."

"We see hunters on the trail all the time," I reminded her. "And people are always gathering... Or, they were until this week anyway."

"I mean they didn't have Walmart or Whole Foods, so they spent most of their time outside searching for supplies."

"Spending all day outside sounds like fun," I said. "You already spend most of your time searching for things anyway. Your keys, your wallet..." Mom probably wasn't ready for the best part; the Witch would never survive our caveman lifestyle. "What ever happened to the Anaschnozzy civilization anyway?"

"I think there was a drought and they disappeared."

"Into the earth like Saint Bernardino?" I yipped.

"No one really knows, but they probably migrated on to Mexico or something. Some people think that the Anasazi homeland became the Aztecs' Aztlan."

"See? They survived."

"Until European diseases killed their descendents."

"*All* of them?"

"Not all of them, but too many."

I'd never heard of anyone actually losing a whole civilization before. When Nature tried to bring its savagery to the human world with something like a sandslide or a tsumommy, I thought people just went somewhere else until they could tame Nature's wildness again. But the boogeyvirus was a kind of wildness that people carried inside themselves, so there was nowhere to escape except from each other. If disease was enough to wipe out a civilization tough enough to live on cliffs like the Anaschnozzy, what did that mean for us? Thank goodness I was traveling with someone who could save the world just by keeping her socks dry.

I watched the wilder-ness flow by out the window and tried to count the towns we passed through to take my mind off of things. I kept losing count, not because dogs can't count that high, but because every time we drove through a town it had been so long since the last one that I forgot how many I'd counted already.

A frightening thought occurred to me. "Mom, could *you* get sick?"

"I guess." She shrugged like it was no big deal. "I'm not so worried about getting sick myself, but I would feel terrible if I got someone else sick. Maybe someone vulnerable, or someone that a vulnerable person relies on."

I was glad we didn't rely on anyone. It sounded risky.

"Lily said they're not even letting family members visit hospitals to say goodbye, or hold memorials for people who've died. I couldn't live with myself if I put someone in that position."

"Nobody knows who's boogeytrapped, Mom," I comforted. "Accidents happen. They can't send you to the pound if they can't prove you're a murderer."

"It's not just that, Spud. Getting someone sick would make this trip a selfish mistake, and I don't want to believe that my existence is a selfish mistake." She flattened a little under the colossal responsibility of keeping the whole world safe against something she couldn't even see.

"So what will we do if you get sick?" I asked.

She tilted her head to rearrange the kaleidoscope of thoughts inside. "I suppose I would drive us home as fast as I can. We have enough supplies to avoid stores for a week, and I could use the dog bathroom so I wouldn't spread germs in any public places. The only thing I really have to touch is gas pumps. I guess I could fill up with poop bags on my hands."

"And that stops the virus?"

"It'd better! If poop bags let germs through, I'm never, ever picking up one of your turds again. I'm just worried about what happens if we get caught."

"They would send us home, right?"

"Home is 1,000 miles away. We'd still need to keep driving and visiting gas stations, so that doesn't change anything."

"They could make us go to a hotel," I sulked. I hate hotels with their uncomfy beds that don't smell like Mom.

"Even if the hotels and campgrounds were open, the guests would be travelers. That's not safer. Our safest option is probably to keep doing what we planned to do all along—wild camping and staying away from interstates and cities. I guess we're refugees now."

"Referees?"

What game could Mom be refereeing? Tiddlywinks? Mom would never tidy up for fun. Duck duck goose? It would drive Mom crazy if the ducks and gooses weren't in the proper order. Certainly not red light green light. Maybe she was playing hopscotch? Or musical chairs? Then it hit me: Simon says! Mom follows the rules very closely, but she doesn't always walk on the right side of the line.

According to Mom, you can tell a lot about what's *allowed* by what's *not allowed* and studying the space between the *allowed* and the *not*. She calls it *law-gic*. If Mom sees a *no dogs allowed* sign below a *PARK HOURS 8 AM TO SUNSET* sign, she reads *DOGS ALLOWED SUNSET TO 8 AM*. That's law-gic.

With everyone trapped at home, the world would need a protector to travel around keeping an eye on things while they were away and to herd everyone back together when it was safe to come out again. That hero would need a sidekick, of course—a referee who knew how to twist silly rules until they made sense again and wield Murphy's Law to make impossible things happen, like bringing rain to the desert. Yes, the fate of the world rested on its globe-trotting hero, Tintin Quarantino and his faithful referee-sidekick, the Weather Jinx.

"If we're referees, does that mean we get to make the rules?" I asked.

"Not *referees*, *refugees*," Mom said.

"Potato-beast, potahto-beast."

"It means people who are forced to wander because they can't go home."

"If you're the referee, does that mean you get a whistle?"

"It was a metaphor," she said, using the fancy word for a lie.

"Well someone's got to blow the whistle on all this. You can't let those rascals cheat at Simon says. The world needs a referee to talk us out of trouble just like you *always* talk us out of trouble whenever the Law comes offsides to hassle us."

"I don't think it works that way," Mom lied again. In fact, Mom had talked us out of trouble the first time we visited Sedona.

During our last Christmas vacation, the Weather Jinx had brought a blizzard to town. Snow may be how clouds deliver white dirt, but the delivery isn't as fun as it looks on TV. The clouds throw it carelessly out of the sky like a drive-by mailman, with no thought to what innocent dog might get creamed by a snowfloof meant for a tree. When snowfloofs land on the road, they make Mom crunch against the driving wheel and yell a lot.

"Dog doo, I forgot about this road!" Mom growled. Her fist was locked tightly to the driving wheel, so when she shook it, her body shook instead, like she was trying to shake sense into the Wagon.

Outside the front window, the road dropped off the side of the mountain and twisted frantically as it fell. Meanwhile, the raindrops recognized the Weather Jinx coming and transformed into snowfloofs the size of dust bunnies. It only snows twice a year in Sedona, and this winter I'd been there to see both.

Back in the Before, driving down a slippery mountain road in the dark had been just about the most dangerous thing in the whole world. The last time this road attacked, the Wagon had carved fresh tireprints into the white dirt while a growing train of blinking cars hitched themselves behind us. Every time the Wagon pulled over to let someone else take a pull, every car in the train pulled over behind us like a big game of follow the leader. The Wagon was so jittery by the time we reached Sedona that it cowered in the first open place it could find beside the road while Mom and I slept off the storm.

That night, the Law had woken me up, and I woke Mom up to scare it away. Mom got out to talk to the lady-Law. She pointed at the snow in the sky and the white dirt on the road. Using law-gic and good grammar, Mom explained that it was all just a big misunderstanding. She promised to leave in the morning if the Law would be so kind as to please let us go back to bed.

The lady-Law looked Mom's chihuahua-sized frame up and down before inspecting the contents of her wallet, probably to make sure that Mom wasn't a poor person. The lady-Law asked her shirt for its opinion. After a long discussion, the Law decided that the Sedonuts were safe with us sleeping among them and invited us to be their guests, just as long as Mom kept her promise and was gone in the morning.

Now that there was snow *and* a boogeyvirus in the air, it was probably best not to catch the Law's attention. The Witch was telling scary stories about how people might need special papers to even leave their houses, and we didn't have magic papers *or* a stuck house handy. It would be hard to convince the Law that we were staying home while the Wagon was wearing its name tags that said, *Hi! I'm from California!*

Once again, Mom hugged the driving wheel so tight that her panting fogged up the front window. The Wagon put-putted at hiking speed down the curly mountain road and a tail of blinking cars lined up to ride in our wagon tracks. As the mountain released its grip on the road, Mom's chest gradually became unstuck from the driving wheel. Her shoulders faded from her ears as the forest gave way to houses and buildings. As street lights appeared, she made circles with her bottom teeth to unlock her jaw muscles.

"It was worth it for fresh, hot vegetables," Mom drooled. "I hope they have brussel sprouts. And green beans! I'd die for some green beans."

"Will they have roast turkey?" I wagged. "Or maybe pork chops? Do you think they'll have pork chops?"

"Tofu! Or any protein drowning in sauce, just as long as it's not beans," Mom gushed. "If they have mashed potatoes, I'm gonna fill a whole container."

My last dribble of drool dropped onto the blanket as a mouth-drying thought occurred to me. It was easy to find town things before the world ended, but now you were supposed to stay outside when you wanted to be inside, inside when you wanted to go outside, and not even the Witch knew if someplace would be open before we got there. Could you have a store if no one was allowed to shop or work there?

"Will Ho Foods be open?" I asked.

"It's a supermarket," Mom said like a threat. "They're calling supermarkets *essential businesses* now, so they have to stay open."

"Wait, I thought you said that working is forbidden. Who will cook the pork chops?"

"I guess work is forbidden for some people, but they're forcing other people to risk their lives to work. Crazy times." She shrugged, as if living in a world that still had tofu with lots of sauce meant she could cope with anything.

Luckily, there were cars in the car kennel and lights behind the Ho Foods door. "I'll be right back," Mom promised with a kiss.

"This is a special occasion," I coached. "Hunt and gather as much as you can drag back to the Wagon."

I climbed into the driving chair and stuck my eyeballs to the door so I wouldn't miss Mom when she reappeared with our feast. While my eyeballs were busy, my ears roamed the car kennel. A woman was filling the car next to me with sacks of treats while her man's waving arms tried to pull my eyes from the door.

"They won't even let you sit inside the McDonald's. They make you take your burger out to the car to eat it," he grumped. "This isn't America anymore!"

I'd always eaten my McRotguts in the Wagon, so I didn't even know there was another, more American way to do it. It was a shame that Mom had left the window closed and I couldn't tell him about the secret window in the back where they'd serve him his dinner without even making him dismount.

Mom's face wasn't hidden behind a stack of treats when she reappeared, so I could see the creeped-out look it wore. Mom always looked creeped out when she came out of stores lately and it was starting to tick me off. *I* was supposed to be the one to have a panic attack every time she left the Wagon. And where were all the bags of takeout? She was only carrying one bag, and I didn't smell a hint of pork chops or *anything* hot and yummy when she opened the door. Not even tofu.

"Sorry, Spud. No pork chops," she said, offering me a cheese stick that she could have found at any old gas station. "The hot bar was closed, and they were completely out of canned food."

"But... but... You promised!" After Oregon, I thought Mom would be more responsible with promises. "Where did all the cans go? Do you expect me to eat kibble for every meal?"

"I did the best I could." She really did look sorry. "Half the shelves were completely empty, especially in the aisles with the crackers and raisins that everyone usually skips. There was a couple with an entire cart full of crates of sparkling water, like that was going to save them from the apocalypse," said my life partner, who buys fuzzy water at every gas station. "I wonder what'll happen if they try to make espresso with it."

"This isn't America anymore!" I said, trying out my new catchphrase for when you don't get something you want.

"I'll make it up to you, Spud. I promise. Wasn't there supposed to be a McDonald's around here somewhere? I think they have outlets and wifi."

"McDonald's is telling everyone to *keep out*, too. I heard a man talking about it while you were inside. That's why this isn't America anymore."

"Damn. I need to charge my laptop," Mom said like she was finally starting to understand how bad things really were. "It'll die soon if I don't find an outlet."

"Didn't you do that while you were inside not-buying my pork chops? You were gone forever!"

"I tried, but all the chairs were upside-down on tables."

"The whole world's upside-down," I agreed.

"Since nobody was in the dining area, I didn't think it would be a problem if I stood quietly in the corner to let it charge, but the lady in the express checkout lane acted like she was going to have me arrested just for standing there."

"How dare she!" I gasped. "Why didn't you buy something first to show that you're not an escaped poor person? Just to set people at ease."

"I had my $200 bag of groceries with me and everything. It didn't matter. I guess we'll have to find another place to sit and use public wifi now that sitting in public is illegal."

"What about my McRotguts? You said you'd make it up to me."

"If we can't find a McDonald's, I'll buy you the first hot dog I see. Promise," Mom said, like someone who hadn't just broken two promises in a row. "Anyone who shops at Whole Foods is used to getting exactly what they want, so they panic at the idea of making do. But we're resourceful. No pork chops? We'll hunt for McNuggets instead. No McNuggets? No problem. We know where to find hot dogs. Shortages are just another puzzle to solve. Bring it on! Scarcity doesn't scare me."

"I thought the plan was to stay away from *scare-cities*," I said. As much as I wanted to go hot dog hunting, this strange new world gave me the willies. No one in the soggy car kennel looked friendly. Instead of invisibility cloaks, they all walked around as if surrounded by force fields of fear and scorn. "I liked it better when we're social distancing."

"I know. I just need to find somewhere to charge up and then we'll get out of town." Mom called on the Witch for help. Her face crinkled and twitched in the screen's glow until suddenly her eyebrows unpinched for the first time since she came out of Ho Foods empty-pawed. "I know where to find wifi and benches, where nobody will tell me to move along!"

"It's hopeless, Mom. If they wouldn't let that big, angry man inside…"

"Not McDonald's, the laundromat!" Mom announced triumphantly. "Some of them even have tables with outlets nearby! Indoors! Can you imagine such luxury?"

"We're saved!" I wagged.

The Witch directed us to a different car kennel with only one bright window surrounded by many dark ones. Mom gathered her stinky clothes and the blankets.

"Back it up or else I'll close the door on your snout," she warned, blocking the doorway with her body and sticking out a hip each time I tried to nose around her.

"But I want to come with you!"

"It says NO DOGS ALLOWED. Here, I'll leave you with dinner." She poured some kibble into a bowl. I leaned in to sniff it. As soon as my nose pulled out of the doorway, I heard a slam.

I was in no mood to protect the Wagon. "Dog food!" I scoffed. "I was told there would be pork chops."

When Mom came back a few minutes later, I was ready to give her a piece of my mind. "Don't tell me," I said as soon as the door opened, "you saw a SERVICE DOGS ONLY sign and now you need somedog to escort you or they won't let you inside."

"I forgot my laptop," Mom chirped, reaching around me for the bag. She slammed the door in my face again.

I sat alone and porkchopless on the bare sleeping mat, watching Mom through the laundrymat window as she tended to everyone's needs but mine. My excitement curdled to anxiety, then to angst, and finally to anger as she scratched the laptop's belly. Why should *I* have to quar-unseen in the Wagon when *she* was the one who was too dirty to be around anyone else? Mom should know better! The reason we go everywhere together is because the world is a scary place without a sidekick. She was probably in there tinkering with our plans right now, trying to plot away the white dirt before I left my mark on it.

With nobody to pat me and tell me what a good boy I was, I had to figure out what to do with the icky buzzing feeling behind my teeth. Maybe a snack? I sniffed the bowl of kibble for signs of comfort or love, but it just smelled cold and dry.

"Phooey!" I grumbled, knocking the bowl so the kibble spilled all over the bed. That felt pretty good, but one of Mom's two-handed face rubs would have felt even better. How dare she leave me alone like this, after all the cool places I'd taken her!

"This is bullplop!" I raged, and looked for someone to back me up. One quick look around the Wagon reminded me that I was alone, so I looked for something to destroy instead. What I found under my upturned bowl was the bunched-up corner of the sleeping mat. I tore a hole in it and found it was filled with the same fluff and guts as my favorite toys.

"I'll show you!" I thought as I tore out more stuffing and threw it into the same pile as the kibble. "I bet you won't even thank me for making the bed better!" I dug like the bed was a beach, spraying kibble and bed guts through my back legs and all over the Wagon. I repositioned for a better ripping angle and got back to work.

"That'll show her," I thought, admiring my handiwork as the knot in my chest melted into a slime of worry. A corner of the mattress under where the pillows go was completely deflated, its ragged ends hanging limply over the new packet of water bottles. I sure hoped Mom liked what I'd done to the place.

My tantrum was long over and I was dozing in a cozy nest of mattress guts by the time Mom came back. The sound of the door opening wagged my tail before it opened my eyes. With my eyes full of Mom and my nose full of fresh laundry stink, I totally forgot about the surprise remodel.

I met her at the door. "I'm so glad you're back," I wiggled.

"What the smell, Oscar?" Mom roared in her road-rage voice. She turned on her dragon voice. "That was BAD! VERY BAD!"

Mom never gets that mad at me except when I run with wild animals rather than her. "What did I do?" I shivered. I tucked in my ears, and slid my tail under my butt, cowering in the corner until she slammed the door again.

I waited for what might have been minutes or years. What if Mom never came back? Maybe she had already found a new life partner and it would just be me and the Wagon alone against the world. How would I reach the driving buttons? Mom was the heart of the Covered Wagon, and I wasn't even sure if it would turn on without her. Could I find my own Witch to order me around and judge me when I was wrong?

When Mom returned, I was back at the door wagging for her. "I'm very sorry I ripped up our bed." I craned my neck to kiss her face. "I promise I won't punish you anymore."

"It's okay, Spud. I get it." She kissed the special spot between my eyes that made everything feel better. "I can't stay mad at you. You're the only one who isn't treating me like the scum of the earth just for breathing."

Mom smooshed her mouth even harder into the kissing place and my nubbin waggled a little as the icky feeling in my chest began to shrink. She gathered up all the kibble and fluff and took it to the trash can in several trips, recharging me with kisses in between. When the fluff was gone, she hid the ragged edges under the sheet and filled the deflated spot with a pillow.

"See?" she said. "Good as new. Come on. Let's go find somewhere to spend the night so we can test out your home improvements."

Chapter 8

Hyper Vigilante

Nature owed me one this time. The last time we were in Sedona, the trail was buried so deep under white dirt that it scared Mom away half way up the mountain. It was barely up to my chin when she insisted that we turn around, promising that we would come back again someday. Now *someday* was here, and I was traveling with a braver version of Mom, who didn't hesitate to walk boldly into puddles, socks and all. Seeing that the Weather Jinx meant business this time, the storm stole away in the night, leaving a clean sky and overcast ground behind.

High on the wedding-cake-shaped mountain, the white dirt glowed like frosting, but here at the bottom there was nothing but brick-grey mud and cacti. The mud squelched through my toes, slipped under Mom's shoes, and gathered in rusty puddles on the trail.

"Do you hear that?" I cocked my head toward a rocky swell. Whatever was hiding behind it roared like a feral washing machine.

Mom had the Witch's stories in her ears and didn't notice the racket until it was too late. The trail turned a corner and dove into a river. The river trickled ferociously through a groove in the mud as deep as a sock and as wide as a sidewalk.

"Oh darn! This keeps happening!" I made my tail sag in fake disappointment. "I guess it's time to go back to town and search for hot dogs."

Mom looked up and down the river for sock-saving rocks. Finding none, she plopped on the bank with the sound older humans make when they sit on something that's not a chair. "Welp, here we go again," she huffed. She took off her shoes and socks, rolled her pants into Knuckleberry Finns, and set herself free from the leash so we could each deal with the river in our own way.

"I didn't agree to this!" I protested from the shore. "You can't just lure a dog with the promise of snow angels and then throw him in a river." I turned and started walking back the way we'd come, hoping Mom would follow.

"Come on, dummy. It's not even deep," she called over her shoulder. "You'll never get anywhere if you let a little thing like this stop you."

"Come back here," I barked.

She found a sitting rock on the far bank and dangled her paws in the water to rinse off the grit. She flossed between her toes with her fingers and used her socks to fan her paws dry.

I wasn't going to cross this time. I really wasn't. I dawdled on the bank, casually sniffing the cacti like Mom would be back at any moment. On the far side, Mom carefully lined her toes up with the holes in her socks.

"Mom! C'mere!" I barked, just like she does when she thinks I'm taking too long to come back from the potty. But Mom never came back. I waited until her shoes were tied and the packpack was on her back. When she turned the packpack on me and started up the trail, I couldn't stand it any longer. I splashed in after her.

"Oh my Dog, I survived!" I panted as I sprinted the last few steps to Mom's side. The water was only below my knees, but I didn't want Mom to get the wrong idea. I shook as vigorously as if the whole river were on my back.

The ground crackled under Mom's shoes as the trail climbed and mud turned to ice. Fluffy wisps started to appear on the cacti like toy stuffing caught in its thorns. Before long, more of it ploofed right out of the mud.

"White dirt!" I squealed. I took a running start and tumbled into snow angel position.

The last time we were here, we only made it to the shoulder of the mountain before Mom gave up. The white dirt had been up to my chest, hiding everything under a blinding blanket so that neither the eye nor the imagination could guess what route the trail must take to the top. Today, we were determined to find out.

The trail sure knew how to build suspense. Mom walked with her nose in the air as her imagination ran wild, trying to figure out what trick of the eye might explain how the trail could land on top of that mountain. The peak above us looked impossible for anyone but a bird to stand on.

Some views are too big to see all at once. The only way to enjoy them properly is to move through them so the different parts can dance together. The higher we climbed, the more the scenery grew around us until there was nowhere for Mom's eyes to rest that didn't tempt her into a picture. A bakery case of iced mountains shaped like cupcakes, croissants, bear claws, and churros were arranged around the valley, competing to steal Mom's eyes. Every time the trail turned, she forgot the wonder from a few steps before and made me stop to pose again, as if she'd never seen me sit in front of anything so marvelous in her life. Even up close, the fluff on the cacti and cushions of white dirt sitting like hats on the pumpkin-grey boulders were a Pied Piper for the eyeballs.

No matter how high we climbed, the mysterious peak never seemed to get any closer. Its steep sides only steepened in my eyes as it stretched away from us. Mom stopped taking pictures as scales of white dirt stuck to the bottom of her pants and a wet stain crept toward her knees. We climbed until all the peaks were looking up at us except the one we were aiming for. Each twist revealed a new catwalk that had been invisible from below.

At long last, the trail led us around the shoulder to the backstage side of the mountain, where the exciting cliffs relaxed into ordinary slopes to make it easier for the workers who hang the sunrise each morning to get to their positions. *So that's how they do it*, I thought with the same sense of wonder as the time I caught Mom pretending to throw the ball and sneakily hiding it behind her back.

As the white dirt got deeper, my fun-o-meter turned up and Mom's turned down until the needles on both fun-o-meters busted their limits. I took reindeer leaps and left behind two snow angels for every cloud angel in heaven. Normally I don't let Mom out of my sight when she's off-leash, but today's fluff-fest was too exciting and Mom wasn't keeping up with the pace of my thrill. Mom hiked behind me with all the late-expedition excitement of Robert Scott.

"This blows. I can't believe this is happening to me again," she harrumphed with the force of a snowblower. "What are the chances that we happened to come here the day after the only 2 snowstorms of the year?"

"I know! Isn't it terrific?" I rolled onto my back and kicked my legs in the air to show how terrific it was.

When I flipped back over to see if Mom had any questions, she wasn't looking at me. Instead, she was looking at a black shadow traveling unnaturally fast through the white dirt. A man as graceful and handsome as an Oscar bounded two-leggedly toward us. His knife-legs cut through the white dirt with the same rockethorse enthusiasm as mine. His fashionable face fur burst open with a toothpaste-ad smile as he passed.

"No better trail the day after a blizzard!" he gushed, like being out of breath was exhilarating, not exhausting.

124

Nothing annoys Mom more than pep. Her jaw muscles rippled as she watched his shapely booty bobble gracefully uphill under lustrous black tights. His good cheer showed the lie in her excuses and she wasn't about to let him get away with that. Mom raised her chin and her face drew to a point. She set her shoulders to *determined* and stepped into his paw holes.

Mom heaved and grunted, scoffed and growled as she stretched her stubby legs to catch each pawprint in the Man-Oscar's effortless stride. I kept her company, following alongside like a gleeful snowplow.

The sun was bright on the ground as we chugged up the last slope onto the flat-topped summit. A cluster of trees wearing white coats two sizes too big for their flimsy branches blocked the view like a curtain. Every now and then, the grove made a plopping sound as the warmer branches dropped their heavy loads. We followed the man-tracks into their shade.

"Eep!" I eeped as a snowblob narrowly missed me.

"Ack! It went down my neck!" Mom acked, digging a dripping clump out of her collar. "That's it, I'm going this way."

My eyeballs lost her for a second as she stepped from the darkness under the trees into the squinty brightness. "Where are you going? The man-tracks go this way. Can't you hear him?"

The Man-Oscar's powerful voice rang out through the clear morning. "…just out for a quick run while the snow's still fresh…"

"After all that work, I want to enjoy the view by ourselves." Mom stomped her own path toward where the white dirt ended and the sky began.

"Ah right," I said, "social distancing."

"Well, yeah," Mom said, like it was obvious. "It's obnoxious when people have phone conversations in the middle of the wilderness."

"Yeah. Ran up here this morning," the wilder-ness said. "What are you doing this afternoon? Wanna come over for some beers and watch the— Oh right. It's canceled. Well come over anyway. We'll fire up the grill."

"It sounds like he's inviting us to a party," I said. "Do you think there'll be snacks?"

"The whole world's shutting down and this self-absorbed blowhard is having a cookout?" Mom grumbled.

"He seems like someone who knows how to have a good time. Maybe he could teach *you* how to loosen up."

"Being happy all the time is a mental disorder," Mom growled.

"You agreed to have dinner with Lily and you'd only just met her, too," I pointed out.

"I hadn't just met her, I knew her from the internet. It's different."

"But you promised me hot dogs," I reminded her. "The internet doesn't make hot dogs. He seems like a fun guy to share a hot dog with."

"He's not inviting us, he's just talking on the phone." The disgust in Mom's voice showed what she thought of people who talked to their witches in public using their mouths rather than their thumbs. "And you made up the part about the hot dogs. For all you know, he's a vegetarian too."

"Not with that beard."

We slogged toward the boundary between mountain and air so that Mom could mark our accomplishment with pictures.

With white dirt covering everything, though, it was hard to tell where the rocks stopped and the sky began.

"C'mere, Oscar! *Up-up!*" Mom tapped a rock far from the cliff like she'd never seen anything so marvelous.

I was more interested in hearing the man-Oscar's thoughts on the game being canceled. "Did you hear something?" I asked the sky in his direction, which just so happened to be in the opposite direction from where Mom was waving the Witch at me.

Mom snapped her fingers like a flamenco dancer to get my attention. "Oscar! Oscar! *C'mere. Up-up!*" she begged like a paparazza, waving her paw over the rock like it was even more amazing than she originally thought.

I ignored her. The Man-Oscar was talking about grilling.

"Fine," Mom said, her voice flattening from a happy teakettle to a gong. She chased after me with shovel-arms, scooped me up like a forklift, and plopped me on the rock.

I stood like a statue with my head sunk low between my shoulders in a sulk.

Mom's voice pretended we weren't in a fight, but she wasn't fooling anyone. "Oscar! Oscar! *Lookit me!* Over here!" she begged.

I thought rock-like thoughts and gazed toward where the voice was coming from.

Mom sighed and put the Witch back in her pocket. "If only people knew how many tries it takes to get some of these photos," she grumbled, like I was the party pooper.

She swiped the white dirt off the rock next to me and sat. We let the soothing burbling of the Man-Oscar's weekend plans wash over us as Mom ate her nut-and-raisin kibble. Even with a mouthful of snacks and no new trail to break, Mom's face still looked dreary.

I took in the sky and the cloud-like summit around me. A thought occurred to me and I perked up. "Hey, Mom. Did you notice?"

She scowled at the bag for not mixing the raisins in right. "Notice what?" she chewed.

"We did it! We came here to see the top of the mountain and we didn't give up, even though we had the same problems as last time. We persisted. We overcame. And we did something we thought we couldn't do. Doesn't that feel good?"

"Know what's funny? I thought I wouldn't have the grit to push through if I stayed positive. Like, if I expected the worst, I'd be prepared for whatever the trail had in store. I never hated the step I was in, but as things got harder, it was unbearable to think that the worst was yet to come. Bracing myself for something I hadn't even faced yet was exhausting, but the idea of giving up was even worse. The struggle in my mind was tougher than anything the mountain threw at me."

"Changing your plans isn't the same thing as danger," I reminded her. "You can't let the things you don't see ruin what's right in front of you."

"I know. But they feel the same."

"Maybe you could enjoy it more if you let things turn out differently than you expected without trying to fix it," I coached.

"Without misery and suspense, it wouldn't feel so rewarding when it ends." She threw the last fistful of trail mix into her mouth without bothering to check that it had the right raisin-to-peanut ratio. "I suppose that's why I like hiking so much. Life is full of uncertainties, but at least in the wilderness you expect the unexpected and can put solved problems behind you." She stood up to look down at the sky, and Sedona underneath. "And there are no downhills in real life. Every day feels like an uphill slog."

Mom knocked the white dirt from her butt, fitted her toes into the nearest heelprint, and let the accomplishment carry her downhill like a sleigh. I ran ahead to spread good cheer to any other hikers we met along the way.

"How much farther?" the uphill hikers gasped.

Look at these poor nincompoops in their department store sneakers, Mom's thoughts said to me, already forgetting her own despair. "Not that far. Only a little more than a mile," she chirped out loud, enjoying how their faces fell like white dirt from a branch. To rub it in she added, "The view is beautiful."

"But you didn't see the view because you were too chicken to get close," I thought back.

'*Still counts,*" her smile said as she tromped away.

By the time we returned to the stream, neither of us hesitated before wading in. My belly, booty, and all four of my legs were already covered with rust-grey mud and the white dirt had soaked Mom's jeans to halfway up her thighs. I even stopped in the middle for a drink, just to show the stream that I wasn't scared.

"It's funny how solving one problem can make another problem go away," I said. "You never cross the same river twice."

Mom was just opening her mouth to make my wisdom her own, when a sound like a bowling strike in reverse cracked the air and rumbled through the valley. It rolled in my ears for too long to be a gunshot, and had too many new sounds inside of it to be an echo.

"Sit, Oscar!" Mom yelled, only she didn't really say *sit*. "Run! Run! Run!"

She didn't need to tell me twice. I shot down the trail as fast as I could go without losing the *ker-plopping* of Mom's steps behind me. Close on my heels, Mom sprinted like a much faster human than she actually was.

We ran until the last pebbles of noise fell out of the air, and kept running until the noise didn't start again. When the air was finally silent, I paused to take stock. I swiveled my eyes in one direction and my ears in the other. "What was that?"

"It sounded like a rockfall somewhere nearby. Like, *really* nearby," Mom said, looking in the direction that the noise had come from. But we were already deep enough into the valley that the scenery was all close-ups.

"I knew it!" I said. "The whole world is falling apart! No hot bar at Ho Foods, you can't sit at McDonald's anymore, escaped veterinarians are wandering the streets, rivers are washing away the trails, I don't even *know* where America went, and even the mountains are coming down around us!"

"The world's not coming to an end," Mom said, as if she weren't still out of breath from running for her life. "Natural disasters, civil unrest, celebrity deaths… they happen all the time. They only *seem* to bunch together because once you notice the first one, you're more likely to notice the second and believe it matters just as much."

"A wise dog always notices what matters."

"It's not supposed to be a good thing," Mom corrected. "It means that your stress-o-meter doesn't go back to 0, so all the scary things pile up on top of each other until they seem much bigger than they really are."

I couldn't be sure the mountain wasn't about to come down on my head, so I kept Mom to my mountain-side to catch any chasing rocks. I thought I would be safer with Mom at my back, but suddenly a monster lunged from behind a rock and threw itself across the trail at my feet.

I porcupined my hackles and shrieked my most ferocious bark.

The monster reared up to look me in the eye. "Come at me, bro," it challenged. It held its ground, waving its hackles to block my way.

"Now you're really asking for it!" I screamed, strategically jumping backward toward Mom so I could hide heroically behind her if the monster made its move.

"It's a log, you dummy!" Mom said, not quite not-laughing. She must have been hysterical with fear.

"Don't you touch her, you evil snake-bear-dragon-beast!" I bellowed as Mom walked past me.

She strolled within inches of the creature as if she didn't have a care in the world. The beast's leafy talons swayed a little as Mom walked by, but it kept its menacing stare fixed on me.

Now I had a new problem: the Thing was between me and Mom, and Mom was calling me. I weighed unthinkable options. I didn't want to fight the monster to the death, but I didn't want to live on this crumbling mountain waiting for the earth to swallow me like Saint Bernardino either. I decided that getting gobbled up by a leaf-serpent was better than a life in isolation and screwed up my courage.

I ran wide, never taking my eyes off of the monster and keeping as much distance between me and It as the trail allowed. It glared at me as I passed, but I must have looked as fierce as a cannonball with my ears back and my tail between my legs, because It didn't pounce when It had the chance.

Once Mom was again between me and danger, I went back to barking and backed away aggressively. No matter what belittling things Mom said, I didn't quit barking until the horrible creature couldn't see me anymore.

Suspense may be fun in movies, but it's a heavy burden in real life. When the villain could be hiding behind every rock, tree, and gas station door, even your own farts can startle you. If the danger's invisible, you never can tell if it's real or just a bad feeling inside. And if it is something inside of you, is it better to let it eat you up inside or unleash it on the world?

"I can't believe you would let me get eaten by that thing," I said when it was safe to stop screaming.

"We might even have time to drive to New Mexico before sunset," Mom said in a different conversation.

"How can you think about sunsets at a time like this?" I whimpered. "What about that *monster?*"

"There was no monster. You were so afraid that the sky was falling that you let yourself get spooked by a silly log. I swear, you're afraid of your own shadow sometimes."

"Look who's talking," I said. "You're the one who's always forgetting what's real and what's imaginary. You think running out of cream for your poop juice is danger."

"I guess that's the difference between danger and anxiety. You can put danger behind you, but you carry anxiety from one problem to the next. Danger made us run from the rockfall, but anxiety made you misplace your fear onto that log."

"Monster," I corrected her.

"Log," she lied.

"I know what I saw."

"Anxiety is real too, even if what you're worried about isn't," she said to even the score.

As we slopped through the last muddy killmometer back to the car kennel, the *wee-woo* sound of a shrieking ambulance filled the valley. Usually, a hysterical ambulance will run away to cry it out in private, but this wailing didn't fade away. Instead, it stayed put just when you expected it to shrink.

We couldn't see the road until the trail made the final turn into the car kennel. Just beyond the entrance, a herd of flashing cars with doors still open were scattered willy-nilly in the road. Men in uniforms were peeking over the edge of the bridge that straddled the ravine beside the car kennel. The people in the dammed traffic behind them also got out to watch them watch.

"Oh. Dog doo," Mom said, slower and more carefully than she does when she realizes that she forgot her wallet.

"What?" I asked. "What's with the party?"

"I don't see a car accident, Oscar. Do you?"

I looked again. All the cars stood on their wheels, and the ones that weren't flashing were lined up neatly without so much as a fender out of place. "Nope. Phew! I was afraid that someone got hurt."

"I'm afraid someone did…" she said. She wouldn't say any more.

Mom shooed me into the Wagon in a voice that said now was no time to ask for pats from strangers. She turned to a man wearing a sunscreen kabuki mask. "Do you know what happened?"

"Maybe someone sprained an ankle or had a cardiac event on the trail," the sunscreen guessed.

I'm a dog, and even I know that they don't send a stampede of police and fire trucks for someone who sprained their ankle. This was definitely the kind of guy who made his poop juice with fuzzy water. "Go back to Ho Foods where you belong!" I shouted through the closed window.

"There were no first responders on the trail." Mom gestured to the uniform-free car kennel behind us. "And why would they block off both sides of the bridge if the emergency were back here?"

The mask stopped doing goofy and did confused instead. We all looked back at the scene, where the noses of all the cars and people were pointed at the same spot—the empty space next to the bridge where the fence was twisted and broken like finish line tape.

"I'm afraid it was a jumper..." Mom said.

Everyone was quiet for a moment before the man walked wordlessly toward the trail, and Mom remounted the Wagon without wishing him a fun hike.

"Wait, what's a jumper?" I asked. "Mom? What's a jumper?"

"You know how sometimes you feel like you've had enough? You're slogging uphill through snow, and then all of a sudden you hit one more obstacle and decide you just can't take it anymore?"

"No. Don't change the subject. Was he scared for his life?"

"Maybe, but I doubt it. Most of the time it doesn't even take that much effort to get past whatever obstacle is in front of you. But knowing that there might be another obstacle, and another one after that, makes you too tired to go on."

"How can you be tired from things you haven't done yet? And why won't you tell me what those Law-men are looking at?"

"Believe me," Mom said. "It's just one damned thing after another, and you get so you can't imagine yourself ever reaching the top of the mountain."

"That's when you're supposed to keep going. So you'll see that it does end, and you'll get to look down from the top of the mountain at all the things you conquered. Speaking of looking down, what are those Laws looking at? Is someone sleeping in their wagon down there? Now? In the middle of the day?"

"Sometimes it's not the pride of overcoming the mountain that sticks with you, but the fear of what you survived that has you jumping at logs," Mom went on. "The imaginary fears pile on top of the real ones until you forget what's real and what's imaginary. Then you'd do anything to get away. Rather than waiting around for something else to go wrong, people gather up all their desperation and do what they think they have to do to make it stop."

"Did someone turn back before they got to the top? Is that illegal now?" I guessed. "Is that why they called the Law?"

"Some things can't be turned back," Mom said. "When you know where you're going, every step feels like progress. But when obstacles block your path in life, every step you take in a different direction feels harder than it actually is. It's not that you can't handle the moment you're in, but the idea that it might never end makes you want to give up."

"Ah, I understand. You're talking about how changing your plans feels like danger again," I said in a life-coachly way. "It takes courage to change your plans when you don't know if it's going to work out." I was starting to figure out what had happened. The mountain must have been too much for someone today. They were probably too tired to walk back down, so they'd taken a shortcut. "But Mom, people are hardly ever *lost* when they're not where they expected to be. There's a difference between being lost and just needing to take a different path than you planned on. Where's this Jumper fellow? I'll tell him myself."

"I don't think he can hear you," she said. She gave the bridgetop party one last searching look, pleading for a way to make it better. Then the Wagon turned away toward the open road.

Chapter 9
A Turn at Albuquerque

Humans have trouble telling the difference between real and make-believe because they learn from fables. If you really want to understand how people see the world, you've got to study their folklore. I'd watched all of humanity's most important myths—*Loony Tunes, Jurassic Park, Friends, Lord of the Rings, Thelma and Louise*—and tried my best to decode the messages hidden inside.

Action movies were exciting, but barking at all those loud noises distracted me from the lesson. Romance was okay, but I couldn't stand to watch someone else getting so much attention when I was sitting right there. Westerns were my favorite. The fancy neckerchiefs and spurs jingling like dog tags when they walked reminded me of myself. I couldn't tear my eyes away from the horses, but what I loved most about westerns were the love stories.

My favorite western was called *Breaking Bad*. It was about a man who loved his family, but still made time to start a new business with his buddy. They made *math*, which was a bad medicine that people took for a thrill. The show followed them on lots of business trips together into the desert, where they taught each other wholesome life lessons about hard work, loyalty, and responsibility, just like Mom and I did.

One of the best characters in *Breaking Bad* is Albuquerque. It looks just like the city nextdoor, yet is surrounded by intrigue and a desert so empty that anything could happen there without anyone noticing. Maybe all that emptiness and not-noticing is why Mom pointed the Wagon toward Albuquerque when Sedona let us down. With the boogeyvirus traveling through chains of people, a city protected by a moat of desert was just the hideout we needed. Or perhaps she just wanted to feel famous.

"Look, Oscar! A sleazy lawyer ad at a bus stop, just like on TV!" Mom bubbled. Usually Mom hates driving in cities, but she was too starstruck by Albuquerque to be annoyed. "Do you think they did that on purpose?" A moment later she gushed, "Look! A seedy hooker hotel, just like in the show!" She'd seen plenty of math heads in the City, of course, but everything looks more glamorous when it's from TV.

"Mom! Mom! There's a hot dog shop in Albuquerque, remember?" The hot dog shop was where Jesse went to meet men with face tattoos and trade business secrets. "It has outdoor seating and everything! Can we go there for dinner?"

"Sure. If it's a real place."

"Oh boy!" I wagged. "I hope I make a Friend with a face tattoo."

"Oscar, what do you think *Breaking Bad* is about?"

"It's about a successful business man who cares very much about his family, just like me," I explained. "It's supposed to teach you about work-life balance. Why, what did you get out of the story?"

"That we really should have affordable healthcare," Mom sighed. After a moment, she asked the Witch's advice on finding the seediest hotdog stand in Albuquerque.

The first place the Witch brought us was dark behind its barred windows and there was nobody with or without face tattoos at the picnic tables. The Wagon and I waited impatiently as we watched Mom walk to the front window and make a visor of her paws to peer inside. She must have seen someone there, because she waved her arms in sign language for, *Look at me.*

When the door didn't open, Mom held the Witch to her face and talked to her instead, all the while staring at her own reflection in the window. She came back to the Wagon empty-handed.

"What happened?" I crowded in closer to sniff for hints of boiled meat.

"They were closed," Mom said in a one-star-review voice. "There was someone inside, but she wouldn't let me in, or even open the door to talk to me. She made me call her just so she could tell me they closed early. They're not even bothering to open tomorrow. She told me all that through the phone while making eye contact through the window. Can you believe that?"

"Rude!" I agreed.

"It's like science fiction or something," her voice said, but her puzzled face seemed more like a scene from a mystery.

"Don't they need someone to eat the leftover hot dogs they're not serving for dinner?"

"How are the staff gonna pay their rent if they can't work?" Mom missed the point, as usual. "Remind me to tip generously from now on."

The Witch led us on a tour of all the locked doors in Albuquerque before Mom finally spotted a sign in an empty car kennel pointing the way to takeout. She came back a million years later with a tub the size of a popcorn bucket and the smell of cheese on her breath.

"They only had a couple of things on the menu, so I got us mac & cheese," she said, scooping a few spoonfuls of mac into my bowl. "I'm sorry, they didn't have any bacon in the kitchen."

I gave the mac a sniff, but Mom had ordered it the way *she* likes it: hold the hot dogs. "But I don't want mac & cheese!" I decided, eating it anyway.

"Me neither." Mom glumly poked at the cheese with her spoon. "I'd give anything for a big salad, but I don't think we can count on any fresh food for a while. We should plan to live off of the water and canned food in the van from now on. Lucky for you, there are hot dogs that come in cans. I've been saving Vienna Sausages for a special occasion."

"I knew you wouldn't let me down!" I wagged.

"Come on. Let's just find somewhere to sleep first so you have plenty of time to lick the bowl when you're done."

Since Walt and Jesse never had trouble finding a secluded place outside of town to do criminal things like cooking or sleeping, I thought I'd be munching on canned sausage in no time. As it turns out, all those convenient car-trails in Albuquerque are pure Hollywood.

The Wagon drove into the sunset and kept driving under a fading sky. It was full-dark by the time we escaped the street lights, and still we drove on into the blackness. The first roadside car kennel the Witch found was so deep into the darkness that Albuquerque was a twinkling Milky Way in the distance. Mom had just reached her paw into the bag where the wiener cans lived when the whoosh-crackle of a car pulling off the road distracted her.

It turned its blinding eyebeams to stare directly at us. A moment later, another set of eyes joined. Behind the growling engines, there was an even deeper rumble that shook the very earth and made my hackles stand on end. Mom froze with her finger on the key to the can and waited to see what would happen.

"Hey! We're trying to eat over here!" I barked.

"Hush, Oscar." Mom patted my head with short, shushing strokes that were supposed to be comforting, but I could tell she just wanted to have a hand nearby to use as a muzzle.

Finally, the glaring eyes looked away and the low growl turned into the racket of a lot of people talking too loud all at once. I heard the *snick-pop* of someone pulling the key on a can.

"It's safe, Mom," I whispered. "You can open my wienie can now."

"Ugh, these drunk college kids could be here all night!" Mom threw the can back into the shadows where the Ho Foods bag was and climbed into the driving chair.

"Where are you going? What about dinner?" I sniffed my bowl just in case I'd missed something in the darkness, but it was as empty as I'd feared.

"There's a campground at the trailhead." Mom turned the key and the Wagon purred to life. "It's only about 30 minutes away. Let's just sleep there."

We drove for what felt like the rest of the night as Mom searched the darkness beside the road for another place to stop. By the time we reached a lone streetlight in the darkness, she was antsy from too much raspberry water.

"You have arri—" the Witch started.

"Oh good, there's a bathroom!" Mom interrupted. She left without telling me she'd be right back and waddled across the car kennel with the jerky, fast-forward steps of a character in a silent movie. A moment after she disappeared into the shadows behind the potty, the blurry edge of the Witch's spotlight peeked around the corner.

Mom stomped back out of the shadows a moment later and pulled the Wagon door open.

"You might as well come, too. There's a sign that says the bathrooms and trash pickup have been canceled *until further notice*." She said *until further notice* in the deep voice she uses to repeat something very stupid. "That makes no sense."

"It's because the boogeyvirus is indoors and people-potties always have doors," I said. "Haven't you been paying attention?"

"You're supposed to be alone in the bathroom," she said impatiently. "The only thing that locking the bathrooms and trash cans does is encourage people to litter and make a mess of the parking lot. I'm not picking up my crap in a bag."

"Don't worry. I'll show you how it's done."

"Going to the bathroom is a biological imperative. Locking the restrooms doesn't make people stop needing one, it just makes them go in less sanitary ways." The Witch's spotlight found the edge of the car kennel and Mom followed it into the bushes. "You're supposed to wash your hands and not touch your face, right? If they really wanted to keep people from spreading germs, I don't understand why they wouldn't just keep the hand sanitizer stocked." She said it like her not-understanding made someone else look stupid.

Mom found a private-ish place behind the potty building while I sniffed for my own spot. It was hard to smell anything over the stink coming from the potty house. An idea followed the smell up my nose and barged into my brain. "If people leave smells behind in bathrooms, maybe they leave germs, too," I suggested.

"It's well ventilated, can't you tell? Even I can smell it. Most people hold their breath in there anyway, so maybe it's the *safest* indoor public place there is. Did you think of that?"

"But what about the flush?" I asked. The Witch had been trying to scare Mom with gross stories about how people potties could blow boogeyvirus into the air when they flushed.

"It doesn't flush, dummy. That's why it stinks."

When I finished my business, Mom unraveled a poop bag before remembering about the trash being locked. She put the bag in her pocket and went back to her rant. She wasn't talking to me anymore, but I tried to keep up anyway. There were so many things I didn't understand lately, and without Mom's rants I might never make sense of it all.

"And what's the point of taping over the fee slot?" Mom scolded. "You don't have to choose between staying open and staying safe. It's a false dichotomy."

"What's a *false de-comommy*?" I asked.

"It means you think you have to pick one thing or the other, when you can really have both. Like thinking that you can't spread money without spreading disease. The economy is like electricity; if you break the circuit in one spot, the lights go out everywhere. Money does no good sitting in the bank just like dog food is no good if you never open the can." So she hadn't forgotten about my hot dogs after all.

"Do you mean to say that the ecomommy relies on other people to open the wiener can for him?" I asked, hoping she'd take the hint. "It sounds like doing good deeds for hungry dogs is pretty important, don't you think?"

"In the past, carrying on through a crisis like this brought nations together and made people proud of their resilience. How do you think most of these trails got here?" She chopped her arm toward the blackness beyond the street light.

"Magic?"

"The New Deal!" she said, like I should have known it all along. "In the depression people needed work, so the government made up odd jobs out of nowhere to put money into their pockets. Those jobs built most of the trails and parks around the country."

143

"But Mom, the boogeyvirus," I said, because that explained everything lately.

"Every crisis is an opportunity to make things better. But you can't look for opportunity if you shut everything down."

"Isn't it nice that the world gets a vacation, though?" I was pretty sure that vacation was the right answer, because vacation was what we were doing, and Mom's always right.

"A crisis is no time for a vacation!" Her paws balled up and her back got a little taller. "The virus is gonna blow over in a few months, and then what?"

"A few *months*? Who can wait that long?" I howled. "This isn't America anymore!" I was starting to enjoy my new catchphrase.

"This isn't just happening in America, Spud. It's all over the world. What I'm saying is that it doesn't have to be like this. People get stuck in thinking there's only one answer to a problem, so they give up when their first answer stops working. Take the camping fees: most people don't even carry cash anymore. Maybe instead of not collecting the envelopes, they could see it as an opportunity to join the 21st century and take credit cards." Her lips curled back like she was ready to bite. "Or take the bathrooms: they've always been gross and stinky, so hand sanitizer would be an improvement, even if lives didn't depend on hand-washing. As long as we're hanging on to the old ways of thinking, we'll never get back to the way things were before."

She opened the Wagon door and we climbed back inside. The sharp smell and wet smacking of hand sanitizer filled the Wagon, dulling my appetite for hot dogs for only a moment. The kibble bag rustled and my mouth started watering again. Mom put the half-full bowl down in front of me and dug through the bag with the canned food in it. Her paw came out holding a can of chili, which she set aside and went back to digging.

I sniffed my dry, naked kibble. "Aren't you forgetting something?"

She turned on the Witch's spotlight and aimed it down the bag's throat. "Where the smell did I put it?" she asked from halfway inside the bag. "I must've missed when I threw the can back." She squashed the bag to better aim the Witch at the shadows behind it and lifted the rumpled-up corners of the blankets. "Seriously, I swear this van eats things."

"But those were *my* wieners," I whined. "You promised!"

"I'm sorry, Spud. Tomorrow. Cross my heart."

Mom was quiet as we ate dinner, but the social studies lecture continued at full volume inside her thought bubble. Every so often, bits of an argument escaped her mouth.

"... do with all that free time, huh? ...Outside, that's where. ...more visitors than ever ...no fees from any of 'em ...fund a whole barrel of hand sanitizer... Stupid, stupid, stupid!"

"Everyone's gonna think you're a genius when you reveal your plan," I said. "You're gonna be a hero!"

"That's what's so scary about it. It doesn't matter what I think. It's completely out of my control."

"Oh good! If there's nothing you can do, there's no sense in worrying." The relief reminded me of the Jumper, who would never see that everything was going to be okay in the end. "Hey Mom, you know how sometimes a mountain looks so steep that there's no way that someone could climb it without falling off, no matter how brave and mighty they are?"

"Sure. I was thinking about that this morning when we were slogging through the snow."

"Maybe the boogeyvirus is like that. Just because we can't see the way out from here doesn't mean that there isn't one."

"Or it could kill us all. Sometimes the path is way worse than you expect."

"But you'll never try to climb anything at all if you let everything that could go wrong scare you out of it. It's not like you have to climb the whole mountain in one leap. All you have to figure out is where to put your paw for the next step. There's always something you can do that'll bring you a little closer to the top, and each step is like another clue. It wouldn't be such a thrill to solve the mystery if you don't put the clues together yourself."

"Sometimes it's not the trail that's the danger, though," Mom said, steering the conversation away before she hit the lesson. "The people who get in trouble are the ones who weren't prepared and run out of food, water, or daylight."

"Or toilet paper," I reminded her. "It's like you were saying about the potties; when something stops working it's not a sign to give up and go home, it just means it's time to change. You'd be surprised how much more you can do if you're okay with things not going exactly the way you expected."

"But it's stressful when you don't know if you're in danger or not," Mom whined. "The stress of not knowing can be worse than the actual danger."

"It's only stressful because you're afraid of being uncomfortable," I coached. "It's like those marathongs I trained you for. Every week we ran farther than ever before. How did we go so far from the car if we didn't know whether we could run all the way back?"

"I'd run marathons before I met you," Mom lied.

Since she hadn't answered the question, I answered it myself. "The trick to doing something hard for the first time is knowing that it's gonna be uncomfortable, and doing it anyway. Training yourself not to think about being uncomfortable is why they put the *thong* in *marathong*."

Mom fell right into my trap. "Uncertainty about what it'll be like when you push your limits is where the feeling of accomplishment comes from," she said, like it was her idea.

"So what if this boogeyvirus, and the ecomommy are like a marathong we didn't plan for? There's no sense in worrying about how awful the last miles are gonna be when we're still running the first. Maybe it'll feel like it's going on forever and we'll never stop running. I bet there'll be a lot of times when we'll want to sit in the shade and wait for the sag wagon. But hopelessness is how you know you're getting close to the finish."

"Real life almost never has finish lines," Mom said. "You just keep running past the point of exhaustion forever and ever, and you never even notice that one crisis has ended because you're already running through the next one."

"But one day, we'll be sitting on the couch together writing the story of today, and we'll notice that we aren't afraid of strangers anymore; that we're free to go where we please again; and that all the potties are unlocked. When we left home, we took all those things for granted. When the boogeyvirus is over, a new Friend or an open potty will feel like a trophy. I bet every day there'll be something that makes us feel like champions."

"But I got rid of the couch when I got the treadmill."

"We might get another one someday," I told her. "You've got to have goals if you want a better life."

"I hope that finish line isn't too far off." Mom gathered up the dishes and threw them in the trash. She tied off the top of the bag so it wouldn't spill chili slime and poop-juice grounds before we found an unlocked trash can. "It's been more than a week and I don't know how much longer I can take this nonsense."

"I bet when we tell these stories, we'll realize that they all had happy endings," I said. "Maybe then we'll realize that we won."

"Dream on," Mom said, reaching for the lamp.

The wind was raging when we woke up. It followed me around the campground as I searched for a potty spot, blurring smells and blowing the splashback into my ankle fur.

"Get ready to hold onto your hat," I told Mom as I jumped back into the Wagon. "You're gonna have to do this whole hike with your paw on top of your head."

Mom was busy setting up the kitchen inside the Wagon, where the wind couldn't blow the stove out. "I changed my mind. We're not hiking today. I don't know if we're even allowed to be here with everything all locked up."

"You can't close nature," I reminded her. "Who's going to catch us? Not the garbage man, the money picker-upper, or the bathroom unlocker, that's for sure."

"Even so, New Mexico is already closed. Who knows how long Colorado will be open for. Anyway, we're less likely to get in trouble for being so far from home in Wyoming. I read that it's one of the only states that isn't planning to close down."

"If you're afraid of getting in trouble, then why don't we just go home like the rules say?"

"And let this thing ruin our trip? No way!"

It kind of seemed like the boogeyvirus had ruined our trip already, but the fire in Mom's eyes told me I shouldn't bring it up. Instead, I asked, "They don't have rules in Wyoming?"

"Nope."

"Can't the Wyomighty catch cooties like Californians?"

"Sure they can, they just have a different sense of responsibility. I'm less likely to get in trouble for breathing somewhere where you're allowed to put cans in the trash. We should stay in places with loose gun laws and no recycling programs if we don't want to get sent home or locked up."

The wind pushed the Wagon relentlessly toward the side of the road as we made our way toward Colorado. Every so often, a gust came along and gave us a vicious shove, just to make a point. It was as if even the boogeytrapped air wanted to keep us in place. The poop juice cooled in Mom's cup as she kept both paws clamped to the driving wheel to prevent the Wagon from being blown off course.

"I should get gas before the state line," she said, fresh cups of fresh poop juice steaming in her thought bubble.

"The Wagon isn't going to faint. It's just faking," I said sullenly, steaming hot dogs filling my thought bubble. Why should even the Wagon get its treats before me?

"I know. But you never know when you'll find a good gas station out here. You don't want to end up at a Sinclair, do you?"

"No!" I yelped. "I take it back!" No snack is worth a trip to a Sinclair station, where there are no cheese sticks or fuzzy water, and there's always a line for the people-potty. The only time Mom doesn't spend a lifetime in the Sinclair potty line is when the troll who guards the key won't let *anyone* use the potty.

The Wagon rolled off the freeway and stopped in front of a juice box. As Mom stuck the straw into the Wagon's mouth, a cowboy at the next juice box called from behind his truck, "California, huh? What are you doing all the way out here?"

"We've been on a road trip for the past week," Mom shouted over the wind. Then, because she didn't want the cowboy to think that her germs would kill everyone in his village she added, "We've been hiking and camping in the wilderness to get away from it all."

"So I guess you don't know what's been happening, do you?" His smile said that it would put the *giddy* in his *giddyup* to see Mom's reaction to finding out that this wasn't America anymore.

"Sir," Mom said, "this is the only road trip I've ever been on where the whole country is talking about the exact same thing. You can't get deep enough into the wilderness to get away from this news."

It was true. Over the years, Mom and I had been close enough to throw a stick at Mexico, close enough to throw a stick at Canada, and all the western places in between. One of the best parts of visiting other places was hearing the exotic ways that people told familiar stories, and recognizing a different side of yourself in the tale. But this was the first time that everyone from Oregon to Arizona and California to New Mexico were all telling the same story in exactly the same way. For once, it was like we were all from the same pack. I couldn't tell yet if that was a good thing or a bad thing.

Mom left the *ha-yuck*-ing cowboy by his truck and went into the gas station in search of fuzzy water and a potty. She was in there long enough that I was starting to wonder if we were at a Sinclair station after all. When she finally came out again, she was carrying an armful of bottles, a steaming cup of poop juice, and a little paper basket that could only mean one thing: She found me a hot dog!

Her fur whipped around her head like wisps of angry thoughts as she hunched toward the Wagon. I stood at attention to give my tail room to wag and smooshed my nose against the window so my mouth would be ready as soon as the door opened.

"HUR-RY!" I barked through the glass.

When she reached the Wagon, Mom put the hot dog platter on the roof to free one paw for the door handle. She opened the door. The wind closed the door. When she opened the door again, a bottle slipped from the crook of her arm. As she leaned over to pick it up, the wind slapped her booty with the door and howled with laughter.

"Slam it!" Mom held the door open with her butt as she threw the bottles at my feet and carefully poured the poop juice into her cup.

"Don't forget my hot dog!" I barked.

When her paws were free, she reached up to the roof. Her arm moved like it does when she's searching for the Witch in the dark, but her paw came back empty.

"Southern ducker!" Mom growled, and stepped back into the wind. I wanted to help search, but the door slammed in my face.

The wind pinned the platter against the cowboy's tire, but the escaped hot dog was making a run for it. Mom chased it toward the street, holding her hat with one paw so it wouldn't blow away while she reached out to catch the fleeing weenie with the other.

A million years later, she came back with my hot dog smelling of hose water and New Mexico. She used some of our precious toilet paper to wipe off the specks of sand, put my dinner back on its platter, and served it to me muttering, "5 second rule."

I licked the delicious slime off the outside, but couldn't fit the whole thing in my mouth.

"Fix it," I told her with the biggest eyes I could.

Mom found a knife and tried to guillotine the hot dog into easy-to-swallow bites, but the brave hot dog wouldn't surrender. It jumped out of the basket and rolled onto the pillow, leaving a scent trail that would fill my dreams with hot dogs for the rest of the trip.

Mom groaned again and used the serving basket as a glove to pick up my brave breakfast like she would a turd in a poop bag. She stabbed it several times with the knife so my teeth would have something to grab onto.

I finished the whole thing in two bites as the Wagon rolled back toward the freeway.

Chapter 10

Retreat

"Colorado's supposed to be very bad," Mom said as the empty desert closed in around us and the last signs of Albuquerque shrank in the back window.

"Okay. Let's not go then," I said supportively.

"We can't get to Wyoming without going through Colorado. I mean, I guess we could go through Kansas, but we'd have to go like 1,000 miles out of our way," she counted.

Good thing Mom always had a backup plan. I'd never been to Kansas, but from the way she said it, I could tell it wasn't the sort of place where a girl, a dog, a Witch, and a moving house would get into trouble. "We went like a zillion miles out of our way to go to Oregon," I reminded her. "Is a zillion more or less than a thousand?"

"A zillion isn't a real number," Mom said territorially. "And we went to Oregon *for* something. It's different. Now we're running away. We should try to get across quickly so we have contact with as few people as possible. Especially if Colorado is as bad as people say."

"*Bad* how? Who says?"

"I don't know. The guy in front of me in line at Whole Foods was one of those annoying jerks who talks on the phone in public. He kept saying that his sister lived in Colorado, and all the ski towns were *very bad.* Whatever that means."

As much as it sounded like Mom was starting another round of the worry game, this one checked out. I'd heard about the Colorado curse, too, way back at the gas-station-general-store in

Nowhere, Utah. Even the Witch agreed. She'd been taunting Mom with mapps showing a stain over Colorado that spread darker and wider by the day as the boogyvirus sank in and set. If the gas station scuttlebutt was true, Colorado was one of the most dangerous places to breathe in the whole, wide west.

"How long is the drive to Cheyenne, Wyoming?" Mom asked the Witch.

"Traffic to Cheyenne is light so I'm estimating eight hours and seven minutes."

"Gosh darn it all to heck," Mom threw the Witch in her lap in disgust. "I knew I shouldn't have slept in. Now we won't clear Colorado till after dark."

"What if you just hold your breath all night?" I suggested.

Mom stole another look at the Witch and sighed. "I don't think we have a choice. Let's at least get past Denver. Nothing good can happen that close to the third-biggest airport in the country." She held up the Witch so I could see the darker shades of grey on the mapp. "Look at all this green north of Denver."

Green was one of those words that I couldn't quite understand. It meant *go* when she was looking at the road, but it meant *a good place to stop* when she was looking at a mapp. One of Mom's best sleep-hunting strategies was to look for where the mapp background behind the highway turned from city-white to grey of wilder-ness. Rules about where you can and can't sleep are born in cities and leak into the wilder-ness on roads, as most civilized things do. The bigger the road, the bigger the leak, and the bigger the leak, the more Law-mobiles floating around. The darker the background, the weaker the rules, so Mom looked for the darkest parts of the mapp and zoomed in on the gaps in between words. When she found a road so small that it was invisible without a magnifying glass, she asked the Witch to take us there. When the

Witch told us we were getting close, Mom would move her search from the screen to the window, looking for dirt roads between the trees where our sleeping won't disturb anyone.

"Is green the light grey or the dark grey?" I asked.

"The whole top ⅓ of the state is green," Mom said, like it was obvious. "There are bound to be a million forest roads. How about we pick an out-of-the-way trail and sleep at the trailhead so we can go for a short run before we leave in the morning? As long as we take the bypass around Denver, we won't have to worry about running into too many people."

With few other cars around, Mom spent more time looking at the Witch than the road, like a TV driver who knows there's no accident in the script. "Loveland, Colorado… That sounds like a one-horse town, doesn't it?"

"Definitely." I hoped that the horse was still taking visitors. "That's the kind of name you give your town when all the official-sounding names are taken."

"Or when the mayor lets his 6-year-old daughter name the place," she said with a nod. Mom was too serious for people who like greynbows and unicorns, even if those people were still puppies. "It's far enough from Denver and Boulder that we probably won't have to worry about city germs and town ordinances, at least."

"You should hold your breath all night, just in case the air is poisonous," I coached. "At least you won't snore."

"I don't snore, you snore," Mom lied.

Mom's sleep-spotting technique was pretty good in California, where she knew all the cities to look out for, but cities had a tendency to sneak up on us when we were far from home. Cities big enough for airports are like giant whirlpools that suck all the roads through them and splatter rules far and wide. By the time we realized that Loveland was another one of the Witch's nasty pranks, we were already in Denver's current.

"Keep the windows closed!" I panted as the glass-and-steel canyons sucked the Wagon through a forest of billboards.

"I told you, it doesn't work that way." Mom turned down the blowers anyway. "We're literally the only ones out on the road. I've never seen a major city deserted in the middle of the afternoon before." Her voice came out thin and shaky. It was hard to tell if she was scared, or if it just sounded that way because she was taking breaths so tiny that her chest didn't move.

She kept rebreathing until the buildings flattened and spread apart.

"Phew!" I left the copilot's seat and flopped into bed for the first time since Colorado Springs. Copiloting is hard work. "How long can I nap before Loveland?"

"Sucks to be you. You're almost there already," the Witch cackled.

"Oh no! It's a tourist town!" Mom wailed.

"Oh no! It's a bluburb!" I joined in.

"We're gonna dieeeeeee!" we howled together.

The town was too big for campgrounds and too greedy for public lands. We would need to find a place to hide out where we wouldn't be busted as referees.

Who me, officer? I practiced. I've never met that mailman van in my life. I'm a Coloradog; have been since puppyhood. How dare some mailman cross the borders of our great state with their nasty California germs.

"I guess we're gonna have to stay in a hotel," Mom said, "… if they're open."

"A hotel is the first place they'll look for us," I panicked.

"Nobody's looking for us."

"Are you sure?"

"No, not really. But I think they just want us to stay put."

"I thought they wanted us to go away. How are we supposed to go away if they're commanding us to *stay?*"

"I have no idea." I expected Mom to ask the Witch for advice like she usually does when she doesn't know where to go, but instead she said, "Let's just see what happens."

The first hotel had no cars in its kennel, so the Wagon kept driving until it found one that was less deserted. This place looked more like a car pound than a car kennel. The Wagon's scarred paint and butt full of stuff blended right in with the mismatched doors, trash-bag windows, and constipated back seats of the other stray cars.

Mom put on the leash and followed me into the lobby. Mom usually does the talking in situations like this, since I'm the one that people think might be dangerous. But now that Mom was a leaky bag of germs liable to kill anyone who came too close, I thought I should take the lead.

"One room, please!" I announced with a hearty *awoo*.

"He's a support animal," Mom introduced me with a bottom-toothed smile. *Support* was the password she used when she didn't know if she was allowed inside on-leash. "I hope that's okay. You're the only hotel in town that's open."

The man behind the counter took a cookie from the jar on his desk to thank me for my service. Lots of people hear *service* when Mom says *support*, but I never correct a man with cookies.

"We're considered *residential* because we do long-term stays," he bragged, puffing out his chest like he'd won a prestigious award. "They're saying we qualify as an essential business."

"All businesses are essential," I told him. "Isn't that right, Mom?"

Mom didn't give him the ecomomics lecture she'd given me last night. "They're actually enforcing that essential business thing?" she asked instead. "How does that work?"

"Oh yes. We got papers from City Hall and everything." The man stood tall like he was proud to live in a town with civilized rules, and prouder that he was an exception to them. "I keep them in my car just in case I get stopped on the way to work."

"There are papers that protect you from the Law?" I asked. "We don't have papers in our Wagon. Maybe an important man like you can grant us safe passage to Wyoming. Please?"

It worked! The man handed Mom some papers and a card. I was about to ask if they really were what I thought they were, when Mom pulled the card out of its holster and wiped it against a box next to the door. "Access granted," the box honked.

I smiled at our neighbors to distract them as I smuggled Mom down the hall. "I love your face tattoo… Great shirt! Did it come like that or did the sleeves rip off when you flexed? …Whatcha drinking there? Is that mouthwash or nail polish remover?" Each time I got close enough for pats, Mom pulled me away, pointing her closed smile but not her eyes at the neighbor.

"The people here seem so fun," I said as Mom used the Card to the City to unlock the door to our hideaway. Inside, the smells of old smoke, bad choices, and sleep farts clogged the stuffy air.

"At least it has a shower." Without a moment to lose, Mom peeled off her crusty clothes and added another layer to the dirt in the tub.

After dinner, I stretched out in the middle of the bed. Mom nuzzled into the sliver of mattress I wasn't using to coochy-coo with the Witch. We lay there, peacefully listening to the muffled voice of the neighbor's TV telling the familiar ghost story of how the whole world was doomed. I was just starting to dream when the Witch woke me with the loudest fart I'd ever heard.

BRRRRRT! Brrrrrt-BRRRRRRRRT! The ringing stayed in my ears after the blast faded.

"What the goose was that about?" I asked.

Mom gave the Witch the look you give someone who doesn't excuse their farts. "It's a public safety announcement reminding us to stay home. It says that the shelter in place order starts tomorrow."

"Good thing we're not in the Stuck House. Everyone in My Hometown is gonna be so jealous that we're in Colorado while they're trapped at home."

"The announcement isn't for California, it's for Loveland. They must do it by GPS location."

"The Witch tattled on us? What a rat!"

The Witch wasn't done ratting us out, either. She blared sirens all night, warning that we'd better skeddaddle. She wouldn't even shut up when Mom hit the *leave me alone* button.

"LOVELAND MAYOR DECLARES SHELTER IN PLACE ORDER GOES INTO EFFECT AT 9AM!" she announced at midnight.

"COUNTY OFFICIALS DECLARE SHELTER IN PLACE BEGINS IN LARIMER COUNTY AT 10AM!" she threatened at a later midnight.

"GOVERNOR DECLARES SHELTER IN PLACE THROUGHOUT COLORADO AT NOON!" she blustered at a third midnight.

"IT'S TIME TO WAKE UP," the Witch shouted while it was still midnight.

"What's the point of staying in a fancy hotel if you're not going to sleep in it?" I mumbled.

"We've got to get out of here." Mom's arm disappeared into the clothes bag and came back with long underwear in her paw. She held them up for inspection before shoving them back into the bag. "We've only got till 9am to get out of town." This time her arm grew back with running tights in its paw. She set the tights aside and went back to fishing. "We've only got till 10am to get out of the county, and till noon to get out of the state, so we'll have to run as fast as we can." Her paw came back with socks, which she laid next to the tights.

"Or else what?" This sounded like the beginning of an excellent western.

"They could pull us over for our license plates. Who knows if they'll throw us in jail just for being here. Or else why would we need papers just to be outside?"

I couldn't wait to find out what happened next. "What will you do if the Law comes after us?"

"No idea. I guess I could just explain the situation and ask for their suggestions. They can't punish us if we ask for help, right?"

It was daybreak when the Wagon crept past the sign at the park entrance. Wooden posts the size of sawed-off phone poles lined the final road to the car kennel, a surrender flag made from printer paper flapping on the side of each one.

"What do they say?" I asked with my heart in my throat.

"I can't read them from here. There was no gate to close off the park, so they're probably telling us to get the hell out or something." Mom checked the mirrors to make sure that no one saw her noticing. "If anyone asks, we can say we got here when it was too dark to see."

Relief washed over me when I saw other cars in the kennel. "At least we won't be the only outlaws hiding out in the park. I hope they don't draw attention to us."

The Wagon stopped with its nose just a breath from another flag-waving post. Mom leaned forward to read it. "It says *NATURE IS OPEN!*" she cheered. "That's the first sane thing I've seen since Utah!"

"Take that, you lying hunk of junk," I told the Witch. "Colorado isn't so bad after all."

Sometimes you just have to see for yourself to know if something is true. I was relieved, but disappointed, too. It was like when someone shouts "MAILMAN" in a crowded living room and you run screaming to the window only to find that it's a false alarm. I was glad I wouldn't have to fight, but a little let down that there would be no glory.

When we dismounted, Mom hid behind the beak of her hat so that no one else in the car kennel could pick her out in a line-up. When she accidentally looked up, a lady a few spots away expertly caught her eyes and smiled. Everyone had the look of someone getting away with something naughty, even the Rangers who came to unlock the potties and take out the trash.

"Go ahead," the Ranger with the mop bucket told Mom as we got close to the potty.

"I'm surprised you're here," Mom warbled, her face turned at an odd angle. It was the tone I was starting to recognize as the sound of not-breathing. "I mean, I'm glad. Thank you. Glad and surprised. It's just... with everything closing down..."

"Yeah, I was waiting for the call that I didn't have to come in today, but it never came. So here I am."

"I'm kinda glad," the one emptying the trash said. "What am I going to do sitting at home all day? Going outside is just about the only thing you *can* do."

"That's just what Mom was—" the leash choked off my words as Mom dragged me into the potty.

"Well thank you so much for everything you do," Mom said, closing the potty door.

"What was that about?" I thought at her. "We were about to make Friends."

"Making Friends is dangerous." I couldn't tell if she was talking about the boogeyvirus or not.

"But they were saying all the same things you were saying yesterday about working and keeping the bathrooms open," I said.

"It's not my business to have an opinion on other people's lives or the laws in a state where I'm not supposed to be." Mom pumped a generous blob of hand sanitizer onto her paws and elbowed the door open.

The world may have been coming to an end, but the sun still rose as usual. It shone on me like a spotlight as we ran up a little hill toward a jagged wall of rocks that stuck out of the top of the hill like the crest on a stegosaurus's back.

"It's called the Devil's Backbone," Mom said. "Do you see it?"

"Where? Is he staying six feet away?"

"No, silly. The rocks." She waved her arm toward the saw-shaped wall. "They're supposed to look like a spine."

I squinted at the rocks and tried to picture it. I guess if the devil were real skinny and spent too much time hunched over his laptop… "The Devil needs to do more lat pulldowns," I coached.

As we ran along the backbone, my eyes ran ahead, past the end of the spine and over his butt cheeks, which were furry with fields and pimpled with tiny farm houses. Behind that, mountains crinkled the horizon. One, bigger than the others, glowed like a second sun rising in the west. It was the kind of scene where each thing looked best as a tiny detail in the bigger picture around it.

"I sure look handsome today, don't I?" I struck a dashing pose while Mom aimed the Witch. "Colorado looks good on me."

Mom's face scrunched. "The backbone looks much smaller in the picture than it does in real life," she said, like the Witch had messed up her order. "It kinda fades into the background."

"Why don't you tell the Witch to make it bigger then?" As far as I knew, the Witch could change anything to make the world look the way Mom wanted it to.

"It doesn't work that way." She scooted to one side and held the Witch up again. "Our minds pick what's most important and make it seem bigger by sort of cropping everything else out. But the camera doesn't know what I'm looking at, so it shows everything exactly as it is. It makes things that are far away look teeny tiny, and things that are too close to drown out what I want to see."

I always knew the Witch couldn't recognize greatness. "So if she doesn't see anything as special, how do you get the love into my pictures? And also the scenery and stuff?"

"I have to put the story together myself. I position my subject—that's you—in such a way that the picture looks the way I want it to."

"So something scary like a big ol' devil's spine sticking out of the earth can grow into the most important thing in the world or shrink to a tiny detail depending on where you stand?" I adjusted my pose the way Mom wanted me to. "And all you have to do to make it less scary is stand somewhere else?"

"Exactly. And it's up to me if I want to tell an exciting adventure story or a cozy feel-good story."

"But what about when something looks scary from far away, but nice and friendly from up close?" I asked. "Like Colorado? Or people from the internet?"

"It's a matter of perspective. People are afraid of the unfamiliar until they see it close up." She looked toward the cozy farmhouses with their teeny tiny farmers trapped inside. "The internet lets you zoom in on anything, but I guess it's always filtered through someone else's perspective. Then again, it can bring connection, too."

"Like Lily?" I asked.

"I suppose. When people see the world through your eyes, they can connect with your ideas. The connection may be virtual, but the feeling is real. Hence, the pictures. I kind of feel like somebody needs to be a witness while everyone else is at home."

"Or a referee," I said. "Where do we need to stand to make the boogeyvirus fade into the background?"

"We'd have to go all the way to the moon." Mom sighed. "I think it's gonna be a long time before we have enough distance to see this whole situation for what it really is."

A visit to the moon sounded like fun, but the Witch would probably tell Mom we couldn't drive there. And Mom would believe her. "It's hopeless!" I huffed. "This isn't America anymore."

"It's not necessarily a bad thing. Distance helps you see something for what it really is. Or, if you don't want to see it, everything else in the frame can drown out the unpleasant parts.

Look at that mountain over there." Mom pointed her eyes at the molehill hulking like a rising moon on the horizon. "That mountain is probably big enough to bury everything from Loveland to Denver a mile deep. If we were standing on it, it wouldn't matter where we looked because everything in the frame would be part of it. But if you *sit* right here, I could hide that whole mountain behind your back."

"You should take a picture, then. So you'll remember what it's like to be a referee in Colorado, and how there's a handsome dog at the center of it all."

"Some things are so big that you can't tell the story with just one picture. It'll take billions of stories from billions of perspectives—both up close and far away—before we really understand what we're looking at. It's gonna be a very long walk, and we're just starting out."

As we made our final approach to the car kennel, a Coloradog bounded toward me dragging a lady behind him. He wagged his butt to signal to his lady that I was cool, and I wagged my butt at Mom to let her know that he was cool. Usually, that's the signal for Mom to compliment the lady on her taste in dogs while I introduce myself. This time, Mom pulled me off the trail and made me *up-up* on a rock to let them pass.

I didn't want to fight in front of strangers, so I *up-upped* like I was told, but my eyes stayed with my Future Friends. "I'll be right with you," I told the dog.

Mom stepped between us and hid him behind her back. I stretched my neck the other way until Mom sidestepped to block my view again. It was almost like she was doing it on purpose.

"Don't be rude," I whimpered.

"No more talking to strangers unless you're off leash, Spud," Mom thought at me. "Otherwise the humans would have to get too close."

Even when my tail wound down and the springs in my legs had shifted to *park*, Mom kept her back to the trail so that her contamomated breath couldn't hurt anyone.

"Good morning," she shouted into the wilder-ness, turning her chin a tick to show the lady that she was talking to her with really bad aim.

"That poop bag back there is mine," the lady told the empty air on the other side of the trail.

"See, Mom? Humans use bags too when they can't get off the trail in time."

"She's talking about the dog, you numskull," Mom thought back.

"She takes credit for everything I do," the dog whispered as he leaned into his leash to catch my scent from a social distance.

"I'm going to pick it up on the way back," the lady explained. "I just don't want to carry it for four miles."

"No judgment here," Mom told the sky.

"Okay, bye then," I called after the would-be Friends. I tried not to let it hurt my feelings that the lady hadn't insisted on just one pat.

We spotted the poop bag a minute later. It looked as out of place next to the trail as Mom in a makeup store.

"I'll just pick it up for her, since we're almost to the parking lot anyway..." Mom reached out and her paw froze. The world stood still while the wheels behind Mom's eyes spun. She stood back up, leaving the poop bag on the ground where it didn't belong.

"Come on, Mom! Do a good deed," I encouraged.

"Ugh! I really want to, but there could be germs on the bag."

"That's what the bag is for. To keep germs in." Silly Mom. She knew that poop bags were made of an impenetrable plastic that wouldn't let germs leak onto her face-touching paw.

"I'm not thinking about what's *in* it, I'm worried about what's *on* it. They don't know how long the virus can live on surfaces. What if I catch It from the bag and spread It to wherever we go next?" Her face hardened with decision. In a brave voice she announced, "The more responsible thing to do is to leave the poo."

"You've *never* picked up other people's poop bags before."

"Fair enough. But this time I *want* to pick it up." She gave the poop bag a longing look. "Everyone's so mistrustful right now. It would make me feel better to do something nice. But doing a good deed could be a bad deed if I get infected, pass the virus to someone, and they die." Her eyes dropped from the poop bag to her toes. "I hate what this is doing to us. It's not just making us suspicious of each other, it's making it harder to be nice."

We fled the poop bag with its load of germs and guilt, and kept running all the way to the car kennel. Mom ran until she could reach the door handle, where she paused only long enough to let me jump in ahead of her. All in one motion, she mounted the driving chair, slammed the door with one paw, and twisted the key with the other to spur the Wagon awake.

"GET THE HELL OUT! LOVELAND IS CLOSING NOW! GO! GO! GO!" the Witch blared as the clock struck nine. Once she'd screamed herself out, she added in her normal voice, "Take the ramp for Route 25 North toward Fort Collins."

"HOLY CRAP, GET YOUR BUTTS OUT OF HERE BEFORE THE COUNTY CLOSES!" the Witch continued as the Wagon reached freeway speed.

"AND DON'T YOU DARE COME BACK TO COLORADO!" she shouted before changing the subject. "Welcome to Wyoming!"

Chapter 11
Why-oh-Wyoming?

Back when the world was free and Mom believed she could predict the future, she aimed the farthest point in our trip at Devil's Tower in Wyoming. More than anything else, she was visiting for the punchline. We watched a movie starring the Tower once, and Mom thought it would be punny in a dad-joke way to spend a day searching for reasons to repeat the tagline, "This means something. This is important."

As the Colorado border closed like the Red Sea in the Wagon's back window, I searched for something meaningful and important in my first impression of Wyoming. The land couldn't decide if it wanted to be prairie or high mountains, so it picked both. Prairie swallowed the mountains until only their sharp tips pierced the sheet of grassland, leaving the chopped-off peaks looking like a collection of busts in a museum. The sky sagged so low that anyone taller than Mom might bump their head on it.

I looked for a landmark, but my eyes slipped over the scenery like paws on a hardwood floor. The boogeyvirus would have to plan its campaign very carefully to go viral in a place like this. Except for the freeway, the empty land must have looked the same as it did to the first wagoneers a million years ago. The few hard-scrabble buildings stayed far apart out of habit. The windows were no darker than anywhere else we'd been, but here the empty car kennels were molting their pavement and hearty lawns grew in the cracks. Wood covered the windows and barred the doors, as if guarding against something more powerful than a hungry person in search of a hot dog.

"I see why you weren't worried about the boogeyvirus here," I said. "This place looks like it's been abandoned since back when this was still America."

Mom shuddered. "I can't tell if it's locked down because of the quarantine, for the offseason, or for good."

Something else was missing from the landscape, too: People, and the things they leave behind. Other than the occasional billboard left over from The Before, the only human things here in the attic of the west were endless wire fences as long as the freeway. The fence was more of a notion than a thing, marking the line where the freeway litter ended and the wilder-ness began. It was practically invisible except where ragged plastic bags stuck to its thorns and stood straight out in the wind like battle flags.

"What in the world could a little fence like that do in all this emptiness?" I asked.

"Funny you mention it. Barbed wire fences played a bigger part in American history than people realize," Professor Mom professed. "Barbed wire is how the pioneers brought private property to the west."

"A puny fence did that?" I asked.

"Think about it, ranches go for miles. How are you going to block off an area that large?"

"Make a fence that someone can't just walk through by ducking," I suggested.

"Out of what? Wood? Where are you gonna find enough trees for that much fence?"

I checked out all the windows, but there were no trees left among all the grass and beheaded mountains. "Why bother? How many mailmans could there be in a place like this?"

"Not mailmen, cowboys. Before the pioneers came along, pretty much everything was public land. Cowboys and Indians alike roamed the western territories camping and… I don't know, prospecting, or beaver hunting, or whatever. When the pioneers claimed the land, there was no way to protect their fields from the cowboys' hungry cattle. Barbed wire gave farmers a cheap way to protect their crops from intruders. Cowboys had to walk their herds around the fences until there were so many barriers that long-distance travel became impractical. It's just one more way that keeping strangers out shaped the country."

I was about to point out that this wasn't America anymore until I realized that this new not-America would probably be even more into fences.

"Look! There's a wooden fence," I said. And what a fence it was! It wasn't wide, but it stood tall as a house and had barely a crack in it, so not even the tiniest cow could slip through.

"That's not a fence, it's a windbreak," Mom corrected.

The fence was only about as wide as a billboard, not nearly big enough to stop all the wind in Wyoming. White dirt piled on one side, but I couldn't tell if it was there to help the fence block the wind or help the wind knock down the fence. You could forgive the fence for thinking it was winning. The white dirt was packed so tightly into the gaps between planks that not even a puff could get through. But the fence tipped under the pressure of a winter's worth of white dirt and wind. One determined gust could change everything.

Something about that little wall trying to catch all the wind in the sky while holding the weight of the world on its back reminded me of Mom.

"Is that what the veterinarian's muzzles are for?" I asked. "To make the air private property?"

"I suppose. But air needs to flow like everything else. If you're always rebreathing your own air, you suffocate eventually."

With each state making its own rules about who was and wasn't supposed to breathe their air, it probably wouldn't be long before someone started building walls between them. I wasn't sure if walls would stop people, or air, or ideas from crossing, but it seemed like something humans would try anyway. I didn't ask Mom about it. Some questions were more fun when you didn't know the answer.

At long last, Devil's Tower sprouted out of the cowlands, giving my drifting eyes something to hang onto. When a hill shaped like a stump pokes out of the ground where it doesn't belong, it's called a *butt*. The southwestern butts in Utah and Arizona are all chewed up like a half-spent bone, but Devil's Tower burst out of Wyoming like it was still reaching for the sky. It was the most magnificent butt I'd ever seen.

I was drawn to it.

"Can we get closer?" I asked.

Mom leaned forward to better see the future. "Let's see."

The Wagon turned and the Witch announced, "In three miles, you will arrive at your destination."

The butt hooked onto Mom's eyeballs and pulled them up from the road. When her eyes could roll no higher, the butt kept pulling her toward the front window for a better view until her chest was pressed to the driving wheel.

"It's bigger than I thought," she said. "I can see why people would think it means something; that it's important."

As she often does when she's inspired, Mom asked the Witch what the internet had to say about Devil's Tower. Just in case there was any news about UFOs or something.

"They just closed it this morning, you fools!" the Witch cackled.

Mom tore her eyes from the sky. "Seriously? It's in the middle of nowhere and 3 miles around. Does it really get *that* many visitors that they can't stay 6 feet apart? Sheesh."

"Wasn't that what the documentary was about?" I reminded her. "How people came here from all over the country to ride in the UFO? Spaceships are public transportation, so they're closed."

"Documentary?" She looked confused.

"Yeah. The one where the sculptor guy and the painter lady go on a road trip to Devil's Tower. They play the alien mating song outside the spaceship, remember? Then the aliens accept the man as their own."

"You mean *Close Encounters?*" she asked. "I can see how a situation like this would bring out the conspiracy theorists, I guess. Especially now that everyone has so much free time."

"Yeah. I bet the first thing everyone thought when they had to quar-unseen was that they should head to Wyoming. Good thing we got a head start."

"Maybe they'll only close the visitor's center and gift shop, not the trails." Mom took a moment to appreciate the wisdom of her lawgic. "They can't close nature, right?"

"We'll never know if we don't check. It's probably a test. Only the bold get to ride the spaceship."

The Wagon slowed to introduce itself at the entrance tardis, but there was wood in the window where a ranger should be. The Wagon nosed closer to the closed gate as Mom and I searched for a clue about what to do next.

A line of knives stuck out of the pavement outside Mom's window, threatening to cut trespassers to ribbons. Outside the copilot's window, a fence ran through the prairie in an unbroken line until it disappeared into the horizon. Between where the tardis gate ended and the fence began, there was just enough room for a Wagon to slip through. The only thing blocking the secret passageway between fence and gate was a cone with a sign sticking out of its neck hole.

"What does the sign say?" I asked

"It says that the park is closed…" Mom's voice trailed off as a thought interrupted her reading. In the same tone as she might say, *and it just might work!* she read, "… except for deliveries!"

"If a dog wanders into a park and no one's there to see him, does he go to the pound?" I agreed.

Mom and I had a history of breaking in when we were locked out. Our rap sheet included "not noticing" when the Wagon "accidentally" drifted off the road right where a locked gate happened to be, and "thinking it was an entrance" when a sand doom spilled over a fence, giving us a secret passageway into a closed park. You can't close nature, after all.

I studied the gap between the gate and the fence again, looking for a trap. It was big enough to drive a truck through. There were no knives, no invincible barricades, only a puny traffic cone guarding the secret passage. The coast was clear. Breaking in would be easier than the last time, when there were so many rocks and bushes in the way.

"This is gonna be a cinch," I said. "Do you think we need delivery disguises, or will the mailman van be enough?"

"I don't know if we should." Mom looked puzzled. She'd never heard anything like that come out of her own mouth before.

"What do you mean? This road is healthy and strong, not broken like the one outside Death Valley. It's covered in pavement and everything. You're not gonna let a little cone boss you around, are you?"

Mom's Code said that we could trespass with a clean conscience as long as we left no trace, trespassed only on public lands, and respected the rules about safety and tidiness, even when no one was watching.

"The other times we snuck in, the parks were closed because of a government shutdown. Rules like that don't actually protect anyone. They're like holding your breath when you don't get your way. I don't mind breaking rules created by people behaving like children, but this is different. It's one thing to commit an act of civil disobedience when nobody can get hurt, but I'm not sure this is a statement I want to make."

"But what about law-gic?" I asked. "How else are you gonna prove that the rules don't apply to us without civil misobedience? Anyway, you can't get anyone sick if there's no one else there. That's what this handy, dandy gate is for, to keep everyone else out."

"What do you think would happen if everyone drove around that cone?"

"It would be like the park was open," I said. "You can't close nature. We'll take only pictures and leave only pawprints, like you're supposed to."

"But what if closing it down is the right thing to do?" She seemed as baffled by her behavior as I was. "There's no playbook for this. Everyone's doing their best to make decisions that no one's ever had to make before." She slumped under the weight of keeping the world safe.

"But we came all this way!" I whimpered. "The Constitution says you're healthy until proven infected. You can't hurt anybody if there's no one to catch your cooties."

"Check your privilege, Oscar. The only reason that it's empty is because other people aren't lucky enough to be refugees like us. They were at home when this started, and they're doing us a favor by staying there. Let's thank them by making our own sacrifices, so that the rangers can stay safe at home."

"But we've already made sacrifices! The other day I waited a whole day and two nights for a hot dog. And what about sleeping under three blankies because we don't have heat? What about living in a house smaller than a parking space? Are you telling me those aren't sacrifices?"

"We signed up for those challenges when we took this trip," she said, like that made a difference. "The virus just makes that choice a little more inconvenient than expected."

"Yeah, but how will you survive without wifi? And electricity? You could die."

"I still have my phone." Mom patted the Witch like a faithful companion. "We can keep up-to-date with the rules without my laptop. That's an easy sacrifice to make if it means we don't have to go home."

"Sacrifices are just choices with resentment. This isn't America anymore!" I huffed into bed with my tail-end facing Mom as she asked the Witch for advice on what to do next.

"Make a U-turn," the Witch ordered.

The Wagon did as it was told, turning its tailpipe on our goal. I watched Devil's Tower shrinking back into imagination through the back window as the Witch guided Wagon to South Dogkota.

Chapter 12

Little Hound on the Prairie

"What do you suppose South Dogkota's like?" I asked as the Witch welcomed us across the border.

"I have no idea," Mom said. "All I know is that hardly anyone lives here and that there are badlands."

I didn't like the sound of that at all. "Well no wonder. I don't want to live on bad lands either. What's so bad about them?"

"Beats me."

Something caught the magnet in Mom's eyes and pulled her toward the front window. On the other side, the ground rose so suddenly that it looked like a tail wagging at the sky.

I tried to smell what I was seeing, decorating the window with nose smears. "It looks like a painting on a teapot. Are we in China?"

"Not China," she corrected, "these are the Black Hills. I didn't expect them to be so… rugged."

I double checked. Mom's supposed to be the color expert, but *black* was one I knew. "They're not black, they're white." It wasn't just the hills, either. All of South Dogkota was covered in white dirt. "Why didn't you tell me it would be like this?"

"I thought this whole state was prairie," Mom gushed in the dazzled voice that sometimes escapes when Nature gets the better of her. "Now we just have to figure out where the trails are."

The Wagon rolled into a gas station so Mom and the Witch could come up with a plan. While Mom was distracted, I studied a billboard beside the car kennel. Four stern-looking dudes stared heroically out of the picture toward the horizon.

When the Witch's time to hog Mom's attention was up, I took my turn. "I recognize Walter White, but who are the other guys?"

Mom looked up for just long enough to see what I was looking at and dropped her eyes back to whatever she was discussing with the Witch. "That's not Walter White, you knucklehead. It's Teddy Roosevelt. Mt. Rushmore is somewhere around here. The other guys are dead presidents, too."

"What's Mount Rush More?" I asked. "Is that why they call it *running* for president? Because you have to rush? … more than the other guy?"

"I don't know why it's named that," she said, too distracted by her own questions to ask the Witch to explain something that someone else was interested in. "The other guys are Washington, Jefferson, and Lincoln. If you ask me, Roosevelt isn't in the same league, but he's something of a local hero."

"What did he do? Did he defeat the bad lands?" I asked hopefully.

"In a manner of speaking." She finally put the Witch back in her lap and ordered the Wagon onto the road. "Legend has it that he was a sickly kid until the outdoor life in the Dakota Territory turned him into a macho man. That's the legend according to him, anyway."

"Teddy Roosterbelt is my favorite president," I decided.

"He created the National Parks," Mom said, ruining it.

"That monster! How dare he block off the best bits of nature just so dogs can't visit."

"Questionable land claims were kind of his thing." Mom had a way of making people in history look like fools for not knowing everything she did. "He was also a bit of a bully. He used to say, 'Speak softly and carry a big stick.'"

"That sounds like excellent advice to me. Except how can you bark softly or any other way with a big stick in your mouth?"

"He meant that he would beat people up if they didn't listen to him."

"But he didn't really mean it about hitting people with a stick, right?"

"Oh, I'm sure he did. The stick itself was a rhetorical device, but he actually challenged White House visitors to boxing matches until one of them practically knocked his eye out. He's like the forefather of toxic masculinity."

"What's a torcal device?" I asked to keep the conversation on sticks.

"It means the stick was fake but the threat behind it was real."

"What a lucky coincidence that the mountain just so happened to look like those four guys!" I marveled. "Cheesology sure is amazing…"

"It's not natural," Mom said, like I should have just known it. "It's a sculpture."

"It's only natural that people would want to remember their heroes," I saved. "Building a country from scratch isn't as easy as it looks, you know."

"That's what bugs me about it. They didn't build it from scratch. I love their work, but it's not perfect. Knowing that there's always room for improvement is what makes it so great."

"In six miles you'll arrive at your destination," the Witch interrupted.

"Ugh! Not again," Mom said in a voice that sounded like she was about to barf in her mouth.

"What?"

"Look at the kiosk. There's no one inside."

"But look, there's nothing blocking the road," I pointed out.

"If there's no one in the booth, it'll be obvious that we didn't pay. We'll have no defense if I get a ticket."

"Do they give tickets in not-America?"

"Who knows. It would be just my luck."

"Maybe a ranger machine can help. Are machines allowed to work during the boogeyvirus?"

Mom jabbed her arm toward the front window to emphasize the point she was about to make. "There is no machi—" When her eyes followed her arm, their indignation turned to triumph. "Look, they have envelopes! Thank goodness for cash."

Even though old-fashioned paper money was banned in most places, Mom had found a black market twenty-dollar bill in a back-alley bank machine that she was saving for an emergency just like this. She told the Wagon to *stay* and reached for the door.

"Don't go!" I begged. "No one's coming for the envelopes, remember?"

"They can't kick us out if we follow the rules," Mom called over her shoulder before closing the door on the conversation.

When she remounted, she stuck the *Get Out of Jail Free* card on the front windowsill and ordered the Wagon to *giddyup*. "Envelopes don't give change for a 20, so I just paid 4 times the entrance fee," she counted.

"What does that mean without the numbers?"

"It means we practically own the place."

"So what should we worry about now?"

"We could agonize about whether the parking lot is plowed. Or whether there's a camping ordinance. Or we could worry about those nasty-looking clouds over there," Mom suggested. "The possibilities are endless."

The car kennel was clear when the Wagon arrived. The white dirt crowded in a wall around the edges, respectfully staying off the pavement. We left the Wagon parked tidily between the lines and climbed through the muddy, stamped-down slot in the white wall where the trail began.

Since she'd already decided to follow pre-boogeyvirus tradition with the entrance fee, Mom tried to follow rules about leashes too, even though no one was around to call her a *good girl* for doing it. The leash jerked as Mom's arms whipped to keep herself head-side-up on the slippery white dirt.

There was a swish and an ack behind me, and the leash jerked harder than ever. When I turned around, Mom, the Witch, and the water bottle were scattered on the ground. Half of Mom's leg was gone, sucked into the white dirt like quicksand. Mom pulled her leg out of the ground and shook the white dirt off of the Witch. She stood up, rubbing her butt.

"Fine, fine," she said, like she'd heard me tell her so. She unclipped the leash and I left her balancing and chopping the air.

I practiced gymnastics in the white dirt, sniffing and rolling, rolling and sniffing like I'd never seen anything so wonderful in my life. A stream sang a tinkling song to accompany my happy dance.

"Slow down," Mom shouted.

Once I'd burned off enough of the zoomies to stay paws-side down, I came back to see what she was on about. "What?"

She looked meaningfully at the river flowing under the bridge of white dirt that we were fixing to walk on. "Just be careful. It's melting season and we don't know if it can hold our weight."

"Good thing I'm not big and fat and drill-shaped like you." I spread my weight evenly over all four paws and pranced across with flair.

Mom watched me go, baring her bottom teeth like she does when I make something look easy that she would mess up. Once I was safely on the other side, I wagged at her to show that only a drill-shaped idiot could mess this up.

Mom put one paw over the hollow part and shifted her weight one atom at a time. Below her, the water whooshed through the roomy tunnel it had bored for itself under the dainty snowbridge. When Mom's leg stayed on top of the white dirt rather than punching through it, she switched from slow motion to fast forward and pitter-patted to my side. If we were in a movie, the white dirt would have collapsed behind her as she ran, but since this was real life, the bridge stayed the same as before except with six extra pawprints on it.

"Good girl!" I wagged.

The next adventure found us where the trail crossed the river without a bridge. "What do we do now?" I asked.

"We cross," Mom declared.

She jumped onto a rock poking out of the water and searched for another stone to aim her next step. The next one teetered when she landed on it. She launched herself clumsily onto shore a moment before it dunked her, dragging her trailing toes through the water. I followed, easing my paws into the icy stream like I was walking on the fragilest of snow bridges.

"*Good boy*," Mom said when I joined her on the far side.

"Are you okay?" I gasped, not sure if we'd just escaped death.

"Yeah. Why?"

"That was a close one."

The river got narrower and deeper as we went upstream. We studied each crossing for traps. Sometimes, there was a gap in the deepest water where a rock was missing. Sometimes the white dirt went all the way across, and all we had to do was decide whether it was a real bridge or a decoy that would collapse mid-river. Whether there was a bridge or not, Mom crossed without hesitation.

"Be careful," I reminded her as she walked onto the most delicate snowbridge so far as if it were made of stone.

"Or what?"

"Or your socks will get wet."

"They're already wet."

"You could lose your balance."

"So? It's only like 4 inches deep. What's the worst that could happen?"

Mom had never asked *me* why those things mattered before. She'd told me that wet socks or falling on your butt were a fate worse than death, and I'd believed her. Now I checked my own paws for signs of drowning, but they were hidden under the elbow-deep white dirt. I pulled out a paw and watched the white flakes turn into wet. Once it wasn't white anymore, I couldn't tell how much of the wetness came from the white dirt and how much was from the stream.

"Knowing the worst that could happen is your job, remember?" I said so Mom would feel like the foolish one. "You told me to be careful."

"I changed my mind. I'm tired of being careful all the time. If we have to be cautious around other people, then I'm gonna throw caution to the wind when no one's looking. Not caring about the things that most people are afraid of is an act of rebellion, too, you know."

Hearing Mom's bravery, the stream turned away from the trail. It wandered into the forest in search of someone less bold to harass, leaving us alone with the hills, whose pointy tips were lost in a mysterious fog.

The sun faded as the mist turned the whole world smudgy like a bathroom mirror. No matter how far ahead of Mom I ran, I could never get far enough to see more than a few steps into the future. Stone towers faded into and out of the fog like stern statues as we walked.

"Do you know what the Lakota called these rock formations?" Mom asked.

"I love this game! They must have *sedimentary* value. The people in these parts don't take their land for *granite*!" I charged on before Mom could make a rule against puns. "Is it Steve Austin? A *Stone* Called Steve Austin? Get it?" I paused for Mom to laugh like they do on TV, but she missed her cue. "Okay, I'll try another one. Do they call them *rock*weilers? *Terrier* incognita? *Schist* tzu? I know! I know! A *rock*-schund!"

Mom's face did patient.

"Wakka, wakka, wakka!" I added, so she might get the hint.

She waited a second to make sure I was done. "They called them *owls* because of their shape, and how they seem to look at you wherever you go. Owls were a symbol of imminent death."

"You're such a bummer. I think they look like hot dogs." Still, I stayed a little farther from the rock-schunds after that. Just in case.

The mominous shapes were the size of park statues at first, but got bigger as we went until they were as tall as buildings. They gathered in clusters that grew like crowds gawking over an accident. Without warning, the ground under my paws flattened and a stadium-sized lump of rock took shape in the mist ahead. Its steep sides blocked the way in the direction that the trail arrows were pointing.

"Now what?" I asked the mist behind me, where I was pretty sure Mom would appear any second.

"It looks like we're supposed to climb it." Mom walked into a crack in the rock no wider than a ladder. Inside, the white dirt was piled against the back wall at an angle that just might be shallow enough to climb. She reached up and patted the wall beside where the slope flattened out. "You first. *Up-up.*"

I took a running start and kept running faster than my legs could fall out from under me. Once I was high enough to reach out and boop Mom on top of her head, the ground flattened enough for me to stand.

I let the speed wind out of my legs for a couple of steps and turned back to Mom. "Your turn!"

Mom stuck the water bottle into the crook of one elbow and turned the Witch's face into her palm so her screen wouldn't smash against the stone as Mom climbed. She held onto the wall with her free paw and stepped up one step, two steps, three steps…

She lifted her leg for the fourth step when, still in a stepping posture, her whole body slid back through her pawprints to the bottom.

She said something about dog doo and put the water bottle and Witch into pockets so her arms were free to behave like legs. She stuck a hand to the rock on either side and pushed hard to wedge herself in. She kicked at the white dirt to see the shape of the rock underneath and after a few practice bounces, she took a jumpy step, followed by a slippery step, and then used her belly as a foot as she flopped face-down at my feet. Her arms became fins as she pushed backward against white dirt, rock, and whatever else would help her slither the rest of the way to my side.

I'd never seen anyone hike like a fish before. "What are you doing down there?"

"It worked, didn't it?" She rolled into a *sit* and gathered three of her legs under her. She stood up with a groan.

"Why didn't you just do it the normal way, like me?" I asked reasonably.

"I tried that. A better question might be, how did *you* do it?"

"You never told me it was impossible."

Mom wagged her head. "We're capable of extraordinary things when we don't know we can't." I couldn't tell if she was talking about me learning to fly or her turning into a fish.

Walking on top of the mountain's craggy helmet got easier with the steep ear flaps behind us. I could tell that we were on top of something tall because the smudgy air was equally empty in all directions. The anti-slip rock and dry white dirt let Mom hike as dauntlessly as if she were on a snowbridge over sock-deep water.

"There's supposed to be some sort of tower up here," Mom said.

"What kind of tower? Like a Rapunzel tower?"

"I don't know. An observation tower, I guess."

186

"Observing what?"

"Danger? Fires? Maybe invading Canadians."

"What's the point of building a tower just for worrying in? Can't you worry from the ground when you need to? Once you've built a tower, you'll feel like you're wasting it if you don't worry enough."

"All that grass on the prairie, I guess." Mom looked into the milky blankness to show me where the grass was. "If you don't have a healthy sense of worry you might not notice a brush fire until it's too late. With those dry prairie winds, a fire could get out of control in seconds. Except now that we have satellites, the observation station is mostly for visitors."

"People visit a place just for the thrill of leisure-worrying? I've heard of making a mountain of a control hill, but not building a worry fort for worrywarts."

"Well there's little hope of seeing anything in all this fog, anyway." Mom took a step onto a patch of white dirt. The ground flicked her paw away. "Ack. Is it just me or is it getting icier up here?"

"Look here, a clue!" I sniffed. A sign grew from the rock in the exact spot where regular rock turned white and glassy. "What does it say?"

"It says, SNOW AND ICE MAY MAKE THE TRAIL IMPASSIBLE BEYOND THIS POINT," she read.

"Nothing is impassable. You just need to think creatively," I reminded her. "What are we waiting for?" I ran onto the white dirt and smeared my face against its slick surface. I pushed my head around like a zamboni, searching for an un-slippery spot to somersault onto my back for a snow angel.

"No way!" Mom said. "I'm not walking on that. We'd slip and fall off a cliff!"

"Don't be so drama-ah-ah—" I started to say, but my face-pushing paw slipped and flopped me onto my side. "I'm demomstrating how much fun it is to play in the white dirt," I saved. I tried to demomstrate a snow angel by kicking all four of my legs in the air, but the darned dirt flipped me until I was lying on my other side, one Oscar-width closer to where rock became cloud.

"Come back from there before you fall," Mom scolded.

The emptiness beyond where the rock fell away could have held a drop shorter than Mom or a cliff a million feet high. The only thing that panics Mom more than looking down and seeing how far she is from the bottom is looking down and *not* seeing how high she is. When I looked back, Mom's eyes were pointing down and she was almost as pale as the sky.

"I didn't know we were so high up," she choked.

I turned back toward the void. "How do you kn—... Oh." The mist shifted and I thought I saw a drop taller than a fall from the moon.

"Let's get out of here." Mom crab-walked away without taking her wide eyes off the emptiness beyond where the ground ended.

"I thought we were being fearless now. Because: rebellion," I reminded her.

It wasn't like Mom not to try something, even if she was scared. Usually she would walk timidly into danger until she was past crying and into bossy, screaming at my every move as she boot-scooted, crawled, or slithered back to safety. I waited on the white lump for her to come back until she was far enough away that I was sure she wouldn't return. She took flinchy-winchy steps, carefully leaving both paws on the ground so she wouldn't get sucked off a cliff. At least she wasn't slithering like a snow-angel-fish again.

When we arrived at the slippery crack, she sent me down first. I ran down the slope, letting my legs roll under me like the Road Runner. When I reached the bottom, I steered to one side to get out of Mom's path so she wouldn't crush me if she came tumbling after like an Indiana Bones rock.

I waited, but there was no rumbling and no tumbling.

I waited some more, but still no Mom fell out of the Mom-return slot.

I would have to step onto her landing strip if I wanted to look for her. I was just about to take a cautious step onto the runway when I heard a whoosh. Two shoes shot out of the crack, followed by two legs. The rest of Mom followed, riding on her butt with her arms in the air like a stickup.

"What on earth are you doing?" my head-tilt asked.

"Sledding." She stood up without the groan and brushed the white dirt victoriously from her tabottom. "That wasn't as painless as I thought. There were some sharp rocks under there."

"The trick to dealing with the sharp rocks is not to see them coming," I said sagely. "Just sit back and enjoy the ride."

As we walked back toward the car kennel, I spotted something in the distance that filled my heart with joy. "Look, Mom! Friends!" I squealed. Besides the Coloradog and his lady, I hadn't made new Friends on the trail since I met Lily. This time, there was no leash to hold me back, so I ran ahead to introduce myself.

"What's your name, little lady?" the one who was a man asked me.

"Bruh, why are there flowers on your jacket?" asked the one who was a dog.

"I'm Oscar," I answered the Man, doing a little hello dance. "Because not many dogs have coats like it, and I like pretty things," I explained to the dog.

"Whoa, you made a boy dog wear a pink coat?" the Man asked Mom. I could tell by his tone that he was impressed.

"Sure, why not?" Mom said. "Dogs don't have gender identities. And they can't see the color pink."

Now that my manliness was beyond doubt, the dog and I played tag while the humans did what humans do when they meet on the back side of a mountain. Mom explained that she'd never been here before, and the Man said he'd never been here before either.

"I'm not gonna just sit at home if I can't work, so I took the dog and hit the road," the Man said. "We'll just keep traveling until it's safe to go home again."

"What a coincidence! Us too!" I said. When I looked at Mom, her face was strained in a mental game of tug. Her thought bubble said she wanted to judge him for being unsafe, but when she tried to come up with a reason why we were different, the bubble went blank.

"Have you been to the Badlands?" the Man continued.

"No, I don't even know what the Badlands are," Mom admitted.

"You've *got* to go to the Badlands," he commanded, like they were made of cheese and bacon. "It's only like an hour away. You can't go home until you've visited them."

"But what *are* they?" Mom asked again.

The Man took out his witch to show why a bad land felt so good. Horror gripped me as he took a step into Mom's boogeybubble. I hoped he didn't notice that she took a mini step back when his face-wiping arm reached toward her and his snot-face leaned in. Both Mom and I held our breath as they looked at his witch together.

Mom stepped back into private air before reopening the vents behind her frozen smile. "Okay, well, have a great trip. Stay safe!" She turned away before he could order her to do anything else.

"So, what's a bad land?" I asked when we were socially distant again.

"I'm not sure. All I saw was him sitting shirtless in the front seat of his truck showing off his pecs. There might've been something the color of dirt out the window behind him."

"Should we investigate?"

"We should probably start working our way back home." Mom sighed. "The Badlands are east of here. We'd be going in the wrong direction."

"But he said we *had* to…"

"I'm a little tired of exploring, aren't you?"

I looked at the owls with all their up-up energy and my legs sighed. "How far away is home?"

"It'll take us at least 3 days to get there, but we have a week if we want."

"How many hikes in a week?" I asked.

"Seven."

"And is three more or less than seven, do you think?"

"Let me put it this way: for every day that we can't find something to keep us on the road, we have to spend a day locked in the house."

I wasn't sure what I wanted. Even though there were days when I was too tired to explore, I wasn't ready to go back to the Stuck House. On the road, there was no knowing when the butt-shredding rocks would hit our tabottoms, so Mom could raise her arms in abandon as the world carried us from one surprise to the next. At home, we would only have the Witch's lies to tell us what was happening in the world outside.

"Okay," I agreed. "Let's break bad-lands before we go home."

The Wagon rolled out of the black-white hills onto the prairie. I kept waiting for the land to do something interesting, but the only thing that happened was that the white dirt turned to grass. There were still cows, though. There are always cows.

Without warning, the Wagon pulled over as quickly and messily as a whale-mobile. I peeked around the arm shelf to find out what was happening in the cockpit. Mom jumped out and ran into the prairie like something had bitten her backside.

I climbed into the driving chair for a better view. "Don't worry, I'll just sit here in case the Law comes along," I said to no one in particular.

While I waited for the Law to ask if I was okay and why the Wagon looked like that, Mom tip-toed through the grass as sneakily as the Hamburgler.

"Holy dog doo, Mom. Look out!" I barked when I saw what else was out there.

A pawful of the biggest, ugliest cows I'd ever seen stood in the grass staring at her. They looked like their father was a yak and their mother was a warthog. They looked like someone had taken a cow and squeezed all of its extra parts up around its shoulders. Their haircuts were just terrible, like Julia Child or Norm MacDonald, but worse. And they wore this frumpy cape—no, not a cape, a *stole*—around their shoulders.

"WHAT THE SMELL IS THAT MONSTROSITY?" I barked at top volume.

Almighty Dog put some beasts on this earth just for chasing. If a critter wouldn't run right away, you had to bow-wow a war whoop and charge them like a cannonball. You weren't supposed to stay real quiet and creep around like you didn't want to raise suspicion. Mom was clueless when it came to wildlife. She always tried *not* to make any sudden moves. When a beast ran away in spite of her incompetence, she just looked disappointed and went back to what she was doing before.

Even though I shouted at top volume through the window, Mom was deaf to my coaching. She just kept waving the Witch in front of her like garlic at a vampire and following the mutants in a slow-speed chase.

"They can smell you, you know!" I barked as loud as I could. "Lemme at 'em! I'll bark at 'em, and I'll chase 'em, and then I'll bark at 'em while I chase 'em! Now! Run now! You're letting them get away!"

Instead, Mom stood up out of her sneaking posture and put the Witch back in her pocket as the deformed cows lumbered into the background.

"GO BACK TO WHATEVER MOO-TANT RANCH YOU CAME FROM, YOU FREAKS!" I screamed.

Mom came back to the Wagon looking as un-disappointed as if she'd actually caught one of the moo-tants. I started quizzing her as soon as she opened the door. "Do you know what the heck those things were?"

"They're buffalo!" she bragged. "Or... bison? Is there a difference?"

The freaks watched boredly from the top of the bluff where they'd stopped as soon as they saw that Mom was done chasing. "I thought bison were ex-stinked," I said suspiciously, without taking my eyes off of them.

"I didn't pay attention in that part of history class. *C'mon.* Get down so you can pose for a picture."

"No way, José. You're gonna run away and leave that curly hunk of jerky to eat me first." I aimed an earth-rumbling growl their way so they would know I wasn't afraid. The king wartcow chewed his gum and looked unimpressed. "DON'T MAKE ME COME OVER THERE!" I stepped aggressively back onto the copilot's chair to show them that I wouldn't hesitate to sick Mom on them if they tried anything. Mom stepped out of the doorway to give me room to jump out and charge, but I just took another bold step backward, deeper into the Wagon. Why put in all that work to train a human if you're not going to use her for protection?

"We should keep away so their ex-stink doesn't get on us," I coached.

"Fine." Mom remounted the driving chair. "You're such a party pooper."

The Wagon remounted the road, but not for long. Every time the road swayed around another bend, the Wagon pulled over again and Mom ejected herself to take more pictures. It turned out that the reason they were called *bad lands* is because they weren't terribly good at being hills, canyons, or fields. I'm not sure you could even call them *lands*, since they were more hole than land. They had no sense of style, mixing back-and-forth stripes like lines in a book with up-and-down creases like tree bark. Maybe they would have been cooler up close, but Mom never let me go more than a few steps from the Wagon.

The umptieth time we dismounted, there was something different in the air. My eyes followed my nose and landed on a pack of sheep staring curiously back at me.

"Mom! Mom! Let me chase 'em!" I barked with so much friendliness that it cracked my voice.

"Hell no! Anyway, you're not allowed more than 25 feet from the parking lot."

"Why not?" I whined. "I was born for this!"

"This is a National Park. No dogs on the trails," she reminded me. "I read something about fleas being a problem…"

"Stop believing the Witch's nonsense! I'm poison to fleas." I puffed out my pest-free chest. "I just had my pill yesterday, remember? And anyway, sheep can't catch fleas because they have wool instead of fur. I'll make them tell you themselves if you'll just let go of the leash…"

"*Some* dogs carry fleas," she corrected, "…and the fleas could infect the prairie dogs."

"There are dogs out here?" I squealed. I couldn't wait to meet one and ask him to show me all the sheep hangouts.

"That's just a nickname. I think they're actually more like ground squirrels."

"There are *squirrels* out here?" I screeched. I'd had this place all wrong!

"No, shut up. This is important. Fleas may be annoying to you, but they carry diseases that can make prairie dogs get sick and die."

"Like the boogeyvirus?"

"Yeah. You could kill someone if you pass on your fleas."

"But I don't have fleas because I take my medicine. The squirrel-dogs can't catch bugs I don't have. Lemme at those sheep. I'll scatter 'em like a bunch of wooly bowling pins!"

Mom wrapped more of the leash around her hand to keep me closer. "That's the thing, we don't know *for sure* that you don't have fleas. Even if you're clean, we can't prove it. So you can't go."

"Innocent until proven guilty, Mom."

"Infected until proven innocent," she countered. "Fleas don't really follow the law, and neither do viruses."

"No fair. If the squirrel-dogs are so delicate, they should stay in their own holes and not ruin the fun for everyone else."

"To be fair, *you're* the one coming from out of town to stick your big nose in their holes. They deserve to be safe from diseases carried by outsiders."

"But you always say it's good to make Friends from other places so we can learn about different ways of living."

"We should respect when we're not invited, and when it's time to go back where we came from." Mom turned so that only the arm holding the leash was left behind.

I turned back to the sheep to see if they'd extend an invitation.

"I guess you're not so interesting after all," they *baaaahed*. They turned their wooly tails and leaped back toward the hole in the earth.

I strained the limits of the leash to follow them. When I could go no farther, I leaned in to watch them drop over the edge of the car kennel and down the striped slope, no doubt on their way to tell their prairie-dog friends how rude Californians were.

Mom led me back to the Wagon and waved me inside. "Let me just make a cup of coffee for the road," she said, slamming the door in my face yet again.

While the water was cooking, Mom wandered around the car kennel, introducing herself to all the other cars. Instead of politely sniffing their butts, Mom pointed the Witch where her nose should go.

"You're supposed to do it with your snout!" I shouted through the window.

She walked to the next car in line and did it again, holding the Witch close enough for a proper sniff. She checked the screen for the Witch's opinion.

"Let me out and I'll show you," I called. "I'll even be in the picture so it turns out better."

Once she'd checked out the butt of every car in the kennel, she came back to review her work. "There are 10 cars in this lot," she held up her hands in the *all gone* sign to show me how many *ten* was, "and only 2 of them are from South Dakota."

"Is two most of ten?" I asked, trying to guess her point.

"No. Most of these cars are from out-of-state."

"You said yourself that South Dogkotans are rare." I was proud to have spotted signs of them in their natural habitat, even if we hadn't found a wild one yet.

"No, I mean these people aren't from nearby. They're from Virginia, Arkansas, South Carolina, Illinois… all over the place. Looks like our secret hideout isn't so secret anymore."

"I thought that everyone was grounded. Don't they need to *stay* in place?"

"Maybe with schools and businesses closed, people are treating it like a vacation."

"I told you! All the referees are coming to South Dogkota and Wyoming, just like the spaceship movie predicted!"

"I don't think it's just South Dakota. Even flyover country is interesting when there's nothing better to do. It was only a matter of time before people decided to escape the madness."

"But they'll kill us all!" I squeaked. "Good thing you took pictures as evidence. They won't get away with this now that the Referee of the Universe is on the case."

"The pictures were just to help me count." She put the Witch in her pocket. "We're hardly in a position to judge."

"We should tell *more* people to travel, then," I said. "To stop the madness."

"I thought we'd be safer on the road with everyone at home. But if other people start hiding out in the wilderness, maybe we won't be as safe there as I thought."

When Mom argues against herself like this, it's best to wait and see who's winning before I pick sides, or else she's liable to fight with me instead. So I waited.

"And if the virus can get us all the way out here, maybe we shouldn't be traveling after all. These people actually decided to leave home even though they knew it was against the rules and possibly dangerous."

"We've known it was against the rules and possibly dangerous ever since Utah. What's the difference?" I asked, excited to find out another reason why we were special.

"Unlike them, we didn't decide to be in this position," Mom narrated. "Maybe we haven't followed the rules exactly, but at least I've been trying to follow the spirit of the rules as best I can under the circumstances."

"I get it. Too many copycats."

Mom had always been a rebel, but how do you rebel when the boogeyvirus changes all the rules? When everyone wants to be part of the pack, you can stand out by being independent. But where's the fun in being one-of-a-kind when everyone's a lone wolf?

"Thank dogness people are coming out again so you can be yourself," I said.

"Now that It's starting to spread, I don't know if it's fair for city people to bring their germs to the country. But it doesn't seem right to tell people they can't come and go either. Sometimes the only way to be beyond reproach is to stay out of the argument altogether."

"Stay out? What does that mean?"

The fight drained out of her before my eyes. "I think it means that it's time to go home," she said with a floppy sigh.

With no more excuses pulling us east, Mom let the Wagon turn its wheels toward the sunset for the first time since our adventure began. From now on, every spin of the Wagon wheel would squeeze us back toward home like the last two drops of toothpaste in the tube.

Chapter 13
Signs of Life

Now that we were facing west, it felt strange to be sucked back toward home so fast. The Wagon crossed Wyoming in one long gulp, and by lunchtime the next day, we were already back in Utah. Mountains grew in the front window and the freeway started to swell from one lane to two, then three. When there were more lanes than I could count on my legs, I had to say something.

"Watch out, Mom. We'll get pulled into Salt Lake City if you're not careful."

Salt Lake City was the worst place to get sucked into at a time when friendship was against the law. It's filled with people so friendly that they'll ring a stranger's doorbell just to meet whoever's inside. They love doorbell-ringing so much that when they come of age, they leave their families behind just to check out the doorbells in other parts of the world.

Despite my warnings, dense buildings grew up beside the freeway as the mountains sucked us closer. After passing a hunerd McDonald's, eleventy-nine gas stations, four Walmarts, thrumpteen parks, and seven hunerd and thirty-twelve houses, the Wagon picked a driveway with a man standing in the center. I couldn't smell him yet, but something about his jeans looked familiar.

I'll never understand how, but like the Weather Jinx can bring a storm to the desert, Mom can conjure a Friend on any street corner just by sitting there and waiting. She did it more often at home, but like with Lily, I'd seen her summon Friends over very long distances before. Mom's Friend-conjuring powers had faded recently, so much that she hardly ever used them anymore. And yet… Where did I know those jeans from?

When Mom opened my door, a rush of memory hit me as I recognized the irresistible smell of Boss Charming! I'd always wondered where he went on the days that he didn't come to see me at the office. My heart sagged knowing that he'd been standing in this lonely driveway all that time waiting for *me* to come see *him*.

"It's you! It's you!" I squealed. "I thought everyone was dead! We're not alone in this world after all!"

I trotted up the walk to the front door. I couldn't wait to give him a tour of his castle.

"Let's go around back." Boss Charming walked away from the main entrance to the gate beside the house. He showed us to a long banquet table in the dog bathroom and pulled out a chair for Mom at one end. The Charming family, like Mom, preferred to keep visitors outdoors. Boss Charming held up a *stay* hand to Mom as he slid the door open just enough to make sure no one followed him inside. "Can I get you anything? Tea? Diet Coke?"

"Just water, please," Mom said, shifting uncomfortably in her chair. Usually she was the one who got the Diet Cokes for Boss Charming.

When I smooshed my nose against the glass door to see if anyone in the kitchen needed help with dinner, there weren't as many sloppy piles on the counters and pawprints on the floor as I expected.

"Aw, your house isn't so messy," I reassured Boss Charming, hoping he'd invite me to sample the delicious smells that followed him back outside.

He put a cup on the table for Mom and a bowl on the ground for me. "So what have you been up to?" he asked, taking his place at the head of the table.

It had been a dog year since we left our normal life behind, and I had more urgent matters to discuss. With all the new rules, there was no way to know what might have happened to all my Friends left in the City. I bumped my head into his hand to get his attention.

"You too, buddy. Have you been having fun?"

"How are my Friends? Do they still live? Or were they trapped by the boogeyvirus with nowhere to turn and no castle in Utah to flee to?" It came out all at once in a screech that made everyone jump.

Much to my relief, Boss Charming reported that many of my Friends *had* fled the City. The office that had been my domain for my whole career was closed and boarded up to keep strays from storming the gates. With no dog to herd them, all of my collies had scattered to the four winds.

"It's funny, some people are loving it and others are realizing, *I thought I would be okay, but I'm really not…*" Boss Charming reported.

"Oh no! Did the virus get them?" I screamed. He jumped again. I didn't mean to startle him, but it was so exciting to see Friends again that I'd forgotten how to control my voice.

"Cheeses, Oscar!" Mom cut in before he had a chance to answer. "Use your indoor voice."

"But we don't go indoors anymore," I pointed out.

"How are *you* doing all alone out there on the road?" Boss Charming asked. "It's a lot to deal with by yourself."

"I'd rather be out on the road than stuck at home," Mom said, looking at her feet like she does when she tells the truth. "I know I can't run away from it, but being on the move at least makes me feel like I'm doing *something*. I'm more afraid of what I'll find when I come home than I am of anything that's happening out here on the road."

Mom and Boss Charming kept speaking in small words like two humans not being paid to talk to each other while one by one the members of the Charming family came to the door to introduce themselves. I graciously offered each of them my butt for scratching, but Mom stayed at the far end of the long table and waved.

"We haven't left the house in like three weeks, and it's driving me a little crazy," Boss Charming admitted. "You're the first person besides family that we've seen."

"What about your parents?" Mom asked. The last time we'd seen Boss Charming, he'd just come back from a week of helping Mister and Missus Charming Senior move to an old folks kennel. Now old folks' colonies were so infested with boogeyvirus that they were following the prairie dogs' example, telling visitors to *keep out* lest they bring in the boogeyvirus like fleas on a stray dog.

"We go and wave through the window. If they need anything, we pick it up for them and throw it over the fence."

People in Utah sure had some strange customs. I was starting to understand why they're so fond of doorbells. If all visitors stay outside, how else are your Friends going to let you know to come to the window and wave? How smudgy would *our* window get if I could only wag at Mom through the glass? The thought froze my heart, so I ducked my head under Mom's hand to make her pat me as she talked.

When the sun set and the air grew frosty, Mrs. Charming stuck her head through the kitchen door. "Where are you staying tonight?"

I was so excited about the feeling of belonging that I'd forgotten that we were referees. The Charming castle was surrounded by miles and miles of houses, so we'd have a long drive to find a quiet place to sleep.

"We'll keep pushing east," Mom said in her business voice to show she had control over the situation. "There's plenty of empty land off the freeway before the Salt Flats."

"Why don't you just stay in our driveway?" Boss Charming suggested.

Mom hid her horror behind a casual voice where only I could hear it. "I couldn't do that to you."

"What are you talking about?" I whispered. "You've shared a kitchen with him Jillians of times at the office, remember?"

"I wish I could offer you the guest room. At least use the guest bathroom to take a shower," Boss Charming insisted.

"That sounds nice, doesn't it, Mom? You haven't had a shower since Colorado."

"You've been working so hard to maintain your quarantine, and we've been out in the world for several weeks." Mom looked around the lawn for a hole to disappear into. "No one knows how this thing spreads. If I got one of you sick—or worse, spread it to one of your parents—I couldn't live with myself."

"She's exaggerating," I reassured him. "The smell isn't lethal. You'll get used to it after a while."

"But we want you to be comfortable," Mrs. Charming said, not knowing that Mom can never be comfortable with a favor.

Mom looked around the patio like a trapped cat. Finally, she said, "If your neighbors don't mind me sleeping in your driveway, and you don't mind me sneaking in to use the guest bathroom, I promise we'll be gone in the morning."

"We'll leave towels out for you and make coffee in the morning," Mrs. Charming promised.

Mom's thought bubble said that it would be more dangerous than the boogeyvirus itself for a filthy disease sack like her to accept so much kindness. Her mouth said, "Thank you. You're too kind. Really."

Mom held it through the night so she wouldn't have to use Boss Charming's guest potty and contamomate his spotless home with her cooties. The Witch woke us before any lights were on in Castle Charming, so Mom set up the Wagon's kitchen on mute to make her own poop juice. When she was done, she carefully latched the stove and slid the foldable TV dinner tray into its slot beside the spare tire. She looked back at the house. There were still no signs of movement in the dark windows, so Mom, poop juice cup, and I all took our positions and the Wagon rolled silently away.

As the Wagon crept through the deserted neighborhood, Mom kept her eyes on the side of the road as if she were looking for a place to finish our short night's sleep. Suddenly, the Wagon turned so sharply that it rolled me hard into the wall. When I righted myself and looked out the window, we were in a crowded Starbucks car kennel. The Wagon excused itself as it pushed around the line of waiting cars to one of the empty parking spots. Mom dismounted in such a hurry that she forgot to tell me she'd be right back.

She ran to the door and yanked the handle. The door didn't open, but a face appeared on the other side. It pointed to a piece of paper on the door and then pointed to the line of cars.

Mom balled her paws in front of her waist and squeezed her knees together in sign language for *it's an emergency*, but the troll behind the glass just closed her eyes, shook her head, and sent Mom back to me.

"There's a steaming-hot cup of poop juice for you right here," I said when she got back.

"Clawed Janet smother shucking pun and a stitch! Another closed bathroom," Mom didn't-quite-yell as she threw herself into the driving chair. "How dare they! What else is Starbucks there for?"

"There was a bathroom at Castle Charming," I reminded her.

"Yeah, but I don't want to soil their bathroom. They were so kind to us."

"What about the people in Starbucks? Aren't they hospitable and kind?"

"Starbucks is practically a public utility. Locking the bathrooms is… is… it's a human rights violation! You can't take away public infrastructure in the middle of a crisis. Where are we supposed to wash our hands, huh?"

"You can always use the dog bathroom," I suggested.

"Not in the middle of a city. Especially Salt Lake, of all places."

"Why? People in Salt Lake City don't go potty?"

"There are people in Utah that wear full-body underwear so that not even God can see their bum. We're gonna have to find some woods to hide in."

Mom bashed urgently on the Witch's screen. "Turn back toward Castle Charming," the Witch ordered. "You will arrive in seven minutes."

"What?" Mom stole a look at the screen and her face burst open with surprise. "It's a miracle!"

"Don't tell me!" I wagged. "We're going back to Castle Charming?"

"No. I picked out a trail in Salt Lake City months ago, just in case we ever found ourselves here without a plan. Apparently I picked somewhere less than a mile from the Charming house, so I won't have to hold it halfway across Utah. What are the odds?"

Sometimes the whole, wide world turns out to be a pretty small place after all.

The Wagon squeezed back through the line of cars and sprinted onto the road with a squeal. The same houses we'd crept past a few minutes before now blurred as we vroomed by. Just before Castle Charming came back into view, the Witch directed us onto a side road that snuck behind the houses and quickly got lost in the trees. Mom squirmed in the driving chair, urging the road to be a little shorter or a little wider, just so she could stop the Wagon and duck behind a tree. Finally, the pavement spread into a tiny car kennel. On the far side, the road shed its pavement and continued naked up the mountain.

Dogs go potty in words, leaving public messages for any passing creature to enjoy, but Mom doesn't like to pee where someone can see. Humans go potty like punctuation, as if its only meaning is a moment of privacy between important things.

We dismounted in a hurry and Mom rushed me down the wide dirt track without giving me a chance to sniff anything. Every few steps, she looked over her shoulder like someone about to do something sneaky. When we were out of sight of the car kennel, Mom pulled me to the side of the trail and unhooked her belt.

She was about to execute the toilet-paper-free maneuver that I'd taught her for self-reliance, when suddenly a truck came tearing around the corner, splattering a fanfare of mud onto anyone squatting beside the road.

Mom barely had time to reach for her pants with one paw and my collar with the other. At the very last moment she stood up, pulling her pants into place and me into her pee puddle so I wouldn't get squashed. We stood beside the road like we were made of wood, and our eyes found the eyes of the man inside the truck.

Now we had another problem. The way that you're supposed to show that you're friendly in the woods is to wave at everyone you see. The wave says, *I see you, and even if I have a gun, I know that you're not a bear.* The closer the truck got, the weirder it was that Mom was looking at the driver's eyes and not waving to him or any of the big grins and small hands waving from the back seat.

Mom had a choice to make: she could put either me or her pants in danger by letting go, or she could let the man in the truck think she was rude. There was really only one choice she could make.

Mom let go of her pants and flashed a palm to Joe White and the seven dwarves. She caught her pants right above her knees and pulled them up again as the truck passed.

"Don't worry, I think you fooled them," I whispered.

Mom flattened her eyes and mouth into lines of embarrassment. "They weren't fooled."

"How do you know?"

"Because they were laughing."

Chapter 14

Wind from My Sails

Mom buckled up her pants and led me back to the Wagon. Without her pulling on the leash, I had more time to look around. The mountain above us was so steep that I had to twist my head at an uncomfortable angle to see where the clouds swallowed the peak.

Mom eyed the piles of white dirt higher up the slope with suspicion. "There's an awful lot of snow," she said. "Maybe we should find somewhere else to run. I bet the Salt Flats would be pretty cool."

The Salt Flats were a patch of Utah where the earth wouldn't load and the ground stayed so blank that you could see the grid lines through it, just like on the Witch's mapps. Any time we drove through the Salt Flats, Mom timed it so we would pass through in the daytime. She liked to take pictures of me on that blank background where there was nothing to distract from my glamor. I'd sniffed the salty flatness around the car kennel, but I'd never properly explored its vacant interior.

"Won't we get lost with no trails or roads?" I asked.

"How could we get lost? The rest stop is literally the only thing you can see besides the road."

Mom asked the Witch to point the way, and we remounted the Wagon. As we rolled toward the exit, I thought I saw something wooly moving between the only two pickup trucks in the car kennel.

The whatever-it-was hid between the butts of the trucks, but I could see its steamy breath drifting up from its hiding spot.

As the Wagon approached, I leaned in for a better view. When Mom's window was even with the gap, the Wagon stopped. Two nomadic hill people wrapped in blanket-capes sat on beach chairs holding steaming cups of poop juice under their noses. When they felt the Wagon stop, they both froze.

I butted Mom out of the way and barked, "No thank you!" as the window rolled down in front of me.

"Back it up!" Mom put her arm across my chest and swept me into the bedroom.

"No! Mom!" I barked furiously. "Social distancing! Stranger danger!" If it wasn't enough to snap Mom out of her recklessness, at least I scared the nomads into beating a hasty retreat. They stood up and took a step back.

Mom waved the shut-up paw in my face. I closed my mouth and squinted to inspect the strangers. Their messy head fur and the dull blush of someone who uses yesterday's dirt as sunscreen told me that they weren't from here. People in Salt Lake City positively sparkle, and there was no toothpaste-ad smile on these faces when they stopped talking. They looked at us with the same suspicion that Mom wears around strangers.

"Remember," I coached at top volume into Mom's ear, "don't bark at strangers. Judge them silently from far away."

"Do you guys know if the trail is clear?" Mom barked through the window.

"The trail to Not the Peak You're Going To?" the lady-one asked.

Mom forgot the name of the peak we were going to. "Um... yeah!"

212

The wooly stranger's sidekick gave Mom a hard look up and down, then studied the sky over his other shoulder to show what he thought of us.

"I hiked up there yesterday," the Danger Stranger said. "The snow's still deep and you have to take it slow, but you can get there."

Mom sized up the Danger Stranger as the wheels in her head turned. The Stranger was about Mom's size, but rounder and jollier. That meant that if Mom started hiking, she would have to do at least as much as this tramp did, no matter what.

"We've been hiking in the snow for the past several days, and frankly I'm sick of it," Mom said, which was sort of like two truths and a lie. It's true that we had been hiking in the white dirt and that Mom had lost her patience with it before the first step, but that was days ago. And who knew if Utah white dirt was the same as the stuff we'd rolled in back in South Dogkota.

"We'll come back in a few months," Mom announced, as if the Stranger in the blanket-poncho were taking reservations. Her finger crawled to the button that closes conversations and the window.

"You should take The Trail You Were Going to Anyway," the Danger Stranger said. "It's clear all the way to the top."

Mom's finger paused over the hangup button. "I've heard that trail is dangerous," she said to give herself an excuse to drive away with dignity if she chickened out. "Is it, like, *really* dangerous? Or dangerous like leaving my house is dangerous?"

All the humans laughed nervously. The two strangers took another step backward and Mom pulled her face back inside the Wagon walls.

The Danger Stranger thought for a moment. "There's one spot where there was a rockslide, but... well... it's hiking."

213

"Thanks! Be safe out there!" Mom shouted through the closing gap in the window.

The strangers' waves wished us safety back.

"But Mom, what if a rock falls on your head?" I asked. "What if you need to go to the hospital, and someone can't have boogeyvirus and dies because you have a rock for a head?"

"Don't we always try to stay out of the hospital?" She pushed the *all done* lever behind the driving wheel. "Nature is dangerous. Life is dangerous. It's not like we go out on every hike thinking, *I sure am glad that there are search & rescue and medevac teams out there, because this cliff looks dangerous and I'll probably fall off.*"

"Yeah, but what if you do? Need to go to the vet, I mean. And someone with boogeyvirus has nowhere to lie down because you're in their bed like Goldilocks?"

"If someone needs help, they should get the best help available, no matter who else is in the hospital that day. Sure, we have a responsibility not to put someone else at a risk they didn't sign up for, but we can't take responsibility for all the danger in the world. Hiking may be dangerous, but we're the only ones we put at risk by doing it. We can't stop living our lives just so someone else can live theirs."

"Isn't that why everyone is staying home, though? People stopping their lives so that other people can live theirs?"

She made a disgusted noise in her throat. "No. Staying home is about the damned hospital beds so everyone doesn't get sick at once. We're just sheltering in place while we wait for my turn to roll the dice."

So that's why Mom was so nervous about breaking the rules all of a sudden; she was afraid that someone would catch her rudely cutting in line at the hospital. As long as she didn't get sick, nobody could accuse her of not waiting her turn. But the boogeyvirus wasn't only in California anymore. If it had caught up to our travel speed, there was nowhere to hide.

"But danger finds us all the time," I said. "I thought you knew the commands to keep us safe."

"It hasn't gotten us yet, has it? And we learn from it, don't we?" She wriggled out of her jeans and pulled a pair of running pants out of the wad of clothes stashed on the copilot's chair. "We turn around all the time when things seem dangerous, even though we could probably figure out how to get through safely. Life is a game of risks and rewards. Most rounds you win, but sometimes you draw a crappy hand. You're bound to have a few unlucky accidents in a lifetime. If you stop your life to avoid every risky thing, you'll miss the best parts. At least in nature you can usually see the danger coming."

I shuddered at the thought of a danger Mom couldn't stop.

Mom's eyes caught mine in the mirror and softened. "How about we pick a safe word, just in case?"

"What's that? A magic spell to keep us safe?"

"Sorta. If something gets too risky or scary, you say the magic word and everything stops. Okay?"

I stopped shivering and let my body get a tiny bit bigger. "Okay."

"So what's our safe word? It's got to be something that you wouldn't say normally so that no one gets confused."

"How about supercalifragilisticexpialidocious?"

"That's a bit of a mouthful. How about, *I'm scared*?"

"I would never say that."

"Then it's settled." She nodded and reached for the packpack.

We didn't need to walk far past Mom's piddle puddle before the trail got down to business. It shrank to barely wider than an Oscar and turned aggressively uphill. The air cut wetly through my coat as we climbed out of the shelter of the valley. With each turn of the narrow trail, there were fewer trees and more rocks. The thinner the trees became, the more wind found its way into my coat until the clamminess felt like it was coming from inside of me.

"It sure is cold." Mom pulled her paws out of her pockets, cupped them in front of her face, and blew them up like balloons. "I think it's getting colder."

People from our part of California are so good at detecting extreme weather that we can identify deadly temperatures long before anyone from another part of the world. Mom can sniff out global warming when it's only *sixey-eight degrees*, which is the number for the boiling point of City people. She carries a hoodie everywhere she goes, in case the temperature drops below *sixey-five*—the number where bodies clench and teeth clatter. If the weather goes below *fiddy-two*, it's just a matter of time before Mom freezes to death.

Dogs aren't as sensitive as humans, but the clammy wind was doing something funny to my paws. Although I could see them and move them, I couldn't feel them. They pranced along under me like the legs of a clumsier dog. "I can't hear my leg muscles," I told Mom, in case it was important.

"This is miserable." She pulled the Witch out of her pocket. "What's the temperature?" she asked in that voice that meant she was getting ready to prove a point.

"It's forty-two degrees outside," the Witch teased.

"Bullplop." Mom poked the accusation into the Witch's face. "It says here it's 35 degrees with the windchill."

"What's *wind chill?*" I asked.

"It's when the wind makes everything worse. It's one of the tricks the weather uses to make you grouchy." Mom packed her shoulders tighter over her ears and trudged on, as if to block out any distraction from her suffering.

"Aren't we having fun?" I asked. I thought we were, but it was hard to tell.

"That's up to you, but it feels like the worst is yet to come." Mom glowered at the clouds climbing down the mountain to meet us.

The white dirt started in slick patches too packed to hold a snow angel. The patches grew until they joined into a slushy layer over everything.

Mom fit her shoes into pawprints that traced an invisible line between a wall-like upslope and a cliff-like downslope. "*The trail is clear* my ass!" she muttered as she punched her bare hand into the white dirt on the uphill side for balance.

"I know! Isn't it a wonderful surprise?" I ran ahead, kicking up a spray like a snowplow until Mom screamed at me to stay close, dammit.

In my excitement I hadn't noticed how far Mom had fallen behind until I heard her calling for me from deep in the distance. When I found her, she was hanging tight to a bush for balance. The white dirt made a mushy sound as her shoe felt around for the solid ground underneath.

"Those branches are thinner than a shoelace, silly," I told her. "They can't hold you if you fall. You'll slide aaaa*aaa*all the way to that valley down there."

We both stretched our necks to look down at where our mountain crashed into a smaller mountain far below. Mom pulled herself closer to the bush.

"You'd better hope it can hold me," she said without taking her eyes off the landing pad. "Your food is in the van and I have the keys."

The next time Mom yodeled for me to *c'mere*, I found her wobbling in the trail of pawprints like a tightrope walker without a balancing stick. She unplugged her back leg from the white dirt and waved three of her legs in the air while trying to keep the fourth in its pawhole. Just when I thought the last leg would lose its place, she aimed her free leg at the next hole and fell toward it. She stuck the landing, but not without burying a third paw in the white dirt for stability. Once she was sure that both legs were plugged in again, she repeated the process on the other side. She looked up to make sure I was still watching.

"Now that you mention it, I can't even tell if you're on the trail," I grinned. "I mean, the white dirt is just as steep where you're walking as..." I looked back at the rocky crashpad to show what I meant.

"It's. very. steep." Each word squeezed out of Mom's mouth in single file on its own puff of air. She looked down again and froze. It was a straight slide to the bottom, with nothing to hang onto or bounce off on the way down. "I'm scared!" She crouched for stability as she slowly pivoted.

"That's not the magic word," I called after her to make sure that she really meant it. Chickening out always made Mom grumpy for the rest of the day.

"You asked about how we stay away from danger? This. This right here is the moment when risk turns into danger," she said, not quite pulling off a know-it-all voice. "I'm scared."

"Chickens say what?"

"What?" Mom said.

If I could laugh, I would. Instead I wagged.

218

"*Supercalifragilisticexpialidocious*, dammit! Let's get out of here!" she surrendered.

I wanted to push on like we used to, back when Mom would climb to the top of a cliff to valiantly save her socks, or when she fearlessly jumped into a monster's gaping jaws to save me. But those acts of bravery were from back when this was America and every heroic tale had a happy ending. Now that an invisible danger followed us everywhere, who knew if stories even ended with *happily ever after* anymore. Mom had said the magic word and I had promised. I took one last look over my shoulder at the dotted line of pawholes leading to the top before following her back down.

Climbing downhill is really just controlled falling. Since Mom never misses a chance to control anything, she was even slower on the way down. She kicked grooves in the white dirt to make sure her paws stayed stuck to the ground. Her downhill hiking technique gave me plenty of time to watch the mountains on the other side of the valley fight with the clouds.

"Hey, look," I called over my shoulder. "I think the sun's coming out!"

Mom looked away from the step she'd been working on just long enough to spot something wrong. "It looks like that storm is coming this way. We should probably hurry."

When the Weather Jinx spoke, the sky awoke. Right on cue, it darkened to a mominous grey and threw down a spat of rain while it gathered its clouds to show what it could really do.

"I sure hope this weather breaks soon," the Jinx jinxed.

"It definitely will. How long can it possibly last when I can see the sun?" I searched the foreshadowing sky for the bright spot I'd seen a moment earlier, but it was hidden behind the smudge of rain. I looked back to make sure Mom was listening. "Right?"

Without warning, the rain turned furious. It fell in fat drops that soaked my fur until I was as defenseless to the wind as a hairless human. I tucked my tail between my legs, but only for warmth.

"Crap! Crap! Crap! This wasn't in the forecast," Mom fumed, as if this were the Witch's first betrayal. "We're gonna get soaked!"

"Too late!" I ran ahead to keep dry under a tree until Mom slithered by. I ran from observation tree to observation tree until Mom was her usual height again. The rain smudged out everything outside this moment as we began to run.

We ran until Mom was wheezing like she was trying to suck the last breath out of the sky. Mom always says that the reason it's hard to breathe in the mountains is because there isn't enough air. But if there was so little air, then why was it blowing through me like ice daggers? I thought that life couldn't get any worse than being soaked by freezing rain, stabbed with icicles of wind, and suffercated by skimpy air, but then the rain started bouncing.

"Ow! It hurts!" I tried hiding in Mom's slipstream, which is usually the best place to escape weather, but Mom's puny bulk did nothing to stop the tiny bee stings falling from the sky.

"You've got to be kidding me!" Mom whined, like there was someone listening who could change their mind about it if she shamed them enough. "It *can't* keep going like this."

But it did.

The wind's breath smelled like zambonis as it huffed and puffed and tried to blow us off the mountainside. The ice grains hissed furiously, collecting on the ground and crunching under Mom's shoes. They fell in waves, lightening up so slightly that I didn't notice the difference until the next wave slammed into me, making me wish I'd appreciated how good life was a few steps before.

The distance back to the Wagon stretched as Mom tried to sprint in pants falling down under the weight of their wetness. She held the Witch and my untasted bag of brunch in one paw and her pants in the other as we scampered soggily downhill.

Reluctantly, I slowed down to let her catch up. "Let go!" I coached. "You can run faster if you let your arms move naturally!"

"If I let go, my pants'll fall down. I'll step on the bottoms and trip on the waistband. If I fall on top of you, we'll both tumble down this hill like Jack and Jill."

I wasn't sure if there was *any* way of going down the hill that would be worse than what we were doing now, but there was no time to argue. I ran ahead hoping Mom would follow my example.

After an eternity and sooner than I thought, the Wagon appeared in the mist ahead. I burst inside as soon as Mom opened the door wide enough for me to fit. Mom tumbled in after me and slammed the door against the cold.

As soon as the sky lost sight of the Weather Jinx, it packed up the zambonis and the clouds melted away. By the time I was toweled off and Mom was wearing dry pants, the distant mountains were already poking whitely into the sky in a way that the clouds had only hinted at earlier.

Mom looked at the view a little too long. I watched a pair of droplets chase each other to the bottom of the window as the Wagon blew the feeling back into my legs.

"I'm not going back out there," I responded to her thought bubble.

"Me neither." Mom sighed. "I'm sure there's plenty to see between here and the Sierras."

The Rockies shrank in the back window. Outside the front window, the land relaxed into the smoother blankness that would eventually turn into Nevada. I dozed, letting the heater blow the damp from my fur. The Wagon's *almost there* click woke me from my daydreaming, and I climbed into the copilot's seat to see if we were approaching a camping spot or just a gas station.

But there was nothing on the other side of the window. Absolutely nothing.

"We're here!" I wagged.

The Wagon rolled off the freeway into what looked more like a research station on Antarctica or the moon than a rest area. Mom opened the door and I ran to where the black road ended and the white emptiness began. I sniffed the air, but there was no freezer-burn smell of white dirt nor prickly smell of desert on the wind. In every direction, there were killmometers and killmometers of nothingness between my eyes and the far-off mountains where the world reloaded.

It felt like freedom to have all that space to fill however I wanted. My paws itched to leave their prints in every tile, but the Salt Flats were too big to properly explore without losing smell of Mom. She plodded behind me at an uncurious pace, capturing as much of the vastness as she could inside the Witch's tiny screen. I rolled as far as I walked, grinding tiny grains of magnificence into my fur so I could take it home with me.

We drifted farther during my floor routine of tumbling, jumping, and abs than I realized. When we found the car kennel again, we were on the far end. Mom and I hiked through the sea of empty spaces. There was only one other car in the kennel, parked far from the potties where few other cars would stop. The lady inside was holding up an empty box of the kind that glass bottles ride in. She twisted it around in the sun as if admiring its beauty.

"I'm trying to see how many calories are in a bottle," the lady told Mom through the open window with a friendly, lopsided smile.

"Is beer diet food?" I thought to Mom.

"I actually know the answer to that question," Mom said out loud. "An IPA probably has about 200 calories per bottle." Mom knows how to put numbers on all sorts of things.

"That's not so bad." The lady looked relieved. I was proud that Mom's counting had helped soothe someone else's stress for a change.

Mom kept the friendly smile on her face as she wished the woman a safe drive home. Behind the cheerful voice, her thoughts judged, "… not bad for 1, but ma'am, you seem to have drunk all 6. In your car. More than 100 miles from anywhere you could possibly live."

"Should I tell her?" I asked, excited to show off that I knew helpful things, too.

"Nah, leave her alone. People are under pressure. They need to get out of their houses to find relief from the constant anxiety somehow. Anyway, she made me happy."

"Why?"

"Because if you've put away a 6-pack of good beer before 4pm on a Tuesday, you've probably got some serious problems," Mom calculated, showing her work as she went. "But she's still thinking about her figure."

"I don't think her figure has been bikini-safe for a long time," I coached.

"Bikinis aren't an essential life skill for women over 30," Mom said like a warning. "Anyone who's day-drinking alone has parts of their life that are out of control, but that lady isn't ready to let herself go. The world's coming down around her, and there may be some huge things that she can't take on right now, but that doesn't mean she has to give in. All is not lost as long as people are still thinking about the future and making plans to improve."

Inspired by the health nut, Mom forgot to be in a hurry and took the time to make her own comfy drink when we got back to the Wagon. While she watched the pot for bubbles, a pickup truck so big that it filled the boundless emptiness pulled in next to us. It continued growling, even after the man inside dismounted. He looked like he had been strong and muscular once, but quit the football team two dog-lifetimes ago. Now, his shirt was inflated with more arrogance than muscle.

He looked Mom up and down, and his eyes said that she was no cheerleader. "What? Are you having a cookout?" he asked with the sneer of a TV bully.

"No, I'm just making a cup of tea," Mom said in a snotty voice that said he couldn't bully her if she bullied him back.

"Psh... that's *random!*" he scoffed, walking to the people potties in a way that might have felt jaunty from the inside but looked constipated from the outside.

"Wow. Cool," Mom said in a voice that meant he wasn't cool at all. She shot a sharp look into his back to deflate his puffed-up attitude.

"That wasn't much of a burn," I whispered when he closed the pooping-tardis door behind him.

"I haven't heard anyone use the word *random* as an insult since I was in like 9th grade," Mom said to make her feelings hurt a little less. "With all the things to worry about right now, that guy's criticizing me about making a cup of tea?"

Mom's eyes dropped back to the pot, where there was still no steam. Despite her brave face, the moldy insult spoiled the love for mankind left over from the Health Nut. She dumped the water on the ground and packed up the kitchen quickly. She mounted the driving chair just in time. The Wagon stole out of its parking space just as the tardis door opened. By the time Biff got back to his truck, we were already long gone.

Chapter 15
Rage Against the Quarantine

We continued our sprint westward through Nevada's furrowed brow, where the land rolls through one unremarkable hill and forgotten valley after another. The hunerds of miles of slow-rolling earth lulled me into a trance of deep thoughts. It wouldn't be long now before we were back in My Hometown at the End of the World.

I liked living at the End of the World before we left. It made me feel like a king to stand in the dog bathroom behind the Stuck House and watch the last mile of a whole continent fall into the ocean. Now that going home meant being trapped in the Stuck House for who-knew-how-long, the End of the World felt more like a dead end than the leading edge of something.

It wasn't just the stuck routine that made me not want our adventure to end. In the time we'd been away, humans had gone from a cuddlicious bouquet of human-mutts to a cesspuddle of plague and suspicion. It was as if the boogeyvirus cast a spell that turned the whole world into grumpy, territorial cats. As long as we lived in the Wagon, I wouldn't have to see what the boogeyvirus had done to My Hometown.

The Witch, who enjoyed nothing more than making trouble, was in awe. She didn't even have to come up with her own imaginary threats anymore with so many nasty words from real people to report on. Every day, she gleefully repeated what our Friends said about how leaving a stuck house was murder, or how everyone who didn't mind their own beeswax deserved what they got. Mom, who practically lived on the internet, was afraid to say anything at all, lest our Friends find out where we were and say those nasty things to her.

But we couldn't hide in the desert forever. We needed to come home to report to my new business posting, and there was nowhere else to turn. There weren't even trails in the empty forehead of Nevada, and California was closing in fast.

"Where should we go tomorrow?" I asked Mom that night as she swiped sleepily at the Witch.

"I don't know. Northern Nevada doesn't have much going for it and it's too early in the season to hike in the Sierras. By the time we get below the snow line around Auburn, it'll be too densely settled and all the trails will probably be closed."

"How do you know they'll be closed? We haven't even checked yet."

"It's California. The state that never met a petty rule they didn't enforce." Mom used to see rules as a fun puzzle, but now there was only surrender in her voice. "Maybe if we go somewhere far outside the Bay Area…"

"But where can you find a place as lawless as Wyoming inside California?" I said in despair.

"Here's a trail in Humboldt County!" Mom sat up taller than she had in days. "It goes along the coast."

"I thought you said they closed all the beaches. Are you sure this isn't another one of the Witch's traps?"

"It's called the Lost Coast. That sounds remote, doesn't it?"

"If it's lost, how are we going to find it?"

"Good point. I guess the coast is pretty hard to miss." Mom got a little floppier. "But it's Humboldt. The county's entire economy has been based on growing illegal weed since the 70s. How well are Humboldt cops *really* going to monitor the trails?"

I never could understand people's obsession with making rules against plants. Some people get their kicks from executing any plant that grows where they think it doesn't belong. I saw a documentary once where the Law dressed as ninjas and swarmed into the woods from land and sky just to weed the forest. They burned the outlaw plants like witches when they were done, just to prove that they weren't messing around. What did that plant ever do to them? It seemed extra silly to be weeding in the forest, especially if you called in the Law to do it.

"Isn't Bumbolt where the people in that movie got murdered for sticking their noses where they didn't belong?" I asked.

Mom's lips bunched on one side of her mouth as she thought. "I'm pretty sure that's less of a problem now that it's legal. It can't hurt to check. Where else are we going to go?"

When people think of California, they think about the beaches on the left and the mountains on the right. They know about the desert in the south and the City in what they call *The North*. What they don't know about California is that the part called *north* is really the middle. There is a whole other half of California above the elbow that hardly anyone knows about. It's filled with bundles of mountains you've never heard of, lakes shaped like strangers' birthmarks, giant trees and dwarfed towns. A place that no one knew about seemed like the safest place for referees who weren't ready to face unreality.

Usually I get a thrill when I see the Sierras crushing together in the front window, but this time I got a funny emptiness in my tummy when the ground started to rumple and turn white.

"Welcome to California," the Witch said. Where you can check out any time you like, but you can never leave, her tone added.

The downward momentum set in, sucking us even faster toward the End of the World. We drove until water softened the air, and the smell of green filled the spaces between buildings. The Wagon rolled through grape fields and redwood forests. When the air smelled of ocean again, a new species of sign I'd never seen before began sprouting among the redwoods beside the road.

"What do they say?" I asked.

"They say, SHELTER IN PLACE ORDER IN EFFECT," Mom read.

"What does that mean?"

"It means, *Go home*."

"Well at least they're being polite about it." I inspected the next several signs as we passed. They were the kind that are made to last, with sturdy faceplates, stalks as thick as the trunk of a small tree, and roots fastened into the ground. "What are they gonna do with all these signs in a few weeks when the boogeyvirus is gone?"

"They're saying it'll be months now, and these signs look permanent," Mom said. "They put intent and funding behind these rules. I thought a community of peaceful outlaws would be a little more open-minded."

"Are we gonna be grounded forever just for being here?" I asked as ninjas swarmed my thoughts. If the Law did all that for a plant that wasn't going anywhere, what would they do for a stresspassing Mom and the dog walking her?

"It's not criminal, but it's a violation of something-or-other," Mom said in her law-gic voice. "I wouldn't call it *il*-legal. More like *extra*-legal."

What a relief. If the Law found us, they would probably give me a medal for being so much more legal than everyone else.

"You have arrived!" the Witch butted in.

230

The Wagon rolled into a seaside car kennel, where shiny papers stuck like scarecrows to every post. The sun reflected off of each sheet's polished shell, hiding its message. The Wagon stuck its nose close to one of the posts like an old person trying to read small letters. Mom leaned forward in the driving chair, squinting into the glare. "Dog doo. It says that if they catch us hiking they can fine us, or even put us in jail for up to a year."

"If they ask, you should choose *fine thanks*, not *jail*," I suggested.

Mom gave me that look again. "A fine is money."

"Do you think they mean dog year, or a human year?" I asked thoughtfully as if I were weighing my options, not tricking Mom into giving me a hint about what we should do next.

"Neither one makes sense!" Mom's paws gripped the driving wheel like she wanted to strangle it. "How can they take you off an 11-mile trail that might only have 1 person per mile…" she held a finger beside her ear to show how many *one* was, "… and put you in a crowded jail, then say the world is safer because of it?" The finger retracted back into its fist. "But whatever. Let's not push it."

The Wagon backed away from the sign and tip-toed out of the car kennel. A block away, a Law watched us drive past from the front seat of his Whale-mobile. The Wagon did its best to look innocent, and Mom kept her nose pointed straight ahead like someone with nothing to hide. If this were a cartoon, she would have whistled and twirled an umbrella.

When we were out of view of the Law, the Wagon slowed in front of a house and stopped in a way that someone who lived there might. Mom summoned the Witch for an emergency meeting.

"We drove through all those woods on the way here," I reminded her. "Let's sleep in there."

"The whole forest is closed." She pointed at a paper badge on the nearest tree. "That's what the signs say."

With all the permanent signs beside the road and the polished signs in the car kennel, I'd hardly noticed the naked paper pinned to just about every tree you could see from the road. "How can you close a whole forest?"

"That's what I'm saying!" Mom said in a voice that usually comes with a stomp and a fist on the table.

I was used to being shut out of nature, but nature had never been off-limits to Mom before. Until now, Mom had always been able to talk us out of a fix by knowing just enough about the rules to pretend she didn't know anything. But that only worked in America where people have rights. For the first time, she was like a weed that someone could rip up by the roots just because they decided we didn't belong. It felt like we didn't belong *anywhere* anymore.

A battle raged in Mom's thought bubble between fury that a flower like her could be treated like a weed, and worries about whether she'd been wrong about thinking herself a flower in the first place.

We drifted back the way we'd come like a canoe without a paddle. There was no time to find somewhere new before bedtime, and with the Law lurking about, we'd have to stay well hidden. With so many signs guarding the road, even Mom's law-gic wouldn't convince the Law that we didn't know we weren't supposed to be there. The Wagon's nose wandered with the current of Mom's thoughts as she looked into the trees for a safe place to hide.

Finally, the Wagon snuck onto an old dirt car-trail mostly hidden by trees. We followed the road a short way until it stopped at the base of a power tower. If the Law spotted us, maybe Mom could convince them that we were fixing the power poles in the middle of the night.

We may have found a place to sleep, but there was still plenty for Mom to fret about. In the game of Simon says, Wyoming was *easy* mode and California was the boss level to beat the whole game. Mom begged the Witch for help, but the Witch was in another one of her sullen moods. No matter how Mom pleaded, all that good-for-nothing would show her was a screen as blank as the Salt Flats.

"If a place is so remote that you have to search to find out if anyone's inside, what does *closed* even mean?" Mom threw the Witch onto the blankets.

I was getting tired of this game. "So? What are you going to do about it?"

"Take my ball and go home." When I cracked my eye open to check for a ball, Mom's arms were crossed and she was pouting. There was no ball.

I closed my eye again and rolled over. "That'll show 'em."

The next morning, Mom set her eyes back to *trail spotting* mode and aimed them at the forest beside the road. "We'll take the scenic route so you can run around on the beach or something along the way," she said. "CHP can't monitor them all."

Before I'd even had a chance to settle into the ride, everything and everyone inside the Wagon tumbled forward as it lurched into a teency-weency parking cubby.

When all was still, I gathered my legs and stood to look out the window. In the back corner of the cubby, a path hid in the underbrush behind a pile of trash and old clothes. Mom looked both ways, checked all the mirrors, and we dismounted.

"Why is there luggage in the woods?" I asked as we walked around the dusty suitcase marking the trailhead. "I thought no one was allowed to travel."

Mom's face said that she was trying very hard not to think about something inconvenient. "Maybe there's a story behind it that happened long ago," she guessed hopefully.

"Yeah," I agreed. "There's probably an airport in here."

"I know I keep repeating myself, but I just can't wrap my mind around why they're 'closing' a trail that they don't maintain in the first place." Mom ducked under a branch with a pair of ripe tighty-whities hanging from it. "There are no services. What's to close?"

I looked for something to distract her from playing the same thought on repeat for the rest of the day. Between us and the road, there were vines, trees, food wrappers, an old boot, a rusty bicycle tire... Nothing in the woods looked like it wanted to be seen, so I pointed to something beside the road instead. "What does that sign say? Isn't it nice that they put it in braille so that blind drivers can read it?"

"It says, *NO SHOOTING*," Mom read. "And that's not braille."

I was confused for a moment, until I realized that there was a clue on the sign. "But how did the bullet holes get through the sign if there wasn't any shooting?"

"No dog doo, Sherlock. A rule isn't worth the sign it's printed on if no one's gonna enforce it." She held up one finger and paused dramatically like she was about to reveal the solution to a mystery. "Those bullet holes tell me that no one's patrolling around here, so nobody who cares about safety and the law will see us sneak in."

"Are you sure that's the message that bullets are trying to tell you?" I asked, but Mom was listening too hard for clues from the trail to hear me.

The trail had the look of a path that wasn't going places. It kept disappearing behind shaggy bushes and matted vines.

"About that suitcase," I said. "Do you think the traveler was going *into* the woods, or coming *out of* the woods? And where are they *sit-staying* now? And do they need their stuff?"

But Mom's imagination was occupied with finding the trail under the bullet skeletons and bottle bones, so she didn't answer those questions either.

Now that we were far enough into the trees that the road couldn't see us, even more trash blossomed on the forest floor. A little ways back from the trail, a washing machine lay on its side with its mouth open while grimy clothes stiffened on the branches above. The clues were trying to tell me something, if only I could figure out what.

I inspected a pile of milk jugs whose sour smell was disappearing into the scent of human pee and dirt around it. "What is this place?"

"Sssshhhhh." Mom's eyes were wide. She cocked her head in high alert. "It's a homeless camp. No matter what you do, don't bark. Who knows if they have an aggressive dog somewhere around here."

"Supercalifragilisticexpialidocious!" I whispered.

Mom was too busy listening for movement in the stinky summer igloo at the end of a cardboard walkway to notice that I'd used the magic word. "They probably set up their tents close to the road for convenience," her thoughts whispered. "I bet the trail continues behind the encampment."

We tiptoed through one scene of destruction after another. I dropped my head to inspect a puffer jacket still floating in the mud puddle it drowned in before I remembered where I was. I ran to catch up with Mom.

"What if they're hiding something you're not supposed to see?" I whispered.

"Hey! Hey! Who goes there?" a tiny voice with a chihuahua accent roared from inside the nearest igloo.

"Let's turn around," Mom thought. She grabbed my collar so we wouldn't be separated if we had to run away.

"Who's out there?" bellowed a human voice, also from inside the igloo.

In her best *howdy neighbor* voice, Mom chirped, "I'm sorry, I thought this was a hiking trail."

"Well it's not," the voice said aggressively but not unkindly, "so beat it."

"I made a mistake. I'm sorry for disturbing you. We're leaving," Mom narrated. Her tone was like the one she might use to say, *Look! They have pistachio croissants at the bakery this week!*

"Wait, where are we going? You're not gonna let him talk to you like that, are you?" I asked as Mom dragged me back to the Wagon. "You can't close nature, remember? Wait here. I'll tell 'em!"

"Nope. Nope. Nope." Mom scuttled past the suitcase and opened the Wagon door, stepping aside to clear my path for a running leap.

I hesitated. "No one will know how brave we are if you run away as soon as someone says *boo.*"

"Not now, Spud. *Up-up.*" It was the kind of voice that you don't argue with. I jumped into the driving chair and Mom followed, slamming the door behind her in the same motion. The Wagon screeched back onto the road like the Scooby Mobile running from a ghost.

I didn't notice how much my feelings hurt until we were safely on the road again. Why would anyone bark at me without getting to know me first? "What did we ever do to those homeleskimos to make them so mad at us?" I asked out loud.

"It wasn't about you, Spud. They just don't like intruders."

"You could have told them that we respected their boogeybubble," I said. "Maybe then they wouldn't have been so aggressive."

"I don't think it was about the virus."

"Then why? Who wouldn't want to meet me? I'm terrific."

"Well…" She wound up her mouth like she does when she's preparing to 'splain something that doesn't make sense. "You know how you bark at service dogs?"

"I hate those goody-goodies. Too high and mighty to sniff my butt…"

"Right. No one likes rejection, but those dogs have responsibilities more important than greeting everyone they meet."

"Greeting everyone you meet is a very important job," I huffed. "They think they're so much better than me just because they get to go inside supermarkets and liberries. I could do those things too, if I wanted."

"Someone else doing their job doesn't mean you're not a good dog. What does it even have to do with you?"

"Innocent guys like me get in trouble because of those self-satisfied snoots."

"Maybe what gets a rise out of you isn't the other dog, but that they stay calm when you can't control intense emotions?"

Mom suggested in a service-dog tone. "Could that be what makes you mad?"

"Well yeah! They're gonna get me in trouble pretending to be good boys and girls like that. It's all an act, you know. You don't see it, Mom, but they're just dogs underneath. I bet they lick their butts when no one's watching."

"It's your insecurity, not the other dog that makes you lose your cool."

"Not me! It's because *you* can't protect me from a judgy look. That's why."

"Right," she said, as if she'd agreed with me the whole time. "People are the same way. They don't just protect what's precious, they also protect what they're ashamed of. Some people don't have it in them to keep up with the responsibilities of money, houses, cars, and their health because there's something stuck on their minds that leaves no room for anything else. Maybe they're doing their best, but others don't understand why they can't just follow the rules like the rest of us."

"But their Friends love them just the way they are, right?"

"Love doesn't always feel loving if someone's offering you help that you didn't ask for. It's easier to hide than to explain yourself to someone who doesn't get it. If you push all your friends away, at least there's nobody to make you feel bad by helping. Nobody to let down if it doesn't work. Nobody to take away your freedom if you can't fix it yourself. The aggression is just misdirection to prevent anyone who comes too close from discovering their secret. That hobo wasn't protecting anything in there but privacy and a whole lot of shame."

"And that makes it okay to be mean to someone who's just hiking by?"

"Sometimes the best defense is to take offense," Mom said.

"And that makes it okay to be offensive?" I asked. "Why should I have to be polite to someone who has such bad manners?"

"They used their words, just like you do when you're on leash and someone invades your personal space." She shrugged. "Everyone's allowed to protect themselves."

It's nice to have a life partner that gets you. "When I can't escape, I've got to tell them somehow," I agreed. "Good offenses make good neighbors."

I hadn't even noticed the End of the World sneaking up on us. Suddenly, there were no more trees and the earth simply broke off and fell into the sea. The Wagon drove straight toward the End. When it seemed like the only place to go was right into the ocean, a crossroad appeared and the Wagon turned to follow the jagged path of the coast. We floated along the highway, bobbing through the waves of wildflowers and cow fields as the ocean bashed itself against the cliffs, too far below to be part of my world. From up here, the waves were just ruffles to remind me how big the ocean really was.

Mom tried to keep the Wagon on the road as she watched the battle between land and sea. *Rumble-grumble-mumble*, said the Wagon's belly every time Mom let its wheels follow her eyes too close to the water.

"Why don't you take a picture? It lasts longer," I harrumphed each time the rumbling disturbed my nap.

"I can't take a picture because I can't pull over because all the pullouts are blocked with caution tape," she grumped.

"You can duck under it," I said. "I'll show you how."

"That tape might as well be an impenetrable wall. Cars can't bend the rules like people and dogs do."

"If you say so…" I yawned. You can't help someone who doesn't want to change her ways.

"Each one of those pullouts holds 1 to 2 cars at the most, and there's nowhere to *go* when you get out of the car," Mom ranted as if I were still listening. "People are gonna stop following the rules if you take things away for no good reason. Quarantine isn't supposed to be a punishment."

"If the tape isn't there for safety, what would happen if you drove through at top speed like in the movies?" I asked.

"We're at the top of a cliff, dummy. Have you ever seen *Thelma and Louise?*"

"Yes, of course. They outsmart the Law by doing what the audience least expects. Where do you think I got the idea from? We can hold hands if you want. One… two…"

Mom didn't reach out her paw to hold mine. "What do you think happens after that last frame, Oscar?"

"It works and they get away, of course. Have *you* ever seen *Thelma and Louise?*"

"I'm not sure you got the point that the ending was trying to make."

After many miles of searching, the Wagon found enough space between road and tape to pull over. It nosed its way into the gap in the tape and casually parked as if it were just thinking about where to go next. Mom and I dismounted and walked onto the beach as if we belonged there, looking for a place to potty away from prying eyes. We took our time coming back, doing our best to look like we'd just forgotten where we parked.

When we ran out of ways to look busy, we reluctantly returned to the Wagon. Mom had just closed the door behind me and was walking around to the driving chair when a motorcycle stopped a little ways away. Its knight dismounted and Mom smiled hello.

"Where are you from?" the Knight asked. I could tell that he was a furryner by the way he made his words like his mouth was full of tennis balls.

"The City," Mom said.

"Eh?" the Furryner asked, taking off his helmet and stepping closer to hear better.

"The City," Mom repeated, taking a step backward toward the Wagon.

"Eh?" the Furryner asked again, stepping to the edge of her boogeybubble.

"The City!" Mom shouted, taking the last step toward clean air. She stood with the butt shelf of the Wagon against the back of her knees, hoping he didn't have any more questions.

"Eh?" The Furryner stepped even closer.

Mom leaned back and her arm shot out as if to shove the Furryner off a cliff. She might have done it, too, if he'd come any closer, but only by accident. They froze for a second, both staring at the *stop* hand at the end of Mom's stiff arm. They realized in the same moment that they had each almost accidentally killed each other.

"San Francisco," Mom finally said, dropping her limp arm to her side.

The Furryner stepped back out of Mom's boogeybubble. "You smart. I forget."

He put his helmet back on for safety and pushed his motorcycle a little farther away. He looked out toward the End of the World and pretended like he was lost in thought. Mom quietly remounted the driver's seat.

"Maybe people aren't as closed off as I thought," she said as she spurred the Wagon to life. "Everything that I know about what other people think comes from social media, but maybe they're exaggerating."

"No one lies on the internet," I reassured her. "I don't think it's allowed."

"People on the internet portray themselves more like how they *want* to be than how they really are," said Mom, who sometimes pretends to be a dog on the internet.

"Why would anyone want their Friends to think that they're the kind of bully that shouts to *stay the duck at home*?" I asked. "That kind of talk makes people not want to play with you."

"Are you asking as a dog who can't pass a service dog without barking, or a dog who preaches love and friendship on the internet?" Mom asked with a trap on her breath.

"Is there a difference?"

"People are just looking for validation. Telling your own truth doesn't mean your opinions always match your behavior. The whole point of the internet is that it gives you a place to say the things you wouldn't dare say to someone's face."

"Like how you're always saying we should be patient and kind, but you think ugly things when you're in a hurry and someone gets in your way?" I asked.

"Hey now. I *think* it, but I don't *say* it."

"Except when we're in the Wagon. Then you say it real loud."

She gave me a look like she was in a hurry to get to the point and I was in her way. "As I was saying, rudeness gets clicks, and clicks stand in for friendship on the internet." That explained a lot about the Witch. "People post extreme opinions when they want to feel heard, but they're mostly just venting."

I was starting to see what she was getting at. "Like how you think your own farts stink less than everyone else's because only you feel the relief of not holding it in?"

"Well said. Behind the internet, there's supposed to be an older worldwide web of empathy and mutual understanding. It reminded us that there were people on the other side of those screens. Now that we're all staying home, the interpersonal web is breaking down. It's easy to lose perspective."

"And hard not to bark at someone who's always yapping and trying to boss you around."

"It sure is," Mom agreed. "Defending an unpopular opinion only makes people less likely to change their minds anyway. After arguing for a while, they get to thinking that what they thought in their worst moment was what they believed all along."

Mom taught me that when things get tense with another dog, I should walk with him. It's easier to understand someone when you're walking the same path together than when you're arguing over a bone. "Don't they see that everyone wants the same thing?" I asked. "They'll get what they want more easily if they all work together."

"You can't walk together if you're stuck at home, alone in your head."

I can't stand when Mom mixes too much right in the wrong and too much wrong in the right. "I don't understand. Am I supposed to be good and yell at people, or nice and kill people?"

"You don't have to choose. You can be safe *and* nice," Mom lied, as if she hadn't just tried to push a man off a cliff for being friendly. "Fortunately, we'll have to worry about it less in a couple of days."

"Why? Is the boogeyvirus over? Thank Dog, I thought it would never end!"

"No, but I start work on Monday, so we'll have less time to travel." Mom's eyes drifted toward the horizon to remind herself that there was still enough room in the world for everyone. "It's probably for the best. It's exhausting having to figure out the difference between right and wrong all the time."

"But I thought the point of being a referee was that you get to decide what's right and wrong," I said. "For a referee, every decision is right. Right?"

From the way she didn't answer, I couldn't tell whether she'd heard me or not.

The Wagon continued drifting toward My Hometown. Now that I thought about it, it sounded nice to have a home larger than a mattress again that wasn't always swaying this way and that. I could nap while Mom made cups of tea, because she wouldn't need to open all the doors to the wind and cold every time she wanted warm, milky comfort. Mom would have electricity coming from the walls and wifi in the air. Even the Witch would have the sky to talk to all the time. Too late, I realized that those things were just bait for The Stuck to suck us in. To have those comforts, we would need to leave the Outside behind. Before I realized what was happening, the freeway widened and the trap snapped shut behind us.

"Is life going to be like it was when I was a puppy?" I asked as we came out of a tunnel. The Golden Gate Bridge filled the front window like the mast of a ghost ship. "You know, back before I was a business dog and I sat at home all day staring at my paws?"

"From what everyone's saying on the internet, I don't think that we'll even be allowed out of the house. Except maybe when you go to the bathroom."

"But how will we get food? I won't have to survive on kibble alone, will I?"

"I think I'm allowed to go to the supermarket, but I'm not sure if there are restrictions on how often."

Something felt horribly wrong as soon as we mounted the bridge. A creepy stillness filled the air, making it hard to breathe. "Holy crow, Mom! Slow down!" I whimpered.

"What do you mean? I'm only going a *little* over the speed limit."

"But you haven't stopped even once. You're gonna hit something if you're not careful."

"What are you talking about? The lane is clear," she said, like *I* was the one talking crazy.

I looked out the front window again. The bridge in front of us was completely empty. There were no clumps of tourists on the walkway nor other cars in the lanes around us. I checked the back window, but it was just as deserted. I'd never seen the Bridge like that before, even in the middle of the night.

We barreled toward the City, whose pavement and buildings covered the hills like a rash.

"I forgot how many people live around us," I said. I'd never thought of it as a bad thing before, but now that anyone could be a murderer, I understood why Mom felt trapped around people.

"Yeah. A virus trying to catch on in one of those small towns would be like trying to light a fire on a wet log. Around here, it could spread like a brushfire on a windy day."

"Don't you mean… *go viral?*" I corrected her. I waited for a laugh that didn't come.

At long, long last, the Wagon rolled over the final hill and came to rest outside the Stuck House. It settled into its usual spot across the street and closed its headlights. Mom and I sat at our posts for one last breath before dismounting. As we crossed the empty street, Mom hit the hibernation button on the key ring. Behind us, the light inside the Wagon darkened as it drifted off into a well-earned sleep.

Part 3
Grounded

Chapter 16

Don't Hold Your Breath

After a long trip, Mom is usually happy to run errands and spend the rest of our time not-driving and enjoying the cozy feeling you get when you know where you're sleeping tonight. Suddenly it didn't seem quite so relaxing to be somewhere without a reason to leave again.

That first morning, I woke up smelling like Head and Shoulders for Men in a bed so big that I could stretch all four legs at once without even touching Mom. After living in a space the size of a Momprint, all that leftover room felt off-kilter somehow, like the wobble of something moving a bit too fast with a screw loose. Four rooms that took more than two steps to cross felt vast compared to the moving envelope that had delivered me to nine states. But then I remembered that these were the only walls I would see for a while, and they started closing in.

I spent the morning napping in my Mom-watching chair while Mom rode her bike indoors and watched other people's adventures for a change. Another shower seemed like a waste after only one sweat, but Mom scrubbed herself from head to toe as she prepared to face My Hometown again. She scrubbed the cooties from behind her ears and between her toes until the steam blurred every window in the house. When she was dressed, she gathered her keys, wallet, and the Witch and looked around as if she was forgetting something else.

"I'm right here." I followed her into the kitchen. "Where are we going?"

Mom opened the cabinet under the sink where the cleaning supplies hid mostly-forgotten. "I'm just going to the grocery store," her voice came from inside the cabinet. "I won't be gone long." Bottles clattered and Mom grunted. She came out with a pair of rubber-ducky-grey gloves and put them in her pocket. The fingers flopped out like tentacles trying to crawl free.

"I'll be right back. You be good." She kissed the spot between my eyes and left me to shelter in place while she went out to hunt and gather.

When she came home, she smelled like vegetables and stress.

"Ohmehgod ohmehgod ohmehgod! It's you!" I jigged when she came through the door. It all came out in a Beatlemania scream. If I had floppy hands like Mom's, I would have flapped them in front of my face to keep from fainting.

When she saw me, Mom squeezed a smile through clenched teeth. "Did you miss me?" I caught a whiff of green beans and tofu as she plopped the bags on the ground to free up her patting hands.

"Boy did I ever! Pat my head! No, my butt! No, my head! No, my butt!" I ran in figure eights to show her how to do it right.

"Sheesh, Spud. I was only gone for an hour," she counted. "How can you miss me when you've been with me every minute of every day for like a month?"

I tried to tell her about all the fears I'd feared alone in this enormous Stuck House, but I was too overjoyed that none of them were true, so it came out like, "EEEEEEE!"

Mom smoothed the zoomies out of my front half and my butt shook out the rest. When I could hold my nose still for a proper sniff, I inspected the bags on the floor. "Where were you?"

I snuffled. "Oh Dog, I missed you so much! I thought you were dead of the virus. What did you get me? Anything good?"

"I sure hope these groceries last, because I'm not doing that again any time soon." Her voice was weary as a soldier coming home from war. Also like a soldier coming home from war, she would eventually yearn for the excitement of the supermarket to break up the monotony of a safe civilian life. But that was all part of a future we couldn't imagine yet.

"You won't leave me home alone anymore? You really mean it?" I squealed. "I mean… Why?" By now I was skeptical of dreams coming true. After all, the boogeyvirus granted Mom's wish to be left alone, and it had turned into a curse that not even Mom would wish for on purpose.

"I didn't anticipate how harrowing it would be during quarantine."

"But you love grocery shopping. It's your favorite kind of shopping," I reminded her. "You went grocery shopping in Arizona. Remember how you didn't die afterward?"

"Yeah, but I'd never been to those stores before so I didn't know what was normal. Plus, the rules were mostly a precaution since Sedona hadn't had any confirmed cases yet. The virus has been spreading in San Francisco for weeks already. I've never noticed how often strangers are in my personal space before."

This wasn't the first time I'd had this talk with Mom. By now I practically had the script memorized. "You just haven't been in a city in a while. You'll get used to it."

"You don't understand!" Mom said, like her life depended on being understood. "Everyone was trying so hard to stay away from each other that they just stood still in the aisles waiting to be alone. I couldn't reach anything because some twit was always in front of what I was looking for, waiting for me to go away."

So this was the version of The Talk where I had to remind Mom about sharing. I'd never been inside a grocery store before, but I'd seen them on TV. People with big smiles pushed tractor-sized food strollers down empty lanes. On TV, no one's stroller ever blocked the cheese sticks and the freezer door never got too foggy if the guy next door took too long picking the right flavor of Eggos. As far as I could tell, the problems with grocery stores were all figments of Mom's imagination.

The problem was that Mom's food aggression was real, even if the challenge from other shoppers was imaginary. Anyone who stepped between her and the baby carrots or veggie burgers once she'd locked on risked being torn to shreds. Not that Mom was dangerous. She knew that whatever she was after would be taken away if she tore someone limb from limb to get it. But *not* murdering is exhausting, and sometimes it takes all the energy you have to be civilized. Mom needed lots of reminders and praise for being a *good girl* when she didn't bite anyone's head off, and long breaks to cool down between challenges.

"Couldn't you just say *excuse me* like you do on a narrow trail?" I suggested. "You can always just step into the freezer case to let them go around, right?"

"There's nowhere to hide with so many shopping carts blocking the way. There's *always* some oaf standing in front of what you want to buy. It helps being small because I can usually just knick around them and be gone with my yogurt or mustard before they even notice I'm there. But now that I can't get close, I have to be patient and, like, *wait* for them to move on. Do you know how long some people spend reading labels? It's like they're gonna be tested on the ingredients before they leave the store."

"But what about the *excuse me* part? Did you try that?"

"No. Because I was holding my breath."

"You held your breath for all that time?"

"No, just when I was near people. But if I said *excuse me*, they might turn around and breathe in my direction," she said, like it was the most obvious thing in the world. "It was safer to wait. Still, nothing makes you impatient like holding your breath."

"I'm sure people were grateful that you were so considerate."

"Hardly! Whenever I walked past someone, they turned their back on me and put their nose right between soup cans or whatever. Half of them just stood like statues with their noses against the shelves waiting for me to go away. They wouldn't even turn enough to figure out whether to go left or right when I reached around to get something. It was eerie, like the end of the *Blair Witch Project*."

"That's nothing new. Witches put people in trances all the time," I said expertly. "It happens to *you* every day."

Her anger slipped for only a moment, but it was long enough for me to catch a glimpse of the sadness hidden underneath. "With everyone acting like zombies and the stress of needing a breath but being afraid to take it… It was a lot."

"Being a *good girl* is hard work. You deserve a reward." In my best *here comes the airplane* voice I said, "Do I smell green beans and tofu?"

She missed the hint as her restlessness ratcheted back up. "Get this!" She held up a finger, warming it up to emphasize a devastating point. I braced myself for the finger to jab at me and the floor many times before the story was over. "So I wanted one of those doughnuts I like, right?" Donuts are like cheese sticks for Mom. When it takes extra bravery to get home without killing any strangers, Mom rewards herself with a donut. "But they weren't in the basket where they usually are, and the whole bakery case was locked." I didn't like where this story was going. You don't get between Mom and pastries. "There was a sign that they had them behind the bakery counter, so I waited in line…"

"Oh no!" I moaned. If this story started with Mom waiting in line, it was definitely going to end in blood.

"I was trying not to breathe, and to stay 6 feet away from everyone, because I'm responsible, right?" She paused and gave me a look that dared me to disagree.

"Right," I said, as you do when someone's brandishing a finger and you don't want them to point it at you.

"… but the woman behind the counter was so slow!"

"She had no idea the danger she was in," I gulped. Mom will do just about anything to avoid asking people for something, especially if what she's asking for is as important as a donut. The asking takes almost all the bravery she has, and the wait to be released turns her into a ticking time bomb.

"I know, right? No sense of urgency!" Mom seethed. Her eyes pointed at me, but the finger waved wide as she gave an exasperated shrug. "I'd been waiting for at least 5 minutes. Holding my breath the whole time, trying to be invisible every time someone walked in the door…" The finger waved at the ceiling like the shot in the air that gets everyone's attention. "… and then this guy walks in and stops right in front of me!"

"He cut you in line?" I eeped, hoping that was the right answer. "How rude! Do you need help burying the body?"

"Well no." The finger dropped and she fired a couple of shots into the floor as she continued, "But this dunderhead, he walks in the door, and—even though there are signs *everywhere* that say you should spend as little time in the store as possible—" she circled the finger to show where *everywhere* was, "… this jackass just *stops* 2 feet in front of me, totally oblivious, and checks his phone."

254

"… And you can't punch him in the nose because you might get boogers on your fist and then touch your face…" I said, to let her know I was still listening.

"Right! And I'm already impatient because I'm holding my breath and waiting for the world's slowest bakery attendant to make a latte. I'm getting lightheaded, and he *still* won't move…"

"So what did you do?" I asked. "Passive-aggressively faint?"

"To get his attention I swept my hands in a *move it along, buster* gesture." She seemed disappointed that the story wasn't ending in the epic battle she'd prepared for.

"And then what happened?" I shivered.

"And then he left and they were out of the kind of doughnuts I like."

"Oh."

"Like I said, it was awful." She uncocked the finger and noticed for the first time that the groceries were still in their bags.

I watched from my Mom-watching couch as she put the food away, slamming the cabinet doors more than usual. She was like a feral creature who, once it had a taste for freedom, couldn't get comfortable with the confinement and structure of town.

She sat. She stood and stalked across the kitchen a couple of times, opening the cabinets and fridge doors only to slam them again. She ripped a banana off the bunch and scowled at it to show how furious she was that it wasn't a donut. The Stuck House was supposed to be the only place where the universe had to obey her rules, but now she couldn't even boss around a lousy banana. She dumped it back in the bowl with a little extra oomph to prove her point.

"Let's go for a walk," she said finally. "I need to burn off these nerves."

"I thought you'd never ask!" I ran to the door to remind her where it was.

As the Mayor, I was dying to check on my constituents and smell all that had happened in My Hometown while I was away. My Trail, which I patrolled at least once a week, was a three-and-a-half-mile path along the last strip of land before earth gives way to sea. Way back in New Mexico, the Witch had briefed us on the brouhaha that erupted when every bored person in California visited My Beach on the same day. A day like that is usually called *summer*, but this year it was called *irresponsible*. So they closed every beach in California as punishment. Only people who didn't need a car to get there were allowed on the beach, which made us exceptional. The Stuck House clung like a barnacle onto the flank of a steep hill, exactly one mile from the End of the World.

I checked over my shoulder to make sure that Mom was coming to the door. "Does this mean that we need to run down the hill?" I asked. "… and then back up again?"

"I think it's okay if we park downtown." Mom is usually an encyclopedia of parking rules, but this time it sounded like she was asking me.

"Won't it look suspicious if we sneak to the beach in a car?" I asked. "What will we say when they question us?"

"I hadn't thought of that. The stores are closed, so we can't say we're shopping."

"And we can't say we're visiting a Friend because that's illegal too," I reminded her, "even if you *had* friends to visit."

"God, I'm not used to proving my right to be out in public. I guess I'll just run with my ID so I can prove that we live in town if I get stopped." Mom found her wallet among the counter groceries that didn't have an *away* to be put in, peeled a card from inside, and slipped it into her pocket.

Instead of the Wagon, we mounted our inconspicuous car, which still had all of its paint and no mirrors out of place to raise suspicion. The car rolled down the steep hill and came to rest in the same beachfront neighborhood where it usually parks.

As we walked, Mom looked from side to side, waiting for the Law to jump out of someone's driveway and demand to see our papers. I strained at the leash to sniff the unfamiliar signs lined up like sentries along the path. Each stood at attention as far from the last as it took to walk in a minute. Their big, heavy letters smelled of aggression and suspicion.

"What do they say?" I snorted.

"They're telling us to *GO HOME!*" Mom read.

"Rude."

"No kidding. I get the sentiment, but there are nicer ways to say it."

There were more signs in front of every car kennel, and a fence of crime scene tape that warned of the dire consequences of parking there. The pier was gated and chained, and there were no fishermen with buckets of fish guts blocking the sidewalk.

I smiled at some of the same people that I usually see on my patrols and Mom waved. They waved back, but went wide as they approached, turning their smiles away before anyone could catch real friendship. It was exactly how Mom behaved when she was at risk of having to say hello to an almost-Friend. Suddenly she bomes very interested in the label on her crackers, reading the ingredients as intensely as a whodunnit until the coast is clear.

At first, I forgot. I thought my neighbors were avoiding Mom's smell until I remembered that she'd already showered today.

The filth keeping my Friends on the far side of the sidewalk wasn't coming from Mom's armpits, but much deeper inside.

When we reached the second hill, I recognized Rick and Diane ahead. Rick and Diane walk the second hill every morning with treats in their pockets, looking for dogs to pat. I'm always happy to oblige.

There's no time for patience when you remember how much you miss a Friend. I raced to meet them while Mom used the leash as a brake, pulling my sprint into slow motion. It was just like that scene where two friends run into a hug while the music swells. As I came into range, I veered to Rick and Diane's side of the trail and slowed down for treats.

Just as our eyes met, there was a yank on the leash.

I looked back at Mom, but she wasn't behind me anymore. She was already a leash-length ahead, barely keeping her walk from exploding into a run. She turned her head away and lifted her paw in a *hello* to show Rick and Diane that it wasn't because she didn't recognize them that she didn't stop.

I pulled back on the leash with all my might. "Mom, wait!" I looked back at Rick and Diane, who were also smiling and holding up *hello* hands instead of reaching for their pockets.

"You guys, it's me. Oscar. Your friend. Haven't you missed me?" I walked sideways as slow as I could to stop what was happening, but Mom's mind was already made up. The only treat I could offer Rick and Diane was a view of my unpatted butt as we walked away.

"What was that all about?" I asked when I caught up to Mom. "Didn't you see that it was Rick and Diane that you were waving to?"

"People's boundaries have changed, Spud. And Rick is pretty old. He's in good shape, but we don't know what kind of health conditions he might have. We'll have to give them space for a while."

"But Rick and Diane love me," I reminded her. "They would never turn their backs on me. You're the dirty one. Can't you stand back or something instead?"

"It's not about how much they love you, Spud. It's about how much you respect them."

"No fair! Love is supposed to add to life, not take the best parts away. This isn't America anymore! I want to go back to the way things were before."

"Me too, buddy. Me too."

My Trail ends at the world-famous Wooden Taco Bell, where you can order quesadillas and fizzy drinks from the beachside window without putting on shoes. Usually, the Wooden Taco Bell is swarming with as many tourists as Alcatraz, but today the beach was deserted and the quesadilla window was dark.

"This is terrifying. Thank goodness work starts tomorrow." Mom tapped the turn-around pole and *about-faced* toward the car. "I don't think I can handle this stress without a distraction."

Chapter 17

Cabin Fever

The next morning, the Witch woke us up before the sun. I needed to let Mom run out her zoomies so she could behave around our new collies, but how? The beach was bound to rile her up more than the run would calm her down, and I had no idea if escaping the Law yesterday was just a fluke.

"Let's not run at the beach today," I coached. "I don't like all the new signs that are hanging out down there these days."

"Me neither," Mom said. "Where do you want to go?"

"How about the Haunted Highway?"

Back in ancient times, the Haunted Highway used to be a road for cars. These days, bushes crowded in too close for a car to squeeze through and roots had chewed up most of the pavement, but you could still smell the rusty skeletons of old wrecks buried in the bushes like a forgotten bone. The ghosts blew in with the morning fog and swirled featherlike through the brush until the sun shined them away around lunch time.

"That trail's at the other end of town," Mom said. "The shelter in place order says that we have to stay within 5 miles of home."

We usually run six miles before work, but I couldn't remember if six was more or less than five. "Five miles by mapp or by car?" I asked.

"Good point. The trailhead is probably only 4 as the crow flies, but then we keep running south, which will take us even farther from the house. The turnaround is certainly more than 5 miles from here, no matter how you count it."

If we got it wrong, would Mom drop dead from the poison air the moment she crossed over the five-mile barrier? But staying home was a different kind of poison. "Aw, that's just another one of the Witch's lies," I decided. "She's trying to trap you again."

"No, I think it's real this time. People are getting really grumpy about it on social media."

"But there's no one out there but ghosts. They won't mind if you have a deadly virus because they're already dead."

"You're right. I think it's fair to measure the 5 miles from where we park, so long as we stay within town limits," Mom said in the same voice she used to get our stories straight in Death Valley.

"Do they have town limits in the woods?" I asked.

"Who knows. The important thing is that *we* don't know, so we have a plausible answer if somebody asks."

We arrived at first light. The car stopped in the milky shadows a few steps from where the road became trail. Mom hit a button on the windowsill and all the door locks thumped in unison without triggering the horn. We looked both ways and scurried into the trees, away from spying windows.

The mist swallowed the pitter-patter of my steps as I ran through a forest as silent as a grave. Even the cough-drop smell of the eucalyptus trees was muted by the gloom.

The trees gave way and the trail opened up like a balcony as Mom's wrist beeped the first mile. On a less ghostly day, this balcony would give me one last look at My Hometown before the trail swooshed back into the forest. After that, there were nothing but hills humping one behind another in a long chain of unbroken wilder-ness all the way to Ellay. On days like today, when My Hometown was swallowed by mist, you could pretend like humans never chopped up the wilder-ness to begin with.

262

Between the second and third wrist beep, we rounded the last shrub at the top of the hill and the world fell away in front of me. Far below, the ocean bit into the land and swallowed everything between here and Japan. I had seen the ocean a million times, of course, but looking at it from up here on the Haunted Highway always felt like discovering the End of the World for the first time.

"Should we keep going?" Mom asked.

"Is it too far?" I looked downhill at the road that would take us effortlessly away from all the mean signs and snot-nosey neighbors. We could let the hill carry us all the way to the dead spot at the bottom, where the Witch couldn't tell us the mean things the internet had to say, and we could pretend everything was back to the way it was before.

"It's too far to go all the way down and back before work," Mom said. I couldn't tell if she was planning an escape or just counting.

"Do we have to go back?" I looked longingly toward the ocean. Despite waves relentlessly pushing its boundaries every day since the beginning of time, the tide always retreated in the end.

"There's no law that says we have to go all the way to the bottom," Mom said, the ocean pulling on her eyes as much as it was on mine.

"Isn't there a law that says we *can't* go all the way to the bottom?"

"Anyone who sees us will be just as guilty as we are." Mom tested a first step toward rebellion.

We stood on the edge, leaning toward the wilder-ness for a long moment. The Witch ruined it with a jarring clang.

Mom jumped, then sagged. "Who am I kidding?" She turned away. "There's no escape. Not anymore. Come on, let's go to work."

Mom turned and let fate pull us back downhill toward the Stuck House, which was about to be transformed into an office. I couldn't wait to see the metamorphosis, but for someone whose greatest wish was about to be granted, Mom didn't seem to be in such a hurry.

After her third shower in as many days, Mom tore the plastic off of a box and pulled out a laptop like a rabbit out of a hat. I stood in the kitchen bright-eyed and waggy-tailed, waiting for my first assignment.

She reverently laid the shiny slab on the kitchen table with a *voilà* flourish. "That's it! We're at work now." She cracked open the lid and the laptop made a warm, welcoming sound. "I'm liking this new commute."

"What do you mean?" I asked, trying to reach the tabletop with my nose.

"Our work is inside this laptop now. We can take it anywhere we go."

"Oh phew! I thought we would be grounded in the Stuck House forever. Where should we go first? I vote for Utah. Or Oregon. Do you think Lily misses me very badly?"

"It was more a figure of speech," Mom said like I was the Weather Jinx bringing rain to her parade. "The whole reason we can work from home is because we're not allowed out of our homes. But look!" She kicked out a leg. "Sweatpants! No more tyranny of buttons and non-elastic waistbands. Isn't it heaven?"

"Dogs don't wear pants," I reminded her. "That's why we're so happy all the time."

Still wearing the heavenly smile of someone with a wonderful secret, Mom turned back to the laptop. It greeted her with a soft, soothing glow.

"So wait, the only time we get to go outside is when we're inside that laptop?" I asked. "Aren't laptops, like, extra big, mega-powerful Witches?"

But Mom didn't answer because her attention was already trapped inside the screen.

When your job is to supervise an office full of people, and your Stuck House is your office, work is much less exciting. I spent the workday on my Mom-watching chair with nothing to do but study the faces Mom makes when she has long, meaningful conversations with her laptop using only her fingers and eyes.

As time went by, there were other signs that Mom was losing it. She started talking to the laptop like it was a person, asking it questions out loud and making gestures like it would help the screen understand her better. You can bark at a screen like it's your friend, but a laptop can't scratch your butt while it tells you how handsome you are. When I butted my head under the table to make sure she was okay, Mom got annoyed and said I was interrupting.

She couldn't help it. It was in her nature to get annoyed, and I was the only one around.

After the Law didn't hassle us for driving to My Trail or the Haunted Highway, we got bolder about visiting other trails in My Hometown. Pretty soon, we were patrolling a different trail every day of the week. It was a dangerous job braving the poisonous air, but it would be more dangerous to be trapped in the Stuck House with a restless Mom. As long as I kept feeding her fresh air and sunlight, she didn't get all wrong in the head like a zoo resident that plucks out his fur or grinds his tusks to nubs on the wall.

As we got used to our new routine, I figured out that I had to take Mom on patrol each morning *before* she laid fingers on the laptop or else it would never let her go. Once the screen was open, she could stare into its warm glow forever as her poop juice went cold and the windows went dark behind her.

Over time, even the boogeyvirus's tyrannical rule started to feel normal. As the weeks went by and wilder-ness took back over what used to be America, Mom's legs, men's faces, and the trails all became shaggier than I'd ever seen them. Weeds and poison oak swelled into places where no one had let them grow before, until the trails began to disappear altogether. Despite its pavement, even My Trail became overgrown as the *GO AWAY* signs multiplied.

I'd always doubted whether people existed when they weren't with me, even before everyone disappeared. Now I knew that people folded into laptops and disappeared into The Cloud until Mom clicked on them again. As time stuck still in our boogeybunker, I began to worry that my friendshapps were getting out of date. If the boogeyvirus ever ended, I might reemerge into a world that had moved on without me, like Rip van Tinkle.

As much as I liked running on trails every day, I missed the excitement of our runs in the City before work. We used to arrive so early that the City still twinkled as we came off the freeway for a landing. We'd leave the car in the loving care of the man who always raised the gate to the kennel as soon as he saw us coming. The car-nanny protected our windows and the change in the cup holder from thieves while Mom and I ran around the City, watching the sunrise behind the Grey Bridge and Alcatraz. When we were done, I'd watch the car while Mom took the packpack into the building attached to the car-daycare. When she came back, wet and smelling like soap, we'd walk to the office together. Back when there was still an office to walk to.

One morning, around the time when the sun started waking up as early as us, Mom pulled out more clothes than usual. She put on her running clothes and packed the extras into a packpack just like she used to in The Before. She carried the packpack out to the car, and this time, instead of turning its nose downhill into My Hometown, it turned uphill toward the stream of roads that all dumped into the City.

We hadn't made this drive in dog-years, and the surprise was too exciting to ruin it by asking where we were going. All that mattered was that we weren't stuck inside a laptop. I sat in the back seat watching the old sights go by and tried to fill the empty world back up with memories. I imagined other cars on the freeway slowing us down and people walking in the crosswalks when it was supposed to be our turn to go. I imagined the silhouettes of people on the empty train that chugged beside the road for a few blocks, and let my imagination paint more silhouettes in the dark windows of the shops and office buildings.

I pressed my nose to the glass as we came in for a landing, anxious to sniff everything that had happened since my last patrol.

"You missed the car kennel!" I wagged. My nose left a smear on the glass as I tried to make sense of the metal curtain covering the entrance.

"Can't go there anymore, Spud," Mom said. "It's closed."

She landed the car in a spot across the street, where anyone could break its windows to steal the precious empty cans under the copilot's chair.

"Not here!" I squeaked. "The car might get covered in meter-maid droppings or beat up by a stray."

"I know, but the garage was owned by the gym, and the gym closed for good a few months ago. They'll be tearing the building down any day now." She looked longingly at the car kennel, without whose shelter the car never would have survived alone on the mean City streets. "We'll have to take our chances with break-ins, but at least they're not ticketing."

I knew that the boogeyvirus had changed things, but I didn't know that they were *that* bad. Meter maids may be pests, but they were also the only people in the City that you could count on to show up on time. If cars could park for two hours and one minute with their wheels pointing any which way, who knew what chaos would follow.

"What do you mean they're tearing it down?" I asked. Imagining the whole City crumbling into the earth reminded me of the last thing Mom taught me before the world closed down. "Is it gonna be like Saint Bernardino?"

"San Bernardino?" Mom asked. "God, I hope not. What put that idea in your head?"

"You said they were tearing the City down. I thought you meant now that everyone lives inside laptops they're gonna throw the City into a hole, just like Saint Bernardino."

Dogs aren't sentimental, but I was glad Mom had brought me back to run our old route again before they chopped down all the sparkly buildings, leveled the hills, and plowed the gingerbread houses into quicksand.

Back when this was America, the first few blocks of our run used to be when we practiced synchronized leashing. In our glory days, we used to impress everyone we knocked out of the way as we ran upstream through the flesh flood pouring from the train station. We would dart between the business bros making googly eyes at their witches and leap over napping strays without disturbing either one.

On this morning, the sidewalks felt king-sized. Only a few stale-smelling people wandered the streets, arguing through their muzzles with invisible ghosts and lamp posts. They built colonies of igloos on the empty sidewalks and landscaped their yards with cardboard. They fenced in their property with shopping carts and bicycle parts. Even before the boogeyvirus, Mom used to hold her breath against the smell of shame and wildness in the damp, shady spots under the freeway. Now we couldn't hold our breath for long enough to get away from the poisonous air in the suburban igloo sprawl.

"Know what the weirdest part is?" Mom gasped when we reached the clear air behind the baseball stadium.

"I can't pick, there are too many."

"Even the homeless people are wearing masks."

"Just because they have a healthy fear of baths doesn't mean their safety isn't important," I reminded her.

"Of course. All I'm saying is that someone who takes a crap on the sidewalk in broad daylight probably doesn't care about manners or hygiene. Each one seems to be missing some critical piece of clothing, but somehow they've all kept track of their masks."

"But they're wearing them over their eyes," I pointed out.

Mom ran wide to keep out of the snore cloud of a man napping on a bench. "Do you know how pervasive a cultural norm has to be for someone to follow it even when they don't notice that they're only wearing one high heel?"

"How are *you* going to keep your muzzle up against all the tourists?" I asked. A few days before, the mailman had brought Mom a packet of neck sleeves that she could pull up and down as she ran. Mom needed the sleeve because, as she explained to me, she would drown in her own sweat, spit, and snot before we got back to the car if she tried to run with a veterinarian's mask. She still hadn't figured out how to make the sleeve stick in place for longer than a breath or two before it fell off her nose and scrunched uselessly around her neck.

"I've been wondering the same thing," Mom said. "But I have a feeling there won't be as many tourists as we're used to." She tried for the gazillionth time to hang her muzzle on her nose in preparation for the crowds as we ran onto the I'mbarkadero.

I'mbarkadero is just a fancy word for a crowded sidewalk with cars passing on one side and boats on the other. It gets its name from a handsome and mysterious dog whose real name no one knew, yet all who met him said they loved him the moment they set eyes on his stumpy little tail. Not knowing his name, they called him the *I'mbarkadero* after the dashing way he used to run around the waterfront, barking at tourists, and scooters, and snakeboarders, and other dogs. But that was in the days when this was America, when you could introduce yourself to someone without them running from you in fear.

Back when this was America, runners would come to the I'mbarkadero from all over the City to run an adventure race that had no official start or finish line. We used to race around clumps of tourists wandering in S's on the sidewalk. We ducked under pointing arms that shot out of crowds, and dodged photographers who backed up without a warning beep. We feinted around farmers carrying crates of vegetables to the market and sidestepped commuters dismounting the boat-bus with their snouts in cups of poop juice, all without being squished by bikes, scooters, or snakeboarders, and keeping a nose out for bad dogs to bark at. On top of all that, there was always another runner a step ahead or behind, competing for the gaps in the crowd and hogging the best lines. It was great fun, and unlike any other run.

But that morning, when we rounded the baseball stadium and slingshotted onto the I'mbarkadero, the race course was deserted—or what passed for deserted in the City, anyway. There was no farmer's market blocking the sidewalk in front of the Furry building, nor men carrying precarious pyramids of peaches through the absent crowds. No poop-juice-snouted commuters hustled up the half-bridge from the boat stop. The lady selling tickets to Alcatraz sat in her tardis playing with her witch.

It was quiet when we reached Fisherman's Wharf, where the tourists used to be so thick that all locals must turn back on pain of torture. Now, the only sound in the air was the clanging of flags wagging their tails against flagpoles as they flapped in the wind. Mom tapped the usual turn-around pole and we *about-faced* to check on the car.

I rushed back the way we'd come, pulling the leash to urge Mom to hurry. From the moment we turned around, every step would bring me closer to my new collies. I still joined every meeting from under the desk like I used to, but these days only Mom's paw reached down for pats and no one could see how cute I was from inside a screen. I could hardly wait to see the joy on their faces when they met me in real life.

I pulled Mom the whole way back to the car, too excited to be patient with her two-legged pace. When we reached our finish line, Mom took the packpack out of its hiding place in the trunk and unlocked a door I'd never walked through before. Still wearing her running clothes, Mom led me up an unfamiliar stairwell, down an empty hallway, and straight to a door that looked just like all the others. Somehow, I knew that whatever was behind this door belonged to me. I pressed my nose into the corner below the knob and waited for it to open.

The moment I felt the door twitch against my nose, I shoved it open and burst inside. "I'm here!" I awooed.

"Quiet!" Mom shushed. "I'm not sure if they've actually cleared you with the building management yet."

I looked around a room as big as a City apartment and as quiet as Fisherman's Wharf. "Where is everybody?" I asked.

"They're still home." Mom dropped her bag in the middle of the floor the way she does when no one's looking. "It's just my turn to water the plants."

"You water plants for a living?"

"Of course not. I think of watering the plants more like an act of faith. If I don't let the past wither up and die, maybe we'll be able to come back to normal someday."

She led me up a flight of stairs into a bathroom. Not the kind of bathroom where you can say hello to your neighbor in the next stall by ducking under the fence, but the kind of bathroom with one potty, one sink, a shower, and the kind of soap that doesn't come from a spout.

"Not in there!" I spread all four of my legs wide and stuck my butt to the ground. "Dogs get baths in bathrooms like that!"

"No baths, I promise. I just can't have you wandering around without me."

I sat on Mom's soaked running clothes and watched a blurred version of her through the shower window as the bathroom filled with steam. There was definitely something strange about my new office. Why did they have a bath room rather than a potty? Why was there a dining table, a fireplace, and an oven? And where was everybody?

When Mom opened the bathroom door, I escaped faster than the steam. Mom followed me back downstairs and banged through cupboards until she found all the supplies for poop juice. While the machine sputtered and choked, Mom opened the fridge. Her face scrunched and her tongue fell out.

"Ugh! Nobody thought to check the milk?" she practically barfed.

"Who's in charge of milk-checking around here?" I asked. "Just say the word and I'll get him fired."

"It's no one's job. This is a startup. Everyone pitches in where they can."

"Is *star-dup* another word for an apartment?" I asked. "Because that's what this place looks like."

"It *is* an apartment. That's where startups are supposed to be born." She took her mug of poop juice to one of the empty desks. "It's a shame we'll never get to work here and have that 'three guys in a garage' experience."

"What do you mean we'll never get to work here?" The disappointment was too much to bear. "I don't get to be an office manager again?"

"Not anytime soon, Spud." Mom looked sad for me but not herself. "The company's outgrown this office while we were all at home. There wouldn't be enough room, even if they were letting offices open again."

"What about when they start the City over from scratch? Will there be a place for us then?"

"It's starting to feel like offices are a thing of the past." She didn't even bother to hide her relief. "Every time the date to lift the restrictions gets close, they push it back again. The safety recommendations are such a pain that no one really wants to bother anyway."

I flopped on the ground with a huff. "But you said the *sit-stay* order was almost over."

"They're saying it's okay to leave our houses, but we're not allowed to actually *do* anything yet. We can't see friends, we can't go to restaurants, and we *definitely* can't gather in big groups like offices." I'd never seen Mom so gleeful at work. "Even if we could, they would make us build plexiglass forts around each desk so we would still be alone, except in less comfortable pants."

"But why, though? We've been so good," I pleaded.

"I know, Spud." She opened the laptop. "Summer's almost here. They can't possibly keep people penned up much longer." She turned her attention to the screen and didn't speak again for the rest of the day.

Chapter 18

Caps Lockdown

As the days and nights passed, I worried how so much time in the Witch's captivity was affecting Mom. I don't know what you call it when someone stays home all day, watches Netflix instead of cleaning up, goes to bed at an irresponsible time, and goes to work in the same sweatpants she slept in. Usually Mom teaches me words for what's wrong with people, but she can't teach something she doesn't notice herself. Without Mom's lessons, I couldn't tell if she was letting herself get stinky and staying in bed past sunrise because she was a good girl who followed rules, or if she just didn't care about pushing against the boogeyvirus anymore.

I was going a little stir crazy myself. All the love I had to give was wasted on Mom in the state she was in. I missed meeting new Friends and spreading joy with little more than a smile and a wiggle.

It had been so long since this was America that wilder-ness was taking over the abandoned places that civilization left behind. It wasn't just the poison oak covering the trails. The news reported on coyotes crossing the Golden Gate Bridge like wily tourists and people in Ellay seeing the sky for the first time in generations. When Mom and I did see other people on our runs, they turned their eyes away and pretended we weren't there, even outside the City where strangers didn't used to wear invisibility cloaks.

One weekend morning, the car stopped in the usual place at the bottom of the Haunted Highway. When I climbed into the copilot's seat for Mom to fasten the leash, there was a crowd outside the front window. A couple of dogs and a couple of people were standing in a very un-ghost-like way, blocking the spot next to the gate where the Haunted Highway began.

"Hey!" I shouted through the window. "Don't you know you're not allowed out of your stuck house?"

Mom shushed me and waved a friendly hello.

"That family could be dangerous," I warned. "They must have passed a hunerd *GO AWAY* signs on their way here." By this time, the *GO AWAY* signs had multiplied so many times that they lined the whole drive from the City to My Hometown, even in the places where there was nowhere to park or walk. "If they can't follow instructions, there's no telling what they might do next."

"They probably live here too," Mom said. "Be nice, they could be our neighbors."

She opened the last barrier separating our air from theirs. "Hi. Good morning. It's good to see you," she said, hitting the button on the key that told the car we'd be back soon.

"She lives so far away that she had to drive here!" the car beeped, tattling on Mom's misdeed in case they hadn't noticed yet.

"The lady is *leaning* on the sign that tells her to go home." I looked at Mom in disbelief. "Are you really gonna let her get away with that?"

Mom silently closed her nose and mouth behind a smile as the dogs and their people stepped out of our way. "I hate those signs," she said when it was safe to open the vents and breathe. "For my part, I'm happy to see people again. There's plenty of room out here for everyone. We'll just keep our distance, the same as we always do."

I looked carefully at the person on the other end of the leash. She smelled like Mom and had the same *pah-dumping* hitch to her stride as always. Only the smile and smooth forehead gave her away as an imposter. "You mean that it's okay to make Friends again?" I asked in disbelief.

"I sure hope so," the impostor said through Mom's mouth. "It's hard to tell a minor inconvenience from the end of the world when all you have to compare it to are the thoughts in your head. Especially when the only people who talk to you are the ones on TV telling you that everything's bad, other people will kill you, and you're filthy disease-ridden scum."

"I don't recall anyone trying to kill us."

"Okay, maybe not literally. But how can we find common ground when even looking at someone's face feels like a fight if only one of you is wearing a mask? I'm looking forward to meeting new people again, and learning from the ones who think differently from me."

Everything went back to normal as we ran through the peeling eucalyptuses with their bark like toilet paper after a cat tantrum. At the balcony overlooking My Hometown, I discovered a bike lying in the poison oak beside the trail.

"Oh no! Do you think it's hurt?" I ran as wide as the brush allowed in case the bike had the boogeyvirus.

"Maybe someone needed to use the bathroom," Mom said, purposely keeping her eyes out of the bushes.

Around the next bend, a man stood beside the trail waving the biggest knife you've ever seen.

"Zoinks!" I jumped.

I peeked around Mom's legs and watched him grab a handful of branches. He hacked savagely at them, grunting and slashing until they came away in his hand. He held the severed branches up in triumph for a brief moment before throwing them on the ground with the dismembered boughs of his other victims.

I relaxed. He was just making himself a salad.

He noticed us behind him. "It was getting too overgrown," he explained as he swung his knife-arm in another wide arc. He held up a pawful of severed leaves to show what he meant.

"Thank you," Mom said meaningfully.

"Should we report him for murdering the mountain?" I thought-whispered.

"Certainly not! Without people like him, you and I wouldn't have anywhere to run," Mom said, like getting away with murder was a decent and admirable thing to do. "We've all been so afraid of each other that we've forgotten how most people just want to help."

"Talking to screens makes people forget that?"

"You can't sit in companionable silence through a screen. The easiest way to get people talking on the internet is to disagree with them. Or agree with them about how awful the people you disagree with are. So everyone has just been sitting at home looking for things to disagree about. Pretty soon it starts to feel like everyone's out to get you and you're paying the bill for everyone else's needs. In regular life, mutual needs usually lead to opportunity. That guy wanted his trail clear, so we get a clear trail as well. Isn't that nice?"

Now I was really concerned. "Are you okay, Mom? It sounds like you're saying that other people make life better, not worse."

"Remind me I said that in a few months when we're stuck in a traffic jam and I have murder in my heart."

We passed one hiker, and then another on our journey to the top of the hill. Since the trails were usually empty, Mom never wore a neck sleeve on our runs around My Hometown, so her naked face was out for all the world to see. Instead, she took a deep gulp of air each time we approached someone and held it so no boogies could sneak in or out. Once they were behind us, Mom kept holding her breath for a count of three before letting it out like a tire with a slow leak to keep her boogeycloud as lean as possible.

"Sheesh, it sure is tough to pass someone going uphill these days," she gasped.

"Wouldn't it be easier to wear a muzzle?" I said.

The muzzle trend had really caught on since I saw my first wandering veterinarians in Arizona. These days, people were so into the craze that they teased viciously when some poor slob showed their whole face in public. Mom would wear her muzzle when she went somewhere without me, like the grocery store, but she still resisted running with a neck sleeve like she resisted pants with inflexible waistbands.

The smile fell off of Mom's face and lines dug into her forehead at the idea of being muzzled. "You've seen me sweat. I'll drown if I run with a mask, and the gaiter is useless if it keeps falling off my face."

"A muzzle is better than suffercating."

"The mask is meant to block my breath, but there's nothing to block if I don't breathe. If I'm not putting anyone in real danger and they still get scared, that's their problem. Anyway, the CDC says I don't have to wear a mask outside," she said in a *so there* tone.

"Your face scares people when they see-dee-see it without a muzzle," I reminded her. "People can't see you holding your breath. The muzzle is like a flag that says *Friend*. Without it, you might bark at a could-be Friend or play with a frenemy by accident." I'd been wearing bandanas for the same reason since long before humans adopted the trend. There are a lot of silly people out there who are afraid of dogs, so to set strangers at ease, beefy loudmouths like me need to dress nicely to show that we're civilized. It's impossible to be scared of a dog with flowers on his bandana, no matter how big he is or how loud he barks.

"Masks don't just block germs. They hide microexpressions and muffle the subtle tone shifts that tell us how we affect other people's feelings," Mom said, hiding her doubt behind big words and a know-it-all tone. "When people see a mask instead of a face, they reduce an entire person down to a threat. It's easy to forget that there are real people who may be warm, kind, funny, and interesting behind those masks. Forgetting how to empathize is a kind of sickness too, you know." She gulped gently for new air, trying not to suck in the exhaust of someone else's boogeyworkout. "Other people can wear masks if it makes them feel better, but now that people are coming out of their houses, I kind of want them to see that I'm more than just a disease vector. Maybe it'll help them remember that we don't have to disagree about everything."

"I thought that being right was the only thing you liked about talking to other people," I said. "You can't correct people without disagreement."

"Yeah, but how can you disagree with someone's face? I can't help my face."

"They can't tell whether it's loaded with boogeyvirus just by looking at you. They think you're trying to kill them."

"Pointing a smile at someone is different from a gun, isn't it? Why should I hide just because someone else finds my face upsetting? What's the point of a concealed-carry smile?"

"What if the face is scowling?" I asked, looking at a woman stalking up the trail with her muzzle pointed directly at us.

Mom sucked in a big huff of air, puffed out her cheeks, and puckered her lips as if she were running underwater. With her boogey-hole pointed away from the stranger as we passed, Mom didn't see the woman stop to glare at us with a look that made my hackles stand on end.

"MASK?" the Scowl barked in a voice like a stab wound.

"I was holding my breath, My Friend," Mom shouted over her shoulder, but not so forcefully that the germs in her shout would hit the lady. She held up her paw in a gesture that could have been a hello/goodbye wave and could have been a sign for the woman to shut up her own face.

"Mmmf marumf arglebargle," the Scowl shouted through her muzzle, but she had already become part of the background. Mom didn't see a reason to waste her breath re'splaining why her face wasn't a weapon and kept running.

I looked back to make sure the Scowl was shouting something like *That's a great idea!* I kept running with my nose facing my butt so I could keep an eye on the Scowl for signs of attack. Mom must not have been paying attention to where my face was facing, because I felt a tug on the leash and turned around in time to see her hit the ground like a chopped-down tree.

"Duck!" She and the Witch both smeared their faces into the dirt and gravel. Mom bounced right up and started running again without even looking down to inspect the Witch's scarred face or the blood on her own elbow and knee.

"Snotty, snippy, toldja so!" the Scowl shouted.

Mom yanked the leash to tell me to ignore the Scowl, but then it occurred to her that she'd actually heard the words this time. She poked a finger in her ground-side ear where the Witch's voice was missing. The kibble Mom wore in her ears to block out everyone but the Witch must have fallen out when she landed. When we turned around to find it, the Scowl was still standing a short sprint away and yelling advice on how Mom should live her life.

"I'd rather you not come any closer, My Friend," Mom snarled, holding up a muddy hand to tell the fink to *stay*.

"I'm *wearing* a *mask*!" the Scowl yelled.

"That's not why I don't want you coming closer," Mom grumbled. She spotted the ear kibble in the dirt, and swooped down to retrieve it, turning tail in the same movement and running away as fast as she could.

"See? Sharp teeth aren't the only dangerous thing about faces," I lectured when we'd put a few turns between us and the Scowl. "Sometimes they cut with insults. Insults that aren't true cut the deepest. Especially when they're loud."

"Maybe some people *do* need muzzles in public, even if they're outside," Mom said, taking my wisdom as her own.

"The muzzle doesn't just keep a dangerous dog from biting," I reminded her. "It's also a warning to keep your distance."

"Exactly. Just because *some* dogs need muzzles, there are people who assume that *all* dogs will just eat them on sight," Mom plagiarized. "We're outside. We were only within 6 feet of her for about a second, and even if I *had* been breathing,—which I *wasn't*— I would still need to actually be infected for her to get sick. Statistically, she's more likely to get hurt by a tree falling on her head."

"Speak softly and carry a big statistick," I agreed.

"Right! She acts like a mask is a badge and she's on patrol," Mom agreed, missing the point. "Like the rules themselves are what stops danger."

"The best defense is to take offense."

Mom's smile was gone and the lines above her eyebrows hardened for good as we ran the rest of the way on high alert for more Simons. She stayed on high alert, even after we'd finished running and the scabs from her run-in with the Scowl had hardened and healed.

I was starting to despair of ever making new Friends again.

Chapter 19

Tahoe-down

Stuck houses around the world had more than a hunerd days notched on their walls by the time Independence Day rolled around. I, for one, was getting pretty sick of independence. Because of the holiday, nobody would be checking on us for four whole days, and Mom needed something to keep her out of mischief.

"Why are you looking at all those places six hours away when it only takes three hours to drive to Tahoe?" the Witch tempted.

Mom fell right into her trap. "I bet it won't be *that* bad this year, since nobody's traveling."

I tried to remember a place so close that was worth the drive. "Which one's that?"

"You know: at the end of that horrible road where people don't know how to drive," Mom prodded, "so they go 20 miles an hour below the speed limit?"

I tried to remember, but the spell had gotten me, too.

"You remember: where we can never find parking, even if we arrive at sunrise?" Mom hinted.

I hmmmmed, but my memory was stuck.

"… the place where all of our friends' bosses have been hiding in their vacation homes since April?"

The only boss-castle I could think of belonged to Boss Charming. "We're going back to Utah?"

"No." Mom wagged her head. "You know, the place where we spend half the time stepping off the trail to get out of people's way, and the other half stepping off the trail to get around people who won't get out of our way?"

She waited for me to remember.

"The one with the mosquitos?" she added.

"Oh, right! Good idea. I don't know why we don't go there more often."

"Me neither. Look at all the great trails up there." Mom gave the Witch a fond scratch. "We'll hardly have to drive at all between trails. It's gonna be so relaxing!"

Mom packed a small bag with the scraps she uses for clothes in summer. After work that evening, we set out for the lake in the sky. When the road had faded to a flashing white line in the darkness, the Wagon slowed and crept into the blackness beyond the reach of the streetlights. Mom was just coming back from checking the shadows for a better hiding place, when a pair of lights paused for a closer look.

"Go away! I have to pee!" I shouted from inside the Wagon. "I can't go with you watching!"

"Hi," a voice said from behind the blinding lights. Mom stepped in front of the Wagon, blocking the light enough that I could just make out the white markings of a killer whale behind the eyebeams. "I just passed by here a few minutes ago and didn't see you, so I wanted to make sure you were alright," the voice explained.

I shouted unprintable things at the top of my bark until Mom spit out her liquid toothbrush. When her mouth was free, she said, "I was gonna sleep here. Is that okay?"

"Oh yeah, that's fine. I just wanted to make sure you were okay," repeated the Whale.

"Yup. Just fine," Mom repeated. She put her hand on the door but didn't open it yet in case the Whale needed anything else.

"Go away! For privacy!" I shouted.

"Okay. Well. Have a nice night," the Whale said. Its eyes shone on Mom's paw not-opening the door for another moment before it looked away.

Mom let me out to potty. I was still mid-stream when the Whale came back.

"I just remembered. There are people that live up that road there," the voice said. Mom looked over her shoulder at the rocky trail that she'd decided was too dangerous for the Wagon to hike on. "They're the kind of people that…" the Whale trailed off, searching for the right word.

"…that don't want to be bothered?" Mom suggested.

"…that don't like folks like me," the Whale finished, making it about himself.

"Oh crap. Okay." Mom waved me back into the Wagon.

"No more driving," I copiloted, sticking my butt to the ground so she couldn't boost me inside. "I'm tired. Let's sleep here."

"No can do, spuddy," Mom said. "Not out here in Conspiracy Country."

I didn't know what a *conspuriously* was, but the way Mom said it made me think it was something dangerous. I hopped inside and saved my questions for later. Once we were safely on the road I asked, "What do people have against whales? Besides that they're nosy and interrupt your sleep?"

"I guess it depends where we are. Out here, it's probably because people are suspicious of the government. Some people think that the virus is a hoax—that it's just a government plot to control us. Especially now that there are all these rules against liberty and the pursuit of happiness. Maybe the conspiracy theorists aren't *completely* out of touch with reality."

"This isn't America anymore," I agreed. It was like what Mom told the cowboy in New Mexico all those months before; you couldn't get deep enough into the wilder-ness to get away from what was happening. The whole world was still watching the same movie, but it was like the sound turned off when they went inside; everybody had to figure out their own story to go with the pictures. By the time they let us out again a dog-year later, everyone was telling a different version of the story. The plots were isolated inside people's heads for so long that the storylines evolved into different species, and the storytellers forgot how to mix their tales together into truth. Instead, people turned vicious and territorial about who got to decide the real reality.

"This van is sketchy enough as it is with its decals ripped off, the blacked-out windows, the mirror that looks more like a satellite dish, and that darned camera," Mom went on. "Being a government vehicle, some paranoid nut could think it's a surveillance van or something."

"Yeah, but did you notice how nice that Law was?" I asked. "Usually professional Simons try to protect the people in stuck houses from drifters like us, not the other way around. That's suspicious, don't you think?"

"I guess it depends on how they look at the situation. Some cops look at us and see homeless transients who are probably up to no good. Others see a woman alone and decide I need protection."

"Protecting from what?" I asked. I'd always relied on Mom to protect me. It never occurred to me that some dumbo might think she needed protecting herself. It would be his funeral.

"Protection from whatever they're scared of, I suppose." Mom shrugged. "We all have boogeymen lurking in the dark corners of our imaginations. The problems that we decide to prevent say a lot about what we're afraid of."

A bright spot appeared in the blackness of the front window. As the Wagon got closer, I made out a people-potty and a picnic table in the shadows. The Wagon rolled off the highway and paused for Mom to decide which of the stalls was least likely to shine a light in her face all night. It was an impossible choice, of course. The lights were always stationed so that no wagon had to spend a night in the dark.

Mom settled into bed and I made myself the little spoon, snuggling all the space from between us. That way, Mom would wake up to comfort me any time a car or potty door slammed in the dark.

A thump under the Wagon's belly woke me. The bed was humming and vibrating, which meant that Mom and the Wagon had been awake for some time already. I lifted my head for a better look at what was under the dense branches gobbling up the early-morning sunlight. Log cabins were tucked into the bed of dry pine needles between the trunks, well camouflaged except for their ice-rink-sized windows reflecting the first light of day. Mom's poop juice leapt out of its cup as we bobbled over potholes that hadn't been repaved since dinosaurs roamed the earth.

I yawned. "This trail must be very remote."

"Not really," Mom corrected. "This is one of the most visited spots in Tahoe besides the lake itself."

"How can that be?" The Wagon jostled and threw me around its belly like it wanted to throw up. "This road can only hold one car at a time. How would people even get here?"

"Look closer," Mom said mominously. "See the *PRIVATE PROPERTY* and *NO PARKING* signs in front of all the houses? That's a dead giveaway that this is an outpost of the City. Most of these places are probably Airbnbs or some tech mogul's vacation home."

I did as I was told and looked more closely, but with nature squeezing into all the crevices and covering everything with branches and pine needles, it still looked like an abandoned settlement that time forgot. When the Wagon could go no farther, it tucked itself into the very edge of a patch of rock-free dirt.

The Witch told us to get ready for a fourteen-mile circle. I looked over Mom's shoulder at the jagged line on the screen. It went up, up, up, with only small downs where it gathered itself for an even higher jump. Pictures like this could show the shape of a hill, but lately, Mom had been looking into graphs like this one as if gazing into a crystal ball that could predict the end of the boogeyvirus. I checked the side of the mapp that tells you how something will end, hoping to see the line come down as suddenly as it went up. Instead of a quick drop back to normal, the graph eased itself down so gradually that you hardly noticed that it was returning to its base. Even at the end, it spiked dramatically here and there to show that it couldn't be rushed.

"Do you want to do it forward or backward?" Mom asked. I couldn't tell if she was asking me or herself. "We could spread the climbing out over several miles so we hardly notice it and then let gravity take over when we're tired. Or we could get most of the climbing over with and then have a grinding downhill for most of the day."

"Tough decision." I considered my options. Mom gets grumpy if things change too quickly, and when they don't change quickly enough. "What do you think?" I asked, hoping for a hint.

"The reviews say that the steep part is *horrible* and *overgrown*, and that there will be a lot of *bushwhacking*," Mom read. "I'd rather deal with that going uphill than down."

"Good idea," I agreed. "I'm glad I thought of it."

Before we even started our hike, we found a real treasure: an unlocked people-potty! Its stink was like a punch in the nose, but Mom acted like it was a breath of fresh air after so many locked doors.

"It's even more fabulous than I remember!" she said, practically twirling with joy as she stepped into the dim cabin.

"Breathtaking," I agreed.

When we stepped back outside, Mom took a big gulp of the fresh, mountainy air before continuing into the forest. A wooden post guarded the spot where the trail pinched down to hiking size. On top of the post, someone had clamped a big bottle with a thin neck and a long beak.

"What's this?" I sniffed the stain at the base of the post. "It smells like poison."

"It's hand sanitizer!" Mom pushed down the bottle's head to make it sneeze a foul-smelling blob into her palm. She rubbed her hands together like a villain anticipating mischief. "Finally! A rational safety measure!"

A few steps away, a family of raccoons was fiddling with the dumpster. They weren't actually raccoons—they were a dog and his two people—but I'd never seen people or dogs trying to break *into* a dumpster before, so they must have been at least part raccoon.

The raccoon-dog charged me like an Elvis fan. "I knew you were still alive!" she grinned. "I haven't seen New Friends in ever so long!"

"Let's wrestle and I'll decide in five seconds whether I like you or not," I screeched before Mom grabbed my collar and put a stop to it. I'd forgotten about social distancing again.

"We just cleaned the bathroom. It's unlocked if you want to use it," the man-raccoon said hospitably. "The darned lock on the dumpster has rusted shut, though. I'm sure there's someone I could call, but it's our first day with the Forest Service and they didn't warn us how bad cell service was up here."

"Nanny-nanny boo-boo! Country dogs don't have to behave like you do!" taunted the dog-raccoon. She danced a little rigadoon while the lady-raccoon tried to catch her without a collar to grab onto.

"Why you little…" I barked.

"What are you, chicken?" the puppy pranced. "Chick-chick-chicken!"

When Mom felt the growl bubbling under my collar, she rolled me up the trail like a bowling ball. "I'm just so glad to see you guys back at work," she said, waving a friendly goodbye to the two-legged raccoons.

I ran into the trees, but checked back over my shoulder as I went. It wasn't the dog I was worried about, but Mom. When we were out of barking range I asked, "What's gotten into you? I thought you made peace with using the dog bathroom. Have you been holding it this whole time?"

"Sometimes it feels like I have. I'm just ready to heal."

"Heal from what? It didn't smell *that* bad in there." I checked her out in my side-eye. Her shoulders rested far from her ears, the lines on her forehead were shallower, and her face looked like it had a smile in its pocket. I couldn't have been more shocked if she'd held out her nose-wiping finger for a bird to land on and then started singing.

"We've all been through a lot," Mom didn't-sing. "I'm just so sick of being anxious, angry, frustrated, and worried all the time. I'm tired of everything being harder than it needs to be, and not knowing when some troll is going to ambush me with their warped sense of right and wrong."

All my life Mom had been wishing for a reason *not* to talk to strangers, *not* to drive to work, and *never* to take off her sweatpants. But when her wish finally came true, she couldn't wait for it to be over. Sweatpants and hibernation are great and all, but all Mom ever *really* wanted was to feel as comfortable around other people as she does in sweatpants.

"I'm excited for more butt scratches from strangers," I joined in. "And to see people smiling at me again."

"It may be a while before we can touch each other, or even see each other's faces again," she corrected to reassure herself that talking to strangers wasn't a necessary step to healing. "But if a mask is what it takes to get back to normal, I can deal with that. I think we're finally on our way!"

The wind was cool in the early-morning shade. It drowned out the Witch's voice so she had to shout for Mom to hear her stories. It blew through Mom's sweat, freezing her front paws into useless stumps. Mom grabbed and flailed at the branches reaching across the trail to pull herself up with paws that couldn't feel the sticks they were grasping for. I bounded up the slope, Mom scritching and slipping behind me. Even with the slippery mud, loose rocks, and overgrown bushes, it was easy to tell where to put your next step by where the bushes were thinnest. That is, until the trail was swallowed by the most aggressive flower bush I'd ever seen.

It was taller than the other bushes, towering high over Mom's head. There was no walking around it; it was stuffed tight into all the good walking spaces and reached around and over us like a long-armed defender trying to block a basket. It flexed its beefy leaves. The flowers stuck out their tongues as if they were hissing.

I stopped and waited for Mom to catch up and give me instructions. The Witch's droning voice told me where Mom was without my even looking, so I turned back to the bush and casually sniffed for clues. A rustling from deep inside the shrub ripped my attention away. What sounded like a giant creature was crashing through the brush.

When Mom saw my ears stiffen, she rushed to my side and grabbed ahold of my collar. The Witch didn't notice a thing and droned on with her story at the same volume, which suddenly sounded much louder than before. It's supposed to be Mom's job to shush the Witch if we hear someone coming, but that tattletale wouldn't recognize Mom's freeze-dried fingers as a living thing. As the Witch nattered on, the rustling among the flowers turned and came toward us. Mom dropped my collar and poked more insistently.

With Mom distracted, I alone was left to deal with the monster closing in on us through the Great Wall of Flowers.

"COME OUT WITH YOUR PAWS UP!!!" I screamed in the voice-cracking bow-wow-wow I save for real danger, like if the mailman actually opens the gate.

Mom clapped her stumps together. "Oscar! *C'mere!*" she snarled in her dragon voice.

I paused just long enough for Mom to catch up, but I kept my hackles unholstered and never took my eyes off the rustling branches.

"I think it might be a bear," I whispered, before bow-wow-wowing again loud enough to shake the mountain.

The flowers trembled. Now that Mom was here, I looked around for the best escape route. If I got away first, the bear would be more likely to gobble her up instead. It would be sad if Mom got eaten, but it wouldn't be so bad to live a collarless life in the woods with the Raccoon family.

"Don't you dare take off!" Mom hissed, hooking her frozen claws around my collar and trapping me for monster meat.

The bush split open and a couple of scrawny humans stepped out. I looked for signs of what breed they were to assess the threat, but their Captain Kangaroo hats and little round sunglasses might have been anything from software engineers to PhD students. Luckily, neither breed is aggressive unless poorly socialized to dogs.

"Cheeses, he never barks at people like that. I thought you were a bear," Mom said without releasing her ice-claw from behind my hackles, which were still twice their normal size.

"I'm glad he did," said the she-bear. "We lost the trail and almost went in the other direction until we heard him."

"You shouldn't go around scaring people like that," I barked. "I wasn't scared, but Mom had to use her dragon voice and I bet she probably sprayed her anal gland."

When the danger had passed, Mom finally let go of my collar and scowled. "What the hell is the matter with you?"

"I thought they were dangerous," I said. "Gol-*ly*, if you hadn't been around to use as a shield, I don't know what I would have done."

Mom's scowl softened. "It's okay to be scared. We all confuse the danger in our imaginations with real life sometimes. But you *really* can't get so worked up that you might hurt someone. What would've happened if you'd bitten one of those nice people?"

"I'd tell them it was an accident and then it would be okay. Once I explain that *whoopsie-daisies, I thought you were the big, bad wolf,* everyone would laugh, wipe up the blood, and keep hiking."

"That's not how it works, Oscar. Accidents happen, but there are consequences when you can't control your behavior and someone gets hurt. Especially for loudmouths with sharp teeth like you."

"Can't you just tell people I didn't mean it? If I wag a little to show I'm sorry, I bet they'd forgive me."

"Have you ever heard of Oscar Pistorius?"

"Another Oscar? Is he a runner, like me?"

"Yeah. A really good one. Or, he used to be anyway. They sent him to prison because he shot his partner and she died. He said he thought she was a burglar, but a lot of people didn't believe him."

"Oh boy, I bet she was real mad when they brought her back to life. But I'm sure they had a good laugh when he explained why he thought she was a mailman."

"You can't take back murder. Accident or not, the result is the same and an innocent person is gone forever." Mom looked sad. "They can't let him keep walking free if he's dangerous when he's scared. That's why he went to jail."

"Why didn't he tuck back his ears to make his eyes look extra big? Or cry to show everyone that he was really, *really* sorry?" I asked.

"He did cry, but it didn't matter. Even accidents have consequences and there are things that being sorry doesn't undo. You don't want to wind up like Oscar Pistorius, do you?"

"I know you'll protect me, Mom. I'm not worried."

I followed her into the flower bush. She let go of a branch and it slapped me in the face, but I forgave her because I knew it was an accident.

"It goes both ways, you know," she said over her shoulder. "Did you know that a lot of people are scared of you?" She stepped out of the bush and knocked the leftover leaves and petals off her hat and sleeves before hiking on.

"Me? But I'm a snuggle-butt. What's not to like? Look at my lovable smile!" I bared my long, shiny teeth as a reminder.

"Some people don't have enough experience with dogs. When they see a dog like you running toward them, they don't see the floppy tongue in your smile and the wag in your tail. They just hear you barking and see a mouthful teeth and think that you're coming to eat them. I live in fear of what might happen if you scare the wrong person, because I can't protect you if an accident happens. That's why I get so upset when you greet strangers like a bat out of hell."

"That makes sense. It's like that nasty dog in the igloo in the woods or that lady who wanted to muzzle you. Some people just turn their ugliness outward when they're scared. If some dumdum can't tell a good dog from a bad dog, somedog might get hurt. Obviously we're all safer sending them to the pound like the Bad Oscar."

Mom wagged her head. "People don't go to jail for being scared of dogs, no matter how wrong they are."

"What? How can that be?"

"Danger is in the eye of the beholder. If enough people are afraid of the same thing, you don't need to be right to convince others that your mistakes were a good idea. Those people don't just get to walk free, they spend the rest of their lives thinking they were right and never learn their lesson."

"But you can't let them get away with that. Someone could get hurt."

"We're trying, Spud. We're really, really trying."

We didn't get lost but once, and then only for a minute or two before the ground evened out and began to behave. Before long, it did what Mom loves best and opened its trees wide to flash a clear view of chiseled mountains against a neon-grey sky.

Without trees to block their way, Mom's eyes climbed the tallest mountains, searching them like a cereal-box maze for a route to the tippity-top. It was a relief that the mountains were so far away and my paws wouldn't have to follow the perilous route Mom's eyes found. It looked slippery up there. I drained my bowl and we sat together for a little longer, taking in the mountains and the sparkly sky-grey lake in the distance.

After a few miles, the trail turned and faced a raging river. We'd crossed a few little streams already, but they all had sock-safe stepping stones. This river was deep enough for the water to have a mind of its own, and there were no hopping rocks to keep a landlubber dog from getting swept away.

I followed Mom up and down the bank, looking for a place to outsmart the river. Every so often, Mom poked a stone with a toe to see if it wobbled, which it always did. Once she had goaded the river into a white fury Mom stopped searching.

"What now?" I asked.

"We get wet," Mom sighed.

Rawr, said the river.

I stayed on the bank and watched Mom stagger over the pointy, slippery underwater rocks as the river did its best to push her over. When I was sure that she definitely wasn't coming back, I splashed in.

Once the river saw that we were worthy, it relaxed into a sparkling lake. It sunned itself, sprawling shamelessly without regard to the ring of equally nude peaks gathered around to gawk. Mom *oohed* and *aahed* at their reflections in the lake as if she hadn't been looking at a less ripply version of the same mountains all morning.

I'd first seen this lake from above a few years ago when I climbed to the top of the pyramid-shaped mountain that was now waving hello from the far bank. From up high, this lake had looked like a skin of water no deeper than a puddle in a flooded car kennel. It beckoned me to run across it just for the pleasure of making a tidal wave.

Now that I was standing on the lake's shore, I saw through its lies. What made it look so shallow from the sky were the Jillians of drowning rocks poking their faces above the water for a last gasp of air. They looked small from the surface, but underneath, their gigantic roots disappeared icebergily into the sky-grey abyss. Some desperately held up a single, bedraggled tree like the cartoon finger of a drowning man showing how many bobs he has left before joining the mermaids. I wondered what other mysteries might be hidden below the gem-grey water, but you could take a lifetime getting to know the heart of a lake, and we still had a long way to walk.

"Hey, Mom. Where's the trail?" I asked, trying to look calm as bugs buzzed in my ears and attacked my eyeballs.

Her eyes climbed out of the lake and back onto the land around our paws. "Oh." She reached for the Witch with one hand while the other slapped it away because there was a mosquito on it.

"You weren't supposed to cross that river back there, you dimwit," the Witch navigated.

"Dog doo. This is the wrong trail," Mom confirmed.

When we reached the river again, Mom searched for the place where we'd crossed before. I could tell by our scent trail that we'd come out a ways down the bank, but Mom has no scents of direction, even when she's only been away for a few minutes. She looked at the river, baffled. Her eyes landed on something and purpose returned to her stomp. I followed her up the bank to where four logs just so happened to fall across the river alongside each other like a bridge.

"What luck!" I said, tromping across before Mom had time to change her mind and go for a swim.

Life is like that sometimes, I thought as Mom tottered across to meet me. Something can be so difficult and uncomfortable that you dread the next time you need to face it, but when you come back and look at it from another side, you see the solution you were missing the first time. The next time people thought that everyone was out to get them, I was sure that they would remember what the boogeyvirus taught us about building bridges. Then, instead of fighting over who started it, everyone would reach out their hands to steady each other and feel the togetherness that washes over you when you cross something deep together and meet safely on the other side.

I was ready for a leisurely picnic in the shade of the Wagon, but we still had miles to hike before we reached the end of the graph. Mom got ever-quieter as we trudged past many lovely lakes and beautiful mountains without stopping for portraits. I smelled the frustration lines shooting out of her like lightning bolts every time we yielded the trail to let a herd of people wander past in the opposite direction.

"Hey, Mom. Maybe you'll be less grouchy and impatient if you eat your snacks," I coached.

"I'm not hungry," Mom growled like a belly.

"What do you mean you're not hungry? We've been hiking all day. What's the point of hiking if you're not going to enjoy extra snacks? Here, give me a cookie and I'll show you how it works."

"I want to enjoy my lunch and a nice cup of tea sitting in the air-conditioned van," she said like a threat. "I'll wait."

The closer to the bottom we came, the more time we had to spend waiting by the side of the trail for more and more people to come out of who-knows-where to block our way. With each stop, the end pulled farther ahead. Mom tried to hold her face still to hide her scowl in case anyone noticed us getting out of the way for them, but they never did.

"Why on earth would you wear fake eyelashes and pancake makeup to go hiking?" Mom scolded.

"Mmmmm, pancakes," I drooled.

They came up the trail in herds, wandering with the grim determination of exhausted tourists searching for the bus to Alcatraz. They wore fashion sneakers on their paws, plastic whiskers on their eyelids, and shirts with slogans over their bubble bellies. They wore cologne, lotion, and fur products that stunk up the mountain, even from a social distance. It might not have been so bad if there were room on the mountain for me to guide Mom safely past them, but the trail was so tight and rocky, and Mom so wobbly, that she was liable to punch a stranger with her flapping if they came too close.

And then there was the breathing problem. Mom held her neck sleeve in place so that someone would need to look deep into her eyes to see the smoldering as she plowed through them like a battering ram. Even with the muzzle in the way, Mom still closed the doors behind her nose and mouth every time a stranger was near so as not to contamomate them. The trouble was that the trains of strangers got so long that Mom could suffercate waiting for them all to pass. If Mom suffercated, who would bring me cheese?

The only way for Mom to safely take a breath was to stop and turn her back on the trail until the danger passed. Nothing makes Mom more dangerous than when she has to wait.

"Downhill traffic has the right of way," she mouthed behind her muzzle so that only I could hear her as we tried to balance together on a trailside rock the size of a pencil tip.

"Step off the dammed trail to take your stupid picture," she muffled as she stood facing a tree with her arms crossed and the eyes in the back of her head shooting fireballs at the photographer.

"What, is the whole class of 2022 out today? What happened to *no large gatherings*," the smoke signals coming from her ears said as she stepped so deep into a bush that she had to swipe leaves out of her eyes.

I strained at my leash as Mom disappointed hundreds of Oscar fans clamoring for my attention. "I think those people wanted to pet me."

"If we stopped to let everyone pet you, or let everyone pass, we would literally never get off this mountain," Mom said as she dragged me past another four-legged hiker leaning in to sniff me hello. "At this rate I bet we'll pass close to 2,000 people before we get back to the van."

I tried to memorize that two thousand people was exactly how many fit on a five-and-a-half mile trail when you stacked them exactly six feet apart. The numbers burned holes in my brain and fell out before I could save them.

Perhaps Mom was right when she said that you couldn't get deep enough into the wilder-ness to escape the boogeyvirus. By now, it had spread so far and wide that even the deepest forests and steepest mountains were teeming with its carriers. It'd crowded the joy out of more than just the wilder-ness. No matter which way we turned, the rules of uncivilization blocked the path back to the way things were before. The only way to get through it was to step aside, hold your breath, and wait for it to pass. But even after all these months, Mom still acted as if the boogeyvirus couldn't catch her if she kept moving. She red-rovered recklessly through barriers and took frantic detours until the twists had tied her hopelessly in knots. The more she struggled to escape, the more tangled she became and the farther the car kennel seemed to get. If only she would *sit* and accept that this was our life now, the car kennel might come before she burned up inside, and we could live happily ever after in whatever safe, comfortable life the New Normal had in store.

As morning became lunchtime, the sun spread the fog thin enough to disappear, bringing the heat with it. I was thirsty for all the lakes and puddles I'd ignored in the cool hours of morning. The bottle under Mom's arm was empty and her sweatshirt was dark around the packpack straps, but to get at short sleeves and the full bottles in the packpack, we would have to stop. Every time we passed a stopping place with enough room for a bowl and all six of our paws, there were already people sitting on the rock meant for us. So I held my thirst as the sun heated my fur like an oven.

There was also a noise coming from higher up the mountain—a sort of manly whoop like the mating call of a hideous bird. The sound was the same every time, like when Mom has a scratch in her brain that makes the same line of a song play over and over in her thought bubble. Except that this sound was in *my* brain. Was I going crazy like Mom?

"What the smell is that woman saying?" Mom grumbled the umptieth time I heard it.

"Wait, you can hear it too?"

heeeeeeeeee-YUP!, the sound said.

"My middle school gym teacher, Ms. McGruff used to talk like that," Mom said. "All the other teachers would avoid her in the halls."

heeeeeeeeee-YUP!

"It sounds like a blister in my ears," I whimpered.

By the gaJillianth verse, the Drill Sergeant had caught up enough to make out the words. "Maaa*aaaaaaaa*aaaaask-UP!" she bellowed.

Again.

And again.

And again.

"Oh, for heaven's sake," Mom hissed. "That's the most obnoxious thing I've ever heard. Maybe she'd be less obsessed with airborne illnesses if she weren't such a windbag."

"She's just reminding people because they can't hang signs in the woods," I said.

"Who does she think she is anyway?" Mom shifted her eyes over her shoulder in a suspicious way. "It's not like everyone on this trail isn't aware of the benefits of masks, and hasn't already made their decision about wearing one. Just let the people breathe in peace."

"Maaa*aaaaaaaa*aaaaask-UP!" brayed the Drill Sergeant.

"Give it a rest," Mom mumbled. "Having some rotten vigilante bellowing in your ear isn't going to change anyone's mind about anything."

"Maaa*aaaaaaaa*aaaaask-UP!"

"You should tell her when she gets here," I said.

"She'd better hope she doesn't catch up, or else I might push her off this damned mountain. And I *agree* with her. Sorta."

"Maaa*aaaaaaa*aaaaask-UP!"

We inched our way through the crowds as the Drill Sergeant closed in behind us. She was practically shouting in our ears by the time we finally reached the crumbling old road where the Wagon was waiting. Mom's shoulders had been creeping closer to her ears every time the Sergeant's orders rumbled through the valley, and now they were almost high enough to be earmuffs. I was afraid she really was about to turn around and fight the old drillmaster to the death, but once we stepped back onto the bombed-out pavement, Mom forgot all about giving the Drill Sergeant something to holler about.

Now, instead of empty nature surrounding the road, cars crouched in every nook and cranny. It looked like a tornado had come through, dropping millions of cars higgledy-piggledy into the forest. Their windows burned the sun back into my eyeballs. More cars rushed to join the mayhem, blocking the exit for the few cars that thought to escape.

Zillions of confused people wandered through the carnage, searching for the car that belonged to them, or a trail to escape the horror. It was so tight that Mom and I even had to yield the trail to cars forced off the road. The cars didn't say thank you any more than the people did.

The tornado of frustration grew above Mom's head, picking up speed every time she had to step aside. "I miss when the world was in crisis and everyone was afraid to leave their homes," she grumbled.

"How can there be so many people and not a single one wants to pet me?" I moaned.

By the time we found the Wagon, there was nowhere for me to lie down in the shade where I wouldn't be squashed by a car. Mom wasn't in a picnicking mood anyway. The cyclone inside her head escaped her throat in scoffs and growls, launched the packpack across the Wagon like a cow in a tornado, and made cheese wrappers miss the trash sack three times in a row. It wound up her muscles like springs and made them snap in jerky motions so that doors slammed and keys jammed.

"Get in the van, Oscar," she growled like I'd done something wrong.

"But I'm thirsty," I said before I noticed the murder still lurking in her eyes. To avoid flying like a cow in a tornado, I held my tongue and obediently mounted the Wagon before asking, "...and what are you planning to do with that cheese?"

"You can eat it once we get going." She hurled herself into the driving chair with such force that the door caught in her slipstream and slammed shut with a bang.

We were only a few miles from a normal road with places to pull over and enjoy a snack, but it took a lifetime to get there. Just like us, the Wagon had to climb into the trees every few steps to let dozens of ungrateful cars pass in the other direction. Mom drove with the fork in her teeth like a pirate carries a knife. My bologna container sat unopened in her lap as the Wagon elbowed its way back up the road.

Finally, the road spread wide enough to make room for all the cars that wanted to use it. The Wagon pulled into the trees one last time and Mom pulled the *all done* lever. She took the fork from her teeth.

"Oscar, if I ever want to come to Tahoe on a long weekend in the summer again, please smack some sense into me." I would have reminded her that paws don't "smack," but she was finally peeling the top off the bologna packet and I didn't want to distract her. She separated sheets of meat from the stack with the butt of the fork and draped them into my mouth like a servant feeding grapes to an emperor. While I ate, she asked the Witch to find us somewhere a little less crowded to spend the night.

"I already told everyone about all the great trails up here," the Witch said. "They're on their way right now."

"Isn't there anywhere that isn't mobbed?" Mom begged, prodding the Witch's filters.

"You might as well just go home," the Witch suggested helpfully.

Mom forgot the torture of the past a hunerd days of solitude in an instant. "Good idea. Someone oughta tell all these people that there's a deadly virus on the loose and it's dangerous to go outside."

Mom began to relax as we rolled out of the mountains and cruised through the marshlands outside of Sacramento. We'd spent many miserable traffic jams in the Before Times sweltering in the sluggish traffic between Sacramento and the Stuck House. Back then, a hunerd miles of traffic used to try Mom's patience more than a whole army of Drill Sergeants. In the peaceful mountains, the Witch used to swear we'd be home in time for laundry, but as we came closer to the City, the traffic would squeeze tighter and tighter, building up to the finale of gridlock on the Grey Bridge that all the other traffic jams could only dream of. As we got closer, the Witch would stretch out the drive, adding a minute here and twelve minutes there, until Mom and I were overflowing with pee and it seemed like the Stuck House was gone for good.

"Traffic is getting worse," the Witch used to announce, as if we hadn't noticed already. "You will now arrive too late to make dinner," she would jeer, so cruelly that sometimes it made Mom bang on the driving wheel. To rub it in, the Witch would remind us that there was no escape. "You are still on the fastest route."

But not today! The boogeyvirus made the impossible possible, breaking the Bridge curse and ending the Witch's treachery once and for all. As the Wagon approached the City, Mom's thought bubble filled with showers and comfy pajamas. I looked forward to finishing my nap in a bed that wasn't humming and swaying. The Wagon careened through the final turn, and the row of seveny-eight trillion toll tardises spread like a finish line across the boundary between freeway and bridge.

The Wagon red-rovered through the tardis line, but instead of coasting over the Bridge for a victory lap, it slammed to a stop just in time to avoid crashing into the wall of cars on the far side. Were they so stuck in the past that they didn't realize we didn't have to live like this anymore?

Mom looked to the Witch for answers. "Don't worry, Spud. It clears up after the meter lights." I wondered who she was reassuring, since I hadn't asked.

She consulted the Witch again when we passed under the flashing lights that used to train people to take turns, back when sharing was a thing you needed to know how to do. "At the tunnel. It's clear after the tunnel," Mom told whoever was listening.

But when we passed through the island holding up the midpoint of the bridge, we found another clog of cars keeping the City just out of reach on the far side. It was like uptillion grannies decided to go for a Sunday drive over the Bridge at exactly the same time.

When I peered through the other cars' windows to give the evil eye to the bridge trolls causing this mess, I noticed something strange. Many of the windows were boarded up with signs or had words painted like nose smudges on the glass. People hung their heads out of open windows, leaning into the wind like dogs and making the *wooooo* sound that means *look at me* in all human languages. People even popped out of roof windows like popes. They waved flags, honked horns, and generally made a big hullabaloo.

"Is this a party?" I asked.

"It must be a protest. Just our luck to turn up right when it starts," said the Traffic Jinx.

"But I'm thirsty and I have to pee! What did I ever do to them?"

"I'm thirsty, too," Mom said to make the suffering more real by making it about her.

Knowing that Mom understood my pain only fed my anger. "Why, it's terrorism to do something so cruel to an innocent dog!"

"It's not terrorism," she said, as if I were overreacting. "They just want to bring awareness to a problem."

"Their problems are between me and the potty. That makes their problem my problem. And you know what? I think they're doing it on purpose."

"Yeah. They are," Mom agreed, but in that tricky way that suggested that being right made me wrong.

"But… But… What kind of civilization lets people get away with being so inconsiderate?" I humphed. "This isn't America anymore!"

"Actually, this is exactly what's supposed to be so great about America."

"Traffic? You can't be serious." Even Mom wasn't dumb enough to believe that nonsense.

"I mean that you're supposed to be allowed to be inconsiderate to make a point. As long as you follow certain rules and don't hurt anyone while you're doing it."

"But they *are* hurting me," I pointed out, sure Mom of all people would understand what can happen when you tell someone who had to go potty to be patient. "Can't they have their peaceful demomstration on the internet where they won't bother anyone?"

"They're not doing it to *you*, Oscar. I have to pee too. And maybe that person in the next car is late to work." Her eyes pointed at a car with two black flags waving like tails and a fist punching the air outside each window.

"They look angry too."

"Maybe that person is hungry." Mom looked at a car on the other side. It had cardboard signs in all of its windows except the one where a man hung out with his mouth open like a goldfish, arms punching the wind above his head. I couldn't read the messages in the windows, but I knew that people in the City often held cardboard signs when they were hungry.

"… And who knows if that person has a condition that makes him incontinent. For all we know, he's had an accident and can't wait for this to be over so he can go home and change his pants."

I peeped through the butt window of the car in front of us and sniffed the air vents for farts.

"Just because we've never had a problem ourselves, that doesn't mean no one else is suffering from it," Mom continued. "You've got to get people's attention somehow. The internet can bring awareness to things, but it's different when you see the faces of the people who are affected. It makes it more real, somehow."

"That's what I mean. Just because they don't have to pee, doesn't make it okay for them to go so slow that I wet the bed. What are they so mad about anyway?"

"Someone died," Mom said, which were the magic words to win every argument. "He didn't deserve it, but they killed him anyway. Now people are mad."

"Aren't his murderers going to jail like the Bad Oscar?"

"Maybe. That's what these people hope will happen, anyway. But now do you see how their problems are bigger than how bad we have to pee?"

"Yes, I see that when some people are having a bad day they think it's okay to make things worse for everyone."

"More like, the more uncomfortable we are, the more power a temporary inconvenience has to make us stop and think." I was starting to think that Mom had lost her mind.

We passed through the skyscraper gates of the City. A whale-mobile was parked in the middle of the freeway, flashing its lights and desperately trying to draw attention away from the rowdy terrorists. The Law stood beside the car waving arms like an air traffic controller to sort the rowdy cars from regular ones.

"Thank dogness you're here!" I wagged. "There are some terrible drivers out today. *Sick 'em!*"

The Law swatted the rogue cars off the freeway. They obediently rolled onto the exit and drained into the City streets to be pumped back toward Oakland. When it was our turn, the Law paddled the Wagon to the other side and we whooshed onto the freedom of an empty freeway. It felt unstable to be moving again, like the moment when Mom lets go of the leash that's been holding me back and I have to sprint out the wobbles just to keep from falling on my face.

"See?" Mom said. "That wasn't so bad, was it?"

"If it wasn't so bad, then why have you been making frustrated noises and banging on the driving wheel?"

"Staying woke is hard sometimes," Mom shrugged.

Woke? So she was still upset about the Law that kicked us out of our sleeping spot last night? "You really need to let things go, Mom."

"Just think of that lone cop standing in the middle of the freeway with nothing but a couple of flags to protect him, facing down hundreds of angry people who came out to protest *him*."

"They could have eaten him alive!"

"You keep saying that this isn't America anymore, but I can't think of anything more American than bravely defending someone else's right to disagree with you." The Wagon stopped at the last abandoned intersection before the Stuck House and waited for the light to notice us. "And did you see how orderly everyone was in getting out of the way? Even though people are mad at the police in general, no one was holding it against that one cop. So yeah, it was annoying, but without the annoyance we never would have noticed that moment. And we learned something from it, didn't we?"

"Sure did!" I fibbed. "You first, what did you learn?"

"That good leadership holds space for disagreement. And that there are worse injustices in the world than a traffic jam."

"Oh. I was hoping you were going to let me stick my head out the window more often."

Part 4
Rekindling

Chapter 20

Mystery

Ever since the boogeyvirus locked us up and threw away the key, the part they called "real" life felt like make-believe. Mom may have enjoyed the months of freedom from bras and pants with buttons, but her paws had been leashed to the keyboard for too long. I was tired of naps, and missed the feeling of strangers' noses and paws on my butt. It was high time for a proper vacation.

To prepare, Mom and the Witch began meeting in the evenings to go trail shopping. They scrolled, tapped, and zoomed until they'd planned a route to Oregon and back. We would start in the unknown mountains of Forgotten California, and come back through the mountains that everyone knows about.

When people think of California, they think about the beaches on the left and the mountains on the right. They know about the desert in the south and the City in what they call *The North*. What they don't know about California is that the part called *North* is really the middle. There's a whole other half of California above the elbow that hardly anyone knows about. It's filled with bundles of mountains you've never heard of, lakes shaped like strangers' birthmarks, giant trees, and dwarfed towns.

When I jumped out of the Wagon on the first morning, the thin air filled my nose with familiarity. This mountain had seen me before!

"Squeeee! I'm back! Did you miss me?" I ran most of a circle before screeching to stop to smell something interesting.

This trail had all of our favorite mountain things in just the right amounts. It climbed to the top of a pass, but wasn't so steep that our legs would burn off or the trail couldn't hold Mom's shoes. It started at some lovely drinking streams and traveled along delicious lakes that mirrored the rocks and sky. There would be soft grass to roll in, bright-smelling wildflowers to sit on, white dirt to wallow in, squirrels chirping in the trees, and chipmunks to chase through the boulders. We would finish in a place made of nothing but rocks and sky, where I could look over the whole world as if it all belonged to me. Best of all was the trailside mystery, that I'll tell you about soon.

We hadn't been hiking for long when I smelled potato chips ahead. Mom was carrying an extra large bag of brunch in her pocket, but her bag-unzipping muscles hadn't warmed up enough to serve brunch yet, so my growling stomach followed my nose. When I found them, the chips were stuck in the paw of a giant turtle.

Turtle-people are a species of stray hikers. Their habitat is any backwoods large enough to lose your Subaru in. Turtle-people have a terrible sense of direction and it's not uncommon for them to wander for tens or hunerds of miles in the wilder-ness before they remember where they parked. Even though they know how badly lost they can get, they don't stay close to the safety of roads and witch service. Instead, they walk foolishly into danger, carrying their homes on their backs.

Turtles aren't bothered by their perilous predicament. They're suspiciously happy and relaxed for someone living such a desperate life. Mom was already vulnerable to falling under their influence, what with her furry legs and bad sense of direction, so it was important to distract her around turtles.

But the potato chips, though…

"Unhand those chips, you brute!" I barked.

316

"Hi, buddy!" The turtle turned around to show its *nice lady* disguise. It held out its free paw for me to smell. How stupid did it think I was?

"Drop the potato chips and no one gets hurt!" I barked, refusing the empty paw.

Mom came up behind me. "Maybe she'd give you a chip if you weren't so rude."

That was the worst thing Mom could say. Now the turtle-person wouldn't think I was ferocious at all. How would I make it drop the chips and run away now?

"You want one of these?" the mutant taunted, pulling a chip from the bag and waving it in front of my nose before finally dropping it on the ground.

I saved it right away.

When my mouth was free again, I barked one last warning. "I hereby invoke the five second rule! You have five seconds to throw those chips on the ground, or else!" I paused dramatically and waited for it to surrender. When it didn't, I started counting. "Five… seven… fourteen… three… nine… eleventy…"

It sneered at me and rustled the bag.

"… eleventy and a half…"

I ran behind Mom to shield myself from whatever happens at the end of a countdown. "… ONE!" I barked, closing my eyes against the blast.

Nothing happened.

The turtle crouched into a play-bow and waggled the chips. "Come on, buddy. It's okay."

"I think it's more scared of us than we are of it," I whispered, making sure to keep Mom in between, just in case I was wrong. "Maybe it'll drop the chips if you startle it."

"Well if you can't say anything nice, don't say anything at all." Mom turned away from the turtle and continued up the trail without me.

Now there was no one to shield me. The turtle's eyes smiled as it bared its teeth. I looked at Mom to see if she was going to let it get away with that, but she hadn't even turned around.

I barked one final woof for the turtle to stay back as I passed, then ran bravely after Mom. She gave me a big mouthful of kibble as thanks for following, but my heart ached for the potato chips. You can't save them all.

The trail was cool in the mountain's early-morning shade, so I trotted past the lovely drinking streams and delicious lakes without tasting them. They would be more refreshing in the heat of the afternoon, and I was in a hurry to sniff the bare rocks ahead for new clues to the unsolved mystery. I kept my eyes on the secretive peak that never seemed to get any closer until we were right at its base. As if changing the channel, the grass, water, and flatness disappeared from one step to the next and we were surrounded by nothing but naked mountain and empty air.

From the bottom, the whole mountain looked like nothing but a pile of loose rocks all the way up to the pointy crown, but somehow the trail always found solid rock for our next step. Beside the trail, rocks the size of soccer balls mixed with boulders the size of SUVs to camouflage the chunks of solid mountain sticking out in between. Besides the lifeless smell of rock, faint whiffs of something that smelled like trouble mixed in with the thinning air.

Mom and I were alone when we reached the stony parapet below the summit. Silence and mystery filled the sky around us. Suddenly, Mom gasp-screamed and jumped backward toward the cliff, almost knocking me off. She'd finally noticed what I'd been smelling for a while.

A deer lay so close to the side of the trail that its antlers could trip a two-legged hiker who wasn't looking where she was going. At least it *had* been a deer once, back when it still had eyeballs and all of its parts were still attached. Now he lay in pieces with his wife's legs, spine, and femurs mixed in with his own. A little farther back, a fawn's head lay on another rock among older skulls, pelvises, and hooves.

"Holy dog doo," Mom panted.

"There was a deer graveyard in the exact same spot last year," I reminded her. "Don't you remember?"

"Last year all we saw were spines and legs. I thought poachers had shot a bunch of deer in the Park and taken them over the boundary to butcher them where they couldn't be seen. But hunters would've taken those antlers." She looked up the rockwall and then at the empty air behind us, searching for a lair. "What could be big enough to drag a full-grown buck over all these rocks?"

"A mystery!" I announced.

I was careful to walk on Mom's zombie-free side as we hiked past the graveyard. If the deer came back from the dead looking for spare parts to put itself back together, I wanted Mom-parts to be conveniently within reach.

We climbed the last of the mountain to where the only thing not made of rock or sky was the sign that said that we were twelve thousand feet closer to outer space and that dogs were allowed no farther. Last year, I collected pats from dozens of turtle-Friends as they hiked out from a lonely dog-free week on Park land. This year, everything beyond the sign was closed and most of the hikers were home with their dogs.

We walked to the very edge of the mountain, where the ground broke off mid-climb and gave way to nothingness. The rock leaned away from the cliff at an angle that hid the emptiness beneath, so Mom didn't go cliff-crazy. Instead, she sat on the edge with the bottom half of her legs sticking into nothingness. I peeked over her shoulder, saw that it was a long way down, and took a step back before *sitting*.

"Why are there trees and grass down there, but not up here?" I asked.

"Because it's covered in snow and ice up here for so much of the year," Mom mmfed around a mouthful of peanuts. "I bet this trail has only been clear for a week or 2. Plants can't grow with snow blocking the sun all the time, and animals can't live up here without plants to eat."

"What about a yeti?" I asked, thinking of the bone yard somewhere below Mom's dangling paws. "I bet yetis eat deer and turtles. When there are no potato chips, that is."

"A yeti is just as likely as anything else, I suppose." Mom put my water bowl and her peanuts back in the packpack. She pulled her legs out of the void and stood up. "Come on, if we make good time, maybe we can find a place to charge my laptop before Oregon."

We climbed back down, past the deer graveyard to where the mountain was alive again with grass and trees. Somewhere among the fresh grass and bear droppings, I sniffed a man, a woman, and potato chips. I found my soon-to-be Friends sitting on grass tuffets, leaning against backpacks with their legs stretched out among the wildflowers. There was a bag of potato chips between them.

"Hi! I'm Oscar. I love potato chips." I ran straight to the lady and gave her a kiss on the face so she would pay me back with a chip in mine.

"Oh, *now* you like me?" she asked.

"Yes, you seem like a very nice lady," I nuzzled. "Nothing like the *last* chipnapping freak. You've gotta be careful out there. Watch your chips. Actually, you can give them to me for safekeeping, if you like."

"You're not nearly as scary as that deer graveyard up there," Mom butted in. "I thought it was poachers, but maybe it's a monster that tears deer apart and eats them?" This was Mom's sneaky interrogation tactic. By turning the mystery into an unclever joke, maybe she could trick them into correcting her and giving up a clue. Or a confession.

"Sasquatch," my Friend said matter-of-factly without taking her eyes off of her sammich.

"Batsquatch," her companion corrected her.

"Is that bologna?" I sniffed.

"Is Batsquatch like the 2020 version of Sasquatch?" Mom asked, trying to play along with a joke that had already gotten away from her. "Like taking something scary and making it way more horrific than you could ever imagine?"

"Yeah, stay away," my Friend said. "He's got Covid."

This was the first time I'd seen the boogeyvirus's work with my own eyes. I'd heard that it was scary, but I had no idea it could tear you limb from limb and throw your pieces off a cliff. I resolved to lick Mom's hands clean more often.

A moment passed while Mom searched for a witty comeback. Her neck sleeve slipped, showing the top half of her frozen smile. When no wit came, she turned to me. "We should get you back down to the car before it gets too hot up here." That was Mom's code that she didn't want to talk to strangers anymore. "Stay safe out there," she called over her shoulder as she walked away.

"Don't let Batsquatch get those chips," I told them before chasing after Mom.

As we walked back down the mountain, we met more Oscar fans. They turned their faces away from Mom to shine big smiles at me, *oohing* and *aahing* at my trendy bandana and itching to pat my rippling muscles. Behind me, Mom pulled up her muzzle and did weird things with her neck to keep it from falling off her nose. Fashion is awkward sometimes.

Here in Forgotten California, everyone hiked with naked faces. "I don't think you need to wear that here," I told Mom. "You would need Friends to catch It from, and you never let anyone that close. Remember what the Witch told you about how the boogeyvirus blows away outdoors?"

"True," Mom said. "But have you noticed that whenever I pull up the mask, people not wearing masks step off the trail for us?"

I hadn't noticed it before, but now that she pointed it out, Mom's muzzle *was* sort of like a superhero mask that magically cleared people from the trail like cars making way for an ambulance. With Mom's muzzle up, I didn't have to *up-up* on a rock every time we saw someone coming, and Mom didn't have to stand with her back to the trail stuffing me full of kibbles until they passed.

The Oscar fans stared agog, thinking Look! Is it a turd? Is it insane? At least it has a cute dog!

"Make way! Make way!" I trumpeted as I paraded down the center of the trail.

They cheered, "Awwwww!" and "What a cute dog!" and "Hey there, fella!" as I trotted by. But none of them reached out to pet me.

"Yield! Yield, I say! She's got a muzzle and doesn't know how to use it. It could drop at any moment, so nobody's safe.

Please, step off the trail and turn your back for safety… and *Hey big fella*, right back atcha, ma'am!"

Only one group carelessly stayed on the trail as Mom approached. A pair of stray turtles were wandering in circles in a little meadow, looking at the ground and not paying any attention to what masked bandidos were charging at them. Mom stopped. Her superhero muzzle fell from her nose. With her whole face showing, Mom stepped back off the trail and I stepped into the gap so the strangers would have someone to pat.

"Your car's not gonna be all the way up here," I told them. "You've got to go farther down the mountain. Go get your packpack and I'll show you the way."

"Lose something?" Mom asked.

The more flustered one raised her arm and our eyes followed it toward a flat rock in the shade of a tree. "We were having lunch on those rocks over there when a bear came along." She raised her arm by a whisker. "We ran into those trees to hide, but it got into our packs."

"Oh no!" I said. "Was your lunch okay? Need me to help you look for it?"

"Did you see which way he went?" Mom asked.

"He dragged my pack into those trees down there," the hungrier one said, swiveling her arm toward a clump of bushes. The branches were too thick for even an ant to slip through, let alone a bear. I sniffed the air for signs of sammiches, but the trail went cold in the marshy water under the thicket.

"Next I saw him, he was running straight up that slope to the ridge," the less hungry one added. We all followed her eyes to where the peak was crumbling one stone at a time into the valley.

"He ran up *that*?" Mom eeped like she didn't believe it, yet didn't think the ladies were lying either. "It seems too loose to hold a 500 pound bear."

"Oh yeah," the Hungry One said. "He was flying."

"Another suspect!" I said. Both Batsquatch and a flying bear would have the motive, means, and opportunity to carry a family of deer into the sky and drop them on the rocks to get at the deliciousness inside.

"My car keys were in there," the Less Hungry One added. Her eyes dropped from the far-off slope to search the grass around her shoes.

"Oh no! If he has your car keys, he could be anywhere in Nevada or Oregon by now," I said. "This is very serious. We'll have to ask the freeway-sign people to tell everyone to look out for a brown bear driving a Subaru Forester. Don't cry, you're about to be famous!"

Mom looked from the marshy thicket up the treacherous landslide beyond. The wheels between her ears spun, working out that if it took her an average of fifteen minutes to find her keys in the Stuck House, how long would it take to find them in all this wilder-ness? "Do you want me to—" she started to say, when all of a sudden her arm flapped and she screamed, "DUCK!"

My new Friends didn't duck, but stepped back from a social distance to an anti-social distance.

"Ow! Duck!" Mom shouted again, wiping her elbow jerkily against her hip and holding it up to inspect the problem up close. "Get off me, you sucker!" She flicked the fingers of her other hand at the spot where her eyes were pointing.

A blob of something waspy flew into the grass.

"That wasn't very cool, Mom," I whispered. "What are you always telling me about barking at strangers? You'll frighten them."

"You saw it, right?" Mom asked the searchers. When she saw the frozen look in their eyes, she pulled her muzzle back up to show she wasn't a threat. Mom may not like people to see her weirdness any more than she wants them to smell her farts, but sometimes there's just no holding it in. "The bee? Or wasp?" she hinted hopefully.

The Less Hungry One sized Mom up, probably trying to decide if she could overpower her in case of another outburst. "You looked like something bit you..." she said cautiously.

Mom hid her arm behind her back where our would-be Friends couldn't see her rubbing the sore spot. "Do you want me to call Triple A when I get back to the parking lot? It'll probably take them a while to get all the way up here. Can't hurt to get a head start."

"It's okay," the Less Hungry One said. "I'll keep looking a little longer. It's a bright teal backpack, I'm sure we'll spot it eventually."

Save me! said her companion's eyes. "Thanks for your help," said her companion's mouth.

"Okay, well, I'll let people know there was a bear sighting in the area on my way out," Mom promised. When we were out of hearing range, she added, "That sucks."

"I know!" I said. "They're gonna have to share their snacks from now on."

"Funny how you can be prepared for anything in the wilderness, but coming back to civilization is usually the hard part." Mom lifted her elbow to inspect the puffy lump growing there. She squinted at it like she was trying to turn her eyeballs into microscopes. "I always forget how much bee stings hurt." She pinched the bump so hard that her whole elbow turned white.

This was strange behavior, even for Mom. "What are you doing?" I asked, checking the trail ahead to make sure no one was watching.

"I'm trying to squeeze the venom out like a zit. That's what you're supposed to do, right?"

"I thought that was spaghetti monsters." A *spaghetti monster* is like a leash come to life. It wags its tail and hisses a warning before the clip end bites you and ends your zoomies forever.

"Oh. Maybe you're right." She tried to put her elbow in her mouth. "Do you think I can suck out bee venom like snake venom? I read about that in a book somewhere."

"I don't know. Dogs don't suck."

Despite all her squeezing and sucking, a white patch the size of my pawtip bubbled up on her arm. By the time we came back to the car kennel, an angry lump the size of a chicken breast had swelled around the white center, until her elbow looked like the Batsquatch of zits.

Mom forgot to be grateful that the keys were still in her pocket because her mind was scattered across the mountains, searching her memory for clues about who made the deer graveyard. She squirmed under the mounting suspense as the road twisted down the mountain.

As soon as the road straightened, the Witch interrupted Mom's puzzling. "You're back online. You will arrive in—"

"Take me to the nearest gas station!" Mom ordered urgently. "We have some googling to do." A dog knows that the fun of a mystery is in the not-knowing, and that it's more exciting to bark through a closed door than to open it and find that the mailman has already gone, but Mom isn't so wise.

A short time later, we sat in a sliver of shade outside a small-town Sinclair station. There was a table just a few steps away, but the electricity was hidden behind the ice machine, so we sat on the ground while the Witch sucked juice from the laptop and the laptop sucked juice from the wall. With nothing to distract her curious fingers, Mom couldn't take the suspense any longer.

"What do you know about dead deer in these here parts?" Mom interrogated.

"Would you like to know about all the Bigfoot sightings in the area?" the Witch asked innocently.

"Yes!" I barked. "Mom, Bigfoot is Batsquatch's nickname. She's saying Batsquatch did it!"

Both Mom and the Witch ignored me. The suspense heightened.

"Are you looking for UFO sightings?" the Witch asked.

"Aliens!" I solved. "That explains everything!"

"There's all kinds of paranormal activity in this area," the Witch agreed. "There have been many reports of unidentified creatures and objects disappearing into solid rock and—"

"That's exactly what I didn't-see!" I said. "What happens next?"

Mom hushed the Witch with a flick before she leaked any spoilers. "Cheese, isn't there anything real on the internet?"

"I found this," the Witch said a moment later, like she expected a treat for it.

Mom looked into the Witch's screen for answers and her face turned a deeper shade of grey.

"What does it say?" I asked. "Was it Batsquatch? The flying bear? Aliens? Who dunnit?"

"It says that the deer migration goes through that pass every year," Mom read, drawing out the suspense.

"No! Don't tell me! Let me guess…" I tilted my head in a *hmmm* and waited, because I know how to do suspense, too. "It's Batsquatch, right? He waits for them in his doorless cave at the tippity-top. When the herd least expects it, he pops out of solid rock and says *Boo!* Then the deer die quickly of a painless heart attack so they won't feel it as he rips them to pieces like a stuffy toy. Right?"

"Nothing like that," Mom said in the voice she uses for bad things that you can make stop by looking away. "They cross the ridge while it's still buried in snow. Every year, a few of them slip. I guess that's where they land."

"That's so sad. They probably die still hoping that Triple A will come save them at any minute." I tried to imagine it, but couldn't. I'd explored the whole ridge, and there hadn't been anywhere scary enough to turn Mom to stone, so they couldn't have fallen by accident. "Who pushes them? Is it the bear? Batsquatch? I give up. Tell me!"

"No one pushes them, Spud. Ice is just slippery. Or maybe a cornice collapses when there's too much weight on top of it."

"Aaah, the old ice twist," I nodded. "I should have seen that one coming. It's the oldest trick in the book: He stabbed her with an icicle… He hanged himself from a block of ice that melted into the puddle at the crime scene… She whacked him over the head with the frozen porkchop and then served it to the detectives…" I let it play out in my imagination like the big reveal at the end of a movie. "But wait, where did they fall from?"

"Remember where we were sitting? That must have been where it happened. There's no other place on that side that's so exposed." She gulped more than just root beer. "Nature is brutal. It doesn't guarantee a satisfying ending."

"That's not a nice story at all." I tried not to imagine Mom slipping and falling off the mountain, but my imagination got away from me. It found her with eyeballs gone and tongue hanging out before going blank. "I liked it better when Batsquatch was the culprit."

"We've gotten so good at staying safe that we're surprised danger still exists at all," Mom said icily. "We think of danger as something that happens *out there*; that you'll only find it if you go looking for it, and you can opt out when it gets to be too much."

"Rules sure are helpful for keeping the danger out of civilization," I agreed. "… if you're into that sort of thing."

"People keep trying to fight off this virus with rules. As if Nature gives a crap," she went on, forgetting that she was new to following the rules herself. "Now that danger is coming for people where they live, they don't know how to cope. The idea that their comfort is insignificant is such an unfamiliar concept that they think some shadowy bad guy must be torturing them for sport." She wagged her head to show how wrong people were. "Deer just accept that danger is part of life and migrate on…"

I wanted to hear what deer-zombies had to teach us about danger, but a medium-sized people-puppy interrupted Mom's train of thought by politely shoving a bottle of soda and a sammich between her eyes and the Witch.

"Here, these are for you," he said carefully, like he wasn't sure if Mom would bite his arm off.

Mom scanned the bags, gnarled wires, gadgets, snacks, and drinks scattered around us. "Oh, uh… I'm not homeless. I just blow a fuse in my van every time I try to charge my laptop."

"Oh," said the people-puppy, still holding out the snacks.

They looked at each other while I sniffed the sammich from a safe distance.

Mom unfroze and tried to look harmless as she gently accepted the sammich. "Thanks. Do you like Coke? It's all yours. Tell your parents you deserve it for being such a big-hearted kid."

The people-puppy turned and ran back to his car, which lit up like a faithful dog when it saw him. "Well that was awkward," Mom said, waving to the boy through the window as his car pulled away.

"Yeah, he didn't even ask if you were a vegetarian," I said, sniffing at the sammich. "Is that bologna? And cheese?"

Mom peeled the bologna and cheese out of the bread for me and started ratta-tat-tatting on the laptop. Eventually, a man who had been pacing in and out of the gas station for a suspiciously long time stopped pacing beside us.

"Could I offer you 50 bucks to drive us to Yreka?" he asked. "Ap-*parently* they don't stock Prius tires at the garages around here. The nearest tire store is in Yreka and they close in a couple of hours. Triple A says that the tow truck can get the car there in time, but we can't ride inside with the driver."

"How many of you are there?" Mom asked.

"Me, my husband, and his mother," the man said, pointing his big sunglasses at a man escorting an old lady across the car kennel.

"I'm sorry. I wish I could help," Mom said. "I don't actually have seats in my van. I don't think it would be a pleasant ride for your mother-in-law."

"Can you believe that they don't have Uber in this town?" he said, like it was a crime no one would get away with if he were in charge. "They don't even have any hotels. There's a motel but…" he shuddered like he was imagining a long fall off an icy ridge. "I don't know how people live like this!"

Mom breathed a sigh of relief that he wouldn't see the inside of the Wagon after all. Guessing he might be less upset if she changed the subject to something familiar, she asked, "Where are you from?"

"The Bay Area."

"You don't say…" Mom caught herself right before the bite made it into her voice. This man wasn't bad, just very lost.

"We're supposed to be visiting friends in Portland this weekend, but we'll never make it now." He seemed to see Mom for the first time behind all the screens and wires. "How about you, where are you from?"

"I'm from the Bay Area, too." What she really meant was, *You seem like you need an interpreter.* "Have you thought about calling an old-fashioned taxi company?"

"I looked on Yelp, but I couldn't find one. They're all in Yreka."

"You could check the phone book. They might have one inside…" She trailed off when she saw the look on his muzzle. "Yeah, you're probably right."

"Where are you headed?" the man asked. A map of all the places on the far side of Yreka formed in his thought bubble.

"The southern Cascades to van-camp and hike for a week."

The wayfarer's thought bubble flashed like he'd just won the jackpot.

Maybe to show that she wasn't a hobo, and maybe just to let him know that we'd be here a while, she added, "I'm just here charging my electronics. You never know when you're going to find an outdoor outlet."

He tilted his head as if it'd never occurred to him that trees didn't have charging stations. He looked at Mom suspiciously, like maybe she was really there to break the window of his Prius and steal the coins in his cup holder. His fingers found the loose loop on his muzzle and lifted it toward his ear.

"What do you do?" Mom asked, hoping that the next line in the script would keep him from thinking too hard.

"I work in tech," he sighed, like such a glamorous lifestyle was tiresome.

"Yeah, me too."

He relaxed and let go of the muzzle strap. Just then, a jumbo tow truck pulled into the dirt patch beside the gas station.

"Oh thank god," the man said, rehooking his muzzle and running to introduce himself.

The couple and the old lady talked to the truck driver through their muzzles. They chopped their arms toward the Prius and then toward Yreka.

The truck driver's face crinkled into a well-used smile that showed where some of his teeth had worn out. He flapped his hand in a *bah!* motion, then flapped it back in a *c'mon* motion. All three of the city slickers went slack with relief and danced around the truck driver in a sort of floppy play bow, yipping, "Thank you! Thank you! Thank you!"

"Look, Mom. They're Friends!" I said.

"Mmmm?" Mom said, pretending that she'd been absorbed in her laptop and hadn't been watching the whole time.

Everyone watched the Prius climb piggyback onto the truck before the two men helped the lady into the truck's cockpit. While his husband climbed in behind her, our Friend looked over his shoulder and noticed Mom watching him. He held up a finger to the truck and came back.

"Thank you," he said.

"For what? I didn't do anything." Mom flapped her hand in the same *bah* motion the driver had made. "I'm glad it worked out. Have a good trip!"

He thanked us again over his shoulder as he ran back to his family and new Friend.

"He was nice," I said once the cloud of dust from the truck cleared.

"Know what's funny? That guy and the kid saw the same scene, but the kid thought *we* were the ones that needed help, and the man thought we were the best ones to help *him*."

"He *did* need help," I pointed out.

"He sure did." Mom shook her head. "I guess that's the problem with this country right there."

"What, that there aren't enough Ubers to bring all the lost cityfolk to the nearest Best Western?"

"I was thinking that the city and country are different worlds. It's selfish to accept free help in a city, because whatever you need is someone else's livelihood. Paying someone to help you out of a fix is a win-win. But country folks pitch in like a deposit, knowing that they may need to ask their neighbors to repay the favor someday. What goes around comes around faster in a small circle."

"Isn't that nice? There's more than one way to care for people. What's wrong with that?"

"Because each way of thinking is rude in the other's world. I was annoyed when that kid offered me a sandwich. I thought he was suggesting I couldn't pay for my own damn sandwich. It took me a second to realize that it was really a very kind thing to do."

"I'm glad you didn't tell him that you're a vegetarian. Are you going to eat the other half?"

"Go ahead." She ripped it into bite-sized chunks as she carried on with her thought. "On the other hand, that guy sure did come off as an insufferable git whining about Ubers and not roughing it at anything grimier than a Holiday Inn."

"He didn't want to bother anyone is all," I reminded her. "And they did find help, so it all worked out in the end."

"Yeah, but he's gonna go home with a story about his close call in this god-forsaken inbred backwater, and how rude the tow truck driver was for not wearing a mask around his elderly mother-in-law. And the driver's gonna go home talking about the helpless fop—except that's probably not the word he'll choose—who made him drive 50 miles with the window rolled down in 100-degree heat, then offered him a $50 tip but didn't tip anything because the driver didn't take Venmo."

"Of course the driver wouldn't use an ugly word like *fop*," I said. "He was a nice man. You could smell it from all the way over here. I bet he'll call them *poor gentlemen who needed my help*. Or maybe he won't say anything at all, because it's not polite to brag about good deeds."

"I hope you're right." Mom pulled the plug out of the wall and wrapped the cord around its anchor. "I hope they both walked away with that nice feeling you get when two cultures make a connection, but no one can make those connections when we're

334

just peeking at each other through the internet and judging others' lives out of context." She slipped the laptop back into the packpack. "I have a feeling that the version that's going to live in those guys' memories is the internet version, not the version you and I just saw."

Chapter 21

Reunion

When the Witch bleated that it was time to wake up, I jumped to attention. "Guess what! We're back in Oregon!" I cheered when Mom gave up on pretending to be asleep. "I thought maybe I smelled green last night, but now that the sun is up, I can smell that it's *definitely* green out there!"

"Grumblegrumblegrumble." Mom used a hat to crush the fur standing straight out from her head.

"Why so grouchy?" I asked. "It's a lovely day."

Mom wiped the sleepies out of her eyes. "It is now, but I can't believe you slept through that thunderstorm last night."

"The what?"

"All that flashing and booming. I was afraid a tree would come down on our heads or something."

"Oh. I thought they were just picking up the trash in the middle of the night."

"They don't have trash day in the forest, you numbskull."

"They could. It was dark when we pulled over, and anything can happen in the dark."

"They don't," Mom said like she was setting a rule. "Places big enough to have trash day don't usually let you sleep in your car. I wish they did, or else I could have gotten an extra 45 minutes of sleep."

Mom made a cup of poop juice and guided the Wagon onto the freeway. When the cup was almost empty, the Witch directed us into a town with more than one gas station and more traffic lights than a dog can count. We rolled through a neighborhood, searching for a stretch of curb long enough to hold the Wagon. There would've been plenty of room to park if it weren't for the overstuffed trash bins waiting beside every driveway like people puppies waiting for a bus. I know adventure is ahead when the Wagon stops in nature, but when we stop in a town and Mom checks for the poop bags before dismounting, I know a Friend is coming to see me. I could hardly wait for Mom to leash up to see who it was.

Poop bags packed, Mom opened the door and I leaped over her lap in a flying dismount before the Wagon had even finished sucking in the seat leash. That did the trick.

"Oscar! Dammit!" Mom ejected herself from the driving chair and grabbed my collar. "What's gotten into you? Get out of the road." She dragged me onto the sidewalk by the collar. While Mom double checked her pockets for wallet and Witch, I perked my ears like two antennae and sniffed the air for the scent of Oscar fans.

"Where are they? Where are they?" I squealed. Without waiting for an answer, I launched in the direction that smelled most like breakfast, dragging a whining Mom behind me.

Suddenly, a bandit popped out from behind a bush. It stood in a star shape, blocking the sidewalk. "Oscar!" it growled.

The bandit was tall and lean, and even though her face was hidden beneath a hat, behind sunglasses, and under a muzzle, I wasn't fooled for a second.

"Oscar! Oscar! Oscar!" The Bandit play-growled as her arms twinkled.

"Lily!" I screeched. I blasted off down the sidewalk with so much force that the leash burst out of Mom's hand. I closed the rest of the distance in a blur, and nearly toppled Lily in a high-impact hug. "How did you get here? You'll never believe all the things that have happened since I saw you last!" I panted over my shoulder as she gave me a ten-fingered butt scratch that went all the way to my ears.

I hadn't seen Lily since she'd tricked Mom and me into running all those extra killmometers in the dooms. When she put Mom up to it, Lily couldn't have known about the dangers of drinking from a shared cup. She couldn't have predicted the risks of using snotty fingers to put unwrapped M&M's from shared bowls into a muzzleless mouth. How could she have guessed at the life-threatening peril of sitting *inside* a restaurant? I'd long ago forgiven Lily for putting Mom in danger, and I was glad that Mom had finally come around to forgiving the extra killmometers, too.

It was hard to imagine that we were so primitive back then. We just didn't know any better. Everything was much better ever since they passed a law that everyone had to eat outside with their dogs.

"Guess what!" I told Lily. "Nature is still open! You don't even have to be sneaky anymore, they'll just let you in the gate like in the old days. Some of the people potties are even open. Wanna see?"

"Let's grab breakfast here so we don't have to eat in the car," Mom suggested. It was one of the best ideas she'd ever had.

"Did you know that some restaurants have *always* let people eat outside?" I asked Lily as Mom tied the leash to a table leg.

"True that," interrupted a German shepherd, who stopped by our table on the way to the potty. "They even have public bathrooms out here." He jumped into the planter that made the outdoor walls of the restaurant and peed on the flowers.

I don't usually like it when Mom ties me up and goes somewhere without me, but with Lily there, I didn't need to bark.

While Mom went inside to order, I taught Lily about breakfast. "Here, let me show you how it works," I coached. "First you say, *I'd like a side of bacon.* Then you ask, *Can I get that with cheese?* Now you try."

Mom came back and Lily took her turn inside. "Don't forget to tell them to put it on a different plate so I don't have to share," I wagged after her.

"Did you hear the thunder last night?" Lily asked as we ate our eggs.

"Yeah. It sounded close," Mom said. "I didn't even know they had thunderstorms on the west coast. I've lived out here for almost 20 years and last night was the first time I've seen lightning."

"It's rare, thank goodness, but it happens. They were saying on the news that it started a fire out by Crater Lake somewhere."

"Sheesh. I hope they contain it quickly," Mom said. "It seems like fire season is getting worse and worse every year."

With breakfasts in bellies, we all mounted Lily's wagon together. Everyone else put on their masks while I mouth-breathed between them.

"You're gonna love hiking," I told Lily. "It's a bit like running, except that it's slower so you have time to pee on more stuff."

I ran from the windows on one side to the windows on the other as we rolled off the freeway and straight into nature. "You can stop there! Or... wait, that's a good spot!" Each suggestion I made squeaked out higher than the last until I was practically whistling.

When we finally dismounted, I could hardly wait to show Lily everything I knew. I ran in circles to demomstrate what expert hiking looked like from all angles while she and Mom swung their packpacks into place.

"You follow this line, where there's no grass and the dirt is packed down. See?" I stood in the middle of the trail where she couldn't miss me and waggled my butt to show what I meant. "You're a natural!" I encouraged, doing a pirouette and scampering down the trail to show the way. When I came back a moment later, I pushed Lily out of the way to get to Mom behind her. "Isn't she doing great, Mom?"

Lily had come all the way from... I still didn't know *where* Lily came from or how she knew we'd be here, but it'd be impolite to let her discover the place for herself without describing it first. So even though we had never been here before either, Mom told her what to expect.

"AllTrails rated this trail as *hard*, but it also said that it's crowded," Mom guided.

"What she means is that most people are wusses," I translated. "So when they say it's *hard*, they probably don't mean it."

"It climbs like 4,000 feet in the first 3 miles," Mom recited, using the Witch as a teleprompter. "Hang on a second, that can't be right."

"That sounds steep," Lily said.

Mom poked the graph so that the Witch would show her the steepness. "It says 52 percent. That's got to be a GPS error," she decided.

"Forty-five means that one of the hill's parents is a floor and the other is a wall," I 'splained it to Lily the same way Mom had once 'splained it to me. "Is fiddy-two more floor or wall than forty-five, do you think?"

"Like you said, people are stupid," the Witch whispered foreshadowingly. "That's why I said it was going to be three miles when I actually meant five-and-a-half. But I don't want to ruin all of the surprises... yet," she added with a silent *moo-ha-ha*.

"At least the whole thing is less than 10 miles," Mom promised. "It can't be *that* bad."

"This isn't so bad," Lily agreed after we'd hiked up a slow, wide trail for a few minutes.

"Sucker! I'll show you!" muttered the Witch, barely able to contain herself.

"We're supposed to turn here." Mom led us into the forest, where the mountain hid behind a thin layer of trees. No sooner did we step into the shade than the steepness began.

The forest crowded in so close that it was hard to see the trail, let alone manage two humans at once. I was glad for the clingy trees because without their roots spilling across the trail to make stairs, it would have been one long dirt slide to the bottom. I climbed in two-legged leaps, clamoring my front paws up the slope until I was standing tall like a human and exploding my back paws under me to complete a leap-froggy move that impressed everyone who saw it. Behind me, the girls climbed in ground-swallowing steps, bringing their knees almost to their chests and grabbing tree branches to hoist themselves to the next step.

Every time we met other hikers on the narrow trail, someone had to step into the woods and cling to a tree to keep from tumbling downhill. When other people stepped off the trail for me, I joined them under the tree. While we waited for Lily and Mom to pass, I would press my butt into their legs with a doggie hug so their free hand could scratch my rocketblasters during the tedious wait. After the girls crawled by, I inspired everyone with a new show of strength as I re-launched up the slope. I collected many new fans on our way to the top.

By the time we came out of the trees and onto the sunny crown near the summit, I was drooling like an enchanted waterfall, Mom's shirt was raining, and Lily looked even more sparkly and vibrant than before. From here, the mountain was too steep for even trees to hang onto. The sun dried us while I led our expedition through the rocks and wildflowers.

"Have you ever seen flowers?" I asked Lily. "These ones are called *feather-flusters*." I tried to roll in them so she would notice, but the mountain sucked me farther downhill than I'd planned. I jumped to my feet and climbed on. "And these ones… oh, these are very rare. They're called *floofs*. They were discovered by Dr. Seuss in the eightieth century." I zipped past them to show how their dainty pedals waved in my wake. "And these little ones here, they're called *1970s linoleum*. It's an heirloom breed…"

"You're so handsome!" Lily told me when she saw how nice the crushed flowers looked under my waggly tail.

"You've sure got a talent for this hiking thing," I told her. "There are people who hike for years without ever noticing how handsome I am."

The people of Oregon had never seen a dog quite so excited to see them either, and they were starstruck by my squealing, wiggling enthusiasm. They rubbed in the compliments while their own canine sherpas sat like obedient sticks-in-the-mud, snobbishly rolling their eyes away while I stole the hearts of their families.

No matter how high we climbed, the mountain just wouldn't quit. Every time there seemed to only be a few steps between me and the sky, I would come over the rim to find more rock reaching even deeper into space. All around me, mountains stuck like fangs into the sky. Behind them, the lopped-off cone of Mt. Hood stuck out like a glowing tongue.

By the time the other mountains were no longer *around* us, but *below* us, there was nothing left of the trail but slippery dirt and rolly-polly rocks. My Fans had nothing to hang onto when I stopped to inspire them, so I was careful to push in the direction of the mountain when I offered my butt for scratching. With my butt facing the mountain, I watched Mt. Hood with each new Friend as it rose like a moon in stop motion above the shrinking range.

Finally, I came over yet another rise and there was no more mountain to climb—only sky above and around me. Hikers were strewn on the ground like bowling pins on strike, and standing tall in the center of the devastation was...

...a mailbox.

"Oh no!" I tap danced urgently as Mom and Lily clawed their way onto the scene behind me. "This must be a mailman's hunting grounds. Don't worry. It looks like he's already eaten today."

Lily and Mom took their place among the spent hikers and I went to inspect the mailbox. It looked more like a shrine than an active mailbox, covered with flags and offerings like it was. It reminded me of pictures from the summit of Mt. Everest except that there were bumper stickers instead of flags. Where climbers lovingly placed photos and gifts in Everest's white dirt, the hikers who conquered Mt. Mailman left offerings of empty drink cans and divorced flip flops.

"What does it mean?" I sniffed.

Mom squinted at the Sharpie inscription on the pedestal. "I have no idea."

"It's a mystery why the native people of this land worshiped the Mailman," I told Lily, who was probably wondering about the history of the place. "Read the inscription to her, Mom."

"It says *f*—... It says *duck*. Nothing else. Just *duck*."

"I don't think even a duck could fly this high," I bragged.

"Let me get a picture of you 2 before we go." Mom held up the Witch in one hand and flapped the other one in the direction of the mailbox to show where we should pose.

"This is the worst part of hiking," I whispered to Lily. "Follow my lead and I'll help you get out of it as fast as we can. What did you do with the hat?"

Lily pulled a crunched up hat out of her pocket and snapped its elastic under my chin. "You're such a good boy, Oscar."

"I know... I know..." I told her. "But she won't let us leave until she gets the picture. I'll wear it this time, but next time it'll be your turn, okay?" I jumped onto the biggest rock just like I knew Mom wanted me to and waited for Lily to find a place next to me.

"How did you learn how to jump on rocks like that?" Lily asked admiringly. She leaned in and I licked the sweat off her face for the camera.

"If you only knew how many rocks she's made me jump on. That Witch is full of nothing but snark and pictures of me sitting on rocks. Let's get another one of us kissing. Muah!"

Once the Witch's appetite was satisfied, we still had to wait our turn to use the trail while a group of triumphant hikers flopped the last few steps to the summit. As soon as the first one saw the mailbox, she turned around to encourage the friend climbing behind her.

"Come on, Deb! You can do it! Just a few more steps!" she cheered.

They hugged when Deb arrived, then both turned around. "Come on, Pam! You can do it" the first lady and Deb cheered.

When Pam arrived, they were ready for her with a group hug and Pam cried for a second. Then, the first lady, Deb, and Pam turned around and cheered, "Come on, Zara! You're almost there!"

When Zara's hug was over, they all turned again. "Come on, Rita!" the first lady, Deb, Pam, and Zara cheered, like they were handing out medals at the end of a marathong.

"We did it! We did it!" they congratulated each other when they were all standing beside the mailbox. They asked Lily to take their picture so they could remember the shared moment of triumph.

Lily and Mom divided up a stack of witches as the ladies arranged themselves in their assigned positions. They assumed the pose that all women of a certain age use in pictures.

"If you look the same in all your portraits, the only thing people are going to look at is the scenery," I coached. I gently red-rovered through them to break up the pose, and Mom snapped a few pictures of their surprise and delight. "Those'll be the ones you like the best," I promised. "You'll see."

Even though the Authorities were constantly reminding us that we were *all in this together*, it was easy to forget about togetherness when the boogeyvirus had you cooped up in your crate all alone. The Women of a Certain Age sharing their accomplishment together gave me an idea: Maybe if everyone joined in celebration when we were all set free, the togetherness of our shared victory would erase all the loneliness that came before. When the boogeyvirus was finally gone, I resolved to congratulate everyone I saw with an exuberant "You did it! You did it!" until there was a smile on every muzzle-free mouth in the world.

To practice, I greeted every person I met on the way down with a big smile and a cheer. All the cheering kept me very busy, so I let Mom supervise Lily. She needed the talking practice anyway. Friendship didn't come easily to Mom, and she'd hardly barked to anyone outside a screen since we saw Boss Charming.

"I don't even want to post on social media anymore. I'm connected to so many people through Oscar that I never would have met otherwise." Mom scratched at the irritation around her bee sting. "Usually I like reading all the different perspectives from different backgrounds around the country..."

"Dogs bring out the best in everybody," I told Lily. "Especially when the dog is me."

Mom didn't like it when my talents overshadowed her genius for finding the worst in everybody. She plowed on as if she hadn't heard me. "... But now I'm seeing a side of people I don't want to see. There's so much ugliness out there."

"It's true," Lily agreed. "All I can look at these days are the cute animal videos. Have you seen the one where the parrot talks to Alexa?"

"No, I missed that one." The parrots in Mom's thought bubble were featherless and repeated uglier things than Alexa was allowed to say.

"She only clicks the stuff that makes her angry," I explained.

"That's the trouble with social media," said Lily. "People always had freedom of speech, but now everyone has a built-in audience, too."

"Don't I know it!" I butted in. "Isn't it great?"

Lily continued as if she couldn't hear me either. "It means that you can say things that you would never say in person. You get validation from some people and baited by others, but you never see all the people who don't engage. After a while, the only opinions in your feed are from people who think exactly like you."

"Or people who trigger you," Mom said from experience. She noticed her scratching and wiped away a spot of blood.

"That's not what it's like on Dogstagram," I said. "Dogstagram is like Black Twitter, but for dog issues. Mostly whether there's equal opportunity in booping, whether or not to conjugate verbs, and if it's *really* that dog's birthday today. They're very complex topics with good arguments on both sides and—"

"I know I could just unfollow people," Mom interrupted. "But isn't that part of the problem? Nobody talks to each other anymore."

"You met Lily on the internet and you're talking to her right now, remember?" I said.

Mom kept on ignoring me. "How are we going to find common ground if everyone is shutting out the things they don't agree with? Isn't it better to have the conversation yourself and form your own opinions, rather than someone else telling you what others think and how you should feel about it?"

Mom was doing that thing she does, which was my cue to un-bum everybody out. "I've been letting you tell me what to do for years and it's working out okay for me. You know what's the best thing about dogs?" I didn't leave time for them to guess, which could take all day. I had a point to get to. "Everyone knows we're there to take their side. Sometimes I tell a story about one thing, and a Friend agrees with me even though they're thinking about something totally different."

"You could leave them be until they drop off your feed," Lily suggested.

"If people are seeing all the right things and still arriving at the wrong conclusions, you've got to correct them," Mom moaned. "Otherwise, how can you hope to fight all the dysinformation out there?"

"You appointed yourself the Referee of the Universe, not me," I reminded her. "It's not *my* job to think for them, silly. I'm just a dog. If you talk to a hunerd people, they'll have a Jillian different ideas about the same thing, and each one has a lesson if you listen for it." I hoped it wasn't awkward for Lily that I was coaching Mom in front of her, but some conversations can't wait. "Agreement is at the root of every disagreement. Even ideas that agree will end up disagreeing if you talk about them long enough."

"Exactly," Mom said triumphantly. "You're just a dumb dog who doesn't understand the nuance of all the horse droppings out there on the internet. You think that rolling in horse plop is fun."

"Maybe you'd be less of a sourpuss if you remembered that every horse turd comes from a pony," I pointed out. "You could argue forever about whose ideas are the best and never declare a winner. Love is what gives you the energy to get up and argue another day. Humans call it *marriage.* " Then I remembered that Mom *had* won that argument once, and that's why we lived alone now.

"You don't roll in horse droppings, do you, Oscar?" Lily asked in a voice that meant she knew the answer was *no.*

"The idea would never even occur to me!" I wagged convincingly. "Dogs don't have ideas, we have feelings. There are Jillians of ideas flying around right now and most of them are horse doo-doo, but there are only a few feelings, and we're all sharing them together."

"Which is why it's so frustrating when people respond in ways that are so obviously against their own values and interests!" Mom threw up her hands as if she were throwing an invisible tennis ball over each shoulder.

"If we're honest about our feelings, then we don't have to convince people what they mean," I said.

"We're talking about facts, not feelings," Mom grumped.

"Most of her ideas never escape her head, so she can't see them change over time," I 'splained to Lily. "If you trapped one of her ideas in a jar and compared it to its relatives still living in her head a week later, you'd see that most ideas are just feelings."

"Facts," Mom corrected again. "I don't get why everyone doesn't see things the way I do. If only they had better information, they wouldn't believe such nonsense."

"Creating an idea is a team sport," I said. "You have to pass a feeling back and forth between a few different players before you start to find any truth in it."

Mom paused her rant and aimed a doubtful look my way. "That's pretty smart, Oscar. Where did you come up with that?"

"Lily said it a few minutes ago while you were thinking about what idea-feeling you wanted to tell us about next. You should really listen to her. She's got some pretty deep wisdom under that hat."

Chapter 22

Superspicion

As the rainforest cleared and the muppet-like moss dried to dust outside the Wagon windows, I wished Lily were still there to watch the world change with me. After climbing back down from the mailman's lair, Lily took us back to the Wagon and went home. Mom and I continued to the empty grasslands on the forgotten side of the state. Like California, Oregon has a forgotten half with even fewer towns and smaller mountains than Wyoming, Forgotten California, or any of the emptiest places you know about. You probably had no idea the Forgotten Oregon is there because almost nobody's been there, and everyone who has forgot about it right away.

"Why isn't Lily coming with us?" I asked. "Do you think it's something you said?"

"She only came for a day hike," Mom said. "Not everyone is into the kind of adventuring that you and I do."

"You don't think it's because you tried to kill her with all that steepness?" I prodded.

"After what she did to us the last time we saw her…" Mom stopped to take the *why I oughta* out of her voice. "If she can handle 33 miles through those dunes, she can take a little steepness. Living without showers and toilets, and sleeping with your feet on the spare tire every night isn't for everyone. Plus, if someone else traveled with us, they'd get a vote in our itinerary."

"What's so bad about that?" I wondered if I had a vote that I didn't know about, too.

"We might go where they want instead of where I want. And what if it sucks?"

"You take us places that suck all the time," I reminded her.

"Yeah, but it's easier to deal with something that sucks when I have no one to blame but myself. Then I don't have to hide how annoyed I am. There's nothing more exhausting than pretending I'm having a good time when I'm not. And it's even worse when the bad idea was mine. Then I have to pretend like I'm having a good time *and* worry about how the other person isn't having fun. That's exponential suck." She paused for a moment to appreciate how much more real her feelings felt when she used math to describe them.

"Okay. Where to next?" I hoped it wouldn't suck.

"It's gonna be a long one," she warned, kicking off a fresh round of the worry game to pass the time.

"You should probably give me extra dinner tonight then. So you don't have to worry about whether I'm hangry."

"The reviews said that we might be out there for 12 hours," she counted. "That means all day."

"You should know better by now than to believe the Witch's lies," I reminded her. Mom thinks her worries are special, just because she's the one who thought of them. She can fill the whole world with booby traps and shadowy monsters just by expecting them to be there. That's why silently yelling at other people who don't notice her worries is important; otherwise they might never learn. Then again, if something *un*expected happens, Mom might go on enjoying herself without even noticing that something's wrong. That's why it's so important to look out for all the things that could go wrong, so that at the first sign of danger she can say, *See? I knew it! I was right all along!* I felt safer knowing that my travel companion controlled all the danger in the world.

352

There's no way to deactivate an imaginary booby trap or vanquish a monster made of nothing but shadows, but that doesn't mean that Mom can let it go. Like carrying a packpack full of rocks helps some dogs hike like *good boys*, I try to give Mom a job to soothe her worries. It doesn't matter what the job is, as long as she feels like she's doing something. "We can pack extra snacks if you're worried," I suggested.

"The reviewers said they kept losing the trail," Mom told me. "We could get lost."

"Why worry about getting lost? You get lost all the time without even trying. You're an expert."

"Getting lost is so stressful and tiring!" Her fingers curled tighter around the driving wheel. "Don't you remember all the times we've been lost before and how awful it was?"

"Getting lost is the part you do without even noticing," I said. "How can you be scared of something you don't notice? It's finding our way back that's a pain. Let's just avoid trying to make our adventure be a certain way and nothing can possibly go wrong."

"Yeah, but I use my phone to find our way back to the trail whenever we get lost. If we're out for a long time, it could run out of juice. Then we could get *really* lost."

"But you keep an extra juice box for the Witch in the packpack just like you keep extra snacks for us," I reminded her. "Here, why don't you plug in the juice box now? That way you know it'll be full tomorrow so you don't have to worry."

"But what if my phone battery gets low and I need to actually *use* the power pack?" Mom asked triumphantly, like it was the impossible question that would win the argument.

"Then you give her a snack. What's so hard about that? Snacks solve most problems, you know."

"If we use the emergency backup power, that means it's an emergency," she said, like she couldn't believe she had to explain something so obvious.

"Doesn't that just mean we're late? I thought it was called *emergency backup* so it would *prevent* an emergency."

"Running late *is* an emergency!"

It's no use arguing with someone who prefers to rack up points rather than solve problems, so I looked out the window. The Wagon crunched the last few miles to the car kennel. "What do the signs say?" I asked, hoping the distraction would throw Mom off her worry game. "I bet they say *YOU'RE IN THE WOODS NOW, SO IT'S TIME TO CHILLAX.*"

The leashes in her neck strained to keep her head from blowing off as she read, "They say there's a fee area ahead and permits are available at the ranger station. There's no cell service out here to buy one online, and I'm not driving 15 miles back to town for a permit."

Now why did they have to go and say a thing like that? I thought. They should know that Moms don't carry old-fashioned money.

"The ranger station would be closed by the time we got there anyway," Mom went on. "The reviews said that the parking lot is always full. Tomorrow's Sunday, which means that backpackers already took all the spots on Friday and Saturday. We'll have to park far away, which will only add to the distance."

"The sign said all that?"

"No, but isn't it obvious?"

Mom is a parking expert after years of practice in the City, where parking is a professional sport. She picks up on meter maid traps that lesser parkers would never notice. I looked around for a parking meter or street sweeping sign, but all I could find were trees. "Where will all the people who arrive in the morning because they didn't sleep at the trailhead leave their cars?" I asked. "We can copy whatever they do."

"I guess they'll park behind a tree somewhere." She looked confused for a second, like everything she knew about the world might be wrong. She caught herself. "But there might be rules against parking in unauthorized areas. Cars can't break rules with impunity like we can, remember?"

"Do they have meter maids in the wilder-ness like they used to in the City?"

"There are rangers. I think they do parking enforcement."

"Are the Rangers gonna take the Wagon to the pound if its technique is wrong?"

"I don't know. Maybe. But you forget, we might already be in distress because we got lost." Mom looked like she was in distress already. "It would suck to be lost all day and come back to find the van is gone with my wallet, all of our water, the chargers, and the rest of our stuff inside."

I tried to imagine it, but the situation Mom was describing sounded more like the middle of a story than the end. "Then how will we get out?" I asked.

"I guess we could ask someone for a ride." She shuddered at the thought. "But then what? I'm already having a bad day, and you want me to ask a stranger for help?" She made her lips disappear and shook her head like someone was trying to make her swallow a pill without peanut butter. "And it wouldn't end there. I'd have to *act* like I'm okay, when clearly I'm not."

"Why would you lie about that?" I asked. "Especially to someone who's already offering to help?"

"Because it's rude to tell someone they can't fix your problems when they're just trying to help. You've got to act like whatever they're doing is helpful even if it isn't, until you feel like *you're* the one doing *them* a favor. So obviously I'd have to escape as soon as possible by asking them to drop us off once we got back to town, even if the van is somewhere else."

"It wouldn't be so bad to live in the mountains. I like it here."

"You don't understand!" she wailed. "I'd probably have to make a bunch of phone calls to find out where the van is…"

"Not phone calls! They're the only Witch torture you can't withstand."

"… And obviously I can't ask a stranger to wait that long. They're not a taxi service." Another wave of hopelessness spread over Mom's face. Her nails went back to picking at the bee sting, which seemed to soothe her. Her whole arm was bigger than its twin by now, and the hole she'd dug in the skin looked ragged and angry. "And they don't have Uber all the way out here. So we'd be stranded again, and I'd have gone through all of that angst for nothing."

"Not for nothing," I reminded her. "It's much better to be stranded in a town than way out in the middle of the wilder-ness. In a town there are plenty of Friends to meet. Maybe one of them will invite us to a cookout." Mom gave me a look and I remembered that Friends were what got us into this imaginary mess to begin with. "Never mind."

Satisfied that the story was back under control, Mom picked up where she'd left off. "How can they take away your transportation back to safety like that? It's unethical!"

"They did?" I looked around the Wagon, which still seemed to be in the woods with both of us inside.

"Okay. I suppose the rangers wouldn't tow someone's car since they'd also be the ones who had to pick them up at the trailhead if they were stranded," she decided. A scab came off and she held up her fingernail to inspect it before wiping it off on her shorts.

My mind was tied in knots from trying to keep up with it all and I couldn't remember what the problem was if the Wagon wasn't kidnapped. "So how will they punish you for leaving the Wagon under the wrong tree?" I asked. "Will they have to kill us to get us out of the way before they kidnap the Wagon?"

"They'll make me pay money," she said, like it was a very vile thing.

"Oh no! And not having money is what got us into this fix to begin with!" I whimpered, starting to see what she was so worried about.

"I mean, we *have* money. It just says that the person I'm supposed to give it to is 15 miles away."

"They're definitely going to eat us now!" I trembled.

"They're not going to eat us," Mom said as if I were overreacting. "The fine probably only costs about 20 bucks more than the permit fee. But money is like battery life, you want to keep as much of it as you can."

"And it's not like you can call them and explain about the bank hiding all your money from you," I said, looking helplessly at the silent sky. "Even if the Witch would let you, they'd never believe you!"

"I could probably talk my way out of it." Mom was starting to turn right-side-out again as her need to be right won over her need to worry. She sounded annoyed that I didn't think she could handle a trifling thing like paying for things. "But it wouldn't be right to ask them to waive the fee when we knew we were breaking the rules all along. I don't want to shortchange the Park Service."

"You're right. You're premeditating your crime right now," I said. "There's no way to win in this rotten situation!"

The Witch butted in, "In a quarter mile, you will arrive at your destination."

Our time was almost up. Impossibility was closing in.

"We could park here, just in case," Mom said. I followed her eyes to a flat patch of dirt under a tree that looked suspiciously like a Wagon hitch.

After the Wagon shut down, Mom remained at her station for a few scratches, listening to the blaring silence left by the engine. "This is perfect. Why doesn't California have more of these? Come on, you needa go potty?"

While Mom leaned against a tree to use an imaginary potty, I sniffed around a suspicious circle of rocks. The middle of the circle smelled like cold fire and the bottoms of all the trees smelled like people pee. "Are you sure it's not a trap?" I asked. "This doesn't smell like a real illegal parking spot at all."

"It's one of those designated wild camping spots, you ninny. They're everywhere up here. When did you become such a worry wart?"

Later that night, Mom absently dug holes in her soup as she studied the mapp. "Should we drive to the main parking area first thing in the morning or hike from here?" she asked.

"Mmmhmm," I agreed, not really listening. I was too pooped to follow her around her thought bubble for another lap.

"We won't have to worry about parking if we go from here, but it'll add ½ a mile to the total distance. That's not so far... or is it?"

"Yip-pee. Extra 'sploring," I sighed, too pooped to follow her around her thought bubble for another lap.

"I guess we can walk half a mile if our lives depend on it." She closed the Witch's screen and the Wagon went dark. "Come on, you needa go potty before bed?"

We dismounted and I sniffed around the clearing for a good spot while Mom went back to the same tree she'd used the night before. Suddenly, the howl of a wounded animal filled the darkness. It sounded close. I froze mid-sniff to listen.

When I turned to listen the other way, I saw Mom's teeth glowing in the moonlight. Her snarl could only mean one thing— The sound came from her.

"What's wrong?" I asked, puffing up my hackles and trying to decide which way to run.

"This tree is covered in sap!" she moaned. "Now I have sap all over my butt and my shorts are stuck to my skin. When I pull them down it's like ripping off a giant Band-Aid. Why is everything so much more complicated than it has to be?"

I'd told Mom so many times that pants were an unnecessary burden that there was no sense in telling her again. She'd tried to 'splain privacy before, but I never understood the point in hiding such useful body parts under pants *and* underpants. Especially if taking off your disguise feels like ripping open a wound. Despite all the lessons I'd given her about proper potty technique, now that the people potties were open again she still preferred to do it her way, with doors to hide behind and store-bought toilet paper.

I left her peeling and hissing in the moonlight and jumped back into bed. When Mom returned, she tucked the Witch under the pillow, put her feet up on the spare tire, and we both tried to sleep through the restless twitching left over in her mind.

The sun, not the Witch woke us up in the morning. "Dog doo!" Mom said, sitting up straight without even checking with the Witch. "I was so preoccupied last night I must have forgotten to set an alarm. The trail's gonna be jammed!!"

She took a poop juice pill from the first aid kit, filled a bag to the zipper with kibble, checked to make sure the Witch's juice box was full, and we set off.

The car kennel welcomed us with a jack-o-lantern's gap-toothed smile. "Hey look, Mom, there are empty spots!" I turned to see if she was relieved, but she wasn't beside me. She was frozen several paces away, staring at a sign and lost in thought.

"Fee envelopes!" she said when I joined her. "Why didn't I think of that?"

"Don't touch!" I squeaked. "Envelopes are the mailman's favorite type of boobytrap. People lick those things. It's probably crawling with boogeyvirus."

"All that fretting about parking… Why didn't it occur to me that there would be fee envelopes?" Mom asked the envelope dispenser like it dispensed advice, too.

The trees were too socially distant and their branches too scraggly to make much shade. Trail dust gathered behind me as I walked, like the cloud that follows a galloping horse when the hero rides in to save the day. It ploofed from under Mom's clunky steps like she was walking with elephant paws. It got in my eyes and stuck to the gooey spots in the crater where Mom's bee sting used to be.

"Why, this trail isn't hard to follow at all!" I pranced. "What were you so worried about yesterday?" I zigzagged across the trail to show her both how wide it was and how silly she was to worry.

"It does all the climbing at the end," Mom said mominously. "We're gonna have to climb like 4,000 feet in the last 3 or 4 miles. It's gonna be like what we climbed with Lily yesterday, only we'll already have 5 miles in our legs when we start, and 5 miles to go when we come back down."

"Bah, you always think you can see the future, but nothing is ever how you expect it to be," I reminded her.

"It says so on the map." She poked at the Witch for backup and read triumphantly, "Here: 13.7 miles, 4,343 feet, 12 hours."

I'm so glad that dogs can't catch math. "Haven't you learned by now that numbers are just something you made up to worry about? If you don't like what they're saying, just make up different numbers. Like this: onety miles, twoteen Friends, and five bajillion, nine zillionty and a half mouthfuls. See? It's easy!"

Somewhere up the slope, a lawnmower-like growl shook the air, each snarl louder than the last. "Do you hear something?" Mom asked.

"I think someone's mowing the lawn," I said, not because it was true but because it's rude not to guess when you don't know the answer to a question.

Suddenly, a motorcycle buzzed around the corner. The Power Ranger on top must have been very lost to be so far up the mountain looking for a safe place to park. He put down his feet to give us time to get out of the way. When he spoke, instead of asking for help and directions, he asked where *we* were going.

"Are you going to the summit?" he asked.

The friendliness almost made me jump. Mom looked him up and down, searching for signs that he was looking for a fight. I guess you could say that Mom was the one looking for a fight, but when a fight finds you, it never seems like you were the one looking for it.

Fights had been harder to spot recently with everyone hiding their hostility behind muzzles and pretending like everyone else was invisible. The aggressive ones could turn on you in a flash if you broke one of their private rules, so you had to pay close attention to subtler warning signs. The most reliable tell was in their eyes, which couldn't fake a friendly sparkle or hide a threatening stab.

Mom looked at her own scowl in the Power Ranger's helmet window and then into his friendly eyes when he lifted the window out of the way. He pulled off the helmet so we could see his naked smile.

When he didn't make any sudden moves, Mom answered cautiously, "Yeah, the summit's the plan. But I've heard that the trail gets sketchy up ahead. We'll see if we make it that far."

"Most people stay on the fire road," he said in a way that showed that he wasn't *most people* and he knew we weren't either. "When you get to the saddle, look for the stick with a string on it. Turn there and you can't miss it."

"Right, the stick with the string," Mom repeated, like that was the most natural trail marker in the world.

"It's wrapped around several times," he reassured her. "And it's a big stick."

He hid his face behind his helmet again and buzzed off in a sepia cloud. Mom held her breath for a little longer to let the dust and boogeyvirus settle out of the air before we continued climbing.

The sun paid more and more attention to me as we climbed. It baked my back and breathed down my neck as I came closer to its place in the sky. I ran ahead looking for lean patches of shade where I could cool off while I waited for Mom to catch up. Finally, the mountain paused its relentless climb into the sun and leveled off. I lay down in the sliver of shade under a scraggly tree and watched the trail drop into the shady side of the valley ahead.

I was just about to point out the silliness of Mom worrying about a tame trail like this when something waving in the corner of my eye caught my attention. It was the same grey as a dead leaf but it thrashed its loose end like a tentacle rather than fluttering. Its other end was hopelessly trapped around a medium-sized stick.

"Mom! Mom! Look! A string! And it's tied around a stick!" I said as she pulled my water bowl out of the packpack. "It's the sign we've been looking for!"

Abandon all hope, ye who enter here! the string flapped.

Behind the stick, the scar that passed for a trail was streaked with the skidmarks of countless slipping paws. It looked less like a path and more like someone fell down the mountain, knocking loose every tree and rock on the way down. It was so steep that when Mom stepped on it, her heel didn't reach the ground. She snuck uphill on her tiptoes.

I thought that such an unruly trail couldn't stay that way for long, but we climbed and climbed for weeks and it never settled. The only sign that anyone might have survived the slippery slope were the tree trunks worn smooth by sweaty palms.

The mountain finally flattened into a balcony wide enough for the trail to fan out like a river into several trail-like smudges. All it took was one step back from the edge to make the mountainside I'd just climbed invisible. The neighbor-mountain looked close enough to reach out and lick it. From here, you would never think that there was a whole valley in between, filled with dusty roads, decoy campsites, car kennels, Mom, and all her worries. I sat inhaling the scene while Mom crawled out of the earth at the pace of a rising sun.

Now we had a new problem. Not only were there many, many trails on the balcony, but most of them didn't look like trails at all. They disappeared behind thick curtains of brush before dropping off the sides of boulders taller than Mom. Where nothing grew, the trail was frayed and torn by greasy black rocks that broke through the threadbare ground and hid any signs of a path. I had to get a running start and cling to their wall-like sides like Spiderdog until Mom could step in and belay me over the top.

Again and again we followed the clearer of two smudges in search of the trail, only to find ourselves at a dead end. We would go back and climb over a graveyard of logs, or around a rock that seemed to dive off a million-foot cliff, and find a pile of rocks waiting for us on the other side to tell us we were on the right path.

Or were we?

We wandered, waiting for the scenery to stick to Mom in that way that made her take a lot of pictures and not want the moment to be over. But Mom's inspiration was as slippery as the oily rocks.

"Isn't this great?" I said as I executed another flawless crash landing. "It's like we could do this forever and the trail would never end."

"Why are we even doing this? This is insane." Mom scooted to the edge on her butt and landed behind me like a sack of potatoes. "This isn't the kind of day I'm trying to have."

"Wait, you already knew you could choose what kind of day you want to have?" I asked in disbelief. "Then why wouldn't you choose to have a great day every day?"

"Some days *great* just isn't one of the choices." Mom's whole body sagged as she said it, like the words made her twoteen times heavier. "We've been wandering around up here for almost 2 hours, but according to the map, we've only made about a ½ mile of progress." She dropped the packpack on the ground with a thump and plonked her butt on a rock next to it.

The moment we stopped moving, a Jillian flies came to buzz in my eyes. My ears filled with the sound they use in movies to show you that something is dead and rotting.

Mom looked at the ground that might have been the trail, or maybe it was just dirt without any rocks or branches on it. Her eyes followed the maze up the dusty wall behind it. The maybe-trail looked like a scream-sore throat feels after a day of ferocious barking. It was even steeper and more coarse than the one we'd already climbed, interrupted here and there with walls of drab-shiny rock to fall from.

"Some days all you can do is decide whether it's worth it to keep fighting or just save your energy for a challenge with a better reward at the end," Mom said.

"But I've never watched a movie where the hero decides to save his energy. What about grit?"

"What about it?" She looked at her hands, which were covered in dark lines. There were dark lines in all of her folding places so that she looked like a pencil drawing of herself, except much older. "I've got grit to spare. And sap in my butt crack. And I want a shower."

"But don't you want to overcome all obstacles, triumph against all odds, and all that hero stuff?"

"Not every challenge ends in a breakthrough, you know. Sometimes winning is just realizing that you're banging your head against a brick wall before you give yourself a concussion." She looked across the parched valley. "I'm not having fun, and it doesn't matter how pretty the view is at the top. I don't care to see it if it's going to take us another 3 hours to get there. We've already gone 5 miles, or 7, or 8 ½, depending on which app you believe. Let's go back."

"But isn't that failure?" I asked, wondering what happened to the Mom who had jumped into the jaws of death in Utah just to see a light at the end of a tunnel.

"Does taking a risk when you're not enjoying it count as success?" It was the kind of question that answered itself.

I went through the worry checklist to figure out where I'd failed. The Wagon was safe from marauding meter maids. We had plenty of water and snacks in the packpack. There were people around to find our bodies if we got lost. We'd solved the riddle of the string and the stick. And we had a mapp to point the way. That left only one thing—the same irritating thing that had been like the sap in Mom's butt crack all year—the wicked Witch!

I tried to sound supportive as I asked, "Is the Witch not feeling well?"

"Nah, we have plenty of battery."

So I was right! The Witch *was* faking it for attention.

Mom carried on before I had a chance to tell her who was really behind her misery. "I don't mind the navigation puzzle when I can see where I'm going, but this is danger without thrill and confusion without intrigue. This story is gonna end with someone breaking their neck."

So even though we hadn't reached anything that you could call a finish line, Mom turned her back on the scratched-up slope and started downhill.

I know that you have to accept Nature's rough drafts to truly enjoy the final masterpiece, but we'd been trying to carry on against the boogeyvirus for so long that I wasn't sure the summit was worth the trip anymore. Maybe that's what Mom meant when she said that the solution to some problems was knowing when to stop fighting. When you're climbing the wrong mountain, it's not the summit that matters, but how soon you realize that you're going the wrong way. That's probably why it still felt like the boogeyvirus was getting the better of us even when we overcame its obstacles. Each victory only brought us closer to the top of the wrong mountain.

Mom minced downhill like someone with her shoelaces tied together. I followed behind to avoid being bowled over by the rocks she kicked loose, or Mom herself if she came loose from the mountainside. The *gah*-ing, *godslammit*-ing, and balancing arm-chops built a forcefield around her as we made a snail's progress back into the valley.

Eventually, the ground started supporting us again and Mom's steps grew back to their normal size. She unflinched her shoulders and the bill of her hat adjusted itself skyward. When I was sure that she wouldn't slip and squash me, I ran ahead to check out the future. Mom squawked for me to come back any time I went too far, so I hiked in suspense at the edge of the squawking zone.

I came around a bend to find a lady and her hiking partner climbing toward me. Her hiking partner had a very long, distinctive face, and I was trying to place where I knew him from before charging in for a boisterous hello when Mom grabbed my collar. I was so absorbed in trying to recognize him that I hadn't even noticed that I'd stopped walking. She pulled me off the trail and snapped on the leash.

Then it hit me. "IT'S A HORSE!" My tail wagged faster as my excitement ratcheted ever-higher. "Oh boy, oh boy, oh boy! I can't wait to bark at him!"

I'd seen horses before, of course, but never so close up. I tried to come up with the most impressive thing to bark at him when he passed, but excitement kept scattering my words. I was still trying to gather them in the right order when something even more amazing happened—The horse stopped right in front of me!

"Hi Oscar," his hiking partner said.

"Hi, I'm Oscar and I'm gonna getcha!" I blurted. It came out as a whistle, but I was too excited to care. They knew my name!

"Sorry! He's a bit starstruck," Mom said, giving me the sign to *sit*.

I clamped my butt to the ground and dug a hole in the dust with my tail. "They're the ones that are starstruck, Mom," I whispered. "Didn't you hear? They already know my name!"

"That's because I've been yelling for you to *c'mere* all morning, you goober," Mom thought at me.

"You're such a good boy, Oscar," the lady said, and my pride puffed up even more. She hadn't told the horse that *he* was a *good boy*.

The horse pretended not to notice the excitement frothing out of me like a boiling tea kettle. He was probably intimidated, but he *stay*ed so that Mom and the lady could talk.

"You used to be able to ride all around these mountains," the horse-lady said. "But now there's no trailer parking anywhere. Everyone comes over from the city and fills the parking lots so you can't turn the horse trailer around. I barely had room this morning because someone parked their dirt bike hauler like a jerk."

"I know all about having trouble with parking and not being welcome on trails," I told the horse, to have something to bond over.

"There are fewer places to ride every year because the Forest Service can't keep up with the blowdowns," the lady continued. "My mules can get around, but not the horses." She patted the horse's neck to tell him he was a *good boy* anyway. "There are rules against using chainsaws on Forest land, so the rangers have to use cross-cut saws. There are only like six guys for the whole district, so they can only clear a handful of trees a year."

"It seems to me that if the Forest Service just asked, people from the city would happily volunteer to break trail," Mom said in defense of Her People. "Office workers are always looking for physical labor to get them outside in the fresh air."

"Or what about any of those out-of-work loggers?" the Horse-lady said in defense of Her People. "There's no shortage of them."

"Right!" Mom agreed, even though she didn't know the first thing about lumberjacks. "Isn't that how we got out of the Great Depression?"

"The Civilian Conservation Corps!" they both said together.

"Jinx!" I barked to show the horse that I wasn't just smart, but quick too. Instead of shushing herself like you're supposed to when you're under a jinx, Mom shushed me and made me lie down.

"Aw, come on Mom. Let me at 'em!" I begged, stretching my nose as high as I could without taking my belly off the ground. "You think it's exciting to startle a bunny or a squirrel? Just you wait till we get this horse going."

Mom didn't answer. She just checked to make sure that I was staying *down*.

The Horse-lady waited patiently until she was sure she had Mom's attention again. "The CCC built all of these trails." She rotated a long arm to show that the trails were all around.

Mom stiffened invisibly. She's always suspicious of a trap when someone talks about history that she doesn't know about, in case they say something wrong that she doesn't know she disagrees with yet. She changed the subject instead. "And I *still* don't understand why the bathrooms are closed!" Mom had practiced this speech so many times that there was no chance that the horse-lady could look at it in a way she wasn't prepared for.

"They're ventilated, and they don't even flush!" The horse-lady nodded the same *so there* nod Mom used when she declared victory in an argument.

"Exactly!" The stiffness fell out of Mom's arms as she waved them for emphasis. "That's just what I've been saying!"

"It's called an *immune system*," the Horse-lady went on boldly. "You need to be exposed to germs to build up immunity, not hide scared in your house for the rest of your life."

"That's just what Mom's been saying! Haven't you Mom?" I looked at her for backup, but her smile was frozen like she had a slow internet connection. It took a second for her thoughts to buffer before the lights in her thought bubble turned off and the exit signs lit up.

The Horse-lady saw it too. "Can Oscar have a treat?" she asked to make peace. She pulled a snack the size of a hot dog from a pocket on the horse's packpack and broke it in half. "My dogs love horse treats." She leaned forward to give one half to the horse and threw my half on the trail.

I looked at Mom. She closed her eyes in a *go on* sort of way. I swallowed it in three big bites to show the horse that I was the kind of guy that you could share a pellet with. When I had hoovered every crumb off the ground Mom turned back downhill.

"Have a good ride on your horse!" she called over her shoulder so the horse wouldn't feel left out.

"He's a mule!" the lady shouted over the horse's rump.

"Shows what I know!" Mom signed off with a wave big enough to be seen from the next mountain.

I'd spent most of the conversation staring at the horse and waiting for my chance to speak, but I'd heard a few things that Mom and the Horse-lady said. When the clip-clopping was out of earshot I asked, "Was that lady a Friend or a frenemy?"

"She was nice. Why do you ask?"

"She said that the internet is ruining her trails because it's bringing City people to the country to fill up her car kennels. But *we* found this trail on the internet, and *we* wanted a spot in the car kennel, too. Is it like the prairie dogs who are afraid outsiders will bring cooties?"

"I don't think she was concerned about the virus, just crowds. I can't say I blame her."

"Isn't there enough room in the world for everyone?"

"Country people are kind of territorial about their land," Mom said, like it was a fact that only dumb dogs wouldn't know. "The reason they live out here is because they don't like crowds."

Mom finally seemed relaxed enough for me to ask about something that had been bothering me since yesterday. "Remember how the Women of a Certain Age were all wearing muzzles yesterday?"

"Sure."

"And do you remember how you pulled up your muzzle before you talked to them?"

"Yeah. The way I see it, someone's either wearing a mask because they're afraid of germs, in which case I should respect their boundaries and use a mask as well; or they're doing it out of respect for my safety and I should give them the same courtesy. It's only polite."

"But where was the Horse-lady's muzzle?" I asked. "Do they not have boogeyvirus in the country? What if they think it's just a fashion statement and they don't know the danger they're in?"

Mom prickled like she was nervous to have this conversation, even in her thoughts where only I could hear. "I'm pretty sure she knows."

"But…" I said, but I didn't know where to go from there. "But…" I tried again, but it was no better the second time. "Are they murderers?" I asked finally.

"Well…" Mom said, but she didn't seem to know where to go from there. "Um…" she tried again, but it was no better the second time. "Murder involves intent, so I don't think that's the right word," she said finally.

"They don't mean to hurt anyone, right?"

"Look, all these Covid restrictions have been hard on everybody. A lot of people feel like they're being told that other people's lives are more important than theirs. I know I feel that way sometimes. And without travel to unite us, different areas are developing their own customs around masks and safety. Difference doesn't have to lead to conflict as long as we understand each other, but without constant exposure to different perspectives, people are turning tribal."

"So she didn't want to hurt anyone?"

"I don't think so," she turned the question over in her mind like she was looking for the key to one of life's great questions hidden on the label of a box of crackers. "People have been saying ugly things, but I do think it's coming from a misguided desire to protect themselves. When you've gotten the message over and over for months that you're a toxic piece of filth that isn't even fit to breathe other people's air, it's gonna have an effect. Some people acquiesce because they want to be *the good ones*, but you can't really blame others for rebelling. It's up to us whether we tolerate or judge people's differences."

"But you said it yourself, it's only polite to wear a muzzle."

"Sure, it's polite where we're from. But in other places people might express respect differently, like by welcoming strangers despite their flaws and cooties. Think of it this way: some cultures think it's disrespectful to show the tops of their heads to God and other cultures think it's rude to wear a hat while you're eating. In countries where yarmulkes, hijabs, or turbans are common, they might think it's terribly rude and dangerous for someone to walk around with the tops of their heads showing, but to a visitor, covering your head might seem unnecessary or even rude. Some visitors would cover their heads out of respect, but others would hang onto the culture they grew up with, and that difference would become part of their identity. It's like that, except we're covering our faces, not our hair."

"Like how my bandana tells people that I'm a polite dog that isn't going to eat them?"

"Exactly."

"Except I wouldn't eat a Friend, even without my bandana," I said. "The muzzles save lives. All the signs say so."

"Masks save lives, and yarmulkes, hijabs, and crosses keep Yaweh, Allah, or God Almighty from smiting you. I guess the danger you feel depends on what you believe and how you deal with the uncertainty of life. Maybe we can acknowledge that everyone's having a rough year in lots of ways that have nothing to do with a virus. Sometimes you can make a bigger statement by not saying anything at all, and the kindest thing you can do is let someone hold a different opinion without trying to change their mind."

"Radical," I said. "But I don't get it. You two agreed on everything. She even shared her horse treats with me."

"You said it yourself yesterday, agreement is the root of every disagreement. Country people blame city people for misunderstanding them and ruining their way of life. And city people blame country people for misunderstanding them and sabotaging their efforts to get back to *their* way of life. That's called politics. It's why people are so angry lately."

"Because the poly-ticks sucking their blood makes them itchy?"

Mom noticed that she was scratching the bee sting again. "Yeah, but probably not in the way that you're thinking."

"Remember how Lily said that people fight about ideas? What if they just shared their feelings? Then they'd know that we're all on the same side and we could all be friends again."

"Right. But there are 2 sides to every story. Politics are the fight over whose interpretation is right."

"Like how you know how to look at a fun adventure and see nothing but problems," I said to show that I understood.

"I guess, but this time *everyone* sees problems. They just can't agree on which problem we need to solve, since the solution to one just makes the other one worse."

"Then you need a third story," I coached. "Has anyone asked a dog yet? When you fleshy folk see nothing but fences and locked gates, it's a dog who thinks to tunnel underneath."

"More like we can't agree what side of the fence we want to be on. Do we save the lives of a few or restore the quality of life of the many? Each one comes with heavy, irreversible consequences, so people need to buy into the sacrifice. Politics is the fight over who gets the short straw."

"How do people decide what side they're on if they don't want to lose something important?"

"You listen to the ideas of people you trust, and when they say something that rings true with your experience and beliefs, you adopt their view. When enough people adopt the same view, that's when we can move forward with solutions. Until then, all we can do is fight."

"Can't people take poly and tick medication every month like I do so they don't catch bad ideas?"

"There's no vaccine for politics, silly. I wish there were."

"But they're making one," I said. "The Witch was talking about it, remember?"

"Maybe you're right," Mom said, "...in a way," she added so she could be *more* right. "Once the vaccine comes, I'm sure we can put all these politics behind us. But that's still a long way off. In the meantime, we need to figure out how to get through this without killing each other."

I replayed Mom's conversation with the horse-lady in my mind, but couldn't figure out where it turned into a fight. "So how do you know who's a bad guy?" I asked.

"Isn't it obvious? The liars, of course!"

Chapter 23

Witchcraft

When we arrived back at the Wagon after meeting the horse named Mule, I collapsed in bed and would have been asleep right away if Mom would settle. Instead, she circled and dug through the blankets like she was the one preparing for a nap. I watched through one half-closed eye as she moved on from the blankets and peeled back the chewed-up corner of the mattress.

I gave up on my nap. "What are you looking for?"

"My laptop charger. It takes a long time to charge off of the van's battery, so I want to plug it in before we hit the… Ah *hah!*" She held up the spaghetti-straw in triumph. She belly flopped onto the bed and reached into the cockpit to plug it into the spare slot under the Witch's feeding straw. "I bet there's enough time for it to be fully charged by the time we get to our next spot. I don't know why I don't do this more often."

She was too proud of herself and I was too tired to remind her why. I rested my head back between my paws and let the Wagon rock me to sleep.

I woke up some time later to Mom hissing about trucks, or maybe it was ducks. When I opened my eyes, Mom was glaring at the Witch in her lap. Like a driver on TV who doesn't have to watch the road, she checked the front window quickly for trucks or ducks and looked back down at her lap for even longer.

"Dog doo!" She pulled the plug in and out of the charging hole, and twisted it around.

"What is it?" I asked.

"Dog doo! Dog doo! Dog doo!" She leaned down so that only her eyeballs peeked over the front windowsill and rummaged in the cubby next to her feet. Her paw came back holding a different plug. She kept movie-driving with her eyes off the road and paws off the driving wheel while she stuck the Witch's leash into the plug, and the plug into the charging hole. She checked the road quickly before looking down at the Witch again. "DOG DOO!"

"What?" I asked again.

"I blew the fuse again."

"Aw, don't be so hard on yourself. I think you're handling whatever it is just fine."

"No, I mean the van blew a fuse. Remember our very first adventure when I plugged too many things into the charger and we had to spend all day at that shady auto shop while a mechanic figured out what was wrong?"

"Was that the day with all the ticks?" I asked. "Because we didn't stay in the Wagon that night, remember? You went into Walmart and bought every flavor of dog shampoo so we could break the world record for Worst Bath Ever."

"Yeah, that time! It was $180 for the diagnostic and $2 for the stupid fuse," she said, as if I wouldn't believe her without a number to measure the problems by.

"And two hunerd for a lousy Motel 6 room!" I repeated to show that I remembered her grumbling. I didn't know what that meant, but sometimes it's more supportive to remember your partner's problems than to understand them.

"Exactly! Well I did it again. I shouldn't have tried to charge my phone and laptop at the same time. It blew the fuse and now I can't charge anything. Even my phone."

"Yaaay!" I cheered. "Ding dong, the Witch is dead!"

"You don't get it. If I can't charge my phone, that means no trail maps, no driving directions, no photos, no music, no audiobooks."

"… The mean old Witch, the wicked Witch," I kept singing. "Ding dong, the wicked Witch is dead!"

"… I don't even know what day it is without my phone. If I don't get this sorted out, it means a 14-hour drive back to San Francisco with nothing but my thoughts to listen to." She shuddered.

"Don't worry, I've seen this movie and there's a shortcut," I said. "You just click your heels together three times and—"

"We're almost at the trailhead and I have enough backup battery for one charge," Mom continued, ignoring my advice. "So I guess we'll turn off the phone and do tomorrow's hike the old-fashioned way. I'll figure the rest out afterward."

"Suit yourself," I yawned. I laid my head back on the blankies and went back to my nap.

That night Mom stared deep into her soup, digging shapes with the spoon and swiping beans around the bowl like Candy Crush. No matter how hard she wished, though, her soup had no answers for what was happening in the world or what the trail ahead had in store. She swallowed her last spoonful of disappointment and we stared at each other until it was too dark to see by. Finally, Mom plugged the Witch into her emergency juice box and tucked her under the pillow. She plugged her swiping finger behind my ear where it scratched pleasantly as it swiped phantom candies until Mom fell asleep.

The sliver of light wedged between the mountains overhead woke us on Mom's first day as caveman. The air seemed softer somehow and the sun was burning slightly more greyly than normal. The smell of camping filled my nose and outside the windows, Oregon looked smudgy like an old VHS tape.

"Is The Covered Wagon a time machine?" I asked as Mom tied a fresh bandana around my neck. "It seems like we're traveling into the past."

"I wish!" Mom said as scenes from before the boogeyvirus played in her thought bubble.

"Is this what they mean by the *mists of time?*"

"This isn't mist. Not in the desert of eastern Oregon."

"Then why is the whole world fading away?" I asked.

"Remember that lightning storm the other night? Before we saw Lily?"

"Right. The one that sounded just like trash day."

"Yeah, you were snoring through the whole thing." Mom showed me the white part of her eyes, like sleeping was an unmanly thing to do. Mom never sleeps through anything worth worrying about.

"What's your point?"

She looked annoyed that we weren't going to talk more about how responsible she was for protecting the world all night with her worries. Eventually she went on, "It's so dry around here this time of year that every one of those lightning bolts started a fire somewhere. It seems like all of Oregon and California are on fire."

"Oh nooo!" I howled. "So it's my fault that the world is going away? I knew it!"

"What are you talking about?"

"I could have scared off the lightning storm by barking at it. And you just let me sleep like a fool!"

Mom softened a little. "You can't scare off lightning by barking at it."

"That's not true and you know it! It's like Smokey Bear reminds me all the time, only *I* can prevent forest fires. I was just so tired from coaching you through all the other disasters. You should have woken me up!"

"It does seem incredible that so many awful things can happen at once." Mom looked toward the scruffy orange sun and baggy dark clouds around it. "Almost like we brought it on ourselves."

We set out to find the house-shaped sign that marked the boundary between car kennel and trail.

"Did you know that before Witches, the native Americans used to use these signposts to mark the way and leave messages to other travelers?" I guided. "Maybe it still works. Can you read the inscription?"

"It just explains how to poop in the woods," Mom read.

"We're already experts at that."

"… and not to leave valuables in the car to avoid break-ins."

"You've got all your valuables right here," I wagged.

Mom clicked a button on the key and the Wagon chirped goodbye. She put the keys in her pocket and, as if by magic, her paw came back out holding the Witch. Even in death, the Witch still had Mom under her spell. She drew Mom's eyeballs irresistibly to her glowing face.

"I thought she was dead," I sputtered. "You promised that we were hiking without Witchcraft today."

"I can hike without audiobooks, but not without maps or photos," Mom said, like I'd caught her doing something nasty but she wasn't sorry. "I'll turn on the low battery setting and keep it on *airplane* mode so it lasts longer, and only turn on the screen when I absolutely have to. Promise!"

"Why do you need her right now, though? There's only one trail."

"But do we know if it's the *right* trail?" As if that settled it, Mom turned her attention back to the Witch and told her to point the way.

"I have no stinkin' idea where you are," the Witch said, not even bothering to give us a blue dot anywhere among the grey boxes. "Why don't you go outside and maybe I'll tell you."

"We *are* outside, you weasel," I barked. "Stop messing around!"

"Are you underground or something?" the Witch asked in a bored voice. I could almost hear her filing her nails as she said it.

The Witch may have the personality of a cat, but you could usually count on her to be a know-it-all when Mom was vulnerable. "Why is she being such a booger-brain?" I asked.

"The mountains on either side of us must be so steep that it can't get a clear signal." Mom's always making excuses for the Witch's betrayals. "Either that or it has something to do with being powered down in *airplane* mode."

"This must be what disappearing feels like." I hoped that Mom still had enough wildness in her to find the right trail by instinct. The Wagon was counting on her, and we were all counting on the Wagon.

We left the house-sign behind, but had hardly taken three-teen steps when we reached another sign with more secret messages on it. This one was covered with a large picture of swirling lines like tree rings. A few tiny words were scattered across the drawing, but not in the usual reading way.

"Uh oh. This trail has a different name than the one we're looking for," Mom read.

"Uh oh," I agreed.

"Oh wait, but look at the shape of the trail on the map." She lifted her arm to show what she meant. "And it ends at a peak called Strawberry Summit. The name of the trail on AllTrails was Strawberry Mountain Peak, and if I remember right, it passed a lake shaped just like that one."

"A clue!" I said, relieved that Mom's instincts might not need a software update after all.

We explored a few steps farther and discovered another wooden post at the side of the trail. Instead of a string, this one had words on it. I sniffed it thoroughly, but found no hints about its message. When I'd finished peeing on it, I looked at Mom. "What does it say?"

"It says that the Strawberry Mountain trailhead is ⅛ of a mile away!"

"We're saved!" I wagged. "Take that, Witch!"

We may have been lost in the woods for more than an eight of a mile (and that's not even counting the length of the car kennel), but it had all worked out in the end.

"Isn't it amazing that someone knew that we would be looking for the trail just here and thought to put a sign out for us?" I marveled at how thoughtful people could be. "I wonder why there aren't more signs on trails so that people don't need to rely on their double-crossing witches all the time."

"There are," Mom said. "I just don't usually look at them."

I was flabbergasted. "Why ever not?"

"Because the signs don't know who you are or what you're looking for. You could accidentally follow a sign meant for someone else and get lost. That's why I never ask someone else for help. Life is just as much about knowing what advice *not* to take, you know."

I went from thinking that Mom was the dumbest person in the world to remembering that she was the *luckiest* dumb person in the world. "Good thing today's sign was for us then," I decided.

We followed the sign's instructions and walked into the forest. Only a few steps in, I noticed a mominous gurgling coming from the trees ahead. It could only mean one thing. We arrived at the banks of a river and I looked up and downstream for a bridge, but there was none. When I looked to Mom for advice, she was studying the rocks and ripples. Suddenly, surprise burst on her face.

"Hang on a second, we've been here before!" she said. "This is that trail where you chickened out crossing the river a couple years ago. Remember?"

I looked along the bank and tried to imagine what it would look like in high definition. The wet rocks sparkled like fool's gold under the orange sun. Then I remembered—The last time we were here I was still a tenderpaw who hadn't learned the secrets of roughing it yet.

The river had been pushy that day, shoving my paws in a direction that I didn't want to go. When the river refused to yield, I refused to cross. I hadn't yet learned that once you slip on a rock and lose your feet, the water holds you up and your paws become fins. Instead, I'd fought for control like Mom always does.

Mom had learned a lot herself over the years. She used to think that she needed a shower *every* week and didn't know that wet socks were just a state of mind. When she thought that dry paws were something she could expect from life, wet socks felt like a great injustice. But the boogeyvirus broke all of that. Once we fell in and learned to accept wet in our socks, smoke in our lungs, and not to count on kindness from strangers, it turned into a kind of freedom. Once you give in, it's quicker to swim to shore than to walk. Though you may come out in a different place than you planned, once you shake yourself off, it's usually only a few steps back to the trail.

"I didn't chicken out," I said. "I stood up to the river. That was a story of bravery. You're remembering it wrong."

"Whatever you say, Spud." Mom aimed at one of the hopping rocks and jumped. It wobbled under her, and she leaped toward the next one to catch her balance. She missed and made a disgusted sound, but hardly slowed down to shake the wet out of her shoe before taking the final leap to the bank.

I courageously mumped from rock to rock behind her and didn't even need a leash to convince me to do it. I jumped dryly onto the sandy bank next to Mom and did a proud jig. "Look how brave I am!"

"Uh, yeah. It's a lot easier when the river is low."

"Nuh uh! I was brave and conquered my fears," I corrected her. "The river only *seemed* smaller because my confidence was bigger."

"And I suppose it has nothing to do with how the first time we came here it was peak melting season in June, and now it's almost September?"

I had to think long and hard to remember what the different months meant. I don't know how to count time, but I do know a little about seasons and how things change. Ever since the beginning, we'd been fighting the boogeyvirus and everything that came with it like we were trying to stand in a river that wanted to wash us away.

When the boogeyvirus first attacked, we'd tried to carry on hiking. But as time went by, we began to swim. As the boogeyvirus spoiled one thing after another, bit by bit, Mom had stopped fighting the relentless current. Her thoughts still doubted that a muzzle was anything more than a good luck charm, but she kept her face hidden all the same. Over time, the push from the boogeyvirus felt less strong as we adapted and Mom found other things to get frustrated about.

I'd never failed before, but I'd watched Mom fail plenty of times; Like the time she stopped being good at her job, or that time she stopped being in love. When Mom failed, she thought it meant there was something wrong with her. If only she'd tried a little harder, or if only she were a little smarter, or lovable, she would have succeeded. So she'd fought and tried to find more ways to change the way things are. When even that didn't work and she had nothing left, she thought that something had gone rotten inside of her. A better person would have fixed the problem by now. But what if it wasn't Mom who had diminished, but the river that had swelled? Or maybe we were wading when we needed a boat. Or maybe it just wasn't the right season.

Mom could read the reviews of all the people who had crossed a river and think, *What's wrong with me if all those boobs could do it?* But she could also think, *That trail wasn't ready for me yet.*

One of the good things about being a writer is that you can think about something for a long time before you say your comeback, and it's still devastating.

"Hey, Mom. The trail just wasn't ready for me yet," I quipped.

"What?"

"You said that snobby thing about me giving up in June when I just needed to wait until August. That's my comeback: *The trail just wasn't ready for me yet.*"

"That was like an hour ago."

"So?"

"What's the key to humor?"

"Wh—"

"Timing!" Mom interrupted. She laughed.

By now the sun was getting high in the sky, but it shone through the trees with the stillness and tint of sunset. Despite days of long hikes over rugged terrain, the wholesome life of a cavedog left my legs feeling springy and fresh. Mom might have felt the same, or maybe the reason she was bounding up the mountain so peppily was to finish the trail before she died of boredom.

A marathong dog like me has ears that can fast all day and live forever on the sounds they find in the forest, but Mom's mind would die of starvation if it didn't have something to chew on. It might distract her from her hungry ears if she had something to look at, so I checked uphill into the future for where the trees stopped and the sun began. But when I looked up, all I could see were layers and layers of trees sitting on each other's shoulders, one behind the other, until they disappeared into the dingy haze.

Mom's eyes followed mine uphill and rolled back down to the trail at our feet. Her chin lifted. "Here's what we're gonna do," she gazed with determination into where the distance would be if the trees weren't blocking the view, "I'll count my paces…"

I sagged. I'd hoped that without the Witch to report to, Mom might let nature fill the space rather than finding extra ways to count it. Maybe she'd lose count by the top and let her instincts back in.

"... and every 100 steps I'll give you a mouthful of kibble," she saved. "Every 1,000 steps we'll stop for water."

"That sounds like an excellent plan! I especially like the kibble part. One question: how many is a hunerd?"

"... and when you're drinking your water, I'll check my phone to see how far we've gone."

"But the Witch doesn't know where we are, so she can't tell you how far we've gone. And anyway, you said you gave her the day off."

"True," Mom paused to give me time to get ready to be impressed, "... but my phone counts steps even when I don't have any apps running. We'll use that!"

"Just like they did in prehistoric times, before they invented watches and witches!" I cheered.

I was about to ask the point of Mom counting her own steps if the Witch could do it in her sleep, but Mom was so pleased with herself that I decided it was more important that she start her challenge with a win. Maybe all that practice counting would come in handy when a house finally fell on the Witch's head and we had to find our way in the world on our own.

"I'll show you how to enjoy the forest in case you lose count," I said. I led her through a googol of trees whose small differences only added to the feeling that they were all the same.

When a tree fainted across the trail, Mom stopped counting so as not to cheat at her own game. *Seventy-two,* she thought as she swung one leg over. *Seventy-two.* She scooted her butt cheek over the log's crest. *Seventy-two.* She reached back for the packpack and plopped it on the far side of the log. *Seventy-two.* She found a grabbing place for each hand. *Seventy-two.* She dropped to the trail. *Seventy-t-oof!* She thumped on the ground next to the packpack. *Seventy-two.* She put the packpack back on her back. *Seventy-three,* she thought as she resumed walking. Behind her, I cleared the log in a single bound.

A deep, creaky grunt came from somewhere in the trees above us.

"Do you hear that?" my perky ears and head tilt asked. "I think it's a bear who just realized he left his cave without his wallet again."

Mom looked suspiciously into the infinitrees. "It's probably a tree moving more than it's meant to. It'll probably fall down soon," she concluded with a self-satisfied nod that she still had what it took to find disaster in everything.

"You and trees have something in common," I said, seeing a chance to teach her a lesson about connecting with nature. "You both groan when you move. And when you forget your wallet."

We stopped and I drank while Mom gave the Witch the briefest of meaningful looks. Usually, Mom thinks stopping is inconvenient, but we stopped again and again on Strawberry Mountain, as if rest were a natural part of hiking. Each time Mom put on the packpack and jiggled the counter in her head back to zero, she hiked like someone with a fresh start and something to look forward to rather than someone starting over after failure.

"What's gotten into you?" I asked. "You usually hate hiking in the trees where you can't see anything."

"I don't know. My legs feel great and time is actually passing faster when I count than if I were distracted. You can cram infinite thoughts into a mile when you're not keeping time, which makes every second feel longer than the one before. Walking 100 steps takes no time at all, and I always know what number comes next. It actually feels like progress."

"Sorta like how every day in the Stuck House feels like a million years, and you can't remember if something happened this morning, yesterday, or a month ago?"

"Yeah. Time sort of loses meaning when everything happens inside the same walls just like it does when you're trapped in your head. You've got to find some way to measure your progress or you'll go crazy."

After we stopped for water the seventh time, the trees thinned enough for some weak sunbeams to leak through. After our eighth water stop, we stepped out of the woody dreadmill onto the shores of a lake surrounded by sharp peaks stabbing at the dull sky. The air stuck to my fur like a sock just out of the dryer. It felt as stuffy in my nose as breathing under a blanket on a warm day. Clouds billowed like smoke caught on a ceiling and the naked sky between the clouds had a flat neon glow that might have worked at sunrise, but the sun was far too old by this time of morning to pull off that look.

"Does it seem like it's getting smokier to you?" Mom asked, pointing at the bubblegum-grey side of the sky.

"Seems fine to me," I said. "Summer is just like that."

Mom looked around with disappointment at all the ruined pictures. A colony of igloos took up all the spots where a dog might pose in front of the scenery. The villagers stood up from their folding chairs clutching mugs of poop juice and climbed out of igloos with pillow-shaped hair. I ran toward the one that looked most like their chief. She was standing tall and barking loud for all to come and see the distinguished guest.

"Hear ye, here ye! Come behold this outstanding canine specimen!" she shouted to the smoldering heavens. Only in her funny dialect, she pronounced it, "Nacho, where are you? Nacho, *come!*"

"*Na-cho kum* to you too!" I barked, carefully sounding out the greeting.

Before I could sit at her feet and politely kiss her hand, a dog came out of the bushes.

"Hi, my name is…" he said before he got distracted by the shouting lady and ran to see what she was carrying on about.

"NACHO! NAAAH-CHO!!!" the Loud One hollered. She grabbed my Friend by the collar as soon as he was within range.

Behind me, Mom yelled, "OSCAR! OSCAR! *C'MERE, OSCAR!*"

"Hi, Oscar," the Loud One and Nacho said at the same time, although the lady was a little more friendly about it.

"Pleasure to make your acquaintance!" I wagged. "The noisy one behind me is named Mom. If you'll please excuse me for a moment, I need to see what she's screaming about."

I found Mom standing on a rock and roaring like she does when she can't see me. Half the time the reason she can't see me is because I'm standing right behind her, so her screaming wasn't a big deal. What was much more interesting was the frisbee next to her on the rock.

"What do you suppose this frisbee is doing here?" I sniffed. I'm not really a *fetch* kind of guy, but picking up a frisbee is a great way to start a game of tag, so I tested its texture with my teeth. Nobody came at first, so I was just about to do the next best thing and give it a good rip when Nacho burst out of the bushes behind me.

"Hey! That's Na-cho frisbee. It's mine!" He cocked his head, trying to decide whether to fight me for it or whether to work it out like a gentleman in a good old-fashioned game of tug.

"Finders keepers, losers weepers." I put my prize down on the rock to pose victoriously with one paw on top of it.

Nyoink! Mom's hand crept up behind me and snatched it from under my paw.

"Hey!" I barked. "Throw it! Throw it! Throw it!"

"Throw it! Throw it! Throw it!" Nacho agreed.

"Please don't let Oscar play with Nacho's frisbee," the Loud One begged.

"Don't worry, I'm giving it back to him." Mom waggled the frisbee. "Nacho! Nacho! You want the frisbee?"

Nacho pointed like a notched arrow. "I want the frisbee! I want the frisbee so bad!"

"Throw it, you tease!" I screeched.

Mom threw the frisbee. It sailed through the air and landed right at Nacho's feet. He nyoinked it up in his teeth and ran back to his village with it.

"Good job, Mom! You did it!" I cheered. Usually Mom throws balls to a spot where there's no one to catch them. I have to chase them and knock them on the ground so they won't get away before she can come pick it up. But now that Nacho had done the hard work, all I had to do was supervise. Nacho and I made a great team.

While Nacho was busy with the frisbee, I came back to the village to get to know his clan.

"Where are you from?" Mom asked the Loud One.

I pushed into her legs to encourage her to add her other hand to the butt scratching.

"We're from Portland," she told my back in a voice loud enough for Mom to hear.

"I'm from My Hometown," I grinned. "It's right near the City. Maybe you've heard of it?"

"We just came down from the eastern Cascades," Mom added. "Was it smoky up here yesterday?"

"We could smell it last night, but a lot more seems to have blown in this morning. Where did you camp?" What she meant was, *How did you get all the way up here so early in the morning? Are you a superhero?*

"Why yes, I am a superhero," I said. "They call me Tintin Quarantino because I'm an adventurous traveler with a fresh and unconventional approach to storytelling that fuses cinematic influences and humor to pay homage to the classic films I admire."

"We slept in my van at the trailhead and got an early start," Mom translated.

Both Mom and the Loud One looked around like they'd lost the next page of the script and it might be stuck under a rock or on a tree limb.

"Welp," Mom said. "We should probably get going if we want to see the top."

"It's not much farther. About a mile," the Loud One said.

"How many steps is that?" I asked, in case the suspense was too much for Mom to handle.

"Enjoy your trip," Mom said, turning away. "I hope the smoke blows out soon."

We turned our tails on the lake and followed the trail out of the forest. Once we'd left the trees behind, it led us up a slope that climbed over the treetops, giving Mom's hungry eyes a blurry panorama to feast on. Faster than I thought, we turned a corner and ran out of mountain. There was no slope so steep and slippery that we might slide off, nor perilous rocks to scale before we claimed the summit. Instead, a trail draped delicately across a couple of boob-shaped humps. The humps dropped off in cliffs to either side, so we had a choice of which direction to keep back from. Beyond the cliffs, a crowd of mountains gathered in the haze, as if to get a better look at me.

When we reached the top, Mom took my most flamboyant hat out of the packpack and looked around for the best place for a picture.

"What's the special occasion?" I asked as she worked a giant indigo-grey feather out of the packpack zipper and tried to stick it back between the jewels where it belonged.

"Because the feathers look dramatic in the breeze, and because there's so much ugliness in the world right now that I want to remember that there's softness and beauty too."

Mom stepped back to admire her work before pulling the Witch out of her pocket and looking for a place for me to pose. Her eyes landed on a patch of bare rock with nothing behind it to block the view. She stepped closer to show me where to *sit* and froze. Stepping one foot back for balance, she stretched her neck out to peek over the edge. The ball in her throat bounced. After a long second, she shifted her weight back and sank into her joints for extra sturdiness.

"Oh dog doo. That's a huge cliff," she announced in the deep voice she uses when she's unsure of herself, as if speaking low would keep her more grounded.

"Nonsense! There are treetops just beyond the edge of this rock we're standing on, see?" I took a step closer and Mom flinched. "That means there's land below us."

"Yeah, but what's *around* those trees?" She didn't wait for me to guess. "A whole lotta nothing, that's what. I don't think there's another level below us, I think there's just a ledge barely wide enough for a sapling and then…"

She stepped backward without taking her eyes off the cliff and settled into an athletic crouch, ready to run away if the cliff made any sudden moves, or maybe just to be more stable in case it tried to pull her off. She tore her eyes away for just long enough to spot a tennis-ball-sized rock on the ground next to her shoe. Her eyes locked assertively back on the emptiness, letting it know to *stay back*. She leaned over cautiously, flicking her eyes at the ground only long enough to pick up the rock. She wound back her arm and threw it. The rock sailed into the smoky sky and began to drop.

"I'll get it!" I volunteered.

"OSCAR, NO!" Her scream froze me mid-jump and pulled my butt to the ground as if by a powerful magnet.

I looked at her expectantly over my shoulder. "What? Are *you* going to get it?"

Mom just cocked her head and listened, so I listened too. A long moment later, a very quiet thump came from the far side of the cliff.

"Mom… where did the rock go?" I asked.

Her throwing arm was still frozen above her head where it let go of the rock, so she pointed with her chin. "It's in those trees. Way down there." She shifted more weight onto her back foot, as if leaning too far forward would catch the rock's momentum and make her topple over several steps of flat ground and over the edge.

My eyes followed the line of her chin into trees so far below that they looked like a piney smudge. "That's impossible! They must be a mile away. You can't throw a rock that far. You have a terrible arm."

Mom finally dropped her terrible arm and wasted precious Witch vitality taking more pictures than she needed to keep the memory. She never took her eyes away from the cliff for long, screaming when I got too close to the edge, and growling when I stepped so close to safety that it blocked the Witch's view of the scenery.

Before putting the Witch to sleep, Mom opened the mapp to see how far we were from the nearest town big enough for a car vet.

"Ah! There you are!" the Witch said. "You're on top of Strawberry Mountain, by the way."

"Where's the nearest town?" Mom asked.

"There's a Sinclair station twenty miles away," the Witch offered.

"Thank goodness," Mom sighed. "That's not far at all, so the GPS won't drain the battery on the way."

"It's going to take you like an hour and a half to get there," the Witch cackled. "If you let me die, you're sure gonna regret it. You'll be cursed with ignorance, and I'll haunt your thoughts forever with worries about all the things you can't control because you don't know about them!"

"We'd better hurry." Mom swung the packpack back in place like someone late for a very important date.

She backed slowly away from the edge, but once we were out of range of the invisible monster that sucks moms off cliffs, she turned her back on the void and rushed down the hill like someone who had more to look forward to than the certain doom of a Witchless life.

We drifted peacefully back down the trail, letting the mountain do the work. Before I knew it, I could hear the stream gurgling through the trees. When we reached its bank, Mom ignored the dry rocks and marched straight into the water, shoes, socks, and all. She untied the sweatshirt from around her waist, threw it into the river, and stomped it to the bottom so it wouldn't float away. She tucked the bottom of her shirt into her sports bra and sat down next to the sunken sweatshirt.

"What are you doing?" I asked in horror.

"I'm cleaning up." She splashed the angry hole where the bee sting used to be and flapped her shorts around underwater. "I'm sweaty and smelly, and so is my sweatshirt. There's sap in my butt crack, and it doesn't hurt to rinse out this bee sting, either."

When she was done splashing, she sat peacefully as the river muck settled into her shorts, and sweatshirt, and bee sting. "Nature isn't always something to be overcome," she said like she was the first one to think of it. "You can use the environment to your advantage."

"*Good girl!*" I said. "Now you're thinking like a caveman."

Mom stood up and twisted the water out of her sweatshirt. She tied it around her waist, where its drips joined the drips from her shorts and ran down her legs into the river by way of her socks.

By the time we reached the trailhead, Mom's shorts were dry and crusty again. We walked back into the car kennel without Mom wasting a single wish on wanting it to be over.

"I can't believe that was more than 5 hours and almost 12 miles!" she said as she opened the Wagon door for me. "It felt like nothing at all! I'm not even hangry."

I was glad I'd given Mom one last Best Hike Ever before the Witch got her revenge.

Mom clicked the seat leash, fastened her paws to the driving wheel, and set her shoulders to *dauntless*. "Now all we need is a new fuse," she announced to show me that she knew how to fix the problem, and to reassure herself that she was still in control of the situation.

"Where do we find one of those, do you suppose?" I asked.

"I don't know if it's the sort of thing you can find just anywhere. And who knows if some small-town mechanic is going to take me for a ride."

"We don't need a ride," I pointed out. "The Wagon can still hike. It's just the Witch that's on a hunger strike."

"No, I mean that some men don't think that women know anything about cars. He may not sell me the fuse and insist on charging a lot of money to run *diagnostics*." She made bunny ears with her fingers to show *diagnostics* meant *big, fat lie*.

"That's when they charge you a hunerd and eighty dollars to plug a machine into your Wagon and tell you what you already know," I said to show that man-dogs know about cars, too. "Joke's on him! You can't plug anything into the Wagon. He's gonna be so embarrassed when he has to ask *you* how to fix it!"

"Yeah, right. Like any mechanic would ask a female for car advice!" Mom scoffed. "Well if we can't find a mechanic to help, we'll have to find a bigger town with an auto parts store. This van is pretty old, though. I don't know if the parts are specialized."

That could mean real trouble. We'd learned that you can't teach old wagons new tricks a few summers ago when the bedside door fell off its hinges. The man who eventually helped us told Mom that it would be very hard to find a prosthetic door for such an old Wagon, so instead he used his big muscles to force it closed. Mom locked it and buried its handle under layers of duck-it tape as a reminder to never open it again. Like a locked door in a ghost story, it had stayed closed ever since. We could live with a lame door, but Mom couldn't live without the Witch forever.

398

"And what if they don't have one in town?" I gulped.

"We'll have to find a city where they have…" she gulped too, "… a dealership."

"No! Mom! Don't talk that way!" I begged. "Call it a *dealer-doo!*"

"It gets worse. At a dealership they *definitely* won't sell me the parts without a diagnostic. Dealer diagnostics are the most expensive of all. *And* they'll make us wait several days. *And* they'll keep the van for hours. Maybe even a whole day!"

"No! Where will we live?" I howled. The last time something like this happened, Mom left me with the Wagon while she went inside to talk to the car-vet. A man smelling of grease and machinery tricked her into giving him the keys and dognapped both me and the Wagon while her back was turned. I thought I'd have to live in that noisy garage forever, but luckily Mom found me and brought me back to the waiting room. What would become of us now that waiting rooms were illegal?

"We'll just have to hope that they have fuses in John Day," she said through locked teeth. "What kind of a name is that for a town? It sounds like a breakfast joint."

"That doesn't sound like such a bad place to be stranded after all," I said. "I hope they have bacon."

I watched Mom's thought bubble for all the ways this could end badly as the Wagon hiked back to civilization. After more than a lifetime, the Wagon pulled into the emergency drop-off spot outside the Sinclair station. Mom unhooked her muzzle from its hanger and hustled inside. A hunerd string cheese wishes later, she came back out carrying nothing but a piece of paper. She unhooked her muzzle to show the smile hidden underneath.

"Did they have cheese?" I sniffed her pockets hopefully. "I mean, did they have fuzzes?"

"No fuses and no cheese, but she gave me directions to a mechanic." Mom held up a scrap of paper.

I sniffed the paper, but it wasn't very appetizing. Mom studied it, memorizing the clues scribbled there before we set off. The Wagon wandered all three streets of the little town as Mom tried to solve the riddle on the paper. When she finally did, she was so excited that she forgot all about dognappers, and left me alone in the Wagon.

I waited a year-long minute for her to return. When the door swung open again, my heart jumped into my throat and my knees turned to jelly. I held my breath, hoping a greasy dognapper wouldn't appear in the doorway. Instead, Mom stepped out with a smile so bright that it shone through the muzzle.

She opened the door and tickled the Wagon under its front windowsill. Before I could ask if she'd found the fuzz, she slammed the door in my face. The Wagon's snout opened, blocking my view of Mom, but I could feel that she was still there by how the Wagon bounced and jiggled as she crawled into its mouth.

The jiggling stopped and Mom appeared in the doorway. She mounted the driving chair, stuck the charging straw into the Witch's mouth and paused momentously to make room for suspense. "This is it, Spud: The moment where we find out if we have to drive all the way home in silence." She took a deep breath like she was getting ready to blow out birthday candles and held it for as long as it takes to make a wish.

I watched her face as she twisted the key.

Bffffft, the Witch farted.

Mom hooted with joy. "It worked! It worked!" she laughed. "I fixed it! Me! All by myself! And it only cost a dollar!"

"Vacation is saved!" I cheered.

She held up a paw and I *high fived* it. She left the Wagon running so the Witch could drink her fill as Mom danced back inside to buy more doom breakers.

"Take that, you two-timing dingleberry!" I muttered, stomping on the Witch's feeding straw and knocking her off the driving chair as if it were an accident. "That'll teach you to sabotage our vacation."

Chapter 24
Where There's Smoke

om's sunglasses stayed on the front windowsill as we drove along the dry side of the mountains between Nevada and California. The air was faded and grey-brown like an antique photo, more ancient even than VHS. We'd been driving all day, and still the smoke followed us. The sky over Nevada on my side of the Wagon was still clear and sky-colored, but the smudge seeping over the mountains from California blurred the peaks on Mom's side. The smell of camping crowded out the smell of trees and it seemed like only a matter of time before the whole world was filled with smoke. Even though the sun was still in the middle of the sky, I could stare straight at it without blinking, like staring at the moon. It wasn't its usual sparkly grey either, but a sort of lava-grey that would have been quite nice on a pair of running shorts, but was unsettling, smoldering so high above the horizon like that. Cars stopped beside the freeway to take pictures of the neon-grey color of it.

The Witch ordered us off the main highway, and Mom's eyes immediately left the road and began searching the trees. Normally, the Law is a lowland creature, but Mammoth Lakes is a rare high-altitude habitat where they herd all the wild wagon-dwellers into hotels. Mom kept her eyes in the forest as we drove the marathong-length loop around town searching for a good sleeping place, but there were already wagons behind every tree.

On the second drive-by, the Wagon found a car-trail that had more space between trees than the others. Mom leaned forward in the driving chair as we crept down the sandy path into the forest, eyes darting from Subaru to car-house, from igloo to

Isuzu. She checked out the neighborhood for signs that dog eyes couldn't see and the muscles on the sides of her face bubbled as her teeth clamped hard. When you accidentally find yourself in a circle of unfamiliar wagons, there's always someone with terrible sleeping technique who spends the night shouting and playing music like the air is all theirs.

"I guess we're sleeping between the drunk college kids and the rednecks tonight," Mom said as the Wagon cleared a spot for itself in the crowd.

We walked into the woods to find a potty tree, Mom keeping her eyes on the ground like she does in the City to keep them from catching a Friend. When we came back, a new car was snuggled so close to the Wagon's butt that it blocked the kitchen door.

"Oh no! What will you do about dinner?" I asked, hoping it didn't mean that my dinner was also trapped.

When Mom saw what I saw, smoke came out of her ears and fury blew the hat off her head. Or maybe the smoke was there the whole time, it was hard to tell. "Forget it." She clamped the hat back down with a paw, not bothering to tuck the stray hairs underneath. "It's probably too windy to light the damned stove anyway. I'll just have nuts and raisins for dinner."

"But what about your morning poop juice?" I reminded her. "Don't you need space to set up the stove?"

"We'll figure it out." Mom opened the door and made a *hurry up* motion. "Let's just get inside and pretend this isn't happening."

She closed the Wagon against the noise of the people-puppy across the way practicing drums on a set of pots and pans. We ate our dinners lying down so that all we saw through the windows was sky. The ferocious wind kept our neighbors inside,

404

so the racket they made wasn't nearly as loud as the wind's howling. Mom poked at the Witch to tell her a bedtime story, but the Witch was giving her the silent treatment.

"Fine. We should just go to sleep anyway." Mom shoved the Witch under her pillow and flopped heavily on top to show that the Witch couldn't dump us if we dumped her first. She said a good-night curse to the wall of cars blocking the road, flopped onto her other side, and pulled the other pillow over her own head.

It was quiet when the Witch woke us in the middle of the night to get ready for our hike. When Mom opened the door, I couldn't believe what I didn't see. Her curse worked! All the other cars had gone to H-E-double-hockey-sticks in the night, just like she told them to.

"Where'd everybody go?" I asked. "Oh no! What if they're already on the trail?"

"I doubt that's what's going on." Mom looked at the moon glowing the color of butt lights on a dark highway. She sniffed the air like she fancied herself a dog. I waited for her to howl. "I think they left because of the smoke," she said instead. "At least that means it won't be crowded."

Mom had plenty of time to make her poop juice in the abandoned clearing before we took our positions inside the Wagon. As we got closer to town, the Witch came alive with all the messages she'd taken during the night. "What the heck?" Mom told the Wagon to pull over so she could give the Witch all of her attention.

"What does she want now?" I asked.

"There are 13 messages from Lily. That's not like her."

Where the hell are you? the Witch buzzed.

Are you safe?

Let me know you're okay!

Mom poked the Witch harder than necessary and spoke directly into her face. "Where are there fires in California?"

"There are fires everywhere in California," the Witch said. "Aren't you paying attention? You're gonna have to be more specific." As if picking one off the pile at random, the Witch added, "Oh, there was this fire in a place called Mammoth Reservoir. Some people had to jump in a lake to escape."

"That one! Where is that on a map?" Mom demanded.

"Mammoth Reservoir? Oh, it's over by Sacramento somewhere." The Witch showed Mom a balloon far, far away from our blue dot.

"Oh phew." Mom's body got a little less pointy. "We're at Mammoth Lakes, not Mammoth Reservoir. Totally different thing."

"Isn't a rese-roar a kind of lake?" I asked.

"Totally different thing," she repeated, a little harder this time. "Lily probably saw *Mammoth* and got confused." She put the Witch back in her lap and told the Wagon to *giddy-up*.

We arrived at the trailhead at daybreak, yet this day came with less light than usual. We dismounted into the shadowy back-of-the-basement dawn.

"Is the sun having a bad day?" I asked.

Mom shrugged. "Summer's ending. Maybe the night's just getting longer."

The trail led us into the cleavage between two mountains. I could tell this was a very pretty place, even without seeing it properly. When I turned to look back at Mom, I could barely make out an even bigger mountain hunched in the distance behind her.

Perhaps there were more mountains behind it, but there was no way of knowing what else might hide in that murky dimness.

"That's Mammoth Mountain," Mom guided. "It's only a couple of miles away, and yet you can barely see it!"

I raised my nose for a better look. It didn't look much like an elephant to me, but it was hard to tell its real shape in all this smoke. "Isn't it impolite to talk about elephants? Let's give it some privacy."

The grapefruit-grey sun rolled up the mountain. It lit the trees with an eerie glow like something in the Wagon's tail lights right before we booty bump it. Its dull rays sparkled like fool's gold in granite boulders and the river reflected its flat light like burning lava. After a while, the sun checked out completely and hid behind the smoke. It felt like the kind of cloudy day that has something worse planned.

Behind the smoke, I smelled that many, many people had passed along this trail recently. The only sign left of them was the faint smell of armpits and their shoeprints in the dust. We did meet other hikers, but they were all turtles coming *out* of the mountains, which was the wrong migration pattern for this time of morning.

"… have time to do laundry at least…" a dusty woman with more hair outside her ponytail than in it told her companion.

"… maybe head down to Badwater instead…" mused a man with a wooly beard to a lady whose outfit matched his.

"… lunch in town before we hit the road?" one man walking in running clothes said to another.

"Where's everybody going?" I asked.

"They're all leaving because of the smoke, I guess." Mom's shoulders twitched, shrugging off a thought like it was a fly in her ear.

Maybe they knew something Mom didn't. I shook off the thought. Mom knew everything. "Why are we going the other way?"

"Probably because they're more sensitive to smoke than we are." Mom thought for a second. "Either that or they have higher standards than we do. Don't think too hard about that."

She didn't have to tell me twice. I stopped thinking about it right away, but it took Mom longer to shed the thought that there was something wrong with not caring about what other people were doing.

After a few miles, the trail made a hard turn and climbed a slope so steep that it seemed no trail could hang onto it for long. The climbing got steeper and steeper, rockier and rockier, until the trail turned invisible among all the steep and rock. Mom climbed slower and slower, using all four paws evenly. The flatter Mom got, the closer I climbed on her heels until she was practically standing on top of me. The ground was strangely unsteady, and I had to step carefully to make sure the earth stayed in place under me. If the ground couldn't hold me, there was no telling what other unexpected things might happen. Mom, too, was having trouble with the trail. By now, she was standing on her front paws more than her back ones, hanging onto rocks with her claws so that her feet wouldn't push the whole mountain away behind her.

"Don't sit there, Spud," she gasped in a way that didn't sound right at all. "If I slip, I don't want to take you down with me."

"Down where?" I peeked over my shoulder. From above, the slope looked a lot more like a cliff. It seemed impossible that we'd climbed so high moving so slowly. "I'll go wherever you go. Please don't leave me here alone."

"Just stay next to me, okay? And don't make any sudden moves."

Mom tested the rocks under each of her paws before each step. Usually, she didn't find the right balance on the first try, or the second, or the third. She grabbed each rock and shook it like a loose tooth, dropping the ones that came free by her side to trip and skip the rest of the way down the mountain until they finally settled with a crackle and a thump far, far below. Before long, it was taking Mom so long to find her next step that the three rocks she was standing on started to inch down the mountain before she found the fourth.

"Oscar! Get the duck out of the way!" she said in a strangled voice I'd never heard before.

I didn't know what she meant since I was at her heels like a good boy, but I stepped aside anyway. When she finally moved her next foot uphill, the rock that it had been holding in place slipped loose. In no time, a herd of rocks was racing in a stampede down the mountain, taking the rock I'd just been standing on with them.

"Are you sure this is the trail?" I asked.

"I thought so at first," Mom panted, "but now I think we've been following the path of a rockslide."

"Why don't we turn back? This seems like one of your bad ideas, and you're no fun when you're wrong."

"I would love nothing more than to turn back, but when was the last time you looked down?"

I looked down again to see if there was something I was missing, but it looked just as get-me-outta-here scary on the second look as the first. This must be what the deer felt like right before they landed in the deer graveyard. Didn't Mom, who's so afraid of heights, see it too?

"It's so loose, I don't know how we're gonna get down," Mom choked. "I'm afraid if we put any downward momentum on these rocks, we'll slip and fall."

I took my eyes away from the bottom so I couldn't imagine what Mom would look like splattered down there. Instead, I looked up to where the mountain gave way to sky. It was closer than the valley bottom, but not close enough. "Then why did you bring us all the way up here?"

"I didn't realize we were off trail until a few minutes ago, and now we're stuck. As dangerous as this is, I think the safest thing is to keep climbing. See, we've just got a few hundred feet to go."

I sighed with relief. "Oh, I was scared for a second because I thought you didn't have a plan. Lead the way!"

Instead, she told me to *stay*. Little by little, she moved sideways to the edge of the slide, where a little bit of solid mountain stuck through the shifty discard pile. She used the mountain like a ladder, pulling herself up one white-knuckled paw at a time and kicking away rocks that came loose under the pressure of her balance.

When she found a solid place big enough to *sit*, she called to me and it was my turn to find a route that worked for my paws. Once I was within patting range, I had to find a rock solid enough to *stay* on while Mom climbed the next section.

After a million lifetimes that ended in a million imaginary splats, Mom's sharp sense of sight picked up the scent of the trail. It was on the other side of the steepest and slippiest part of the slide. And it was below us.

Again, Mom told me to *stay* while she kept climbing.

"The trail is below you, silly," I thought after her, not daring to bark in case the force of it caused more of the mountain to come loose.

"If I go straight across, I'm going to slip and take half the mountain down on top of me." She thought each word carefully, as if letting her thoughts move too quickly might send us both cartwheeling to the bottom. "The only way to cross is to keep going up and to the right until I'm above the trail."

She kept moving slower than the glacier that created this mess until she made her way to the other side, where solid mountain again poked through the river of loose rock. She called me over and I tip-toed across stones hardly bigger than my paw. They made a sound like dishes as they shifted and slipped under me. Time didn't speed up to its normal pace again until I was touching Mom. I sat so close that I was practically on top of her. Her fleshy bulk felt like the only solid thing on this mountain and I wanted as much of it holding me up as possible.

We leaned into each other, looking down at the trail not-that-close below us. "What now?" I asked.

"Sit behind me and go exactly where I go." Mom waved her hand behind her to show where she meant. I tucked in so close that my toes scratched her butt and her shoulder blades scratched my chest.

We sat like a bobsled team with our hearts beating next to each other. Mom took a deep breath, and let the mountain take its course.

We used all eight of our legs as brakes as the mountain carried us down a slope as tall as a house and dropped us on the trail in a cloud of dust and smoke.

We stood on the solid ground for a long time, just making sure that we were both really alive. Mom crumpled down next to me and put her forehead on my forehead in that way that she does when she needs to block out everything but love. She plugged her fingers into the soft fur behind my ears, and told me she loved me once for every time she'd thought of death that morning. She kissed the spot between my eyes, put her forehead back on mine, and told me I was a *good boy* just as many times.

When all the trapped screams had finally melted from her mind, Mom stood up again and looked around.

"We're going back down now, right?" I asked.

Mom followed the trail with her eyes until they lost track of it a short way below. It wasn't much easier to spot from up here than it was when we lost it a lifetime ago.

"We must be 1,000 feet up," she counted to soothe herself. "I need more time to calm down before I'm ready to try that again. Let's see what's at the top."

We'd climbed so high trying to escape death that it only took a minute of normal walking to reach the top, where the trail was flat and the ground covered in serene lakes. It must have been a very lovely place in modern times, but with the smoke acting as a filter and fear still crackling in my veins, it felt more mominous.

I sat on a rock and watched the world fade. The boogeyvirus had taken so much: my officeful of collies, the smiles of new Friends, our freedom, and Mom's invincibility. Now nature was disappearing, too. Perhaps the next time I left the Stuck House, there would be no wildness left at all, only witches and the lies that they spread.

"Is nature ruined?" I asked, searching the sparkle-less lake for signs of hope.

Mom looked where the sky was meant to be. "There's been a lot of destruction, but it's not ruined. Just injured enough to leave a scar."

We watched together as the mountains on the far side of the lake faded like the Cheshire Cat, leaving only the outlines of sharp teeth in the gloom. After a while Mom said, "You know what it's like to have a bee sting?"

It was a strange time to play the guessing game, but I played along anyway. "Surprising? When it's okay to say bad words? Ouchie? Itchy? Puffy? Something to do with venom?"

"Itchy, right." Mom picked absently at the scab on her arm. "When it's irritated, you can't think about anything else until you scratch it."

"Duh. What else would you do with an itch?"

"Fires are a little bit like that—just a tiny pinpoint of inflammation in a vast world. They only seem bigger because you can't think of anything else until they're put out." Her eyes stayed lost in the missing mountains as she picked slowly in time with her thoughts. I wondered if her mind was behind her fingers or her eyes. "Wildfires aren't like housefires," she went on. "Firefighters can't put them out, only contain them."

"Like scratching an itch," I said. "But the more you scratch, the itchier it gets."

"At least you feel like you're doing something. And doing something is a kind of relief, even if it only distracts from the problems you can't fix." She picked off a scab and inspected the tender skin underneath. "I guess what I'm trying to say is that like everything else, no fire lasts forever. It seems like the most important thing in the universe when no one can control the spread and the world is filled with smoke, but we forget quickly when the fire is out and the smoke clears."

"But if you scratch too much, you'll get a scab that takes even longer to heal."

"But at least you're healing," Mom said. "Maybe it isn't good to move on too quickly, especially when relieving your discomfort creates a whole new set of problems to recover from.

Maybe scars and charred logs remind us of what we learned during the times we'd rather forget."

"As long as the itching is gone, you know you're gonna be okay," I encouraged.

"Yeah," Mom said. I wondered if she was agreeing with me or her own thoughts. "But imagine it from the point of view of the bee. Something enormous and unexpected enters your world and it's terrifying. You fight for your life, but no matter how brave you are, you're gonna get swatted away. A minute or two later, you'll die alone in the dust, far from your hive. The disaster will carry on, and your bravery won't count for a damned thing."

"Wait, are we the bee or the one getting stung?" I asked. "Are we still on fire?"

"I thought I was saying that this, too, shall pass."

"I thought you were saying that you should be more chill and not blow your stinger on fights you can't win." I didn't give her time to answer, in case that guess was wrong. "But how can we chill when smoke has erased the whole world and there'll be nothing left when it's over?"

"The smoke is filling *our* whole world, but it's not everywhere. We're so small and can only see such a short period of time that we can't imagine these things at the scale that nature sees them. I bet there's no trace of it in Peru, or Timbuktu. It's blowing east, so we probably won't even see it at the coast. All this smoke will be a distant memory by the time we get home." She looked back toward where the land dropped away. "*If* we make it back home." She scratched behind my ears and I leaned my head on her shoulder so she could get the right spot. "*When* we make it back home," she decided. "What seems like the end of the world now is just a short irritation in the scheme of things."

"But we *live* at the End of the World," I reminded her.

"Which means there's nothing west of us to burn. The rainy season starts in a few weeks, anyway. Then they'll put the fire out and all this smoke will clear in no time. It's here one day, gone the next. Afterward, we'll see that everything we thought was lost was here all along."

"Maybe we shouldn't be here today so we're not gone the next," I said. "I mean, if the wilder-ness is so dangerous right now, shouldn't we go wherever all the other hikers went until it's safe?"

"I'm really not sure... This isn't what we planned for, but the wilderness is uncontrollable. It's like you said, if you only see it on its good days, aren't you kind of missing the point? You need to see nature in action to appreciate its power, right?"

I chewed on that. I thought that's how we'd always lived, but when I tried to come up with examples, I remembered plenty of trails that were still waiting for us because the white dirt was piled too high, or the Weather Jinx brought rain, or the trail was steep and turned Mom into a chicken. "Is that why people are such wimps?" I asked. "Because chickening out gives you something to look forward to?"

"What do you mean?"

"You people have it so good. You can open the Food Fortress all by yourself and buy hot dogs whenever you want. You get to go to an office and eat free snacks while you hang out with your Friends in meetings, or play on your keyboard for hours. You can drive wherever you want, and when you get there, people let you inside the buildings so you don't have to wait in the car. No one ever takes your toys away as soon as you find the squeaker." She served me a fistful of brunch to give herself time to remember why all that was a bad thing. "You talk about how stressful it is to have too much choice, but you complain when life makes a choice for you," I went on. "The one time life took your choice away, you had a meltdown. Everyone did. With everything you *can* do, why get so bent out of shape the few times that life says no? Doesn't Nature playing hard-to-get just give you something to look forward to?"

"I guess time feels so short and there are too many things to do."

"You just said that we have all the time in the world. Isn't it exciting to think about all the things that could possibly happen in that time?"

"Isn't it disappointing how many things we'll never get to do?"

"You can't be disappointed if you don't expect anything," I said. "Look at me. I'm never allowed to do all that cool stuff without permission, so every time the Food Fortress opens its gates, it's a delightful surprise."

"I hate surprises," Mom said. "You make it sound like freedom isn't worth the responsibility that comes with it."

"You know those pigeons in the City?" I asked.

"What about 'em?"

"Some of those guys are pretty messed up—missing feet and eyes and stuff. But I've never seen a pigeon sulking. They lose bits of themselves or they grow new lumpy bits that don't belong, and they just say, *This is my life now. Maybe I can use this peg leg to club Larry when we're fighting over smashed chips outside the Taco Bell tomorrow.* It's no use complaining about the way things are."

"Accept and adapt," Mom said thoughtfully. "Like stoicism?"

But I was just warming up. I ignored her made-up words. "Everyone's been so grouchy about the boogeyvirus because they didn't plan for it and they can't make it stop. So people do what

they always do when they want to control something dangerous—
they make rules about where the virus can and can't go. They say
that it's in some stores, but not others. That it spreads by talking to
strangers, but not your family. That it can only spread in parks with
gates to lock. But the virus *is* wilder-ness, and wilder-ness doesn't
follow rules."

"You forgot to mention how it's not in bathrooms."

"You can sulk about how other people are doing it wrong
until you pee your pants, or you can be like a dog and get excited
about everything you find rather than worried about everything you
don't know yet. If you refuse to do something until everything goes
your way, you'll be waiting for an awfully long time."

"Okay, I promise. I won't try to bend the world to fit my
will anymore." She looked at the sky. "Just please, please get us out
of here safely."

"Where to, then?"

"I was kind of hoping the problem would solve itself if we
waited long enough." She *had* let me sit at this lake for an awfully
long time, despite it being so hard to breathe. "Let's see if there's a
trailhead up here. Maybe we can hitchhike back to the van."

"Don't hitchhikers usually get murdered?" I asked.

"I'll take my chances if it means not having to go back the
way we came," Mom gulped.

"Wouldn't you rather die than ask someone for help?" I
asked.

"It's a tough choice."

"Ha! You chumps!" the Witch interrupted. "There's a
parking lot a couple miles that way, but the road to get there is
closed. You're trapped!"

"Maybe there's a longer way around." Mom tickled the Witch to put her in a better mood. "Any trail has got to be safer than what we just came up."

"You're ten thousand feet in the sky and everyone went home because of the smoke," the Witch scoffed. "What are you going to do, fly home?"

"I don't see a way out," Mom said to me as her eyes continued begging the Witch to *say it ain't so.* "I know it's early, but we haven't seen anybody else coming this direction all day. I don't think we can count on anyone coming along to help us. As sketchy as it was, I think we're gonna have to find our way out of this one on our own." Her face went greyer than the smoke as she turned back toward The Inevitable. "Let's hope the trail is easier to find on the way down. We'll take it nice and slow. Inch by inch if we need to." Then, so she would have something to live for that wouldn't be too disappointing if she died and left it unfinished, she added, "If we survive, at least we'll still have time to do laundry when we get home."

We walked along the lake to where it became a stream, which became a waterfall, which fell off the same cliff that we had to climb back down. When we reached the edge, Mom leaned forward to look at the impossible path below us. She jumped back, startled.

My hackles prickled.

A labradoodle climbed into view. "Hi guys! Golly, that sure was steep," he panted.

"Is it dog-friendly up here?" the man behind him asked.

"A hell of a lot more dog-friendly than what you just came up," Mom said with eyes wide and eyebrows high. "Is there a trail that goes all the way down?"

"Of course." The man tilted his head like Mom had said something confusing. "Although it gets a little sketchy down there a ways. How did you come up?"

"You see that scree field?" Mom pointed her chin at the pile of rocks that definitely did not look like a trail from here. "I clung to those rocks and climbed all the way to the top of that moraine before I finally found the trail." She shook out the fear and looked the man in the face so he would look closely at her face, too. "I am Claire, by the way. Claire from near San Francisco. I drive a white Dodge van with California plates. This is Oscar. Nobody knows we're here but you." She held his eyes for a long second when she was done talking to let him know that she'd told him a very important message that he might need to deliver someday.

Mom and the man reminded each other to be safe, and the labradoodle and I reminded each other to have fun. They went toward the lake and Mom and I went back in search of the trail. We started downwards, looking around before every step so the trail wouldn't have a chance to escape while we were distracted. For a while, Mom walked with only two paws on the ground until the trail dove under a blanket of white dirt the size of a small car kennel or a large driveway.

We looked down the white dirt to where the trail came out on the far side. Because of Mom's silly two-legged walking style, this steep white dirt would be too slippery for her. A good life partner thinks about his Mom's needs and not just his own. It's called *empuffy*.

"Oh no! How will you get down?" I empuffed.

Mom studied the hill for a minute. She climbed onto the top edge of the white dirt and sat down. "On my butt!"

She lifted her heels and started sliding. Unlike when we'd ridden our tabottoms back onto the trail earlier that morning, she used her paws not as brakes, but as paddles to speed up. When she got to the place where the white dirt ended, she stuck her shoes hard into the gravel and let her butt slide off the ground, back into the air above her legs. She took a few steps to catch the momentum, shook the wet out of her shorts, and turned back to me.

"Your turn!"

I started walking after her, but pretty soon I was coming down the same way.

"Weeeeeeeeeee!" I thought loudly until I landed on the rocks next to Mom.

The next time the trail disappeared under more white dirt, I said, "You're definitely going to slip and fall here. Look how steep it is." The white dirt started high enough on the uphill side of the trail to block any chance of escape, and dove across our path all the way to a stream a ways below. The stream rushed headlong toward where the ground disappeared altogether, turning it into a waterfall just beyond where the white dirt ended. The mountainside above the white dirt was too steep and crumbly to walk on and everything else was better suited for sledding than walking.

"Yippee! I get to be a sled dog again!" I jumped onto the slope and started sliding just like before.

"NO!" Mom shouted, so sharply that I dug in my paws hard and stopped short. "If you slide down that way you're just gonna plop into the river and fall over the waterfall. This time we need to go *across*, not down. You've got to think ahead, Spud!"

I didn't remind her that thinking ahead was her job.

She grabbed the rocks next to the uphill white dirt and started climbing, hanging from her front paws and using her back legs for balance like she had earlier that morning. She went up, up, up until she was standing at the head of the white dirt a little ways above the trail. As she reached across the top-most part of the white slide, one of her back legs slipped, leaving a dirty streak in the frosty whiteness. She whimpered and hugged the mountain closer for a moment before pulling her stray leg back in. When she recovered, she carefully worked her way on feet, hands, and butt back down to the trail on the far side before calling me to follow.

I walked across the white dirt like normal.

There was no white dirt the next time the trail disappeared, just air. The trail had either fallen off a cliff, or hidden under a bush. Mom studied the ground carefully for hints about what to do next while I studied her face carefully for the same. We looked for a long time before Mom started climbing down the cliff. I followed her as the rock got steeper and steeper. She hugged the mountain as she waved her foot into the abyss, searching for the next rock to stand on.

"Wait here." She held up her hand in the *stay* sign. She kept her hand up as she disappeared beneath it. Finally, Mom pulled the hand out of sight so she could use it to hang onto the next rock.

There was a lot of clattering and smashing. A second later, a cloud rushed down the lower mountain so far below that it looked like the setting of a different story.

When the cloud spent itself, I heard a voice call from the abyss, "Oscar, *c'mere!*"

I looked down, but didn't see anywhere to land even my front paws, let alone a runaway dog ramp if my brakes failed. Did she want me to take the same route as the rocks?

"I don't know how!" I whimpered.

"Okay, I don't know how you get down here either," the Voice said carefully, like it was trying very hard to stay calm. "I was hoping you had a better idea. I'm coming up. *Stay!*"

Many lifetimes later, Mom climbed out of the cliff, hanging onto bits of the mountain no bigger than a chihuahua's paw.

Our party was safely back together again, but we still didn't know where to go. Mom studied the bush where the trail might be hiding. She ducked under a branch and studied the rocks and white dirt underneath for a very, very long time.

"I think it's okay to keep going," she said.

"Where?"

"Beyond that bush. We'll deal with whatever comes after it when we get there."

I found my trail and Mom found one that was better for her.

"This doesn't look like the trail either, but at least from here I can see the trail farther down," Mom said. "If only we can get to it."

I looked down, down, down through the smoke at a faint trail miles below. Just then, the mountain under one of Mom's shoes started a surprise sprint to the valley. She pulled her leg back like she'd stepped on something hot and hung on to an outcropping of the solid mountain for balance. This stampede brought even bigger rocks down as it went, making more and more noise, and leaving Mom hanging by her armpits and elbows.

I sat and Mom hung still as statues as we watched the rocks crash through the smoke. In the background, an ant-sized hiker stopped to watch the show from below. When the dust settled, the ant-hiker turned and walked the other way. Mom tested different standing rocks until she found two that worked. She took a deep breath and we kept inching down.

Just like on our way up the slide, Mom was doing a weird smacking thing with her mouth like someone had tricked her into eating medicine.

"What's up with you?" I panted.

"I'm so scared that I have dry mouth," Mom rasped. "I've only been this frightened a few times in my life."

"Isn't it exciting?" I asked, hoping she'd say yes so I would know the pounding in my chest and the sick feeling in my tummy were a good thing.

"Fear is only exciting when you're not really in danger." Mom said in a voice about to snap. "This is very serious. If either of us loses our footing, we may not survive." I wasn't sure if she was reminding me or herself. "We'll be safe if we can just get down to where that hiker is. Easy does it."

"Maybe you should bark at it and ask it to wait," I suggested. "It can help me if you fall."

But asking strangers for help was still more scary than whatever had turned Mom's mouth into a desert, because all she did was smack her lips and plan her next step.

We inched and slid, and Mom boot-scooted and squawked, until little by little we didn't have to plan each step. Eventually Mom began to walk on all twos again, one step at a time at first. When Mom no longer had to arrange each step in advance, I caught the smell of lunch ahead. In an instant, terror turned to hunger in my belly. I ran to investigate, with Mom trotting right behind me.

The lunch lady looked up when she heard my thundering paws. "Hi! I'm Oscar and I didn't fall off the mountain, even when Mom screamed at me," I announced. "I'm very brave, so I think you should pet me on my tabottom and maybe give me some of that sammich."

"Hi," Mom called as she caught up. "Do you mind talking to me for a few minutes?"

I was so stunned that I almost forgot about the sammich. Mom? Asking a stranger to talk to her? For no reason?

The lady put the leftover lunch into her packpack without sharing and stood up to Mom's level. I closed the gap and gave her my waggly butt to scratch so she would know that we weren't stranger-eating dangerous.

"I thought I was gonna die up there," Mom explained quickly so the lady wouldn't think she was the kind of person that would talk to a stranger if it weren't a real emergency. "It would make me feel a lot better to talk to someone while I calm down."

"Um..." the Lunch Lady agreed.

She never turned all the way toward Mom, but the Lunch Lady matched Mom's pace so they could walk side-by-side, and I led the way. Mom and the Lunch Lady talked about normal things like driving, and muzzles, and their favorite trails, and how great dogs are, until Mom remembered how these things were important to her.

It turned out that the Lunch Lady was the very same ant that had chickened out when she saw all those rocks that Mom kicked loose fall off the mountain. And Mom thinks that she has no effect on the world! She probably saved the Lunch Lady's life.

"Don't feel bad, Mom chickens out a lot too," I told her so she wouldn't feel like a wimp. "Sometimes the bravest thing to do is to chicken out."

"You made the right decision," Mom said through her teeth. Her teeth wouldn't let go of each other for many hours yet. "I wish I hadn't gone up there. Absolutely nothing is worth risking my dog's life like that."

The whirlwind inside Mom didn't calm down until we were almost home. The lights came down over the City in bright, velvety greys. Even when night made the air invisible, I could tell that the gloom had followed us by how the smell of camping blotted out the smell of ocean. When we reached My Hometown, the street lights shined cones into the thick air like heads drooping under the weight of a Cone of Shame.

My hackles were still buzzing from the mountain when we walked back into the Stuck House. One eye recognized it as the same home where I'd always felt safe. The other eye saw it as a stranger might see ruins, as the pawprint of what a long-ago life left behind.

While she waited for the dryer to finish, Mom asked the Witch to tell us more about the fires.

"You're such a sucker," the Witch said. "The fire was just on the other side of that peak you were looking at this morning. The one behind the lake. The fire's burned an area one and a half times the size of the San Francisco Bay by now. Bahaha, you should see your face!"

"Holy dog doo, Oscar. Those stranded people who had to jump in a lake were walking toward where we were, just from the other direction. Talk about the wrong time to go to the mountains!"

"Sounds like we were in the *right* place at the wrong time," I said. "See? Luck isn't about avoiding danger. It's about how good it feels when it doesn't get you."

Chapter 25

Orange

"With all the forests in California closed for fire season, we'll have to get better acquainted with familiar places instead," Mom said the next morning as she dug through drawers for her running clothes. "And maybe meet some people here, too."

"I've sniffed every inch of this town," I humble-bragged. "I know everything there is to know about everyone who's ever peed here."

"Maybe you should get to know the people themselves, not just the distractions they leave behind." Mom checked the key bowl by the door to see if she'd remembered to leave the car keys there for once. As usual, the Wagon keys were there, but not the keys to the around-town car. "I'm always in such a hurry to get stuff done so we can hit the road that I hardly know anyone here in town." She started digging through the laundry, shaking shorts and jackets and listening for the jingle of keys.

"I bet Rick and Diane have missed me terribly." I ran to the door before she could change her mind. "Let's go find them right now."

"There's this trail on the far end of town that I've been meaning to check out." She pulled the car keys from the pocket of shorts she'd worn so long ago that I hardly remembered them. "I was thinking we should go there this morning?"

"You mean there are districts of My Hometown that I've never visited and you didn't tell me?"

"It's paved. I thought you wouldn't be interested." She shrugged. "It's down in the headlands by that old World War 2 lookout. You know, the one that sits like 10 feet in the air because the ground eroded around its foundation?"

"You mean Rapunzel's tower."

"I'm pretty sure it's an old war thing, but let's go check it out to see who's right," Mom challenged, turning our disagreement into a game.

Walking to the car, I picked up on something fishy. Wasn't it suspicious that the air didn't smell fishy at all? I held up my nose and sniffed for a clue, but the stink of campfires drowned out everything. Instead of little spittles of ocean breath settling on the car overnight, it was dusty with grey flakes that didn't drip, but fell like feathers when Mom opened the door.

It's normal for it to be a little dreary in the morning, when the ocean fogs up the air in its eagerness to meet the day. It's not normal for the morning to never come at all. The air glowed the color that a fire shines on a wall, and although the morning was getting on, the streetlights never turned off. As we drove across My Hometown, my eyes strained to see beyond what was right next to the road. Familiar rocks, bushes, and sidewalks appeared under the streetlights, but anything behind their cones of light looked like the smudges an eraser leaves behind. The ocean was nowhere to be seen.

"Isn't it usually lighter at this time of morning?" I asked.

"I know it's early, but this is wild." Mom squinted at the flat nothingness ahead, where the road faded away. "It's like a scene out of Cormac McCarthy. And why is it orange?"

So that's what *orange* meant! It was one of those human words I heard all the time but never understood. I sniffed a big noseful of the foul, revolting, monstrous air and thought about *orange* so I would remember for the next time. When I had it memorized, I asked, "What's a Big Mac McCarthy?"

"There's this story. It's about a boy and a man. Some world-ending catastrophe happens before the story starts—I don't know what, the book is kind of vague on the details—but there are fires, the sun and plants disappear, and everything is covered in ash. There's also disease, so most of the people are dead. Everyone who's left is afraid, desperate, and violent."

I relaxed a bit. "So all this has happened before. How does it end?"

Mom didn't answer the question so she could tell the story like it belonged to her. "It's about a father and son's love for each other. They walk along the road all the way to the ocean. There's some sense that the ocean will bring safety, but that part isn't really explained."

"That sounds just like us!" I looked toward where the ocean should be, glad that we were already almost at the happy ending.

Mom continued her book report. "I think the moral is supposed to be that love is the only thing that can save us in a post-apocalyptic world. But, like, not in a mushy way."

"What's a *pup-eclip-trick*?" The word confused my tongue. "Is it a word for the healing power of dogs?"

"*Apocalypse* means the End of the World as we know it."

"Look! I can almost see the pup-eclipse from here." There was just enough light now to make out the waves beating themselves against the sand behind the Wooden Taco Bell. The water was the dark, oily grey of heavy metal in the rusty air. "You know the End of the World, Mom. We run by it all the time."

"No one calls the coast *the End of the World* but you. I meant it in the sense of the sudden collapse of civilization after a disaster. Or, that's what it means in literature, anyway. I'd never seen an apocalypse in real life before, but this year's been more like something out of a book than anything I've ever experienced."

Now that she mentioned it, it did feel like the whole world had been fighting for breath ever since I left my old office for the last time. Even though I'd never seen the air turn orange before, I recognized the burnt sienna oppressiveness like you do something that you've only seen out of the corner of your eye as it stalks you from the shadows. Until now, we'd escaped, but its stranglehold had tightened with each twist of the plot until now it was here in My Hometown to suffercate us once and for all.

First, we'd tried fleeing civilization, back when it was just the boogeyvirus—an invisible curse that choked its victims from the inside out. The fresh air protected us for a while. When the curse caught up and sent us home, we were safe as long as we stayed in the Stuck House. But being stuck is its own kind of suffercation. To break free, people had to hide behind stifling muzzles that muffled their words, hid their faces, and smothered their spirit. If you could believe the loudest ones, the muzzles smothered their breath, too. When one of its faceless vigilantes came to muzzle Mom, she didn't fight, but turned and ran away. And again, when anger, hurt, and traffic choked the Grey Bridge with cars that overflowed with people screaming from sunrooftops that they couldn't breathe, we choked back our impatience to make room for the grief of others who needed it more. It was almost like there wasn't enough air for everyone, and some had to hold their breath so that others could breathe. You never knew whose turn it was to catch their breath, but our turn never seemed to come. And then, finally, the very air went rotten with smoke. When fire filled the world and everyone else went home, Mom and I didn't turn back. We alone stood up to the poisonous air, let it fill our chests, and breathed it right back out again. We nearly didn't make it out, and now it had come for us at home to finish the job.

"Do the Boy and the Man find what they're looking for in the ocean?" I asked, thinking of all the rivers we'd crossed, and the important lessons they'd taught us. If a little river could teach a big lesson like not fearing wet socks or waiting till the time is right, what could a whole ocean teach you?

"Not really. There might have been a giant squid, but I think I made that part up. Now that I say it out loud, it doesn't seem consistent with the narrative style. That's what I love about McCarthy's storytelling, all the most significant parts are in the subtext so you fill in the gaps from your own imagination."

"Those are the best stories! I love it when you're looking for one thing, but you find something better than you imagined and realize that the answer was inside you all along. And how does it end?" I asked again.

"You don't want to know." There was a moment of silence while Mom translated what I didn't want to know into something that I did. "But you learn that love protects us from evil, and connection to others is the path to salvation."

I was about to ask her if she'd even finished the book, but the car pulled off the familiar road into an unfamiliar car kennel, and I had more important things to wonder about. I climbed into the copilot's chair and pressed my nose against the window, but all I smelled there was smoke.

"I've always wondered what was over here." Mom opened the door and the smell of burning mixed with the faintest whiff of fish.

"No, you thought that you've already seen everything worth seeing," I reminded her, because I listen to Mom's thoughts even when she's not listening herself.

Not all adventures pop outways. Some expeditions suck into themselves, with episodes made of details rather than landscapes. With the orange glow blotting out everything beyond sniffing distance, the world shrank down to just Mom and me.

What we discovered, yard by yard, was a path tracing the End of the World mid-fall from land to sea. I sensed an imposing solidness to one side and a hollowness beyond where the rocks suddenly ended to the other.

As we ran, the smoke conjured new details that disappeared ghost-like back into the shadows after I passed. Trees with heads shaped like wind hung onto the cliff's edge by their roottips. There were benches where a dog and his Mom could watch for giant squid, back when you could still see the ocean. The hilltops were lost in the fox-grey sky. Rock walls strained against their wire cages.

"Hey, I *have* been here before!" Mom said, like she'd only just discovered that we were a few miles from home. "This used to be the road before they built the tunnel. These narrow, blind curves were hell to drive on. Every so often there would be a big landslide and everyone in Half Moon Bay would be stranded for weeks." She looked at the flimsy cage doing its best to hold back the mighty mountain. "This must be the spot that was so unstable."

"It's still a road," I pointed out. Unlike the Haunted Highway, this pavement was smooth and its paint unchipped. Its steep and twisty path wasn't a problem running at dog speed, but a clumsy car clinging to the mountainside at highway speed could make Mom's teeth stick and the leashes in her neck pop. I checked her neck now, but it was hidden under the muzzle.

"I don't think you need the muzzle," I coached. "No one's here."

"The mask is helping, for a change. I can't breathe this filth. Like you said, you can't always wait for a perfect day. You've gotta take the bad with the good, right?"

Ahead, I could barely make out the shadow of Rapunzel's tower as a dark spot in the murk. The prehistoric civilizations of My Hometown had a solemn tradition of watching for giant squid from Japan, so they built hovels throughout the hills, where they could watch in comfort. Helmet-shaped fortresses squatted like toadstools in the forest, hidden but for the bright hieroglyphics and sacred inscriptions painted on their walls. The difference between Rapunzel's Tower and the ordinary fortresses was that Rapunzel's Tower was perched on top of a sandy trunk narrower than its floor. It sat like a lighthouse in a flat, open area right at the edge of the cliff, drawing the eyeballs of any dog, tourist, or bird who passed by.

I'd seen Rapunzel's Tower from the road many times, but never up close. Despite the dream-like VHS-feeling of the morning, the tower seemed more real from outside the car than it did zooming past the window like a movie background. When we were under the shade of its floor, we stopped running to inspect the inscriptions. A Mom-sized painter wouldn't be able to climb that high. Only a giant could have painted the messages on its walls.

"What do the hieroglyphs say?" I asked.

"Most of the ones I can read are about smoking weed."

"This might be important," I said. Maybe the world catching on fire was just the beginning, and these ancient inscriptions held clues about what was to come after the Great Smoking. "Do you think *all* the plants burn, or just the weeds? Are there any instructions on how to stop it?"

"Nah, it's just drunk kids. Or, I guess they were high."

"They must have been, to reach all the way up there."

"It wasn't always like this. It used to be on the ground 75 years ago, but the wind wore away the sand underneath over time. It's basically a hoodoo."

"That's what I'm trying to figure out: *who do that*? And how did they make it float?"

"Its base won't hold up much longer. It'll fall into the ocean one of these days."

"I knew the world was falling apart!" I looked at the tower for a long moment, waiting for Rapunzel to unfurl her fur, invite us inside, and settle the bet. But no hair-stair came. Maybe Rapunzel had given up waiting for visitors, too. After half a year of being locked up with Mom in a tower of sorts, I could understand how she might start to believe that no visitors would ever come.

Now that we were living in a world without sun, where the street lights never turned off, would there ever be an end to the troubles? Maybe this really was the End of the World. I wished that Mom had finished that Big Mac McCarthy book so she could tell me how the story made it from here to a happy ending.

Mom turned away from the tower and looked into the bushes on the other side of the highway. "It looks like the trail keeps going over there." Her eyes pointed through the mist to a gate among the bushes. "Wanna see where it goes?"

Mom listened both ways and we rushed across the highway. After only a few steps, the bushes hugged closer and blocked out the towers, roads, and other traces of civilization. Only the smoke remained as the earth carried us upward into the orange air.

The trail was so narrow in places that lonely vines reached across it to reconnect with their leafy friends. Perhaps it hadn't seen enough runners to finish becoming a trail yet. Or maybe it was going the other way, forgetting the paws that carved it and fading back into wilder-ness. When the hill weighed down Mom's steps so much that running turned to walking, the brush parted and I recognized the curious triple phone tree that marks the one-mile mark on the Haunted Highway. We stepped onto the familiar balcony where ghosts look back at My Hometown one last time before the sun sucks them back to heaven.

434

I peered through the orange, trying to make out the places where I usually run patrol. Now that the sun was higher, I could make out the shadows of hills and the lacey whiteness where the ocean met the land. From up here, My Hometown looked more wild than not. The houses and streets that made up my life were slotted into the spaces left over between hills and ocean. I knew the Stuck House was down there somewhere, but the smoke and distance made it as invisible as a tiny, unimportant detail in all that wilder-ness.

Mom looked up the Haunted Highway with the hungry eyes of someone seeing it for the first time. "I had no idea that the trail system south of the tunnel connected back to the other trails in town," she said. "I wonder if we could connect them all into one big run that starts and ends at our front door."

"That would mean running a very long way to go nowhere special," I said. "The nice thing about being from somewhere is that you don't have to enjoy it all at once."

"I suppose you're right. At least not today. We've got to hurry or I'll be late to work."

Every trail changes when you run it in the opposite direction, especially when it's on a hill. In some places, the earth was so crumbly that it lost hold of Mom's shoes. She growled deep in her throat and punched the air wildly to catch her balance.

Scrit, Mom's shoes said.

"Duck!" Mom shouted.

Tisk, tisk, tisk the gravel warned as Mom fell from one leg to the other trying to catch herself after tripping.

"Damned goat trail," she growled. One of these days, Mom wouldn't catch herself, and she'd tumble into the ocean growling last words about ducks and dog doo dragging me by the leash behind her.

"Did all of California look like this once?" I asked.

"Yeah." Mom's paw slipped toward another cliff. She waved her arms until her wayward paw stomped into a bush that caught its escape. "I don't know how they got covered wagons over this terrain."

"The wagon trains didn't travel in lines like roads, right? They followed the earth like trails do."

"Sure. But eventually we got better at making straight lines to get places faster. That's called progress."

"I bet that's why everyone is so peevish lately," I decided. "Because the road they usually take is blocked, and now it's an emergency because they're gonna be late. What does progress do when there's a mountain in the way?"

"They use machines to cut through it. Like the tunnel they built to avoid landslides."

"So when your path keeps getting blocked, the answer is to hide underground where nothing dangerous can reach you?"

"I wouldn't put it that way," Mom corrected. "Progress is solving a problem that keeps happening rather than just living with it. I would think that a life coach like you would know that already."

"I thought that maybe the lesson was that sometimes it's best to stay safe underground until the danger has passed. That's why they told everyone to hide at home."

"Tunnels aren't meant to be shelter," Mom corrected again, forgetting that something can be two things at once depending on the problem. "You've got to come out on the other side eventually."

"Exactly," I said, so that we were both right. "The answer isn't always to get over it. Sometimes you just have to get through it. Maybe the reason everything has been so hard lately is because we're not getting over it, we're tunneling to the other side. When we do break through, perhaps we'll look back to the old way from a different direction and find beautiful things we couldn't appreciate before. Don'tcha think?"

"I guess. But today it's hard to see anything nice. This whole year has felt like a knee on our necks and I'm out of breath from all the running away." Mom let her eyes drift up the caged mountain toward the orange sky. "We can't dig that tunnel by ourselves. It's one of those things that can only be finished when everyone's tunneling in the same direction. And I'm losing patience with all this division."

"Don't worry, Mom. I'm sure the tunnel-building people always finish their projects quickly and without drama, since everyone is depending on them."

"I don't think you've quite grasped the concept of government."

Part 5
Cooldown

See more photos

Chapter 26

The Race

There are two hard parts of a marathong: the part that's hard for Moms and the part that's hard for dogs. A Mom-athong starts with a checklist of all the hard things she'll have to endure, like pacing, and chafing, and grape Gatorade, and the neck cramp at the end from shivering while they look for the bag with her sweatshirt and keys in it. Mom-athongs get easier as you go, because each trial is like a river—once it soaks into you, you have one less burden to worry about. Mom went through her runs doggedly checking off one misery after another until finally the river washed her clean of worries and she got her sweatshirt back.

Marathongs are a different kind of difficult for dogs. We can't read checklists, so for us, a marathong means following Mom until your legs get crabby and it dawns on you that this run might take longer than you thought. The burdens and discomfort pile up until it occurs to you to try something different, like sitting in a shady spot, or drinking from the river rather than crossing it, or sitting on a rock for a little longer than usual after a picture. But no matter what you try, Mom always tells you to keep going. So you trudge behind her, wasting no movement until the end finally comes, long after you stopped looking for it. And yet, the extra snack at the end will be the most delicious you've ever tasted, which makes the whole thing worth it.

The boogeyvirus marathong had us running both ways at once. There were trials, but no checklist to tell how much was left before the finish. We passed each challenge with a dog's strategy of trial and error, stepping boldly into rivers and resting in the shade of the Stuck House. But with no signs to point which way to turn

439

and no one telling us where the finish was, the wet socks, sunburn, and grape Gatorade only added to our burdens. No matter how long we endured, the boogeyvirus just teased, *Keep it up, you're almost there.*

One night, weeks after the first rain storms had put out the fires, when the smoke and summer fog had cleared from the air, Mom was all tucked into bed. I was helping her get a good night's rest by pinning her under the blankets, when suddenly the door to the Stuck House burst open.

I jumped up, but was too startled to bark. "What the goose?" my head tilt said.

"Grumblegrumblegrumble," grumbled Mom.

Without me to keep Mom's straightjacket fastened, she escaped the blankets and closed the door.

"Who was it?" I pinned her back where she belonged, but kept my head up and my ears cocked for signs of ghosts.

"It was the wind," she mumbled. "Can't you hear it? I must not have closed the door tightly. Come on, *lay down.*"

But what dog could *lay down* when he might need to wake his Mom at any moment to protect him? Mom pretended to sleep, but I sensed her mind sitting at attention, too. Her arm escaped the blankie and pulled me into little-spoon position. She rested her chin between my ears and her thought bubble leaked numbers into my head.

"Let's play a game," I thought to her. "Let's think about all the things we've learned this year. Round 1: Oregon. What did you learn in the dooms?"

"I learned that people lie and get away with it every day."

"Wrong. The correct answer was that you've got to keep going if you ever want something unpleasant to end. Let's try another one: What did you learn in Utah?"

"That dry socks are just a state of mind."

"I'm sorry, the correct answer was that you shouldn't let your fears stop you from chasing what you want. Okay, I'll give you an easy question: What did you learn when we got back home?"

Mom tightened her arms around my chest to squeeze more love in. "I learned that you can be unwelcome in a place where you thought you belonged."

"And the mountains, what did you learn there?"

"That rednecks don't appreciate how the Great Remote-work Migration can breathe new economic life into their communities?"

"Wrong again! The correct answer is that we're all heading for the same finish line, but we might take different paths to get there. Okay, here's an easy one." I yawned to let the suspense build. "What did you learn from that time we almost fell off the mountain?"

"That danger isn't just something abstract that happens on TV and we need to be more careful."

"More careful? What makes you say a silly thing like that?"

"I've always thought of danger as something I could leave *out there* and visit it on my own terms. But now that the air is clear, there's still no end in sight. It feels like it's only a matter of time until it gets us, too."

I must have dozed off, because the next thing I knew, her thoughts were back to chasing their tails in the same rut they'd been running through for weeks. *God, I'm gonna be so tired tomorrow. I don't want to run in this wind. I hate wind. I hate running. I hate feeling tired. I wonder how many votes they've counted in Pennsylvania. Why is it so close? How could anyone vote for* him? *I'm so tired of this. I'm so tired. God, I'm gonna be so tired tomorrow...*

Mom had gotten sucked into a very suspenseful show called *The Election*. She'd been watching it before bed all week, and after lights-out she lay awake wondering how it would end. I hadn't seen the world so wrapped up in a show since *Game of Thrones* spoilers used to chase Mom from the lunch table at work every Monday. Unlike *Game of Thrones*, Mom was too impatient to wait for the season finale to binge the whole *Election*. She tuned in to each episode as soon as it dropped, as if something terrible would happen in real life if her favorite character didn't win. The suspense was taking over our lives.

Part of the problem was that *Election* didn't follow a schedule like an old-fashioned TV show. A new episode could drop at any moment, so Mom checked with the Witch a million times a day to make sure she didn't miss a thing. She couldn't look away, even when there were no new episodes to watch, because there was always someone spinning numbers into fan fiction or *blah-blah-blahing* a theory about what something in the most recent episode could foreshadow in the next.

When her thoughts went into reruns and still no one burst through the door to gobble us up, I finally put my head on my paws and went back to sleep.

After running through "a very close race" all night, the next morning Mom's thought bubble was empty. She dug through drawers like a zombie, pulling out the right number of clothes but in the wrong combinations. She laid out two pairs of shorts and no shirt. Then, a shirt and a hat that didn't match either pair of shorts.

"What about the threeteen Jillian reasons you listed overnight for not running?" I asked. "Why don't we stay home and eat brunch in bed?"

"I do laundry on Sundays. You can't do laundry when your sock drawer is still too full to close all the way," Mom explained, like it was obvious. "What's the flattest trail around here? I don't have the energy to run uphill."

"Have you ever looked out the window?" I asked. "There's nothing flat around here. Not even the beach is flat."

Mom thought about that and it did something to her face like she'd swallowed throw-up. Her face let go. "I know! Let's go to the dog beach!"

At the Dog Beach, a dog and his life partner could run for miles using only the leash in their imagination. Mom would take off her shoes so she didn't have to worry about sand or water getting in her socks and we would run fearlessly, letting land and ocean take turns between our toes.

"But you don't wear socks on the dog beach," I pointed out.

"After all the dangers we've faced this year, maybe I can handle an overfull sock drawer after all. At least the beach is wide enough that I can keep 6 feet away and won't have to pull up my mask all the time. I'm so sick of having to worry about that damned mask. I'm sick of it all!"

"No! But we've been working so hard to make sure you don't get sick!"

She looked very sad all of a sudden. "There are other ways a person can be sick besides a virus."

Mom put on her running clothes, pulled a fresh pair of socks from the drawertop pile, closed the drawer another whisker, tied a bandana around my neck, and we turned to face the world she'd spent the night trying to block out.

When she opened the door, the screen flew open faster than Mom could catch it. Everything outside was bent in the wind as if an invisible giant were sitting on it. The same air that had breathed fire not long ago was now blowing ice. I rushed to the car as frigid combs raked through my fur. I felt better the instant I jumped into the quiet air in the back seat.

Mom looked back toward the Stuck House. "Hang on, I forgot something." She slammed the door in my face and ran back inside.

She came back a century later wearing a long-sleeved shirt. Things don't change much in My Hometown from one season to the next, so I tell the difference in the seasons by the differences between what Mom wears from night to day. It was the first time she'd run in sleeves since Utah. Without even noticing the time passing, we'd come back to the season when sleeves bookend the day.

The vast car kennel was as full as ever when we arrived at the Dog Beach. Sunlight sparkled in the sea of cars and flashed like sequins on the skirt of the dancing ocean beyond the cliffs. "The weather doesn't seem so bad," Mom said in the moment between silencing the car and opening the door. Sometimes life is like that. Something seems scary while we're inside the Stuck House listening and worrying, but if we actually venture into it, the howling wind and driving rain aren't nearly as bad as the Witch made Mom think. Mom might not even notice anything wrong if the Witch hadn't gotten her all worked up about it.

Mom's long sleeves stuck to her body like spandex in the wind as she held the door for me. "Remember how you said things aren't as bad as you thought when you turn off the TV and check them out for yourself?" she asked as I dismounted.

"You heard that?"

"You were right!" She struck a determined pose. For a moment, the wind made her look dauntless. Then, it blew her hat off and she just looked hatless.

Mom's head fur whipped like streamers as she chased her hat across the car kennel. By the time she caught up to it, she had the unruly hair and wild eyes of a mad scientist. She fit the hat back on her head to keep the madness inside and turned toward the ocean.

I stayed behind Mom for shelter as we jogged across the car kennel to where the land dropped away. Beyond the cliff, the ocean looked ragged and frayed. The wind pulled Mom's legs this way and that until they bumped together like the tinkle tubes on a windchime. A fierce gust held me midair in freeze frame, then dropped me closer to Mom's heels than I expected. When her heel popped up for the next step, I took it on the chin.

"I thought everything was supposed to be better now," my eyes said when Mom looked back to make sure she hadn't kicked my teeth in.

"They are, but it's going to happen slowly," she shouted over the wind right before we leapt off the cliff together.

Falling down a cliff isn't always as bad as it seems from the top. A set of sand stairs led from the car kennel to the Dog Beach, so we never fell more than one step at a time. The farther away from the car kennel we dropped, the more the wind relaxed.

"See? All we needed was shelter," Mom said. "We need a good wind to blow away all that smoke. This is just the beginning of a long process of clearing the air. If we can shelter ourselves from it, we might just ride this thing out after all."

"I don't remember what it was like when there wasn't danger in the air," I said, blinking the grit out of my eyes.

"Yeah, we've been running into headwinds for so long, I'm not sure I remember how to live without something to fight against. It'll probably be a while before we remember what it's like not to be constantly in crisis."

I jumped off the last sand stair onto the beach, where it was a mostly-calm sunny day. Uncountable dogs dug in the sand, splashed in the waves, and chased each other in lopsided loops. Their people threw balls or crouched to introduce themselves to dogs they were meeting for the first time. There wasn't a muzzle in sight, as if the Dog Beach were a place where more than just the dogs were free to be themselves.

I ran through the crowd, pushing other dogs out of the way and introducing myself to their people as Mom trudged around the outside of the group where she wouldn't have to talk to anyone. Here, where the sand was weak and messy, pushing off felt like digging in. A frisbee flew overhead and sand smeared under my paws as I tried to knock it out of the air before anyone else could catch it.

Lower down, where the sand spent half its day as beach and the rest as sea floor, the waves made the sand strong. A dog could run easily on the sturdy ground, leaving a line of pawprints to mark his progress. Once he'd moved on, the tide would wash all traces of him into memory, leaving a fresh, blank world for the next dog. When Mom reached the sturdy sand, she turned her shoulder to the waves and started to run. She called for me to follow.

Running on the soggy sand next to Mom was a happy feeling that reminded me that there was enough room in the world for everyone. The ocean smashed itself against the land like a berserk beast trying to break out of its cage, but by the time it lapped over my paws, it was as gentle as a kiss. No matter how hard it tried or how loud it roared, it made progress in inches and gave up ground as soon as it was gained.

Today, the ocean was especially cranky. Instead of settling the ground, it stirred up the sand within its reach, turning it into quicksand. I ran beyond the range of the unruly waves, letting the drying sand slow me down to Mom's pace. Beside me, Mom struggled through the soggy muck that greedily sucked at her paws, leaving only faint ripples where her pawprints should be. A dogtective on our trail would think that Mom had left me to walk all alone.

"Ugh! Why?" Mom groaned. "Why is everything so much harder than it needs to be lately? It doesn't matter how hard I push, the earth just sucks up my energy with every step. It's like I only get weaker and stucker the harder I try."

I was about to tell her why when two wrestling dogs distracted me. They were doing it all wrong!

"*Stay close*, Spud," Mom said, forgetting about her problems only long enough to boss me around.

Mom tells me to *stay close* around other dogs because she thinks that I'm an *sasshole*, which is her word for a referee that no one invited to the game. With the ocean crowding in on one side and the cliffs herding us close on the other, there was no room to stay out of the ring and pretend I didn't notice all the rules they were breaking. Especially the rule about how they should be playing with me. With the Referee of the Universe by my side, it shouldn't have been my responsibility to tell the wrestlers what's what, but Mom was too wrapped up in her own misery to notice. Someone had to set them straight. So I joined in their game anyway. I barked thrumpteen fouls and screeched niney-twelve penalty shots. When they paid me no nevermind, I gave them each red cards.

Being a referee is fun, but it's stressful when other dogs and the universe don't listen. I wasn't sure how long I could keep control of the situation with no one paying attention to me, but Mom was taking forever to pass. I could hardly hear her gaspy shouts over my robust barks. Finally, she plopped far enough ahead that I could run after her without it seeming like I was running away.

"And don't let me catch you doing that again!" I shouted so I'd have the last word, and the first, and all the other words in between.

When I caught up to Mom, her eyes were fixed on something that was both straight ahead and inside her head. It was the face she made when she was looking into the future. I followed her eyes to where the cliffs met the sea a short way ahead.

Mom charged straight for the barrier without slowing down. She only stopped when the water was too deep to continue running. A wave bashed into the cliff, barely far enough away for the exploding spray to miss us. Mom gave the wave a hard look. It sucked in its foam and quietly slunk back into the depths. She looked at her wrist. "Dammit. We've gone 2.95 miles. If only we'd been here half an hour earlier, we could have gone an even 3," she counted to show the size of her disappointment. "No matter where we go, it's like the walls are closing in."

"Oh no!" I took a step back onto dryer sand. "Pretty soon there'll be nowhere safe to turn."

"Not like that. It's just bad timing." Mom looked annoyed that I was making her play defense on the Worry Game. "At high tide, the water gets to the places where the sand is less settled and stirs everything up. The ground isn't as stable and there's less beach to walk on, so everyone's forced into each other's way." She looked

448

more tired than ever, even though her breathing was almost back to normal.

"Why would our run be different if we came at a different time?" I asked.

"Tides come in cycles, sort of like rivers. If we'd gotten here earlier, the way wouldn't have been blocked." Mom stretched her neck as long as it would go, trying to see what was beyond the rocky barricade. "If we wait long enough, the tide will go out and we'll be able to get through."

"How long do we have to wait till everything isn't harder than it needs to be?" I looked for a comfortable place to sit in the meantime.

"Not long now, Spuddy. No matter what, the tide's gonna turn once they call the election."

"And then everything will be better?"

"Not right away." She looked up from the ocean's rage to the top of the cliffs, where the wind scoured the land of anything not stuck in place. "There's a lot to heal from, but at least this agonizing uncertainty will be over."

"Are we still talking about the tide?" Mom often confuses what's going on inside her mind with what's going on outside. It's a condition called *metaphor*.

"Maybe not." She took one last look at the cliff blocking her way and came to join me on the dry sand. "The nice thing about an election is that it's a decision we all make together. Nobody gets everything that they want, but at least you come out with a consensus on where we should go from here. A lot of crap is gonna wash up when the tide goes out on this disastrous year. There's gonna be a lot of cleanup to do. At least we'll all be cleaning it up together."

"Come on," I said. "Let's make like the tide and turn around."

We turned back toward the part of the beach where all the people were—people who weren't working so hard to escape. I ran ahead to check out anything nasty that might have washed onto the beach while my back was turned. With the way things were going, who knows what sea monsters might wash up.

Sure enough, something was off about the distant group hiking through the waves up ahead. The dogs were unnaturally large and the human shapes, although still taller than the dogs, weren't grouped right. And no one was running. Or swimming. Or fetching. I sniffed the breeze to find out more.

"MOM! THEY'RE HORSES!" I barked with glee. "Or maybe mules. Do you think horses carry treats like mules?"

"Oh lord," Mom groaned, getting the tone all wrong for excitement. "This is just what we need. I didn't bring a leash."

"Don't worry. I'll bring 'em to you without a leash," I wagged. "You just wait right here and I'll take care of the whole thing."

"Don't you dare!" Mom's voice was sharp enough to cut off my dramatic chase. "*Stay close.*"

"Oh goody! Horses! Horses! Horses!" I panted, stretching the imaginary leash as far as it would go without making Mom snap at me.

"No!" Mom commanded. And "*Stay close!*" And "*Eeeeeeeeeeeasy.*" When we were so close that I could smell every hair on the horses' rumps, she said, "*Eh-eh-eh!*" which is what she says when she can see my thought bubble and disagrees with what's there.

The horse parade took up all the good wet sand, so Mom got on my wave-side and herded me onto the dry, shifty sand. I wanted to introduce myself to the horses, but suddenly Mom's two legs ran faster than four. I ran even faster and she matched my pace, keeping her body in the way, no matter how fast I ran. Her face wore grim determination, like she alone was blocking the four horsemen at the End of the World from riding into the City.

One horse was already gone behind me. To cut Mom off before the next one, I ran faster still. And still, Mom matched my speed.

As we pulled alongside the third horse, his jockey turned a friendly smile on Mom. I heard Mom think that she wanted to show the jockey the finger that doesn't mean *hello*, but we were in a dead sprint and she didn't have a finger to spare.

Now we were in the home stretch, with only one horse left to chase. The lead horse stepped out of the waves and started squeezing toward the cliffs, cutting Mom off and forcing us deeper onto the bad sand.

"Oh for heaven's sake," Mom gasped like a final prayer. She looked at me and made the *boop-boop-boop* noise that means I should pay attention because things were about to get real.

This is it! I panted. The horse is playing right into my paws. Now Mom will have to yield, and I'll be barking between those hooves in no time!

Then—I kid you not—Mom signaled for me to follow and ran *between two horses.*

"Really? You really mean it!" I was too gobsmacked to be excited.

"*C'mere*, Spud!" Mom said in a stronger voice than I thought was left in her. I followed, taking it all in as I merged through the parade of horses.

When we reached open water on the other side, Mom and I sprinted through the ankle-deep waves past the lead horse's nose and cut him off to reclaim the land. With the last horse behind us, we let the sand absorb our speed and eased into a victory lap.

"Phew, that was close," I panted.

"I think I'm gonna puke," Mom gasped.

A tie goes to the first competitor to claim victory (everybody knows that), so before Mom could catch her breath I announced, "And I won! I was eleventy thousand, seventy hunerd and eighty noses ahead. Which is one more than I needed."

I looked over my shoulder to savor the sight of Mom as a sore loser. She plodded on, rescuing each step from the quicksand an instant before the unsupportive world collapsed and the earth swallowed her like Saint Bernardino. Her body slumped and her breath came in ragged gasps. "Why is everything so much harder than it has to be?" she whined again. "It's like every time you think you're done, something happens that means you have to fight even harder than before."

"What are you running from?" I coached. "If you don't like horse racing, just slow down and you'll be surrounded by horses. You win either way."

Mom looked over her shoulder and the jockey on the nearest horse smiled at her. Her mouth twitched into something between a polite smile and a snarl. She turned back toward the crowd of frolicking dogs and laughing people, and the fight left her stride. She let the sand suck up the rest of her momentum and hit the *all done* button on her wrist without waiting for her watch to beep the end of the last mile.

I smiled at everyone we passed on the walk back to the sand steps. Even with all the other good boys and girls around, each stranger had a smile and a compliment just for me. "See?" I told

Mom. "You can run around playing referee and worrying about how no one plays by your rules, or you can just look for the people who play nice to begin with. It doesn't matter how many enemies there are if you find people to love you just the way you are."

"Yeah, yeah, yeah," Mom said. "Right now all I care about is that there are more of our people than there are of *them*. And that our people voted. Let's go home and see how the counting's going."

Chapter 27

Epidog

Just like everything else that year, *The Election* season ended in a cliffhanger and a warning: *To be continued…* And just like everything else that year, no one wanted it to continue as much as they just wanted to know how the story would end. Mom stayed captivated by each of the Witch's retellings, imagining all the ways the story could play out and getting more prickly when each retelling didn't answer her questions. After a while I wasn't even sure what we were waiting for anymore, let alone whether it would happen.

"Why are you still watching that show?" I asked. "All the suspense is over. You already know how it's going to end."

"But I *don't* know how it's going to end!" Mom said through stuck teeth. "I can't stop until they admit that I was right all along. Who knows what they'll try next if they think no one's watching."

Mom had been Referee of the Universe for so long that she'd forgotten it was a responsibility that no one assigned to her in the first place. For weeks, she'd been living in two competing stories: one where her patience was rewarded and she was crowned right, and the other, where everything ended with the plot twist to end all plot twists. If Mom's side lost, all the rules that civilization had created to protect itself since the beginning of time would turn out to be imaginary. It was a lot for a support dog to keep up with.

Maybe that's why she was so obsessed with rules and routine, because they were the only things left that were all hers. They could close the world down, lock up nature, burn down the wilder-ness, and make poison out of the very air around us, but as long as we didn't leave the Stuck House, there was nothing else to lose.

But too much routine can be its own kind of prison. Before I was a business dog, I too used to sit around the Stuck House all day waiting for things to happen. Since my life wasn't very exciting back then, smaller things felt bigger. Getting a treat was more of a treat, but all the moments that I *didn't* get a treat were more disappointing, too. And there were a lot more moments without treats to be disappointed about. It didn't matter that the stolen treats were only in my imagination, the rage that someone wanted to take them was still real enough to bark about.

"We didn't know how good we had it," Mom would say every now and then when she saw something on TV that would be impossible in real life.

"No one expects the Spanish Inquisition!" the Witch announced.

While the Witch laughed at her joke, Mom said, "Imagine a world where it was funny for a group of strangers to burst into someone else's home! Someone could be killed if you tried that today."

"Wait, what happened during the Spanish Imposition?" I asked.

"They murdered a lot of people. But that's not the point. It's like watching an episode of Friends to relax, and they cut away to the New York skyline with the Twin Towers. Reminders of loss are more jarring when you don't expect them."

"But what about shorter buildings that are still there?" I reminded her. "Even with everything that the boogeyvirus took away, there's still more than enough left over. You could be grateful for what you still have."

"Oh yeah, like what? The office is closed, probably forever. Stores and restaurants are closed, half of them for good. Even the damned mountains are closed."

But if Mom was wearing long sleeves again, that meant that the mountains would have been closed by now anyway. "What about the desert?" I reminded her. "Is the desert still out there? Maybe we should check."

"The desert's too far away. We need at least 4 days… Hang on a second!" she looked at the calendar on the wall and remembered what it was there for. "Thanksgiving is next week! I completely forgot!"

Mom and I had a tradition of spending every Thanksgiving in the desert near Las Vegas. We hadn't been to the desert since the first invasion of the boogeyvirus, but what's a tradition if not a connection to The Before? And what's Thanksgiving if not a time when you're supposed to eat treats to celebrate that you still have treats to eat?

"Hooray! I can taste freedom already," I drooled.

With the decision made, Mom pulled our winter gear out of the closet and loaded it into the Wagon. She bought a brick of bottled water and many more cans of soup and wet food than we could eat in a long weekend. One afternoon, she closed her laptop earlier than usual and we set off for the desert. Hours passed as buildings gradually disappeared from the windows and the land turned dry and sandy.

"Are we almost there yet?" I asked when the Wagon's control panel lights turned on. I'd forgotten how stiff a whole day of driving made me.

"Just a few more hours." By Mom's voice, I guessed that was a short way. "I thought we'd stop at those dunes in the Mojave that we never got to explore last year."

"The ones where we met Lily?" The way I remembered it, Mom never wanted to see those dooms again.

"Not those ones…"

"Oh! You mean the pink ones that were actually white?" The way I remembered it, I'd convinced her to accept the dooms as they were, without waiting for them to put on their formal colors.

"No. You remember, that time the road was too rough? We left the van behind and walked the rest of the way on foot."

"Oh! You mean the *un*-certain dooms. Where we walked all those boring miles and turned around as soon as it got sandy because it was getting late and you had to work the next day?"

"That's right. I was thinking that if we went at the beginning of our trip, we'd have the whole day to deal with the unexpected."

"Why do we need so much extra time?" Before she could answer, another question bumped the first out of the way. "Wait. What about the road?"

"What about it? I bet it'll be in way better shape than it was last time with everyone taking road trips this year."

I checked her thought bubble, where millions of beefy truck tires rolled over a Wagon-eating ditch, packing down the loose rocks and softening the steep edges until it was barely a dip. "But what if the road is the same as before?" I asked. "Or worse? What then?"

"I know I promised we'd play it safe on the side of that mountain, but I miss the thrill of trying new things. We're too precious with this old van anyway. It can probably handle more than I think. I've gotten a lot more practice off-road driving this year, and we've survived dicier stuff than that. It's like you're always telling me, I've got to get out of my own way and trust my ability to work things out."

"I told you that?" The way I remembered it, Mom finished that long-ago adventure proud of her accomplishment. When she was too chicken to push the Wagon across the ditch, we got out and walked the rest of the way. If we'd stayed on the roads the Witch told us to follow, it would have been five miles in each direction. Instead, Mom used a magic spell she called *trigomometry* to cut the distance in half. We walked wild through the desert and found our way all the way to the dooms by sight. It was the first time Mom ever found anything without someone else's trail to mark the way.

"We've been relying too much on other people's advice about what's safe," Mom said with a confident nod. "When have we ever met a problem that I can't solve by keeping my wits about me? What's the worst that could happen?"

That word *safe* reminded me of something. "What would someone less witty than you do if they got in trouble out there? What advice would you give them?"

"There was cell service, remember? I used it to find the way back to the van. I suppose they could call for help…" …*like losers!* her thought bubble added.

Something about that didn't add up for me. How would *we* get out without calling for help if we needed it? But since dogs can't add, I did the reaction Mom's face told me to do. "Ding dong, the Witch is dead!" I wagged.

By now, everything outside the Wagon was total blackness. With the Witch giving directions, Mom let the flashing cursor in the middle of the road lull her into a trance. Now that Mom's thought bubble was finally quiet, I gave in to the Wagon's rocking and dozed off.

"Exit here," the Witch announced, breaking rudely into my nap.

The Wagon exited into nowhere.

"Continue on this road for thirty-four miles," the Witch ordered.

I climbed into the copilot's chair. "Do you think thirdy-four miles is longer or shorter than those flashing lights up there?"

Mom looked through the front window at the two dots bee-booping back and forth like a game of catch. "S'riously?" She looked to the Witch for an explanation.

The Witch pointed straight ahead like everything was normal.

As the Wagon got closer, its eyes lit up a sign between the lights. "What does it say?" I asked.

"It says that the road is closed to through traffic," Mom read.

"Does that mean we have to turn back because it's too dangerous?" I was sick of signs bossing us around.

"It means that there's a way through if you know where to look for it." Mom squeezed her eyes to peer into the shadowy desert that blinked in and out of existence each time the light caught on that side. "Look!" she said after a few flashes. "There's definitely a way around. You see how the dirt's packed down beside the gate?"

My eyes followed hers out the window, but all I saw were layers of emptiness appearing and disappearing into the night. "It's awfully dark out there," I said so I wouldn't have to admit that I didn't see the solution. "The last time a sign told us that the road was closed, you said it was because we couldn't count on anyone to rescue us if we got in trouble out there. As soon as you even

460

thought about breaking the rules, the Law showed up to tell us to move along. Are you sure it's not a trap?"

Mom wagged her head as if shaking off a silly thought. "Totally different thing. When something is closed *to through traffic*, that means it's open to people who belong there. They couldn't close the road completely or else those people would be trapped. Through traffic is going to Joshua Tree, but Joshua Tree is a National Park so we can't go there," Mom said, like not being welcome made us special. "We're *aiming* for the middle of nowhere. That makes us the exception to the rule, which means we're allowed." She sat back in the driving chair as if to say, *I rest my case.*

Something still bothered me, but I couldn't put my paw on what.

The Wagon crept timidly into the darkness until its eyebeams lit on tireprints in the dust. It lined up its wheels and rolled with purpose over the tracks until its tires were back on the pavement and the fence was behind us.

"See?" Mom said. "We're perfectly safe."

I watched the bee-booping lights get smaller in the back window. "But if the road is closed, won't other people turn back before their tires get a chance to flatten out that scary ditch that stopped us last year?"

"What? Suddenly you can tell the future?" Mom asked like an invitation to a fight.

I looked out the front window the way that Mom does when she's predicting the future, but as usual, it didn't work for me. Instead, all I saw was the past. "No, I can't see the future," I admitted. "All I see are those flashing lights again."

"Crap, really?" Mom's body flopped in that way that means shenanigans aren't cute anymore.

This time, the Wagon didn't stop. It just slowed for as long as it needed to find the secret passageway.

When the bumps under the Wagon smoothed again and I didn't have to concentrate on balancing anymore, I nudged Mom's elbow to pat out the bumping in my chest. "Are you sure we shouldn't turn around?"

Mom sat tall in the driving chair as if it were a throne. "Don't worry, I know exactly where we are. Isn't that right?" she asked the Witch.

"This is the only road to where you're going," the Witch confirmed.

"Suck-up," I muttered. I went back to bed, letting Mom and the Witch finish their game of truth or dare without me.

Despite my worries, Mom's prediction came true. Every time lights dammed the road, there was always a secret passageway around the gate to the regular pavement on the other side. After jumping on and off the highway ten or fiddy times, the Wagon stopped to catch its breath while a choo-choo train as long as a race crossed our path. Boxcars chugged through the Wagon's spotlights while Mom squirmed in the driving chair and counted the centuries. When the caboose finally passed, the bee-booping lights looked both ways one more time before lifting the gate and going dark. The Wagon crossed the tracks, but this time the pavement didn't follow us into the darkness.

"The road's gonna start getting sketchy from here on out," Mom said.

"We're not at the sketchy part yet?"

"Don't be such a nervous nelly." Mom guided the Wagon to an empty place in the blackness and pulled the *all done* lever. "The best thing about the wilderness is that you only have to figure out one move at a time. Now that we know the road isn't really closed, we can put that worry behind us and rest easy."

With confidence filling her head and nothing but wilderness around us, Mom drifted peacefully into sleep. When the sun returned in the morning, it shone straight through the front window, turning the entire desert into shadows on a white screen. We followed the glare as adventure knocked on the Wagon's belly, quietly at first and then faster and more violently. Mom groaned with each sucker punch and squinted harder to find the next rock before it found us. By the time the Witch made her first announcement of the morning, Mom was squinting so hard that her face looked ready to turn inside-out.

"Continue on this road for thirteen miles," the Witch ordered.

The Wagon rattled over machine-gun dirt and rocky landmines for what felt like forever. Each time we had to slow down to find our way over a pothole or around a big rock, time stretched to hold the suspense as the world shrank into the inch in front of us. The space between obstacles got shorter until it felt like we'd been staggering blindly down this road for weeks. Then, the road crumbled away completely. There was a drop half a wheel high, followed by nothing but a stream of sharp rocks disappearing into the glare. The Wagon stopped.

Mom squinted into the shadows in the front window for a moment before giving up and pulling the *all done* lever. She released the seat leash. "I'm gonna get out and look."

"I'll help," I said so I wouldn't have to admit that I didn't want her to leave me alone.

In front of us was a strip of wildness as wide as the Wagon was long. The ditch was filled with rocks—some the size of softballs, others the size of basketballs, and all ready to shift and roll if the Wagon dared step on them. Mom poked one of the bigger rocks with her shoe to see how heavy it was. It twitched and settled into the same place it was before she nudged it. She looked at the Wagon's bellyheight and turned back to the softball- and basketball-sized boobytraps. After studying the cheesology of the ditch for a long time, she stood up and announced, "I think we can get across!"

We remounted and Mom commanded the Wagon to *back it up* so we could get a rolling start. She took a deep breath, adjusted her grip on the driving wheel, and ordered the Wagon to charge. We all braced for impact.

The Wagon filled with bangs and crunches as the road savagely kicked its underbelly. Mom's head rolled on her shoulders as I rolled from one side of the bed to the other and back again. The Wagon made the final leap out of the ditch and landed with a thud. It kept rolling.

"I think we're gonna make it after all!" Mom hooted triumphantly.

"Turn right," the Witch commanded, cutting off Mom's celebration. I may not know how to drive, but I know that when the Witch doesn't say the name of a road, it means either we're *almost there,* or we're so deep in the wilder-ness that places no longer have names in human language.

The Wagon turned and the squint fell from Mom's face. Her mouth did *The Scream* while her eyebrows did gymnastics. "Aaaah, I thought my face would be stuck like that forever!"

"How much longer?" I asked.

"In two miles you will arrive at your destination," the Witch said.

But the Wagon didn't seem so confident. It swayed like it had just chased its tail for an hour and was too dizzy to stand.

"What's wrong with the Wagon?" I asked.

"It's this sand." Mom steadied the driving wheel with stiff arms and kept her eyes fixed straight ahead. "Sand is a bit like snow. You may slip and slide a bit, but you won't get stuck as long as you keep rolling."

"Does sand melt?" I asked.

But Mom wasn't listening because not-stopping took all the concentration she had. The Wagon staggered obediently on until its wheels finally found solid ground in the tiniest little car kennel you ever did see.

"See?" Mom shifted the Wagon triumphantly into *recovery* mode. "The trick to not getting stuck is to just keep moving."

Again, there was something about that that didn't feel right, but I still couldn't put my paw on why. "But we did stop."

"Right. We stopped *after* achieving our goal," she said like she was letting me in on a clever secret.

I looked back at the Wagon prints in the sand. "But, like, what if the ground is too sticky and you *do* get stuck?"

"Sand isn't sticky, it's slippery," she said, like it couldn't be both. "It's like a river, we might slide off course, but as long as we keep moving in the direction we want to go, we'll get back to *terra firma* eventually. Like I said, once you've solved a problem in nature, you can put it behind you for good."

I didn't like the sound of *terror-firma*. "What if the Wagon gets hurt on the way back?"

"Then I suppose we'll figure it out like we did the last time we were here." She pulled down the corners of her mouth and did a lopsided shrug. "Aren't you always telling me that I spook myself by seeing danger where it doesn't belong, and that's how I miss out on the best experiences?" She looked at the desert like it was a stray dog she planned to tame. "Isn't this lovely?" Just beyond the car kennel, giant dooms curled out of the ground like the heaps of straw Rumplestiltskin weaved into gold. The gold-grey peaks looked like a less crinkly imitation of the ragged mountains on the horizon behind them.

"Yeah, but..." but what was squigging me out was still just out of my wisdom's reach. So I stopped asking questions and waited for the thing that was bothering me to come closer so I could sniff it properly.

We left the Wagon to recover and turned toward the sand. Mom set her eyes on the tallest doom rising like a great pyramid out of the sandscape and we set off.

The side of the doom was as steep as any mountain, but it sucked in enough of our paws that there was no danger of slipping to the bottom. Instead, it buried our tracks before we even made them, as if determined to keep its shape no matter who tried to leave their mark. If I dug a hole or built a sandcastle, my work would disappear back into the overall design before anyone had a chance to discover it.

When we reached the summit, Mom made me stop for a picture with two legs planted victoriously on each side of the pointy ridge. I sat as if on a throne and the point flattened into a cushion under my butt. I stared confidently into the distance as Mom and the Witch climbed around me in circles taking pictures. The dooms were the only tile that stood out in all of that vast emptiness between rumpled horizons. You could rearrange all of the other tiles between us and the mountains and no one would ever know the difference.

I stared at the doom's peak between my paws and waited for Mom to tell me she was *all done*. The crease wasn't solid, but made of Jillians of grains of sand coming and going. Underneath the grains I could see, baJillians more were stuck in place, waiting for their chance in the sun. Only the fortunate ones got to ride wind up the slope to see the desert they were a part of. The lucky grains that reached the tip only got to stay there for a moment before the wind pushed them down the other side to make way for the next. All around me, baJillians and baJillians of sand grains rushed around, constantly on the move, and yet the shape of the dooms never changed.

I wondered if the story of the dooms was about a single grain trying to reach the top and stay there, or about the whole doom directing countless unpredictable events in a pre-destined plot that none of them knew about. I wanted to ask Mom about the story of the sand dooms, but she would probably need to count all the grains before she could answer.

When Mom told me I was *all done,* I leaped off the side of the doom just to see if I could still fly. For a moment that could have lasted forever, I did. Then my paws landed and the sand caught me gently for just long enough to blast off again.

We hiked *Choose Your Own Adventure* style, making our trail in whatever shape looked most interesting until we'd turned so many times that we lost track of where the car kennel was. We could see the Wagon from the top of the Great Pyramid, but down here in the middle of the swirling dooms, it was hard to get our bearings.

"Where to?" I asked.

Mom raised her arm toward a distant mountain that was bigger than the rest. "I recognize that mountain over there as the one closest to the road."

We turned and walked the way her arm was pointing. Here and there, bushes grew in the flat sand, marking the beginning of regular, solid ground. With less to keep her mind busy, Mom asked the Witch's opinion.

"You don't need her," I said. "We just walk toward the mountain, remember?"

"The van is just a tiny speck in this enormous desert. If we're off by just a fraction of a degree, we'll miss it," Mom warned. "Even a slight muscular imbalance could be enough to set us off track."

"Think of all the adventures that you'll miss when you decide exactly where you want to go ahead of time," I said. "If you don't wander, you miss all the things you don't know to look for."

"True, but what's the alternative? If you don't take the most direct line toward your goal, you could miss it completely and be left wandering forever."

All this time, I thought that Mom was wandering in search of happiness, or at least a fun time. It never occurred to me that she was aiming for something else. But what? Then again, aiming at the wrong thing is another kind of wandering. Perhaps every wrong turn was still a step toward where we were supposed to be. Maybe the point was to wander in circles, learning lessons on each lap, until we finally learned enough to recognize the path we were meant to follow all along.

"Have we been wandering aimlessly this whole time looking for our path?" I asked. "Did the boogeyvirus lead us astray?"

"There is no path. What do you mean?"

"Life was normal, and then we went out of our way to the dooms in Oregon," I said. "Nothing was ever the same after that. Maybe that's when we got off course and we never noticed."

468

"It does have a kind of poetic resonance, doesn't it?" Mom said, missing the point.

"No, I mean that's when things started being harder than they needed to be, remember? They promised that we would only have to run fifteen and a half miles, but we had to go much, much farther than that. Maybe that's when we stepped off the right path, and why nothing has been how we expected it to be."

"I don't think that's how it works. There's rarely only one true path. More often than not, getting blown off course is a sign to aim for a different goal. If you stop chasing the impossible, you might find an easier path to something better."

"But the very next day you turned your back on the path that was calling you and took the easy way out. Are you sure we haven't been on the wrong track ever since?"

"I guess we'll only know when we get there." She looked at the distant mountain. "But this story will be a dead end if we don't find the van."

"What if we didn't look for it? What if we just let the desert lead us wherever fate wanted us to go instead of following the Witch's dirty tricks?"

"Do you know how far we'd have to walk to find help? I suppose if we keep walking toward that mountain, we'd hit the road with the ditch in 2 or 3 miles, but I didn't see any lights on the way out here besides the road work signs, did you? With the main road closed, we can't count on anyone going past the roadblocks. The nearest man-made thing is the railroad crossing more than 13 miles away. We could try to flag down a train, but who knows if the conductor would be paying attention out here in the middle of nowhere. We'd need to keep walking a few more miles to Route 66, but since it's closed, we'd probably have to walk another 30 miles back to the freeway before we saw anyone. Best to let the GPS lead the way."

I couldn't follow all those numbers. "But we could walk it, right?"

"That's close to 50 miles," she counted. "It's theoretically possible, but not with the food and water I have in the backpack. We'd need to find the van first. There are enough supplies in there for at least a week."

I looked back toward the distant mountain for guidance. A twinkling against the drab desert caught my eye. It was the Wagon reflecting the sun like a beacon. Even though we were wandering, we weren't lost after all!

The Wagon always looked sleek and shiny like a space-aged egg from far away. Even though I knew every smell and streak, this sparkling version was a better portrait of how it looked in my heart than the grimy, banged-up thing that made the Law come knocking.

Mom looked at her wrist. "Oh good! We can still be in Las Vegas by lunchtime."

She made herself a fresh cup of poop juice and we took our positions inside the Wagon. Thank dogness we'd already solved all the dangers along the way and there would be no more surprises on the slippy sand, bumpy road, train tracks, and dotted pavement.

The Wagon backed into the middle of the car kennel and turned its nose toward civilization. It took a running start and launched into the sand. We had only been moving long enough for a deep sigh when the Wagon gave a satisfied little wiggle and settled in like it was naptime.

"You've got to keep moving," I reminded Mom.

Rrrrrrrrr, purred the Wagon in a tone that sounded less like contentment and more like panic.

"Oh dog doo," Mom said slowly, like speaking at a normal pace might cause something to go terribly wrong.

"Does this count as stopping?" I asked.

Mom dismounted without answering my question and disappeared below the windowsill. She was much dustier when she reappeared a very long time later.

"We're stuck," she announced as she climbed back into position behind the driving wheel. "We're really in deep, but there's hardpan about six inches down. I dug out the wheels and all the sand I could reach underneath to clear a sort of track to more solid ground." She woke up the Wagon. "It'll be okay, if only we can get moving again…"

"Ready, set, go!" I cheered.

"I am," Mom said through her teeth.

"No you're not. See? We haven't moved."

"Maybe we can reverse out of it?" She moved a lever but the Wagon paid her no mind and went on whine-purring.

Mom's whole body made a fist and the Wagon's whine got more shrill, but still we didn't move.

Mom let go. With a sigh, she turned the key and the Wagon went silent. She spread wide the Wagon gates and let me back into the desert.

I inspected the Wagon while Mom discussed our options with the Witch. The first clue I found was that the Wagon's belly was on the ground, which wasn't how it usually sat.

"*Up-up*," I commanded, but the Wagon didn't move a muscle.

I didn't know the sign language Mom used to communicate with the Wagon, so I sniffed around some more in search of another idea. "Eureka! I know what the problem is!" I declared.

"The sand ate the bottom half of the wheels so they can only roll on one side!"

"Yes, I'm safe. But I'm in trouble," Mom told the Witch.

"I think we have to lift it from the top and move it a few Wagon-lengths that way," I suggested.

"It's okay, I have food and water if I need to be out here for a few days, but I'm hoping you can send someone with a winch…"

"The Witch can't help here," I told her. "She has no arms to push with, nor feet to drive with. You need to try a new style of moving. The usual way isn't gonna work."

"Not a *witch*, a *winch*," Mom said with her eyebrows crossed, which meant *shut up, I'm on the phone.*

"A wench? Will she be strong enough? I don't see how a girl would be any better at—"

"A winch, a winch!" Mom repeated. "As in something to pull us like a fish on a hook. Yes."

I couldn't tell if she was talking to me or the Witch. I decided she was talking to me. "Where are you gonna find one of those all the way out here?"

"Yes, I think a winch on a 4X4 truck should do it. Thank you. I'll give him my GPS coordinates when he texts me his number." Mom put the Witch in her pocket and stared blankly at the distant mountains.

"What's the plan?" I asked. Mom always has a plan.

"Spud, I just did something I thought would kill me," she said without taking her eyes off the mountains.

"Talk on the phone? Yes, I heard you. *Good girl.*"

"No, I mean—"

"Oh! I know what's been bugging me!" I interrupted before she gave away the answer. "You kept saying we wouldn't get stuck, but we did. Then you said the only way out was to call for help. But you hate the phone, and you'd rather die than ask for help. Are we gonna die?"

"… I just asked for help!" she finished like she could hardly believe it herself.

"Oh no! You'll have to let someone else do something that you'd rather do for yourself," I empuffed. "You're already having a bad day and now you'll have to act like you're okay when clearly you're not."

The toughness drained from Mom's whole body at once. "Yeah, well, there's no getting out of this one without help."

I looked around and noticed that no help was on the way. "Now what?"

"We wait." If there's one thing that Mom hates as much as asking for help, it's waiting. "What should we do on our adventure?" she asked to turn the wait into something less terrifying.

"Why don't we go play in the dooms some more?"

"Nah. I've got sand in my shoes." Mom kicked the ground to scoop a little sand onto her shoe for extra realness. "How about I drink my coffee and we write?"

"I guess," I shrugged, lying in the shade of a bush.

Mom tore off the tag and opened the pop-out chair that had seemed like such an exciting idea when she bought it years before. The most inspiring part of the chair was the hole in the armrest meant to hold a drink. Mom imagined it would be very nice to sit in the wilder-ness drinking a drink and thinking a think, but it was only the *idea* of the chair that Mom loved. Outside Mom's imagination, we never stopped moving long enough to sit in it. Instead, Mom drank her drinks from a dented cup and thought her thinks in the driving chair as the Wagon carries us to the next adventure. Each chip, stain, and dent in the cup and the Wagon were like a badge of faithful service, and neither one had failed her until now.

With everything arranged perfectly for a relaxing day, Mom sat her big butt in the chair. The chair's bones clenched under her weight, pulling on the armrest and dumping the cup of steaming poop juice into her lap. Her lap was also where her laptop was.

"Ah! Ah! Ah!" Mom screamed. She shot out of the chair, throwing the laptop into the sand. She screamed again and sat down to pick up the laptop from the muddy puddle before poop juice turned it into quicksand. When her butt touched the chair again, more poop juice poured into her lap and she made another noise that letters can't spell.

Mom wasn't much in the mood for writing after that, so she paced while I watched her closely from the shade of my bush. She stared toward the road. She looked down to ask the Witch a question. She shut the Witch up so the answer wouldn't distract her from staring back at the road.

I dozed, Mom paced, and eventually we ate. Mom's butt dried, and then it got wet again when she sat back in the chair. She paced until it was dry again, and then she made a fresh cup of tea to replace the poop juice that her pants had drunk. Finally, I heard a distant crunching and spotted a far-off sparkle.

The twinkle flashed as it climbed over the ditch. It passed the turn without slowing and disappeared into the desert like a shooting star.

I looked to Mom for an answer, but she was already lifting the Witch to her face. "Where's he going?" I asked.

"Hi, I'm the idiot stuck in the middle of the desert. I think you just passed me," she told the Witch without taking her eyes off the near-distance where the truck disappeared. "Yeah, Cadiz Dunes parking area. Okay. Katie's Dunes, then. That's right. Don't worry, you'll see me."

I wanted to ask who Katie was and whether she was the wench we needed, but Mom was still staring at the spot where the star disappeared like she was trying to conjure a miracle. I'd heard of people making things happen just by wishing for them hard enough, but I wasn't sure if those stories were make-believe. If anyone in the world was stubborn enough to will the impossible to happen, it was Mom.

Let there be light! Mom's thoughts grunted as they strained against the spot. I sat quietly next to my bush and watched for signs of a dream coming true.

And lo, a flicker appeared in the spot where Mom's eyes were pointing. The flicker grew to a glimmer, then a glitter, then a gleam. When it made the turn toward us, Mom's teeth released their grip and her eyes fainted in their sockets. "Thank God," she whispered to the sky.

"How did you do that?" I asked when the shock passed.

"I told him to turn around. Didn't you hear me?"

"I heard you talking to… hang on a second!" It was so obvious, I couldn't believe I'd never noticed it before. Only the Witch knew where we were going when we met Friends like Lily or Boss Charming in far-off lands. "You mean the Witch can summon Friends?"

"Of course. What do you think phones are for?" Mom gave me a look like it was the most obvious thing in the world. She turned her eyes back toward the miracle and waved her arms above her head like an air traffic controller.

I had so many questions, but a truck appeared behind the comet and Mom forgot all about me. As the truck came closer, she waved her arms more frantically until she looked more like a car wash windsock-puppet than an air traffic controller.

She kept flapping until the truck was close enough to see its captain's bulky silhouette through the front window. Mom's eyes dropped to the tattoo on the truck's upper lip and her arms froze in midair like she was being held at gunpoint. The truck's entire snout was covered with a painting of an eagle soaring out of a rippling flag. The eagle's wings stretched from stars to stripes as its sharp scowl and pointy beak aimed threateningly at anything in the truck's path.

"Look, Mom! It's America, come back to save us!" I cheered. Unlike the men on the road to Yreka, I hoped that Mom was smart enough to know a Friend when she saw one, but I wasn't sure. The suspicious glint in her eyes was the same one she'd used to size up the friendly Power Ranger on the day I met the horse named Mule. "Don't forget," I whispered, "you've got to act like whatever they're doing is helpful, even if it isn't. It's the polite thing to do."

"Oh cheese," she muttered, dropping her arms but not taking her eyes off of the cocky eagle. "This should be interesting."

The slamming door snapped Mom out of the eagle's trance. Instead of a wench, a big man stood beside the truck.

I ran to greet him. "Hi, are you Katie? I'm Oscar. Thanks for coming."

Behind me, Mom prepared to assert her dominance by showing she was in control of the situation. She huffed and puffed to inflate her big, bad business voice. "Hi, you must be Ruben," she commanded, in case Katie thought he was somebody else. Before he had a chance to notice that the Wagon was sitting on the

476

sand like a duck sits on a lake, Mom squared her shoulders and announced, "I really ducked up."

Ruben stood with his big arms crossed over his chest and took in the scene. Mom waited for him to tell her that this desert was no place for a little lady in a soccer mom's van.

"Do you think you can get us out?" Mom asked a little more timidly.

"Is that thing front wheel drive?" Ruben asked.

Mom looked at the Wagon. "Um, I forget," she said so she wouldn't have to admit that she never knew in the first place. "I think so."

Ruben looked the Wagon up and down, and I thought I saw admiration in his face. "How did you get all the way out here in that thing? My truck has all-wheel drive and even I was a little worried that I'd get stuck. Are you out here all alone?"

"The dog is with me." Mom looked at me. "But he can't help me push."

I smiled at him and wagged a little harder. "I'm The Dog, but you can call me Oscar."

"Dogs are the best hiking buddies." Ruben played my ribcage like a set of bongos. "My boy Bruno used to do everything with me, but I had to say goodbye to him a few months ago."

"Did he go away to college?" I asked.

Mom's eyes softened as they watched Ruben remember Bruno. "Stop! You're gonna make me cry, too!" she said, and the puddles in her eyes showed that she meant it.

Ruben got back into his truck and carefully turned the eagle's rude stare away from us. He returned draped in chains with the biggest fish hook I'd ever seen.

I offered to help Ruben dig under the Wagon, but Mom grabbed my collar and told me to watch from the driving chair instead. So I leaned out the window to watch him crawl around in the dust, barking encouragement every time he knocked on the Wagon from below.

Mom stayed outside, trying to figure out the most helpful place to put her paws. Her back paws kicked the sand as her front paws moved from hips to cheeks, then tested whether it was better to clasp them in front or behind. She crumpled like a chair every time Ruben grunted with effort, as if folding up would hide her from the shame of not doing it herself.

Finally, Ruben asked Mom to *up-up* into the driving chair and returned to his truck.

Mom woke the Wagon and stuck a hitchhiking thumb out the window. From the window of the truck, Ruben hitchhiked in return.

The truck started rolling and a moment later, the Wagon lurched like a crash landing in reverse. We began to roll.

Ruben's truck used the chain as a leash to pull the Wagon through the sand, yanking on it every so often like Mom does when I'm distracted by a pee spot. Each time it did, the Wagon dutifully followed, until the sandy road became rocky under its paws.

Once we were back on solid ground, the truck stopped and the Wagon *sat* obediently behind. When Ruben dismounted to unleash the Wagon, Mom and I got out to say goodbye.

"I can't thank you enough for coming all the way out here on Thanksgiving Day to save my ass." Mom handed Ruben a card from her wallet. "And especially for not making me feel stupid about the whole thing."

"I'm impressed that you got this far in that thing," Ruben said, looking up from his clipboard. The Wagon proudly shined the sun back into his eyes. "Most people wouldn't even try with a minivan."

"But we never would have made it out again without your help." Mom accepted the clipboard that Ruben was offering and scribbled on it before handing it back.

"I'll stay with you until the highway." Ruben ripped a paper off of the clipboard and handed it to Mom. "I don't want you to get stuck again and have to pay another thousand dollars."

"Thank you again," Mom said in a voice that showed how small a thousand could be. She checked the paper to make sure it had Ruben's address before putting it in her pocket so she could send a reward closer to the size of her gratitude. "And happy Thanksgiving."

"Happy Thanksgiving to you too, buddy." Ruben ruffled my ears and patted in the goodbye.

Everyone remounted, and Ruben's eagle led the way back down the bumpy road. Every time the Wagon had to slow down to pick its way over the tricky terrain, Ruben's surefooted truck slowed to let us catch up, just like Mom and I do for each other on the trail.

When we crossed the train tracks back onto a real road, Ruben's truck started shrinking in the front window. When we reached the first Road Closed fence, Ruben's paw poked out of the window and waved a final goodbye before disappearing into the desert.

When we reached the freeway, the Wagon stopped for Mom to read the signs. One way led back to California and our Stuck House at the End of the World. The other led to Las Vegas and the desert where this story began, once upon a time.

"Do you know when we were here last?" Mom asked thoughtfully as the Wagon turned away from the sinking sun.

"Yesterday?" I guessed.

"No, I mean before that. This is the same route we took into Vegas right before everything shut down. Remember that day with the nosy cops that wouldn't leave us alone? Now that I think about it, that morning was the last time anything felt normal."

"Oh," I said, because I didn't know what else to say.

The Wagon chased its shadow toward *happily ever after* as the sun watched us through the back window.

"I can't help but think that there's a lesson we're supposed to learn here," I said. "What does it mean when you think you can do everything yourself?

"…and you run all over the West looking for a place where no one can disturb you?

"…until you get so stuck that you need someone to leave their Thanksgiving dinner behind to pull you out?

"…and then they don't even make you feel dumb about it.

"What's the word for that again?"

Mom needed to think about it, so I gave her a hint. "Is it something about not doing everything yourself? Or maybe it's something about Friends? Do you think it's about Friends?"

"The things you come up with, Oscar!" Mom said, like I was suggesting something silly. "Obviously, the lesson is that we need a truck."

THE END

Glossary

bluburb (*n.*) the flabby outer layers of a city where the houses, the dog bathrooms, and even the people are bigger than in a city.

It's against the rules to sleep inside a covered wagon in the bluburbs.

boogeyvirus (*n.*) an invisible, evil force that travels on microscopic boogers, infecting people with suspicion and fear. *The boogeyvirus was a kind of wildness that people carried inside themselves, so there was nowhere to escape except from each other.*

butt (*n.*) When a hill shaped like a stump pokes out of the ground where it doesn't belong.

There are butts all over the southwest, but none that looks like Devil's Tower in Wyoming.

car kennel (*n.*) a safe place for your car or wagon to stay when you need to leave it alone while you're away from home.

As we rolled toward the exit, I thought I saw something wooly moving between the only two pickup trucks in the car kennel.

cheesology (*n.*) the study of how the Earth was made, usually while thinking about cheese. Since most living things think about cheese more or less constantly, cheesology is more commonly used to refer to the study of rocks, even when cheese is the more important part of the thought.

"What a lucky coincidence that Mount Rush More just so happens to look like those four guys! Cheesology sure is amazing.

the City (*prop. n.*) a place with gigantic buildings, two bridges, zillions of people, and some pigeons. People from far away sometimes call the City *San Francisco*. People who call it *Frisco* are not welcome in the City.

From the sandy canyon bottom, the rocks had seemed like buildings in the City—close together, but each one standing on its own.

civilization (*n.*) a magical spell that makes humans the most powerful of all beasts, strong enough to defeat any danger. To keep the spell alive, everyone must say or do the same thing at the same time, like a worldwide game of Simon says.

Most people spend so much time in civilization that they forget it's all in their imaginations and they can step out of it at any time.

collie (*n.*) a Friend you make at work.

A new group of collies sat unsupervised at the lunch table, probably dropping chicken and hamburger on the floor.

contamomate (*v.*) to make impure, harmful, or unusable through contact with something unclean or bad, usually Mom.

Mom kept her back to the trail so that her contamomated breath couldn't hurt anyone.

demomstrate (*v.*) to show someone less competent than yourself how to do something correctly.

I ran in circles to demomstrate what expert hiking looked like from all angles.

diagnostics (*n. pl.*) big fat lie used to take more money than something should reasonably cost.

"He may not sell me the fuse and insist on charging a lot of money to run diagnostics." She made bunny ears with her fingers to show diagnostics meant big, fat lie.

dog bathroom (*n.*) the open-air potty beside a stuck house traditionally only used by dogs. When traveling, the whole world becomes a dog bathroom and may occasionally even be used by humans.

What's gotten into you? I thought you made peace with using the dog bathroom. Have you been holding it this whole time?

doom (*n.*) a hill made out of sand; (*n.*) a devious torture device when all you were hoping for was some pretty pictures and an easy run.

On every climb, Mom shook her fist and whispered threats about the nasty things she would do if the dooms didn't cut it out.

dreadmill (*n.*) a piece of furniture that takes up as much space in the living room as a couch and lets you run great distances without ever leaving your stuck house.

I sat in my Mom-watching chair and coached Mom through her morning workout on the dreadmill.

dysinformation (*n.*) information that is deliberately false or misleading, usually spread by witches with the intent to make people feel angry and off-balance.

The humans spread dysinformation to convince dogs that a treat broken in half was actually two treats, telling them not to believe their growling bellies.

ecomommy (*n.*) the worldwide exchange of activity that inspires humans to do things for each other and spreads money like boogeyvirus. When the ecomommy is broken, humans get very irritable.

Money does no good sitting in the bank just like dog food is no good if you never open the can. Therefore, fancy wet food is essential for a healthy ecomommy.

empuffy (*n.*) the quality of thinking about your life partner's needs and not just your own.

Dogs drooling when someone else eats something delicious is an example of empuffy.

End of the World (*prop. n.*) where the land ends abruptly and falls into the sea.

I liked living at the End of the World. It made me feel like a king to stand in the dog bathroom behind the Stuck House and watch the last mile of a whole continent fall into the ocean.

exstinked (*adj.*) no longer having a member of your species or tribe to leave their stink on the world.

Even if you find their pawprints, you'll never smell a dinosaur's stinky feet because they're all exstinked.

Friend (*prop. n.*) a friend who stands out from all of your other adoring fans because you have known them for long enough to know the special things about each other's personalities and create memories together that you don't share with anyone else.

Mom was too clumsy around people to make Friends without supervision. That's why I was hired.

furryner (*n.*) stranger who talks funny and doesn't follow all the rules, but in a cute, harmless way.

I could tell that he was a furryner by the way he made his words like his mouth was full of tennis balls.

grey (*n., adj.*) a color besides black or white. Synonyms include, red, orange, yellow, green, blue, purple, indigo, puce, magenta, periwinkle, mauve, etc.

High on the mountain, the white dirt glowed like frosting, but here at the bottom there was nothing but brick-grey mud and cacti.

Grey Bridge (*n.*) the other bridge in the City — not the famous bridge, the other one that goes to Oakland. The one where the traffic is from people who live here, not tourists.

The car-nanny protected our windows and the change in the cup holder from thieves while Mom and I ran around the City, watching the sunrise behind the Grey Bridge and Alcatraz.

greynbow (*n.*) a trick of the human eye that makes them believe that there are more colors in the world than black, white, and grey.

Mom told me not to drink from puddles with greynbows in it. Dogs are colorblind, so I don't believe in greynbows.

homelesskimo (*n.*) a culture who lives in summer igloos full time. Their natural habitat is under the freeway overpasses of large cities, but they occasionally live in wilder-ness areas, too.

The homelesskimos built colonies of igloos on the empty sidewalks and landscaped their yards with cardboard.

I'mbarkadero (*n.*) a fancy word for a crowded sidewalk with cars passing on one side and boats on the other. It gets its name from a handsome and mysterious dog whose real name no one knew, who used to run around the waterfront, barking at tourists, and scooters, and snakeboarders, and other dogs.

She tried for the gazillionth time to hang her muzzle on her nose in preparation for the crowds as we ran onto the I'mbarkadero.

juice box (*n.*) a contraption that feeds machines like witches and wagons.

As Mom stuck the straw into the Wagon's mouth, the cowboy at the next juice box called from behind his truck, "California, huh? What are you doing all the way out here?"

killmometer (*n.*) an imaginary version of a mile that only comes out on special occasions, like a race. Unlike miles, killmometers don't measure a consistent distance, but grow and shrink depending on how hard the race is and how you're feeling at the time.

So if you agreed to run twenny-five killmometers, and we've run twenny-five killmometers, I guess we're all done.

laundrymat (*n.*) a luxurious amomodation for not-dogs with indoor benches, outlets for charging your laptop, and occasionally wifi.

I sat outside the laundrymat, watching Mom through the window as she tended to everyone's needs but mine.

Law (*prop. n.*) humans who roam the streets waking up sleeping dogs to ask nosy questions in the middle of the night. The Law may also hunt by daylight. Unlike a Simon, the Law wear special matching outfits, drive matching cars with killer-whale-like markings, and have a more sophisticated communication network.

As we walked, Mom looked from side to side, waiting for the Law to jump out of someone's driveway and demand to see our papers.

lawgic (*n.*) following the rules very closely to detect when they don't really apply to you.

According to Mom's lawgic, you can tell a lot about what's allowed *by what's* not allowed *and studying the space between the* allowed *and the* not.

liberry (*n.*) a building filled with nothing but lousy old books that only allows service dogs inside, as if any normal dog worth his fur would be caught dead in the place. They don't even let you bark!

The service dog thought he was so special just because he was allowed in supermarkets and liberries.

mailman (*n.*) a sneaky, murderous beast who wanders neighborhoods (often while the humans are away) hunting for dogs who are home alone so he can eat them for lunch.

It was like when someone shouts "MAILMAN" in a crowded living room and you run screaming to the window only to find that it's a false alarm.

mapp (*n.*) a Witch's warped representation of how the world should be, paying no mind to reality.

We were so new to traveling that we didn't know about AllTrails or saving mapps for when the Witch wasn't talking to us.

marathong (*n.*) from the Greek root *—thong* for "something that isn't too uncomfortable as long as you don't think about it too much," a marathong is a run that you know is going to be uncomfortable but you do it anyway.

"It's like those marathongs I trained you for. Every week we ran farther than ever before."

math (*n.*) a bad medicine that some people take for a thrill and others take to deal with unbearable emotions. Math uses numbers that dogs don't know. See below for a list of not-imaginary numbers.

In Breaking Bad, *Walt and Jesse cook math. Mom likes to count things because math makes her feel like she can predict the future.*

mominous (*adj.*) having a dangerous quality that only Mom can sense. Possessing the type of danger that only exists in Mom's head.

"Among other things…" she said mominously.

nyoink (*v.*) to snatch something quickly in a playful way, usually without permission.

He nyoinked the frisbee up in his teeth and ran back to his village with it.

packpack (*n.*) a bag for carrying water, snacks, and other supplies on a human's back. Packpacks tend to be the same size or smaller than a full-grown raccoon, while larger packs up to the size of an adult sow are called *backpacks*.

She dropped the packpack to the ground and pulled out all of the empty bottles, lining them up in the sand.

people (*pl. n.*) a being whose thoughts, feelings, and experiences contribute to the collective game of Simon says that creates civilization. Colloquially, *people* refers to humans, but is also correct when referring to wise and friendly dogs, especially if they are very handsome.

Dogs are people too.

poop juice (*n.*) a warm, milky drink with a pungent smell that humans take in the morning to prevent themselves from turning into zombies and to help them… you know (hint: It's in the name.).

The poop juice cooled in Mom's cup as she kept both paws clamped to the driving wheel to prevent the Wagon from being blown off course.

potato beast (*n.*) the handsomest breed of dog with a muscular body that is the same shape and hardness as an uncooked potato.

Potato beasts are the best breed of dog, and Oscar is the best of them all.

quarunseen (*v.*) to stay away from people because your presence could   kill   someone.

We spent the rest of the evening quarunseening in the Wagon and waiting for Utah and Mom's hair to dry.

reasonable amomodation (*n.*) a business dog who accompanies his life partner to work to make sure she overcomes her separation anxiety and behaves as expected to in a business setting.

I was what they call a reasonable amomodation, which means a dog who trains a reactive human to behave around other people.

Simon (*prop. n.*) a nosy person who takes it upon themselves to inform you of rules that don't need enforcing, as in a game of Simon says.

Simons print their rules on signs to recruit people to play with them and post them on the internet so witches will tell far-away Simons all about their accomplishments.

snow (*n.*) the sparkly bits that flake off of clouds and turn everything underneath fluffy with white dirt.

I watched the rain trying to turn to snow as the slush under our wheels got chunkier and grew a white crust.

'splain (*v.*) to establish dominance by explaining something to someone who probably already knows it.

She wound up her mouth like she does when she's preparing to 'splain something that doesn't make sense.

stuck house (*n.*) a house without wheels that is in the same place all the time. Spending too much time inside of one tends to lead to a yearning for adventure. See also:

Stuck House (*prop. n.*) the stuck house that Oscar lives in.

I tried to tell her about all the fears I'd feared alone in this enormous Stuck House, but I was too overjoyed that none of them were true, so it came out like, "EEEEEEE!"

suffercate (*v.*) the stifling, uncomfortable feeling that you can't breathe.

Mom still closed the vents behind her nose and mouth as the group of strangers approached. She hoped she wouldn't suffercate waiting for them all to pass.

summer igloo (*n.*) a portable shelter made from fabric or skins when it is too warm for ice, used for sleeping in the wilder-ness or under bridges.

The villagers stood up from their folding chairs clutching mugs of poop juice and climbed out of summer igloos with pillow-shaped hair.

tabottom (*n.*) A sled that is also your butt.

"I was sledding," his hapless sidekick replied. She stood up and brushed the white dirt victoriously from her tabottom.

"That wasn't as painless as I thought. There were some sharp rocks under there."

trigomometry (*n.*) a magic spell that cuts distances in half.

If we'd stayed on the roads the Witch told us to follow, it would have been five miles in each direction, but Mom used trigomometry to make the walk shorter.

tsumommy (*n.*) a very, very large wave, usually sent to annoy landlubber dogs and soak his companion's socks.

When Nature tried to bring its savagery to the human world with something like a sandslide or a tsumommy, I thought people just went somewhere else until they could tame Nature's wildness again.

turtle (*n.*) a species of stray hikers found in any backwoods large enough to lose your Subaru in. They have a terrible sense of direction and it's not uncommon for them to wander for tens or hunerds of miles in the wilder-ness before they remember where they parked. They walk foolishly into danger, carrying their homes on their backs.

Turtles are suspiciously happy and relaxed for someone living such a desperate life.

wagon (*n.*) a car that is also a house so you can carry your life with you as you search for adventure.

Wagon (*prop. n.*) Oscar's wagon. Short for the *Covered Wagon* because it is old, round and white.

The Wagon screeched back onto the road like the Scooby Mobile running from a ghost.

white dirt (*n.*) rare dirt with magical properties that regular dirt doesn't have, including smelling like freezer burn and zambonis, preserving perfect buttprints when you roll in it, cooling you down on mountain hikes, and tasting delicious. White dirt occurs when snow stays on the ground after falling.

You'd have to be a real fuddyduddy to dislike white dirt. Mom can't stand the stuff

wilder-ness (*n.*) what's left over outside of civilization, where no one gets to make the rules and anything can happen. *Wilder-ness* is both a place and a state of being.

To hear most humans talk about it, the wilder-ness is a dark and frightening place. If there were no civilization at all, wildness would just be a fact of life, but the wild feels wilder right after you've broken the spell.

witch (*n.*) a small device that follows humans wherever they go, pretending to be helpful but actually spreading rumors, lies, and passive-aggressive criticism.

Witch (*prop. n.*) the Witch that Lives in Mom's Phone. An especially devious specimen of the species.

That Witch is full of nothing but snark and pictures of me sitting on rocks.

Numbers

Dogs can't count higher than ten, but that doesn't mean that we don't understand quantities. Below are some numbers that dogs use.

twenny — a medium amount. It usually means "some, but not too many."
Oscar ate twenny hot dogs, but he could have eaten more.

twenny-five kay — not the same thing as 17.7 miles.
Twenny-five kay is only supposed to be fifteen and a half miles. No more, no less. We should be done by now!

forty-five — if a hill is forty-five degrees, its grandmother was a wall and its grandfather was a floor.
"It says 52 percent. That's got to be a GPS error," she decided.
"Is fiddy-two more floor or wall than forty-five, do you think?"

fiddy — another medium number used for things that you can't see to count them.
Oscar's fiddy colleagues couldn't all fit around the same lunch table, so he had many lunch shifts to supervise.

fiddy-two — the number of degrees it takes for someone from San Francisco to die of cold.
If the weather goes below fiddy-two, it's just a matter of time before Mom freezes to death.

sixey-eight — the boiling point for people from San Francisco.
Mom can sniff out global warming when it's only sixey-eight degrees.

a hunerd — a sorta big number, but not *that* big.

Instead of taking a hunerd pictures, you could just take one and look at it for longer.

millions — a big number, but not super-duper big.

It looked like a tornado had come through, dropping millions of cars higgledy-piggledy into the forest.

zillions — more than millions.

Why work so hard to gather zillions of memories if you're gonna ignore the versions you don't like?

Jillians — so many that no one could count that high.

There are Jillians of ideas flying around right now and most of them are horse doo-doo.

baJillians — even more Jillians.

All around me, baJillians and baJillians of sand grains rushed around, constantly on the move, and yet the shape of the dooms never changed.

gaJillian — so many Jillians that it's like a Jillian of Jillians.

By the gaJillianth verse, the Drill Sergeant had caught up enough to make out the words to the song she was singing.

If you've enjoyed spending this book with Oscar, please share your experience by leaving a review. Your reviews help other dog lovers find Oscar's work and give him a warm, fuzzy feeling that sets his tail wagging.

If you'd like to join Oscar on more adventures, you can find him at the links below:

Oscar's blog and website: dogblog.wf
Substack: oscarthepooch.substack.com
Facebook: facebook.com/poochoscarthecoach
Instagram: instagram.com/poochoscarthecoach
Pinterest: pinterest.com/oscarthepooch
Email: oscar@dogblog.wf

About the Pawthor

Oscar the Pooch is not only an author—he's a phenomenon. Known globally for his way with words, hilarious wit, and profound wisdom as much as his dreamy eyes, spellbinding smile, hunky muscles, and irresistible dream-butt, Oscar rose to fame by sharing his unmatched brilliance and captivating good looks with the world. He brightens the lives of millions through his blog and social media presence, inviting his Friends along on his adventures and offering profound life-coaching insights and eye candy along the way. His devoted fan base can't get enough of his advice on everything from snack management to fitness.

Oscar began writing in 2015, when he discovered how many people in a Facebook running group needed his guidance and encouragement. His social media posts quickly evolved into a blog so that his wisdom could reach a wider audience. His stories are now serialized in weekly installments so his fans are never lonely. You can read his stories at dogblog.wf, or at the links on the next page.

Oscar has a Master's Degree in being a good boy (which is what you call it when your puppy school professor suggests that you repeat the class after graduating), and his expert observations of human behavior have contributed immeasurably to the world's understanding of humans' most perplexing customs and norms. He is also an accomplished Greeter and Supervisor of Snacking in his professional life.

When he's not escorting Mom on adventures, Oscar lives in Pacifica, California, where he spends his days napping, eating searching the kitchen floor for snacks, and posing for photos with flowers on his head.

Made in United States
Troutdale, OR
10/26/2024

24134023R00309